The Bonbon Girl

Linda Finlay

ONE PLACE. MANY STORIES

HQ
An imprint of HarperCollins*Publishers* Ltd
1 London Bridge Street
London SE1 9GF

This paperback edition 2018

1
First published in Great Britain by
HQ, an imprint of HarperCollins*Publishers* Ltd 2018

ISBN: 978-0-00-826297-6

Printed and bound in Great Britain by
CPI Group (UK) Ltd, Croydon, CR0 4YY

To my Bonbons, Jack, Heather, Darcey and Chloe.
With special thanks to Darcey for naming this novel.

Prologue

Colenso watched as the rising tide advanced towards the Devil's Frying Pan. The turbulence created by rough seas surging through its entrance was legendary. Her father had chosen his spot well. Desperately she tugged at the ropes binding her hands, only to wince as the damp hemp tightened, cutting deeper into her flesh.

As white-tipped waves swirled ever closer to her feet she shuddered. In the distance she could hear the sounds of the organ from the travelling fair. Loud and brash, its purpose was to attract the crowds, and judging from the shrieks of laughter coming from the villagers on the green it was doing its job. Nobody would hear her screams and Kitto, dear unsuspecting Kitto, would be waiting for her.

The light was fading, the wind rising, bringing with it a thick bank of rolling mist. She licked her salt-coated lips. The crescendo from the waves pounding the tidal cave and reverberating around the serpentine rock was deafening now, blotting out all sound of the fair. Her father had promised to return for her decision before the tide was in full spate but, intent on his mission and wishing her scared witless, she knew he was deliberately cutting it fine. He'd have a wasted journey though, for she had no intention of changing her mind. Her heart belonged to Kitto, and without him her life would serve no purpose. She would take her love to the grave if need be. And if it was deemed to be a watery one then so be it.

Spray from the advancing swell covered her feet before receding to allow her respite, albeit momentarily, and she gave a laugh that came out as a high-pitched shriek. How ironic that her name Colenso should mean 'from the dark pool' for now it looked as if she would be returning to it much sooner than she'd thought.

Chapter 1

Cadgwith, The Lizard, Cornwall

> 'An' it harm none, do what thou will'
> *Wiccan Rede*

With these words ringing in her ear, Colenso put the bread to bake then set about making the pastry for her pasties. Today was a special day and she had a plan. Excitement bubbled up as she mixed swede, potato and onion with the scraps of meat old Buller the butcher had given her in exchange for helping him earlier that morning.

'Don't forget the herbs, Colenso. Marjoram for love, rosemary to stimulate the heart, sage for wishes, and best put in a pinch of parsley for lust.'

'Really Mammwynn,' Colenso chided, colour flooding her cheeks. Her grandmother believed her beloved herbs were the answer to everything, nurturing varieties that by rights shouldn't even grow let alone flourish on this wild peninsula. Then she remembered and looked up with a start. Sure enough, the room was empty for her beloved Mammwynn had passed on at Samhain last October. Being the festival that marked both the end and beginning of their year and a time of celebration for those who'd gone before, Mammwynn would have thought it perfect timing. But Colenso had loved her grandmother dearly and still felt her loss keenly.

'Oh Mammwynn, I do miss you so,' she murmured, dashing a tear from her eye. 'The weather's been bitterly cold this winter and many of your plants are lying dormant so I'll have to use the ones I've dried.' As she reached up to take a handful from the clothes pulley above her head, she felt the slightest of touches on her shoulder and knew her grandmother approved. Crumbling them into the mixture, she finished making the pasties adding a decorative finish to the biggest with a flourish. She hoped Kitto, her beloved, would appreciate it.

As the aroma of baked dough filled the air, she removed the loaves to cool, added the pasties to the tin and slid it back into the hot recess of the Cornish stove that was her mamm's pride and joy. It had been her father's wedding present to her and about the only thing he'd ever bought her, she thought, staring around the room with its hand-me-down dresser and rickety table and chairs. The tiny window let in very little light even on the brightest day and there wasn't enough space to swing a rat. Imagine the luxury of living somewhere with room to put her things, not that she had many, Colenso sighed, as she set about tidying up. Mamm worked on call as the Sick Nurse and after sitting in with old Mrs Janes would appreciate returning to a clean room with their evening meal prepared. Her Father and elder brother, Tomas, laboured long hours at the works and were forever hungry.

She wondered how her younger brother William was faring. How she missed him. With only thirteen months between them, they'd always been close until the dreadful night he'd taken their father to task for squandering his entire weekly wage on drink. The fight that had ensued still made Colenso shudder and she didn't blame Will for running off to make a better life for himself. Tomas was hardly home these days either.

Pushing the door of their tumbledown cottage closed, Colenso shivered and pulled her bonnet down tighter as a gust of February wind threatened to send it spinning down the lane. Checking the cloth was still covering the pasty, she hefted her basket over her arm and made her way down the rutted track and on past the huddle of thatched cottages. Their thick serpentine, stone and cob walls were designed to keep out the worst of the squalls and misty weather that frequently swept over The Lizard. The shoemaker's shop with its array of boots, rang with the sound of scutes and nails being hammered into heavy leather soles. She stepped over the wooden bridge that spanned the stream and across the Todden, which divided Little Cove from Fishing Cove. It was a fair walk to Poltesco and the serpentine factory where Kitto was employed as a trainee marble turner, but if she hurried she should be in time to join him for his noontime break. She'd have to dodge her father though, for he disapproved of their association, wanting better things for his daughter. However, she had an excuse for visiting the works as she'd been told there was a new batch of cuttings waiting to be collected. Extra money to eke out the family budget was always welcome, and with Kitto's help she would fashion them into buttons and souvenirs ready to sell to the visitors that swarmed to the area in the summer months.

Since Queen Victoria and Prince Albert had purchased items of serpentine for their Osborne House home on the Isle of Wight, the local stone, which displayed the brightest colours of green and red when polished, had proved popular.

Waves pounded the shore and she wrinkled her nose at the oppressive odour of fish and bait emanating from the cellars below. Gulls screeched as they circled the few fishing boats bobbing in the bay, their nets cast wide. Thankfully it was too early in the year for the pilchards to arrive. She far preferred working the Lizardite, as the rock was known locally, to salting and pressing the silver fish that, whilst providing the necessary food and oil for lighting, tainted her hands and clothes.

'Morning, maid. 'Tis a fine day for it.' Colenso jumped as the West Country burr broke into her thoughts.

'Good morning, Mr Carter, Mr Paul,' she replied, stepping to one side to let the two fishermen pass carrying their gulley laden with nets and baskets. Dressed in their customary blue ganseys and flat caps, they eyed her quizzically.

'Taking your young man something nice, I 'spect, this being a special day an' all,' the second man grinned, sniffing her basket appreciatively.

'Really, Mr Paul, I'm not sure what you mean,' she demurred, feeling her cheeks colouring. The two men gave her a knowing look.

'Listen to 'em birds, maid,' Mr Carter called. 'They be choosing their mates too.'

'Wish I were a youngster again. Give him a good run for

his money for a beautiful maid like thee, I would.' As their guffaws of laughter rang around the cove, Colenso felt her cheeks growing hotter.

'If you'll excuse me, I must get on,' she muttered, hurrying on through the village and out the other side. Honestly, was nothing around here secret? She remembered Mammwynn saying you only had to sneeze at the top of the hill for someone to be enquiring after your health by the time you reached the bottom. Her hand strayed to the star-shaped necklace at her throat.

'Heed what it tells yer, maid, 'tis never wrong,' her grandmother had whispered, fixing her with that gimlet stare before her eyelids fluttered closed for the last time. Well, it hadn't told her anything yet, she thought climbing the steep hill towards Ruan and skirting the ancient church dedicated to Saint Rumonus, nodding to villagers as she passed. Hearing the clock chime the half hour, she quickened her pace, her mind racing along with her steps. She and Kitto had been walking out for some months now and although he'd been loving and more attentive of late, he hadn't mentioned taking things further.

'*Just needs a bit of encouragement.*' Mammwynn's voice urged. Well hopefully today would give him that.

Hurrying down through the wooded valley, she rounded the sweep of the cliff and saw a schooner anchored off shore waiting for the shallow draught barges to transfer their loads of stone. The sprawling works were set in the cove below and plumes of smoke curled their way upwards from the tall chimney adjoining the machine shop. Passing the mill and gurgling stream that drained most of the Goonhilly

Downs, she began descending the steep track the horse-drawn wooden carts used to transport their blocks of quarried stone. Her ears were assaulted by the sound of saws, chisels and hammers mingling with the rumbling and splashing of the waterwheel. The clamour from the grinding and sanding of the stone got ever louder. Men shouted orders, though how they could be heard above the noise of the sea beating on the shingle was beyond her.

Suddenly, at the blast of a hooter, the clanking of the machinery ground to a halt, workers downed their tools and the valley was filled with the blissful sound of silence. Ignoring the descending dust, men squatted on slabs of stone to eat their noon pieces, eyeing Colenso speculatively as she picked her way through the dirt and debris towards the workshop. However, before she reached it, Kitto appeared in the doorway. Dark-haired and handsome despite the dust covering his working clothes, Colenso's heart quickened at the sight of him. When he spotted her, his face broke into a wide grin, and, heedless of the jeers and catcalls from the others, he ran over to join her.

'Well, you're a pretty sight to brighten a fellow's working day,' he greeted, wiping his hands on his apron.

'I heard there were cuttings to be had,' she told him, trying to keep a straight face.

'And there's me thinking you'd come just to see me,' he sighed, shaking his head.

'Actually, I've brought something special for your noon piece,' she told him, unable to keep up the pretence.

'Something special, Cali?' he asked using his pet name for her. It meant 'beautiful', and that he should think of her that

8

way still surprised her, for she had the same dark colouring as many others on The Lizard. However, her delight soon turned to despair for he'd clearly forgotten what day it was. 'Come on, let's find somewhere quieter to eat,' he suggested, taking her arm and leading her towards the thicket, away from prying eyes.

'If My Lady would care to take a seat,' he said, sweeping aside a low branch and gesturing to a felled tree trunk. 'Something's smelling good,' he added, looking hopefully at the basket on her lap as he squatted beside her.

Colenso hesitated. Suppose he thought her gesture stupid? But he was waiting expectantly and lifting the cloth she passed him the pasty she'd so painstakingly decorated. He stared at it for a long moment then his lips curled into a grin.

'You did this for me?' he asked, tracing the pastry heart with his fingers. Then, unable to resist, he bit into the pastry and sighed. 'Delicious and meat in it too?'

'Well, I thought with today being … I mean …' her voice trailed off uncertainly as she saw him quirk his brow questioningly. Yet he could no more keep a straight face than she. 'I love it and I love you, Colenso Carne,' he declared, reaching out and squeezing her hand. 'Happy Valentine's Day. I'm famished and you must be too so let's share this before it gets cold.' She started to refuse but it had been a long morning and she was hungry.

The outside world receded as they ate in companionable silence, their eyes meeting then quickly drawing away again. Along with the fragrance of herbs, the air between them was filled with suppressed excitement.

'My, that was good,' he declared, wiping the last crumbs from his lips. 'I shall be a lucky man coming home to … that is … I've been thinking it's time …' He thrust a package into her hands. 'Look, I'm no good with fancy words but hopefully this will explain.' He stared at her, brown eyes shining with emotion.

Heart soaring, she smiled, running her fingers over his gift. It seemed they had been thinking along the same lines after all. But just as she began to unfold the wrapping, the hooter sounded. 'Not now,' Kitto groaned. 'I'd better look sharp, the new manager started today. We're turning pillars for a large shop up country and he's ordered they be shipped out tonight. Goodness knows what time we'll be working till. Sorry Cali, this isn't the way I'd planned to do this,' he shrugged, pointing to her present. 'Can I see you tomorrow? After I've finished the Sunday chores for Mother. I know how your father likes a nap after his noontime meal so perhaps we could meet on the Todden? Talk about …' Again, he gestured to the package before darting a quick peck on her cheek. Then, at a shout from one of the others, he turned on his heel and ran back to the workshop.

Disappointment mingled with excited anticipation as she stared at the package in her hands. She was tempted to open it right away but knew if she didn't collect the cuttings others would. Bending to retrieve her basket, she felt the point of the necklace stab her chest. Gazing ruefully down at her ample bosom, she sighed. Why couldn't she have been born dainty like Mammwynn and Mamm?

Lifting her skirts, she picked her way through the dirt and debris until she reached the factory office. She could hear her father shouting orders to other labourers further down the valley, but luckily could see no sign of him. However, as she left the building, her basket heavy with the cuttings, she again felt that stabbing in her chest. Looking up, she saw a man of middle years, stroking his moustache as he stared at her intently. Dressed in a dark suit, cravat at his neck and sporting a bowler hat, he stood apart from the others with their grime encrusted aprons and rough working clothes. But it was the look in his eyes that sent shivers slithering down her spine.

'Might I enquire who you are, young lady?' the man asked, lowering his glance until it was addressing her chest. His voice was brisker than the local dialect she was used to.

'Colenso Carne, sir, daughter of Peder, labourer here. Why do you ask?'

'I saw you leaving my office and want to know what you were doing there.'

'Your office, sir?' she replied, wishing he'd stop gawking at her body. Finally, he raised his face, his lips lifting into some semblance of a grin.

'Indeed. I am the new manager here,' he declared, moving closer. 'And as such I insist on knowing what you have in your basket, Miss Carne.'

'Only cuttings, sir. They were left for me to collect.' She lifted the hessian back for him to see.

'You mean you have been pilfering our fine English marble?' he asked, quirking a brow. She opened her mouth to protest but he ignored her. 'Be sure we shall meet again, Miss Carne,' he added, the steely glint in his eye belying his smile. With a curt nod, he strode inside, leaving her seething.

What an obnoxious man. Meet him again? Over her dead body. She'd make sure she had nothing more to do with him, she thought, hefting her basket over her arm and stomping her way back up the hill.

Chapter 2

Colenso stamped her way back up the track and had reached Ruan before she'd even begun to calm down. The new manager's high-handed attitude was unnecessary and uncalled for. Pilfering indeed. Why, she'd been collecting bits of trimmings and offcuts for months now, spending her precious spare time fashioning and polishing items for the nascent tourist trade. Although she failed to see why people would want to holiday on a peninsula which, at this time of year, was often shrouded in swirling mist, the trees bent and twisted like little old men by the prevailing winds. Still, if they were keen to purchase souvenirs to take home, why shouldn't she provide them? It was satisfying and contributed much-needed money to the family food pot at the same time.

Realizing she was passing Mammwynn's final resting place, she felt her spirits rise. What better place to open her present from Kitto, she thought, hurrying through the rickety gate that led to the sheltered piece of land where her grandmother had grown her beloved herbs. She settled herself on the wooden bench that stood as if waiting for its owner to reappear, and stared at the cairn of stones sited on the exact spot Mammwynn had insisted she be placed. Not for her a plot in the churchyard. 'Why waste good money?' she'd cried. 'My spirit will have long since returned to the Summerlands. I shall be reflecting on lessons learned here and finding out what is yet to come, not worrying where my old body's rotting. Better it be returned to the ground here where it can help nourish all these,' she'd said, her hand making a sweeping gesture around her cherished plants. Colenso sighed as she took in the sad state of them, all withered and wasted. Then she recalled how Mammwynn had explained they were merely resting and would thrive again. There's a proper time for everything and everything has its season, she'd said.

'*Tell me all.*' It could have been the wind whispering in the rowans that bordered her patch but Colenso felt sure it wasn't.

'Kitto loved his pasty Mammwynn, and guess what? He had something for me too,' she cried, taking the package from her basket and holding it up for the woman to see. Then unable to wait any longer, she tore off the wrapping and smiled. Fashioned out of the serpentine stone was a heart, carved with their initials. It must have taken him ages, she thought running her fingers over the gleaming red surface.

'Oh, Kitto,' she murmured. No wonder he'd been dismayed when the hooter sounded. 'It seems we were thinking the same, Mammwynn,' she announced excitedly. The rowans rustled vigorously, as though dancing for joy, and she felt warmth steal through her chilled limbs.

'Before I leave, I know you like to be kept up to date with what's happening. Well, there's a horrid new manager at Poltesco. He's got an upcountry voice and doesn't look you in the face, just sneers like he's better than us. Not only that, he accused me of stealing his rotten old offcuts,' she sighed, but as she got to her feet, she again felt that stabbing at her chest. 'Oh Mammwynn, I'm too large to wear your dainty necklace,' she cried. The rowans stopped their rustling and everything went still. Suddenly the air felt oppressive, as if a storm was brewing and grabbing her things, she hurried for home.

Hoping to share her news with her mamm, she burst into their living room, disappointed to find it empty. She dumped her heavy basket on the floor then busied herself adding wood to the range and setting out the plates ready for their family supper. Although family was a somewhat of a misnomer now that William had left home and Tomas spent as much time as possible away from their domineering drunk of a father.

When she was satisfied everything was prepared, she rummaged through the bag of trimmings to see what could be used to fashion into trinkets. As ever, most of them were too small to be of any use although a few looked promising. Then, she spotted the paper package and clutching it tightly to her, ran upstairs to the room she shared with Tomas.

It was cramped, containing two beds, a tiny chest and the tattered curtain strung up along the middle to protect her modesty. Placing the heart on the shelf, she threw herself down on the woollen blanket and thought about her meeting with Kitto earlier. He'd clearly been trying to say something. Had he been summoning the courage to propose? Although he was kind and loving, he wasn't given to sentiment. Suddenly she heard the back door clatter open.

'Colenso, get down here now.' As her father's angry voice carried up the stairs, she quickly hid Kitto's present under her pillow. Goodness, she must have dreamed away an hour or more, for it had grown dark and she hadn't even noticed.

Slowly she descended the stairs to find her father had lit the lamp and was sitting in his chair drumming his fingers on the table. Grim-faced at the best of times, he was looking positively severe.

'What you bin up to?' he snarled, hazel eyes eyeing her suspiciously. 'Mr Fenton pulled me aside as I was leaving work.' Frowning, he clamped his mouth over his pipe. Nervously, Colenso watched the curl of smoke disappearing into the clean clothes hanging beside the herbs on the wooden airer.

'Mamm not back yet?' she asked, knowing how much her mother hated him smoking in her kitchen.

'Don't change the subject,' he growled, his eyes narrowing. 'Don't know what you've done but you're to come to his office with me first thing Monday morning.'

'But I haven't done anything wrong. I only collected the cuttings you said were waiting,' she said, gesturing to her basket.

'Well, you've to take them back and samples of them gifts you make,' he added. Just then, the door clattered open again and Colenso's mother hurried into the room. 'You're late, woman,' he barked, turning his attention to his wife. 'And not for the first time this week.'

'Sorry, Peder,' Caja puffed, clearly out of breath from hurrying up the lane. 'Mrs Janes took her time passing and then I had to lay ...'

''Tis supper I want, not excuses,' he grumped, drumming his fingers on the table again.

'Yes, Peder,' she replied, scuttling over to the range.

'It's all right, Mamm, I baked pasties this morning,' Colenso said seeing how tired and drawn she looked. Not for the first time, she wished her father would show more consideration for her mother, especially as it was his spendthrift ways that caused her to work all the hours she could. 'I'll make a brew to go with them.'

'You're a good girl,' Caja replied, smiling gratefully.

'Pah, you won't think that when you hear what she's been up to,' Peder scowled.

'I only collected the cuttings as usual,' Colenso explained as her mamm looked askance. 'It's not my fault that nasty new manager took exception.'

'Well, old Coxie never minded. Perhaps he was just exerting his authority, him being a new broom an' all,' Caja mused.

'This one's horrid. He's got probing eyes and a nasty sneer. Reminds me of a ferret …' Colenso began, only to be interrupted by her father.

'We'll have no more of that talk. You'll show respect to Mr Fenton come Monday morning, my girl, or you'll feel the weight of my belt. Now, where's my food?'

Knowing from experience that his threats weren't idle, Colenso snatched up the pot and hurried out to the pump. There wasn't anyone to stick up for her either, for Tomas had taken to staying out until their father had gone to bed. Hopefully, it wouldn't be long before she'd be free from her domineering parent.

*

The next day, as soon as they'd finished their midday broth, her father slumped in his chair and closed his eyes. When his snores and snorts rang out, setting the bowls on the dresser banging together, Colenso tidied her hair then removed the apron protecting her Sunday-best blouse. Although it was far from new, its gold sheen brought out the amber flecks in her dark eyes. Kissing her mamm goodbye, she threw her shawl over her shoulders and headed towards the Todden. She was so excited, she hardly noticed the sea fret hanging over the headland or the biting wind keening in from the east. Hunched in his heavy serge jacket with his flat cap pulled tightly over his head, Kitto was pacing the green impatiently but, as soon as he saw her, his face broke into a wide grin.

'Thought you were never coming,' he murmured, taking her arm and leading her away from the fishermen's cottages where the windows stood staring like prying eyes.

'I said I would, silly,' she smiled.

''Tis silly I am, is it?' he grinned. Then he became serious. 'And is silly what you thought of my present?' She pretended to consider, but he was staring at her so anxiously she shook her head instead.

'I thought it was lovely,' she told him. 'In fact, it's the nicest one I've ever received,' she teased. To her surprise, instead of bantering back as normal, he just nodded. Arms linked, they wandered up the lane, strides matching with the ease that comes with being comfortable in each other's company. A couple of times he cleared his throat as if about to speak before shaking his head. For once Colenso remained silent, knowing he would say what he wanted in his own good time.

As if by instinct they found themselves in Mammwynn's little garden and Colenso settled herself on the seat.

'Colenso.' His voice was gruff with emotion and she turned to face him. Except he wasn't beside her. 'Colenso.' This time she realized the voice was coming from her feet, and looking down she saw Kitto on bended knee staring up at her. 'Will you marry me?' he asked.

'Why Kitto, of course I will,' she cried. 'Now get up off that damp grass before you take a chill.' Grinning, he sprang onto the seat beside her and held out a ring. She had to stifle a giggle when she saw it was one of his mamm's brass curtain rings, but let him put it on her finger anyway.

'This is just a token, Cali,' he murmured. 'I love you and promise to save hard for a proper ring.'

'All I want is to be your wife, Kitto,' she smiled leaning closer. As his lips came down on hers the rowans rustled their approval and she felt a deep sense of contentment.

'We can have our handfasting ceremony right here,' she murmured happily.

'Of course, where else? Although you do realize we won't be able to wed until I've seen my siblings settled.' He stared anxiously into her eyes and, knowing how seriously he felt the responsibility for his family's welfare, she sought to reassure him. It wasn't his fault his father had been caught sheep-rustling and deported two years previously. His mamm had borne the humiliation of losing both her husband and farmhouse home with dignity, making the best of life in a dilapidated hovel on the outskirts of the village. Although she took in washing and cleaned at the hostelry when needed, it was Kitto's wage that paid the rent and being apprenticed, that wasn't much. However, provided he continued putting in the long hours required, his prospects at the serpentine works were good.

'I understand, Kitto,' she assured him. 'Still, Alys is applying for a position as scullery maid at Bochym Manor next month. She'll live in, get well fed and who knows, she might even get to see our dear Queen Victoria and Prince Albert should they decide to stay there again.'

'She'd love that,' he grinned. 'It was them that popularized our local stone, you know.' Colenso shook her head. Everyone knew it was the royal visit and their subsequent purchases that had breathed new life into the industry. However, Kitto was still musing. 'Give anything to see that serpentine ha-ha in the grounds, meant to be a right feature, it is.'

'Well, Cury is only a few miles away so if Alys gets the job you can offer to take her.'

'That's a thought, but there's still Wenna and Daveth.'

'Who are growing up fast,' she assured him.

'Mother always looks on the bright side too,' Kitto smiled. 'I can see why she loves you almost as much as I do.' He leaned closer, his lips claiming hers once more.

'And Mamm thinks the world of you too,' Colenso murmured when she'd recovered sufficiently to talk again.

'I shall need to ask your father's permission,' Kitto grimaced. Colenso nodded and swallowed hard.

'It will be fine,' she assured him.

'Do you really think so?' he asked, doubt furrowing his brow.

'Of course,' she replied, crossing her fingers and hoping hard. 'I've to see this new manager of Poltesco with him tomorrow so will try and pave the way for you then.' But the thought of facing her father must have been playing on his mind, for he didn't even ask why she'd been summoned.

'Best not tell anyone till I have spoken to him, though.'

'Don't worry, only Mammwynn knows and she can't say anything, can she?' Colenso chuckled. The rowan rustled harder, making her laugh even more. 'Or perhaps she can,' she spluttered. 'She always said you were a devilish rascal, Kitto Rowse.'

*

The next morning didn't get off to a good start as Caja was sent for to help with a birthing.

'But I ain't been fed yet,' her father grumbled.

'Don't worry, Father. I'll see to it,' Colenso assured him as her mamm, torn between her duties as wife and sick nurse, dithered uncertainly.

'Best keep your news to yourself, the mood he's in,' she whispered.

'But how …' Colenso began, staring at her mamm in astonishment. Caja gestured to the ring on her finger and winked before scurrying out of the door.

On the way to the works, hurrying to keep up with her father's long stride, Colenso waited for an opportunity to broach the subject of Kitto. Despite the damp mist that clung to her clothes, she was so happy she felt like a soap bubble ready to pop.

'Don't know what you're smiling about, Colenso Carne. Being summoned before the manager ain't nothing to be proud of. 'Specially a new one,' he snapped. 'Years I've been trying to gain a rung up the ladder. Toiled long hours, I have, earning enough to make a better life for you and your mother.' Colenso bit her tongue. That he earned a reasonable wage might be true, but them seeing any of it was quite another matter. Mamm was forever saying the hostelry was her father's mistress, swallowing his money like a bottomless pit, leaving them scrimping to pay the rent man and put food on the table.

'Ouch.' She jumped as yet another stone stabbed her foot. As ever, a new pair of boots or at least decent soles were long overdue, for she'd long outgrown her brother's old ones.

'Stop wittering and get a move on, maid,' her father snapped, glaring at her over his shoulder. It would help if he carried her laden basket, but should the thought even cross his mind, which she doubted, he would consider it beneath him. Her breath rose in little white puffs in the cold morning air as she endeavoured to keep up with him. They were joined along the way by other bleary-eyed workers carrying knapsacks over their shoulders, the scutes on their boots ringing out on the rock-strewn path as they tramped towards the mine. Some called out in greeting and Colenso waved back, but her father sullenly ignored them. Colenso sighed. Mamm was right, it certainly wasn't the right time to tell him about Kitto.

Finally, as the straggle of workers rounded the corner, the mist lifted and they saw another schooner waiting in the bay.

'God knows how he thinks we'll cut enough stone to fill that. We only sent one off Sat'day,' her father grumbled as he stamped his way down the rough track to the factory and its adjacent workings. 'Bet he'll dock my pay for taking you to his office, an' all.'

'I can go by myself,' Colenso assured him.

'Pah, you're female,' he spat. 'What would Fenton make of that? Managers deal man to man,' he added, squaring his shoulders.

'Yes, Father,' she replied, hefting her heavy basket onto the other arm as they picked their way carefully towards the office.

To her father's annoyance, rather than be shown inside, they were told the manager was busy and they should wait.

'Who the hell was that?' he asked, frowning at the dapper little man who, after imparting his message, scuttled back inside leaving them shivering in the freezing cold of the early morning.

Chapter 3

'Costing me money, this is, Colenso,' her father snapped, staring at the work going on around them. They'd been waiting outside for ages and Colenso's hands were red with cold while her ears rang with the constant noise of sawing and banging. 'I'll dock it from your allowance,' he growled, clamping his mouth on his pipe.

'My what?' she exclaimed, staring at him incredulously. But footsteps crunched on the stones behind them and he'd already turned away.

The funny little man reappeared and beckoned them into the office, almost bowing to the manager before scurrying away. As the door closed behind him, Peder's scowl turned to a syrupy smile.

'Good morning, Mr Fenton, sir. I have brought my dear daughter Colenso to meet you, like you asked,' he gushed.

Henry Fenton looked up from the papers he'd been studying, a gleam sparking momentarily as his eyes drew level with Colenso's chest. Gripping her basket tighter, she quickly looked away and stared around the room, which seemingly overnight had turned from a dingy dumping ground to a neat and tidy office. Even the windows had been wiped, although they wouldn't stay clean for long with all the dust and grime that was constantly blown around.

'Correction, Carne, I ordered you to bring her to see me,' Fenton pompously pointed out, bringing her back to the present. Picking up a pen with his soft, white hands, he sat and studied them. Evidently he didn't intend doing any manual work, Colenso thought, taking in the cut of his charcoal suit and matching silk kerchief in his top pocket. And his manners were sorely lacking too for, despite there being two other chairs, he didn't invite them to sit.

'I hope you are settling in …' her father began.

'I didn't ask you here to talk about my well-being, rather to discuss the matter of theft from my premises,' Fenton replied crisply.

'I'll have you know I am not a thief,' Colenso cried. 'I only took the cuttings I was told I could have.'

'Quiet, girl,' Peder ordered.

'Quite, Carne. Now,' he said turning to Colenso. 'I'm in charge here and do not recollect giving you permission to remove anything from the premises.' The eyes that surveyed her were as grey and forbidding as the granite cliffs. Clearly grey was his colour, she thought and would have laughed if her stomach wasn't tying itself into knots. 'The first thing I did when I arrived was to have all the materials checked, and it would appear there are quantities unaccounted for. Now, empty out your basket,' he ordered, gesturing to the space in front of him. Colenso looked at her father, who shrugged. Slowly she placed the small sack of cuttings she'd collected on Saturday, plus brooches and buttons she'd recently fashioned, on the desk before him.

'As you can see, there are only a few offcuts and trinkets ...' her father began.

'You can go about your work now, Carne,' Fenton cut in. 'An important order needs shipping out tonight so you'd better look sharp. You don't want your wages docked more than necessary, I'm sure.'

'Yes, sir. No, sir,' Peder stuttered. Three bags full, sir, Colenso thought as he hurried from the room like a schoolboy anxious to please his teacher.

Once the door had closed behind him, Henry Fenton sat back in his seat and studied Colenso thoughtfully.

'Tell me a bit about yourself, my dear,' he said, his voice softer now. Colenso frowned, suspicious at the change in his demeanour.

'Do you have any brothers and sisters?' he asked.

'Um, five, sir.'

'Five?' he repeated incredulously.

'Well, two brothers living and three sisters in the churchyard.'

'Your sisters live in the churchyard?' he asked, his brows rising.

'Yes, sir, two were born dead and one lived for six months.'

'Oh, I see. And you live at home with your parents and brothers?'

'Yes,' she replied, wondering where this was leading.

'How old are you, Miss Carne?'

'Seventeen but I don't think ...' she began, but he continued speaking.

'I expect a handsome young lady like yourself has many followers?' he asked, nose twitching as he looked her over like she was a prize filly. Buxom she might be but handsome? Was he having a laugh at her expense? But that gleam sparked in his eyes again, making her shiver.

'Only the one,' she mumbled.

'Goodness, the young men around here must be blind,' he exclaimed, leaning forward and picking up one of the trinkets she'd fashioned. As he did so, she noticed a shiny spot on the top of his head. Why, he was going bald, she thought, stifling a giggle.

'You find all this amusing, Miss Carne?' he asked brusquely, his eyes turning hard again.

'No, sir, I'm just feeling a bit faint, having been stood outside in the cold for so long.'

Impatiently he gestured for her to take a seat. Her eyes widened in surprise but she did as he bade.

'I see some of these have been turned – and expertly too,' he said, studying a rounded stone fashioned into a brooch. 'Tell me, are you a marble turner perchance?' His lips curled into one of his sneers and she knew he was mocking her.

'No, sir, but you …'

'So presumably you have help from one,' he cut in. 'And presumably that person is employed here at the works?' He turned his penetrating gaze upon Colenso but determined not to give anything away, she didn't reply.

'I see,' he replied. 'Well, Miss Carne, you should be aware that as manager, I will make it my business to find out everything about the people employed here. In the meantime, perhaps you'd tell me what you do with these, er, trinkets,' Fenton asked.

'Sell them to the tourists,' she murmured.

'Indeed. And do these tourists pay well?' he asked, sitting back in his chair and eyeing her speculatively.

'Quite well, sir,' Colenso replied, not sure where this new line of questioning was leading.

'And tell me, Miss Carne, how much of the sale price you receive do you give back to the works?'

'Give back?' she murmured. 'I don't understand.'

'Well, it stands to reason that if you sell property belonging to Poltesco then any profit should be given back, should it not?'

'But they are only odd cuttings you would otherwise dispose of,' she sputtered, her nails biting into her hand as she strove to keep calm.

'Cut offs, cuttings, edges, edgings, what's in a word?' he shrugged. Then he leaned forward, his eyes narrowing. 'The fact remains that you have been taking materials that belong to the works here. Works that I am now managing, Miss Carne.'

'But I was given permission to take them,' she protested, rising to her feet.

'Not by me, you weren't. As far as I'm concerned, you have taken property that doesn't belong to you. Worse, you have been profiteering from it. The question is, what am I to do about it?' he asked. There was something about the way he was studying her, almost as if he was assessing her, that made her feel increasingly uneasy.

'I don't like the word profiteering, sir,' she protested, endeavouring to keep her voice steady.

'Nor do I, Miss Carne, and I shall have to give serious thought to the matter. Be on your way. You'll hear from me further when I have decided what action to take.'

'Action?' she cried.

'Indeed,' he agreed, that gleam sparking in his eyes as he once again addressed her chest. Angrily she began to collect up the cuttings and trinkets, only for him to shake his head.

'Leave those here where they belong,' he added, before waving her away. Remembering the long hours she'd toiled polishing the rock until it gleamed with colour, she opened her mouth to protest, but he'd already turned back to the papers on his desk.

Feeling sick to the stomach, Colenso left the office, instinctively heading for the workshop. Then fearful that Ferret Fenton might be watching, she veered sharply towards the track. It wouldn't do to get Kitto into trouble. Besides, it was Monday, the day she helped Emily Tucker with her sewing and she couldn't let the old lady down. At least the work would be indoors, she thought. Like most women in the village, she was adept at juggling different jobs to earn a few extra pence, only knowing what day of the week it was by where she was meant to be.

As experienced dressmakers, Emily and Clara had built up a thriving business visiting ladies in their houses and measuring them for their new clothes. Sadly, Clara had recently succumbed to influenza, leaving Emily snowed under with unfinished orders. Knowing Colenso to be a dab hand with the needle, her mamm had offered her services in return for a few shillings and offcuts of material. Offcuts, the word kept sounding in her head as she sped down the lanes of Ruan. How dare that horrid man Fenton accuse her of stealing.

By the time she let herself into Emily's stone cottage with its thatched roof badly in need of repair, Colenso was red with rage. The front room that best got the light had been turned into a sewing room, and Emily, silver tendrils escaping her bun, and customary tape around her neck, was already about her work, a roll of crêpe cloth on the stool beside her. She looked up from a swathe of black serge spread out on the table in front of her.

'Ah, there yer are, Colenso. I thought yer weren't coming,' she muttered through a mouthful of pins.

'I'm sorry but I had to …' Colenso began.

'Tell me later, lover. Got a new order, as if I haven't enough already,' she moaned good-naturedly. 'Lady Carwell's mother died at the weekend and I've been commissioned to make her mourning outfits. Her driver is calling for them later today so if yer can sew a veil to the back of that whilst I finish here that would be grand,' she said, waving her hand towards a fur hat on the dresser that was somehow squeezed into the corner of the room.

'Everyone wants things yesterday,' Colenso grumbled, still out of sorts after her visit with Fenton.

'Well, the poor woman didn't ask to die,' Emily replied with a reproving look.

'No, of course not,' Colenso murmured and, feeling chastened, settled down to her task. She began stitching, her needle stabbing in and out of the fabric as if she was poking that horrid Ferret in the eyes. She didn't know what was worse, his creepy staring at her chest or being accused of theft. After a while, her nerves began to settle and she found herself sewing in time to the ticking of the little ormolu clock on the shelf above her.

'Ther's done,' Emily said some time later, shaking out

the folds of the mourning dress and eyeing it critically. 'Her Ladyship's going to wear her black fur over it for the funeral tomorrow. If yer've finished that, yer can add some tulle to the neck and wrists,' she said, passing over the folded garment while casting a critical eye over Colenso's work. 'Now, I'll makes us a hot drink and then yer can tell me why yer were fuming like a chimney when yer arrived.' Colenso watched as the woman got awkwardly to her feet. Judging by her red-rimmed eyes and stiff back, she'd been up working for hours.

'Would you like me to do it?' she asked, feeling guilty for bringing her earlier bad mood into the room.

'No, ta, me lover. It'll do me good to stretch me old bones. Besides I need the privy,' she added with a girlish grin.

As Emily shuffled stiffly towards the door, Colenso unfolded the tulle and began pinning it onto the dress. Even plain black serge could look attractive when it was good quality and nicely trimmed, she mused. Her thoughts turned to what she was going to wear for her handfasting ceremony. A deep red would be in keeping and complement her dark looks, or perhaps purple with flowing sleeves. The ties that would bind her and Kitto together could be made in matching material. Perhaps Emily would advise her, though of course she wouldn't say anything until she'd spoken to her mamm. With any luck her father would spend the evening in the hostelry and they could begin making plans in peace. Although it would be some time before Kitto finished his apprenticeship and his siblings were settled, it was exciting to think that one day she would become his wife.

'Here we are, lover, chamomile tea to soothe your mood, though yer looking brighter now,' Emily said, eyeing her shrewdly as she set the tray carefully on the shelf. 'Best put yer sewing down, don't want Her Ladyship's dress getting stained. 'Made us a bit of luncheon while I was at it.'

'Thanks, Emily,' Colenso said, pushing the dress carefully to one side. 'I'm famished.'

'Yer always is,' Emily laughed. 'Come on, eat up then yer can tell me what's wrong. Looked like a dog who'd had his bone took earlier, yer did.'

They ate their bread and cheese in peace, each lost in their own thoughts. From the way Emily kept glancing at the empty chair beside her, Colenso knew she was thinking of her sister. She was sipping her tea when Emily got to her feet again.

'By the way, yer can have these offcuts, if they're any use,' she said, passing over some squares of material.

'Oh,' Colenso muttered, her eyes filling with tears as she stared down at them.

'I thought yer'd be pleased not upset. Yer don't have to take them if yer don't want,' Emily frowned.

'But I do. It was the word offcuts that reminded me ...' she broke off as a lump rose in her throat.

'What's up, lover? Come on, yer can tell Auntie Em,' the older lady said, patting Colenso's shoulder.

'The new manager at Poltesco, he ... he ... called me a thief cos I collected the offcuts on Saturday. But I was told I could take them like normal,' she shook her head.

'No wonder yer was hopping,' Emily murmured, passing her a clean kerchief. 'Wipe yer eyes, I'm sure yer father'll explain he's mistaken.'

'Huh,' Colenso sniffed. 'He was there and didn't stand

up for me at all. All he did was grovel like the manager was some kind of god. Then, when he'd gone, that horrid man accused me of profiteering cos I sell the trinkets I fashion to the tourists.'

'But if they was odd bits of no use to the works then they'd just be thrown out, surely? I mean, these offcuts of material here aren't any use to me, but they'd be the start of a lovely patchwork quilt if yer has the time to sew them together. I mean, I guess yer'll be thinking of yer own nest now,' she said, grinning wryly at the ring on Colenso's finger.

'Nothing gets past you, Em,' Colenso said, her spirits lifting. 'But you're right, I shall go and tell Mr Fenton exactly that tomorrow. Now I'd better get back to my sewing or you'll be docking my wages too.'

'Only when yer've calmed down, lover. I were worried poor Lady Carwell's hat was going to be full of holes the way you were stabbing that needle through it. A word to the wise though, I've heard that new manager stops at nothing to get his own way.'

Colenso felt the necklace stab at her chest and that feeling of foreboding settled over her once again.

Chapter 4

Having stayed late to help Emily pack up Lady Carwell's mourning clothes ready for her driver to collect, it was dark by the time Colenso arrived home. The candle was flickering in the window and, despite it having been a long day, her heart quickened at the thought of discussing Kitto's proposal with her mamm. A cosy evening by the warmth of the range making plans for the handfasting would be a welcome pleasure. She might even heat some elderflower cordial as a treat for them both.

However, when she entered the room, her spirits sank for her father was sitting in his chair. To her surprise he greeted her jovially, a smile replacing his usual sullen look.

'Ah Colenso, there you are.' She darted a look at her mamm who shook her head. 'That nice Mr Fenton called me into his office and we had another chat about them things you've been making and …'

'Look, Father, I'm no thief,' she cut in, her temper rising again. 'I only took the offcuts you said I could have.'

'Calm down, maid. Seems the manager's taken a shine to thee and thought of a way you can make it up to him.'

'Make what up? I've done nothing wrong. If anything, he

should apologize to me,' she frowned, slamming her basket on the table.

'No need for that attitude, maid,' he grunted, tamping tobacco into his pipe. Ignoring him, Colenso turned to her mamm.

'Do you need any help with supper or have I time to sort out my things?' she asked. From the appetizing aroma filling the room she guessed they were having root stew and her stomach rumbled in anticipation.

'Finish listening to what your father has to say,' Caja replied, shooting her a warning look.

'You mean there's more?' she asked turning back to face him.

'There is, maid. Mr Fenton is prepared not to call in the constable if you go for afternoon tea at his house on Sunday. Play your cards right and the Carnes could be on the up,' he crowed, rubbing his hands together.

'I have no wish to set eyes on that man again, let alone be entertained by him,' Colenso cried.

'Now listen here, my girl, it's either that or be sent to gaol for theft. Take your pick. Fenton also let slip his friend were Justice of the Peace at Falmouth,' he said, giving her a hard stare.

'Like I said, I've done nothing wrong so I'll take my chances.' To her astonishment he smiled, his manner becoming conciliatory.

'Look, maid, this is your opportunity. For some reason he finds you attractive. I've seen the way he stares at your ...'

'Father, please,' Caja spluttered.

'Well, if she has charms he wants then she should make the most of it. That's how you women work, isn't it? What's that in your basket anyhow?' he asked, leaning over and pulling out the bundle of material.

'Offcuts, I mean remnants Emily gave me,' Colenso said, making to take them from him.

'Not so quickly, maid,' he said, studying the cloth carefully. 'This is good stuff. You can make yourself a nice top to wear on Sunday. Som'at to show off those, er, womanly assets,' he leered.

'I'll have you know this material is to be the beginning of a quilt for when Kitto and I wed.'

'Wed! You'll not be wedding some apprenticed worker, not when there's the chance of walking out with the manager of the works. Think about it, maid, you could be set up for life and see us all right too. After all we've done for you it's the least you can do,' he wheedled. Seeing the set of his chin, Colenso knew she was treading on dangerous ground but the subject was too important to let it rest.

'Look, Father. Kitto is going to speak to you, ask for permission …'

'Oh, so that's what he wanted,' he snarled, his demeanour changing. 'Hanging around outside earlier, he was. Sent him packing with a flea in his ear, I can tell you. Told him never to darken my door again.'

'But …' she began then stopped as his eyes darkened, his hand going to his belt.

'If you've been out sewing you'll have been paid som'at, so give it here. All this jawing's given me a thirst,' he barked, holding out his hand.

Reluctantly, Colenso delved into her pocket and passed over the few precious coins Emily had given her.

'Just look at them 'ands,' Peder snorted. 'You looks like a common washerwoman. Mother give her som'at to smooth them. A fine man like Fenton don't want a woman with rough 'ands. And what's this?' he asked, his eyes narrowing as he took in the brass ring on her finger.

'I told you, Father. Kitto and I are to be wed and ...' she began, snatching her hand back.

'Over my dead body,' he growled. 'You can take that excuse for a ring off right now. You'll marry who I says, maid, and that be final. Mother, talk some sense into this daughter of yours,' he snarled.

'Mamm ...' she began, looking imploringly at her mother, but her father shot out of his chair and seized her roughly by the shoulder.

'Come Sunday, you'll have a new top to wear, one a proper man like Fenton will find tempting.'

'But I see Kitto on Sunday afternoons,' Colenso protested. His grip tightened, making her wince. 'It's Fenton you'll be seeing. Do I make myself clear?' It was only when she nodded that he let go of her. As the door slammed behind him, banging the bowls together on the dresser, Colenso turned to her mamm. 'I've never heard anything so despicable. I'm not an animal to be paraded around and sold to the highest bidder.'

'I know that, Colenso,' Caja sighed. 'But it seems this is the only way to prevent Mr Fenton calling in the authorities.'

'But I've done nothing wrong,' she cried for what seemed like the hundredth time.

'I know you haven't, but Mr Fenton thinks otherwise and he's the manager. Who are they going to believe, eh? Best you humour him, at least for now. We'll take you to Fenton's house on Sunday afternoon, be pleasant to the man and we'll take it from there.'

'But what about Kitto?'

'I'll let Mrs Rowse know you'll be busy on Sunday. You really have no choice, Colenso. Besides, once you've visited Mr Fenton he might decide you're not for him after all.'

'Well, he's certainly not for me. He's old with a balding head, and the way he gawks gives me the creeps,' Colenso shuddered.

'You saw how determined your father was,' Caja sighed. 'Still, it'll only be for an hour or so and we'll stay with you. Now, I think there's a pot of your grandmother's calendula salve in here somewhere,' she said, rummaging in the drawer.

'Mammwynn wouldn't insist on me going to Fenton's house,' Colenso cried.

'No, but she didn't have to live with your father, did she?' Caja replied bleakly.

*

Sunday, the day Colenso had been dreading, arrived seemingly in the blink of an eye. At her father's insistence, she'd spent the past few days trying to improve her appearance. She'd been confined to the cottage and forbidden to fashion any trinkets from the rough offcuts of stone in case she scratched herself. Her hands had been slathered in thick salve and covered in cotton gloves to give it the best chance of sinking in. This had made sewing cumbersome, but when she'd complained her mamm had shrugged and said this was her opportunity, reminding her to brush her hair a hundred times and rub her teeth with the powder she'd mixed from bark, salt and liquorice root to whiten them. Then this morning she'd been made to bathe in water infused with the magnesium from ground-down serpentine to freshen her skin, and gargle with a tincture of clove to freshen her breath.

She'd pleated one of the squares Emily had given her and sewn it into the front of her best blouse, secreting the others away to make a quilt for when she and Kitto set up home together. Now she had to suffer the humiliation of standing in front of her father as he cast a critical eye over her appearance.

'Shame she couldn't have lost a bit of that podge, Mother, and why isn't that top showing a bit more …' he muttered, gesturing to her front.

'I am not some prize filly,' Colenso snapped, thoroughly disgruntled by the whole charade.

'That you're not, maid,' he snorted. 'Can't turn pigskin into silk, can you? And I thought I told you to take that stupid curtain ring off.' As Colenso opened her mouth to protest, they heard the sound of hooves outside. 'Do it now, Colenso,' he ordered. Seeing the set of his chin, Colenso reluctantly removed the ring and placed it in her pocket. 'Let me escort you to our transport, Mother,' he added grandly.

He led them outside to the waiting pony trap, where the driver, stiff-backed and straight-faced, touched his hat in deference.

'See, maid, this is the life we could have if you acts right,' her father grinned, climbing grandly up as though it was the finest carriage in Cornwall. Then, as they made their way down the lane, neighbours staring in surprise, he proceeded to nod and tip his cap like a country squire.

'I hope you've got some good conversation ready, Colenso. Mr Fenton'll expect some witty repartee, won't he, Mother?' Repartee? Since when had her father used fancy words, Colenso thought.

'That he will, Father, but our Colenso's a clever girl and won't let us down,' Caja told him. Dressed in her Sunday best with a new ribbon trimming her bonnet, she looked livelier than she had for a long time. 'And this breeze will have added colour to her cheeks by the time we arrive.'

Colenso hardly heard them, for her stomach was churning like it was making butter. She was missing Kitto and couldn't help wondering how he'd be spending the afternoon. They should be curled up together on Mammwynn's bench, making plans for their future. Instead here she was, being bowled through the country lanes, past her grandmother's final resting place and the church and cottages of Ruan, with her father crowing like a cockerel while Mamm simpered beside him. If Mr Fenton was expecting lively conversation then she'd make sure he got it, she vowed, remembering how Kitto had told her about the weathering of serpentine on the grand buildings of London.

'The stone may be hard but for centuries it's been exposed to blasts and storms. It is used to rain, fog and sunshine. Maritime climate exempts the area from extreme cold and there is serious question over its durability in the frosty conditions that prevail in the towns up country.' Remembering how he'd become quite emotional about the action of a hard frost on thin slices of serpentine, she smiled. That should knock the sneer off the Ferret's face.

As the cottages were replaced by stunted trees, the lane

turned rougher and the trap began rocking alarmingly. She gripped the sides, wishing she was on foot, for this little conveyance would surely never make it down the steep track to Poltesco. However, before they reached the turning to the works, the driver veered sharply right. Tucked into the sheltered side of the valley was what looked like a huddle of cottages. As they drew to a halt, Colenso could see it was actually one large angular single-storey building, constructed mainly from dressed serpentine. Rows of square windows suggested numerous rooms inside, and plumes of smoke curling from each of the three tall chimneys hinted at grand fireplaces. It was a far cry from their humble home and, feeling somewhat overwhelmed as well as apprehensive, she clambered down, shivering as the wind blew in from the sea. The waves thudding on the rocks below echoed the pounding of her heart and once again she wished she was with Kitto, his hand holding hers as they made plans for their future.

Her musing was interrupted by her father digging her in the ribs as the door was opened by a tight-lipped housekeeper. Disapproval oozed from every pore as she looked them up and down with a sniff.

'Do you want me to hang them, er, shawls on the stand?' she asked, looking relieved when Colenso shook her head. Whether it was correct or not, she intended keeping herself as covered as possible. The housekeeper led them quickly down a hallway bereft of any pictures or ornamentation, and into the sparsely furnished front parlour. A fire crackled in the grate, lending cheer to an otherwise dreary room.

'Your, er, visitors,' she announced disdainfully then, with another sniff and rustle of starched petticoats, withdrew.

'Ah, Mr and Mrs Carne, welcome,' Henry Fenton said, putting down his newspaper and rising to his feet. 'And you have brought your charming daughter, I see.' His nose twitched, his eyes glittering as they greeted the swell of her chest. 'Would you like to divest yourself of your wrap?' Again, Colenso shook her head and was gratified to see a flash of disappointment before he smiled again.

'Good of you to invite us Mr Fenton, sir,' Peder said. 'This is Caja, my wife.'

'What a delightful name,' he smiled.

''Tis the Cornish for daisy, Mr Fenton, and I'm pleased to meet you, sir,' Caja beamed, bobbing a little curtsey.

'And Colenso you have already met, of course,' Peder said, giving her a nudge towards him.

'Indeed. And what does your name stand for, my dear?' he asked, giving her a wide smile. It was as if their previous exchange had never taken place.

'It means "from the dark pool",' Colenso replied.

'Very appropriate for your exotic colouring, my dear,' he smiled, that gleam sparking in his eyes once more. Exotic? What did that mean, Colenso mused, returning his smile through gritted teeth. And as for names, with his twitching nose and piercing eyes, 'Ferret Fenton' was certainly appropriate.

'Do take a seat. My housekeeper, Mrs Grim, will return with a tray in fifteen minutes,' he told them. 'Now, Caja – I may call you that?' he asked.

'Why yes, sir, of course,' she simpered, settling herself daintily on the edge of a chair beside the fire. 'What a charming home you have here.'

'Thank you, although as you will see from the furnishings, or rather lack of, it sorely needs attention. Now, do forgive me if I discuss Poltesco matters with your husband. I'd like to dispense with business before we partake of refreshment.' Without waiting for her to answer, he turned to Peder. 'You were telling me about your ambitions, Carne.'

'Yes, Mr Fenton, sir. I have been labouring at the quarry for many years now – my undying loyalty, your works have. Long hours I labour shifting them heavy blocks, even saw and rough-shape when time is pressing, I do. It's down to me spurring your men on that Poltesco orders are met.'

'Indeed, Carne?' Fenton replied with the merest quirk to his brow. 'Well, such loyalty certainly deserves recognition. And you, my dear,' he said, turning his gaze on Colenso. 'Tell me how you spend your time, when you're not fashioning my offcuts, that is,' he laughed.

'First of all, Mr Fenton, I'd like to make it quite clear that I am no thief. Any bits of serpentine I have used for my trinkets have been given to me.' He studied her for a long moment then grinned.

'Bravo, well said, my dear. I like a woman who stands up for herself. As I have already intimated to your father, I'm a reasonable man and sure I can be persuaded to overlook the matter in return for …' He stopped as the grandfather clock in the corner of the room struck the quarter-hour and the door opened.

The housekeeper strode into the room carrying a tray of crockery along with a plate of saffron buns, followed by a young girl of about six, staggering under the weight of a huge teapot. Deftly, she placed the things on the table then

43

turned the full force of her glare on the girl, who flustered and tripped, spilling dark liquid on the rug. As her eyes widened in fright, Colenso jumped to her feet and took the pot from her trembling hands.

'Lady guests don't help,' Mrs Grim snapped, her voice laden with reproach. 'Do you wish me to pour, Mr Fenton?' she asked.

'As I'm holding the pot, I might as well,' Colenso replied before he could answer. The woman's lips pursed in disapproval as she looked uncertainly at her boss.

'Thank you, Mrs Grim, that will be all,' he replied. With a brisk nod, the housekeeper marched from the room. As the little girl scuttled after her, Colenso winked, gratified to see her smile back. It was only when her father glared that she realized she was still standing in the middle of the room, pot in hand.

Quickly she poured the tea and handed it round.

'Idiot,' her father hissed as he took his cup from her.

'Remember your place,' Mamm whispered. However, judging from the way Ferret Fenton's lips were twitching, it appeared he found the situation amusing.

'Delicious buns, Mr Fenton, sir,' Peder said, helping himself then spraying crumbs over his lap. 'Our Colenso here is a dab hand at cooking and baking. She made the revels for both the Grade and Ruan Church feast days,' he boasted.

'Revels?' the manager frowned.

'They're the same as those, really,' Colenso said, pointing to the buns. 'But with saffron so expensive, we only bake them for high days and holidays.'

'Indeed? Well, as I consider today to be a high day, Miss

Carne, let us enjoy the fruits of Mrs Grim's labours,' he chuckled.

'Ah that's good, Mr Fenton, sir. Fruit buns and fruits of her labours.' Peder's raucous laugh boomed around the room, spraying more crumbs everywhere. Not for the first time that afternoon, Colenso wished she was anywhere but here.

Chapter 5

'I hope you and your family have settled well on The Lizard, Mr Fenton,' Caja enquired, breaking the ensuing silence. Knowing she was probing, Colenso shot her mamm a warning look.

'Alas, I am a widower and not blessed with family. However, I'm gradually settling in, thank you. Though, as you can see, this house is sorely in need of a woman's touch,' he shrugged, his eyes sliding towards Colenso, who looked quickly away. He turned back to Caja.

'Those threadbare drapes at the window, for example, were left by my predecessor and I really need to employ the services of a seamstress.'

'Why, our Colenso's also a dab with the needle. Helps Emily sew Her Ladyship's attire, she do,' Caja beamed.

'Does she now? You are indeed useful with your hands, Miss Carne.' As his speculative gaze sent shivers sliding down her back, the necklace stabbed at her chest. Despite her resolve, she'd found herself unable to remove Mammwynn's gift but now, as the Ferret sat gawping at her, she wished she had. Pulling her shawl tighter around her, she jumped up and went over to the curtains. Then, as she studied the material, her eye was caught by the vista from the window.

'Why, you can see virtually the whole of the works from here,' she cried, staring down at the extent of the factory buildings, derricks and stream. The iron-framed overshot waterwheel with its wooden leat was supported on a huge timber framework that rose like a monster out of the basin of the pond. She could even see along the full length of the wooden jetty where the flat-bottomed barges were moored ready to transport the heavy stone out to the schooners. Being the Sabbath, nothing but the water was moving, but just how much the works had grown was evident.

'Why, it's enormous,' she cried.

'And I have plans to extend it further,' Mr Fenton boasted, puffing out his chest. 'There'll be more buildings erected and something done to that stream, which I understand weakens in the summer and slows the wheel. Can't allow production to fall.'

'You can spy on us workers from up here, then,' Peder exclaimed, having risen to join her.

'I prefer the word oversee, Carne,' Mr Fenton replied mildly. 'As I've said before, I take my responsibilities as manager seriously, very seriously indeed.'

'Of course, Mr Fenton, sir,' Peder mumbled, returning to his chair. 'And what other plans do you have?' Colenso saw the spark in her father's eyes and realized he was hoping to find out if there'd be anything in it for him. Although different in class, the two men clearly had similar objectives. However, the manager wouldn't be drawn.

'That's enough talk of shop for one day,' he said, seemingly amused by his own words. 'You are here as my guests,' he added, turning back to Caja. 'In answer to your question, I have been made most welcome, thank you. Although I must confess that having spent most of my time sorting out the works, I've yet to see anything of the surrounding areas. Not being from around these parts, I wouldn't know where to start. Perhaps, if I were fortunate to have the company of someone who knew the best places to visit, it would be different.' He shrugged, letting his voice trail away as he took a sip of his tea.

'Our Colenso here would be the perfect person to escort yer, Mr Carne, sir. She do know all the best spots,' Peder said excitedly. 'One turn deserves another, what with yer seeing me get on at the works, like.'

'Oh, I couldn't possibly impose,' he demurred.

But you will, Colenso thought, a feeling of doom descending like a dark cloud.

'She would be delighted to, wouldn't you, Colenso?'

'But I'm busy with my handfa ...' she began.

'She'd love to, Mr Carne,' Caja cut in. 'There's nothing you'd like better, is there?' she added, shooting Colenso a pointed look.

'And would you be chaperoning me, Mamm?' she asked sweetly.

'Goodness, maid. I'm sure there's no need for that, Mr Fenton here being a respectable man, like,' Peder said quickly.

'Well, if that's agreed, I will call upon you next Sunday, Miss Carne, and you can direct me to places you think will be of interest. I understand that the church towers around here are mostly constructed of blocks of unpolished serpentine rock – and of course, you are knowledgeable on that subject, are you not?' he smiled, giving her a knowing look.

'Indeed I am, Mr Fenton,' she agreed, ignoring his obvious reference to the trinkets she fashioned from offcuts. 'Both Grade and Ruan Church are built of the stone and the pulpit and lecterns are fine examples of polished serpentine workmanship.' If she had to spend time with this pompous man, then she'd make sure she did it in public. There were always villagers in the churches on the Sabbath and she'd feel safer in the company of people she knew. It seemed Ferret Fenton had other ideas though.

'Afterwards we could drive somewhere quieter, partake of afternoon tea, really get to know each other better,' he suggested, grey eyes glinting silver as they roved over her body. Respectable indeed, Colenso thought, gritting her teeth and pulling her shawl even tighter. The twitch of his lips told her he knew exactly what she was doing but he rose to his feet, saying: 'Well, it was good of you to come but I really mustn't detain you any longer.' Picking up a silver bell, he shook it and immediately the housekeeper appeared.

'Show my visitors out please, Mrs Grim.'

'It will be my pleasure, sir,' she said, turning on her heel and hurrying down the hallway.

'Thank you for the tea, Mr Fenton, sir,' Peder said, ushering the others out after the housekeeper.

'Don't know why you looks like you're sucking on a lemon, maid. You're just the same as us,' Peder whispered, catching up with the housekeeper as she stood waiting with the door open.

'I don't see how you make that out,' she sniffed.

''Tis easy, maid, we're both workers for Mr Fenton, aren't we?'

As she sniffed again and firmly pushed the door shut behind them, Peder turned to Colenso.

'Play your cards right and you could be her boss one day.' Bemused, Colenso could only stare at her father, but before she could think of a suitable reply, he'd climbed into the waiting trap, her mamm following after him.

The shadows were lengthening as they made their way back up the driveway and through the country lanes. Silhouettes of twisted trees rose out of the dimpsy light, their knots like evil eyes, reminding her of the way Ferret Fenton had gawped at her chest. Gently she fingered her necklace. 'How I wish you were still here, Mammwynn,' she whispered. Then her father's raucous laugh rang out, rousing the roosting rooks and making her shudder. How she hated him for putting her in such an impossible situation. Drawing the ring from her pocket, she placed it firmly back on her finger where it belonged.

To her surprise, a light was flickering in the window when they arrived home. It must mean her brother was back, she thought, her spirits rising. Sure enough, he was hunched over the table studying some papers, a half-empty mug of cold tea beside him.

'Oh Tomas, am I glad to see you,' she cried.

'Hey, little sis,' he grinned, his dark eyes lighting up. ''Tis flatterin' to get a greetin' like that. You're shaking – what's up?'

'You wouldn't believe …' she began.

'Remembered where you live, then?' Peder growled, striding into the room. 'What's that you're reading?'

'Evening to you too, Father,' Tomas said, a wary look replacing his grin as he hastily folded the papers and put them in his pocket.

'Tomas, you've come home,' Caja whooped, throwing her arms around him. ''Tis good to see you son. I'll make us a brew and we can have a nice old catch-up. You won't believe where we've been.' Letting go of her son, she hurried over to the range.

''Tis unusual to see you all dressed up of a Sunday evening. And was that a pony and trap I heard outside?' he asked, staring at them curiously.

'Yep. The Carnes is going places,' Peder told him, unable to contain his excitement.

'Sounds like you've already been,' Tomas replied.

'Ha son, very funny. Now listen up,' he said, tossing his cap onto the nail and settling himself down at the table. 'You'll never guess what?'

'Colenso's walking out with the new works manager,' Tomas quipped.

'How do you know that?' Peder exclaimed, his brows almost disappearing under the flop of greying hair that fell over his forehead.

'I was jesting, Father,' Tomas sighed, shaking his head.

'But 'tis true,' Peder boasted. 'And if she plays her cards right, we'll be out of this cot and into something bigger and better come Michaelmas.'

'What?' Tomas gasped, starring at Colenso in astonishment.

'In fact, if your sister really turns on the charm, she could make that midsummer and save us the quarter's rent,' Peder carried on gleefully.

'But I thought you and Kitto …' Tomas began.

'We are …' she began, only to be interrupted once again as Peder jumped to his feet and stood glaring at her.

'No daughter of mine's wedding a foreigner Duck and that's that. Geese we be, and proud of it.'

'For heaven's sake, Father, 'tis merely the stream that separates us Grade Geese from Ruan Ducks. Besides, Kitto only lives on the edge of the village,' Tomas laughed.

'In a down-and-out hovel,' he snorted. 'Anyhow, I ain't having no interbreeding in the Carne family,' he glared.

'But you just said he was a foreigner, you can't have it both ways,' Colenso began. 'Besides, Mammwynn was born on Ruan side.'

'Yeah, and look at her with her herbs and potions. The woman was crackers. Or should that be quackers, being as how she were a Duck,' Peder chortled.

'That's enough, Father. I'll not have Mamm spoken about like that, God rest her soul,' Caja cried, banging their mugs down hard on the table. 'Besides, I use herbal remedies to heal my patients.'

'Sorry,' Peder mumbled, looking anything but. 'Fenton's a man of breeding. Come from up country, he has.'

'Yes, and there's rumours as to why he left,' Tomas said, giving his father a sharp look. However, Peder was in his stride and even if he'd heard Tomas's remark, he chose to ignore it.

'Taken a shine to our Colenso, he has, and is calling on her next Sunday. Play our cards right and we could be rolling in it,' he crowed, rubbing his hands together.

'Is this true, our Col?' Tomas frowned.

'I don't want to …' she began.

'You'll do as your darn well told. Just seventeen, you be. A child. Until you become an adult 'tis up to me to decide what's best for you,' he said, clamping his mouth around his pipe and tamping tobacco into the bowl.

'So, I'm old enough to earn money for your drink, but only a child when it suits you,' Colenso retorted. Seeing her father's hand go to his belt, she jumped to her feet. 'You kept me prisoner here all last week but I promised to help Emily with her sewing tomorrow and I intend to so.'

'Of course you will,' Peder replied, a smile replacing his scowl as he struck his tinderbox. He puffed on his pipe, sending spirals of smoke disappearing into the clothes on the pulley above. As Caja opened her mouth to protest, he leaned forward and stared hard at Colenso.

'You'll need som'at new to wear when you go out with Fenton, so be sure to get more of that quality material from her.'

'But they were surplus offcuts. I can't expect her to give me any more,' Colenso told him.

'Then take some,' he snapped. 'Used to pilfering, ain't you?' Unable to believe what she was hearing, Colenso stared at him in disgust. 'And then you can spend the rest of the week making something more fetching than that effort you're wearing now. A man likes to have something womanly to look at.'

'Really, Father …' Tomas began.

'Who asked you to pipe up? You're only a cutter but your sister has a chance to better herself,' Peder glowered.

'Well, thanks very much,' Tomas replied but his father had already turned to Caja.

''Tis up to us to assist our dear daughter, Mother, so Colenso will spend her time keeping house and getting our meals.'

'I already cook most of them, Father,' she pointed out.

'But you always does the same things. A man like Fenton needs a wife who can entertain, put something tempting on the table.'

'I have no intention of doing things just to please old Fenton,' Colenso cried.

'Listen here, maid. That's exactly what you're going to do. If you let this chance slip through your fingers I'll ...' He rose to his feet and towered over her. As he began unbuckling his belt, Colenso fled up the stairs to her room.

Cradling the serpentine heart to her chest, she threw herself down on her cover and stared at the grimy ceiling. Heedless of her father's wiles and Fenton's threats, it was Kitto she was going to wed. Her father's moods were more changeable than the weather. As for her mamm, she'd always liked Kitto, and Colenso couldn't believe she'd sided with her father.

As for bettering themselves, whilst they didn't live in the best of cottages and there was always more week than wage, they'd always got by. Of course, if her father didn't frequent the hostelry so often, life would be easier. But to make her walk out with that Ferret Fenton, whose eyes never got higher than her chest, was despicable even by his standards.

Shouting from below followed by thumping on the table woke her. As ever, it seemed her father and brother couldn't be in the same room for long without coming to blows. Wearily she undressed and, tossing her clothes on the floor beside her, climbed under the cover. The weight of her necklace felt heavy but, as ever, something stopped her from removing it. If only she could remember exactly what Mammwynn had said when she'd given it to her.

'Hey Col, you awake?' Her eyes flew open to find Tomas lying on his bed beside her.

'Must have dropped off,' she murmured.

'Before Mamm comes up, tell me what's been going on.'

Briefly she filled him in about Kitto's proposal, Fenton accusing her of theft, then insisting she go for tea before inveigling his way into calling upon her next Sunday.

'He's horrid, Tomas,' she shuddered. 'I can't believe Mamm's encouraging him.'

'You know Father's temper. She'll do anything to avoid riling him. It's why William left. Not sure I can put up with much more meself.'

'I'm scared, Tom. Please promise you won't leave?' He stared at her closely for a moment then nodded.

'I'll not leave yet, sis,' he promised. 'I'm surprised at Kitto letting you go to Fenton's though.'

'He doesn't know.'

'Why not?' She could feel his sharp look peering through the darkness. 'He'd look out for you, thinks the world of you, he does.'

'I didn't get the chance to tell him. Besides, I couldn't risk upsetting Fenton. He threatened to call the constabulary in.'

'But you're innocent.'

'I know, but they'd start probing and … well, Kitto turned some of my trinkets on his lathe.'

'Jeez. What a mess. Still, I don't like the idea of you walking out with that man, Col. He already has a bad reputation. Word has it he's got the quarry owners on side, started up some sort of alliance. I don't know all the details but I intend to find out. Whatever it is, it'll be bad news for us at the works, you can be sure of that.'

Hearing the scraping of chairs on the flagstones below, he jumped up and drew the dividing curtain.

'Don't worry, I'll find out what's going on, sis. Now, pretend to be asleep,' he whispered as they heard their father's tread on the stairs. He came to a halt outside their door and Colenso froze, but luckily he had other things on his mind.

'Hurry up, Caja,' he called. 'A husband don't like to be kept waiting for his rights.'

As his raucous laugh bounced off the walls, Colenso hid her head under her pillow and desperately tried to get back to sleep.

Chapter 6

Colenso was being chased by Fenton who was being chased by Kitto. Round and round the serpentine works they ran. Fenton, rapacious arms outstretched, was gaining on her by the second. '*You're mine, mine, mine,*' he was shouting. Unable to keep going any longer, she ran to the end of the jetty and jumped. As the cold water closed over her, she woke with a start and lay in the darkness, trembling and disorientated. She blinked, trying to dispel her dream but the images persisted and she knew she had to see Kitto. Quietly, so as not to wake her brother, she slipped on her clothes, then boots in hand crept out of the room. The snores and snorts emanating from her parents' room told her they wouldn't be rising any time soon and, tiptoeing down the stairs, she threw on her shawl and bonnet and slipped outside.

Apart from a pearlescent loom to the east, the sky was black as soot. Not a soul stirred, although she knew it wouldn't be long before the villagers rose to begin the new day. Determination lending urgency to her steps, she sped past the neighbouring cottages, their windows still shuttered and chimneys not yet smoking, over the wooden bridge that spanned the stream and on through the village. Then her ears pricked. She could hear footsteps running towards her. A shadowy figure emerged out of the darkness. Heart pounding like waves on the beach below, she swallowed hard.

'Colenso?' To her surprise, Kitto came slithering to a halt beside her. 'What are you doing out at this hour?' he asked.

'What are you doing here?' she asked at the same time. They laughed then stood gazing at each other, breath rising like steam in the early morning air, until he broke the silence.

'I had to see you. Make sure you're all right. I waited ages yesterday, and when you didn't come I skirted round the back of your cottage so as not to bump into your father. He gave me a right old ear-bashing the other afternoon. Warned me not to visit again, or words to that effect,' he shrugged. 'Anyway, couldn't see any sign of you, so I went home. Spent the afternoon patching up our leaking window. Where were you, anyhow?' he asked, dark eyes staring into hers.

'You won't believe this,' she muttered. 'We had to go for afternoon tea at Mr Fenton's house.'

'You mean as in the works manager?' he frowned. 'But why? I mean your father's not exactly on the same level, is he? Sorry if that sounds rude but ...' he shrugged.

'It's true,' she agreed, jumping at the snap of shutters being pulled back. As candles began flickering in the cottage windows, she knew the men would soon be making their way to the works. 'Fenton accused me of theft,' she admitted.

'What?' Kitto gasped, staring at her as if she'd grown another head. A door opened behind them. 'Come on, we can't talk here,' he muttered. Taking her arm, he led her towards the shelter of the adjoining stables. 'Now, tell me what's been going on,' he demanded.

Quickly she told him everything, from her meeting in Fenton's office to the invitation to tea, although she was careful to keep the manager's intentions to herself. Then she frowned.

'Mamm promised to let your mother know I wouldn't be able to meet you.'

'Didn't get any message. Mother would have passed it on if she had. I don't like the sound of this at all, Cali. You're my girl … I mean, you are, aren't you?' he asked, treacle eyes staring deeply into hers.

'Of course I am,' she cried. 'I love you and can't wait to be your wife, Kitto.'

'Then as soon as I get to work, I'll go to Fenton's office and have it out with him.'

'But he saw the things I made and knows some have been skilfully turned. If you do that he'll put two and two together. Even if he doesn't call in the constable, he'll like as not sack you. You can't afford to lose your job, Kitto.'

Silence descended as he processed all she'd said. There was a soft whinny and the smell of straw and horse emanated through the wooden slats as the animals stirred. Finally, he let out a long sigh.

'You're right. Nobody will take on a partly trained apprentice.' As they stared at each other helplessly, the horses gave another whinny and a nearby door clattered open, followed by the banging of others. Then came the ringing of booted feet on the rough country lane as the men began their trek up the hill towards the works. 'Got to go, but you can be sure I'll give this some serious thought. Can we meet later?' he asked.

'I'm sewing for Emily today. She's up to her eyes with

orders so I'll be working late,' she told him. 'How about tomorrow? I'd better not risk coming to the factory, so I'll see you on Mammwynn's seat when you've finished work.'

'Right,' he nodded. 'I still can't believe you've been to Fenton's house,' he muttered, shaking his head. 'It doesn't feel right. Why do I get the feeling there's more to all this?'

If only you knew, she thought as an image of the Ferret's glittering eyes rose before her, making her shudder.

'Don't worry, Cali, I'll get it sorted,' he murmured, pulling her closer. For one blissful moment she was enfolded in the warmth of his arms and then, with a quick peck on her cheek, he was gone. She watched as he ran towards the line of workers snaking their way out of the village. Why was life so difficult? One minute they were planning their future, the next that horrid Fenton had arrived, making her life a misery. And she still had to tell Kitto about the forthcoming outing on Sunday. It wasn't fair, she fumed, heading towards Emily's cottage.

'Cripes, maid, yer early, and looking wild as a winter storm,' the woman greeted her through a mouthful of pins. 'Still, unless yer at death's door, yer'll have to wait till later to tell me what's wrong. We've got a busy morning ahead. Mrs Jeans is coming for her dresses and yer know how particular she is. I offered to deliver them as usual, but it seems her son has business over at Ruan so he offered to convey her. Convey,' she laughed. 'They were her very words.' Despite her mood, Colenso couldn't help smiling at the woman. 'Now, I've pinned up the hems so if yer can stitch them and add pearl buttons to the bodices, I'll get on with the skirt for Miss Cardew.'

Although Colenso's hands automatically performed her

tasks, her mind was running amok. The thought of another long week confined to the house, doing only light chores so as not to redden or scratch her hands, was more than she could bear. As for making an appealing top for that odious manager to gawk at her in, the very idea made her shudder.

'Someone walk over yer grave?' Emily asked.

'Might well have done,' she sighed.

'Well, the smoothing irons are hot so yer can get them hems pressed, that should warm yer up.' Colenso couldn't help smiling at the woman's humour as she picked up one of the heavy irons with the thick cloth and spat on it. When it hissed, she wiped the sole, spread out one of the dresses on the table and set about her task. By the time they heard the knock on the door, the garments were ready.

'That'll be Mrs Jeans,' Emily said, getting stiffly to her feet. 'Let's hope she pays cash rather than insisting on having an invoice sent. Gives me extra work when I could be sewing, and goodness knows I can do with the money,' she grumbled. 'Yer go and make us a brew while I see to her. There's a heel of bread and some cheese on the side to go with it.' Colenso smiled gratefully, for in her hurry to see Kitto, she'd quite forgotten to break her fast.

'Well, there's a turn-up for the books,' Emily smiled as Colenso returned with the loaded tray. 'Mrs Jeans not only paid on the spot, she wants another dress made – a fancy one for entertaining, no less. She's brought some lovely emerald satin material and wants it trimmed with black fringing. Naturally she needs it immediate, like, so there's more work for yer this week.' When Colenso didn't respond, Emily frowned. 'Thought yer'd be pleased.'

61

'I would, only Father ordered me to stay indoors for the rest of the week. I've to sew another top, a more appealing one this time, and make different dishes to increase my cooking skills. He says they're too limited,' she sighed.

'Get away with yer. Young Kitto's that besotted he'd think yer was appealing if yer wore yer bedcover,' Emily grinned. 'And I can't imagine him complaining about your cooking either.'

'It's Father. He wants to impress the new works manager.'

'Oh?' Emily narrowed her bird-like eyes. 'Would this be anything to do with them accusations of theft he made?' Colenso nodded.

'He told Father I could make it up to him by going for afternoon tea at his house. It was ghastly. Mamm simpering, Father kowtowing, Fenton gawking. And that's not the end of it. He's asked for me to show him the local sights on Sunday. When I started to refuse, Father told him I would. He says it's a good opportunity.'

'I'd like to say I'm surprised, but I'll not lie. Always one to feather his nest at another's expense, if yer'll excuse me being candid, maid.'

'But Mamm backed him up.'

'Well, she would, wouldn't she? I mean she might be the sick nurse and a capable one at that, but she'll not stand up to yer father. Course, she were different before she married him.'

'What was she like then?' Colenso asked. Emily took a sip of her tea, a faraway look in her eye.

'Happy, spirited, do anything for a lark,' she said eventually. Then she grinned. 'One day she took your mammwynn's bloomers off the washing line and sewed up the ankles.

Keren never realized till it were too late. Hopping she were, literally,' Emily chuckled.

'I can't imagine Mamm being mischievous, or laughing,' Colenso replied, her eyes widening in surprise.

'Well, that's the thing, see. The right man will make a woman blossom and grow, but the wrong one'll crush the life out of yer.' Colenso stared at her in surprise. How could someone who'd never married know about such things? 'Seen it happen too often,' Emily added as if guessing her thoughts. 'So, make sure yer choose the right man.'

'Oh, I will,' Colenso assured her, an image of her dark-haired, treacle-eyed Kitto rising before her.

'And if it's who I think it is, make sure yer tell him about that outing. Honesty's everything and it wouldn't do for him to find out from someone else.'

'I intend telling Kitto when I see him later. Though I can't see him being pleased about it. Still, if I accompany Fenton this one time, I'll surely have paid my debt for this perceived theft.'

'Hmm, I wouldn't be too sure,' Emily frowned. 'Now about that appealing top yer father expects yer to make,' she added, stressing the word appealing. 'Does yer have the material to make such a thing?' she asked before taking a sip of her tea.

'No,' Colenso admitted, not wishing to admit what her father had suggested.

'And did he suggest where yer might get some, by any chance?' As the woman stared at her closely over the top of her mug, Colenso felt a flush creeping over her cheeks.

'Thought as much.'

'But I wouldn't …' she cried.

'Don't worry, maid. I never thought for one moment yer would.'

'Besides, I don't want to wear something that reveals my …' she gestured to her chest. 'The way Fenton gawks at it gives me the creeps.' She leaned forward to pick up her mug and the necklace stabbed her. 'Ouch,' she cried.

'What's up?' Emily asked, concern wrinkling her brow.

'It's this necklace Mammwynn gave me, it keeps digging into me.'

'If that's yer grandmother's pentacle yer wearing she reckoned it always prodded her when evil threatened. Said it never lied.'

'That's it,' Colenso cried. 'She said to heed what it told me cos it never lied. So, it's got nothing to do with my size?'

'Yer a Cornish maid through and through, and proud of it you should be too. Yer Kitto thinks yer beautiful and so you are. He's a good man.' Then she became serious. 'However, there are men who are not so honourable, and this Fenton sounds one of them. Mind yer heed that warning.'

'But what am I to do? Father will kill me if I don't do as he says.'

'I'm guessing yer mamm's no help?' Colenso shook her head and Emily sighed.

'A true friend to me yer grandmother was. Used to pass many an hour listening to her talking about her beloved herbs and plants. Real knowledgeable, she were, and her nettle unguent were the only thing that eased my old joints,' she said her hand going to her hip.

'I didn't realize. Mamm has all her receipts so I'll get her to look it out,' Colenso offered.

'Thanks, maid. Now, eat yer food while I think of a way we can outwit that old pessack.' Colenso smiled as she picked up her bread. A rotten old pilchard described Fenton perfectly. He was ancient and probably smelled of decay, although she had no intention of getting close enough to find out. She'd just finished eating when Emily shouted, making her jump.

'Got it, me lover. We'll design a top that teases but protects your modesty at the same time. Now listen up, this is what we'll do.'

*

Dusk was falling as Colenso made her way to Mammwynn's seat. She'd spent the day sewing the top Emily had designed for her and concocting a potage from a gaverick begged from old Mr Paul and flavoured with dried herbs. Her father hated all things crab, but he'd told her to try different things, hadn't he? Lost in thought, she sat on the seat, the shadows lengthening around her. Surely Kitto should have been here by now?

'Oh Mammwynn, if only you knew what's been going on,' she sighed. A sudden gust of wind shook the rowan branches. Unable to keep still any longer, she dropped to her knees and began tugging at the weeds that were sprouting between the plants. It was heartening to free the brave little dog violets, red valerian and yellow Alexanders that always bloomed early. Perhaps she'd pick some and make a salad with the pungent leaves. She smiled as she imagined her father's face if she did. The work was soothing and it was satisfying to see the plot beginning to look neat and tidy again. Why, even the herbs were showing signs of new growth. Blow father and his ruling she shouldn't get her hands dirty, she thought, staring down at her grime encrusted nails.

It had grown quite dark and still Kitto hadn't arrived. Disappointment flooded through her. Surely, he wasn't getting his own back for her not showing up on Sunday? The necklace stabbed her chest.

'No, he wouldn't do that, would he, Mammwynn?' she murmured. The rowans waved their branches wildly, the necklace stabbed again. 'Oh Mammwynn, I know you're trying to tell me something, but what?' An image of Kitto's grim-faced determination the previous morning rose before her and she felt a frisson of fear snake through her body. Something was wrong. Shivering, she pulled her shawl tighter round her then, all thought of salad and food forgotten, she ran as fast as she could to Kitto's hovel on the hill.

It was in darkness and, heart hammering, she banged on the door.

Chapter 7

With only the stars to brighten her way, Colenso hurried through the dark lanes, thoughts tumbling round her head like the weeds around Mammwynn's plants. Why hadn't Kitto turned up? Where were his mother and siblings? Why was the hovel in darkness? By the time she reached home and lifted the latch, the church clock was chiming six.

'Where've you been?' her father snarled. Still in his coat, he was sitting at the table eating his supper, knapsack at his feet. 'And what the 'ell's this muck? Come in starving after a hard day's work and what do I get? This gloppy gloop, that's what.' He lifted his bowl and for one moment she thought he was going to throw it at her. 'You knows how I hates crab,' he added petulantly.

'That's all the fishermen caught. Besides, you told me to cook something different, Father, so I did,' Colenso retorted, her mind still on Kitto.

'Yes, som'at fancy for when you entertains, not the guts of a gudderin' gaverick. And a man shouldn't have to come home to an empty house neither. Gawd knows where your mother is. Where've you been anyhow? I told you to stay indoors and make som'at decent to wear on Sunday.' Colenso let his tirade wash over her as she quickly slipped her ring into her pocket before taking off her bonnet and shawl and hanging them on the nail by the door. Why he expected life to revolve around him she'd never know. And it was so cold in here. Would it have hurt him to stoke the fire? As she bent over to riddle the range, his arm snaked out and grabbed hold of her shoulder.

'I asked you a question, maid,' he growled. 'And what the 'ell's this?' He frowned at her earth-encrusted hands.

'I needed some air after being cooped up indoors so I went to see Mammwynn. Weeds were choking her plants and …' she began.

'I'll blinkin' choke you, girl. Didn't I tell you to look after them hands? Mr Fenton don't want a maid with roughened skin. He wants a lady, someone who takes care of herself and wears fine clothes. Someone he can show off when he invites his quarry-owner friends to supper.'

'I'm not some displaying peacock,' she snapped. His eyes narrowed to slits. 'Get and wash them filthy mitts, then show me what you've sewed,' he ordered, but Colenso was already taking herself out to the pump. If only she could take herself out of here forever.

She winced as the icy water stung like nettles. Ignoring the chill wind blowing in from the sea, she stood staring up at the star-studded heavens. What could have happened to Kitto? It was the thought of seeing him that had kept her going through the long, lonely day. And why wasn't Mrs Rowse at home? Usually she'd be preparing supper for when Kitto returned from the works.

'How many hands you washing?' As her father's strident voice reverberated across the yard, she let out a heartfelt sigh and made her way back indoors. 'Now show me this top you're making and it had better be good or ...' his voice trailed away as he fingered his belt.

Removing his bowl, which despite his protestations was now empty, she wiped the surface of the table.

'Hurry along, girl, I'm already late for my appointment.' And we all know where that is, she thought, carefully laying out the teal silk bodice she'd cut and tacked. 'Well, I'll be ...' her father whistled, hazel eyes gleaming in the candlelight. 'At least you had the sense to swipe some decent stuff. He'll go goggle-eyed when he sees you in that. Won't be able to keep his hands off you.' The very idea made Colenso's stomach turn but her father was beside himself. 'Seize the chance, maid, and you'll be wearing finery like this all the time. A works manager be a far better catch than some apprenticed turner. Especially one with grand plans.'

'I don't suppose you saw Kitto today, Father?' Colenso asked, trying to keep her voice casual.

'So happens I did,' he replied with a gleeful grin. 'Got called into Fenton's office, didn't he? Still there when I left an' all,' he crowed. 'Well, I'm off to celebrate, maid. You can tell your mother I'll be late,' he added, ramming his cap on his head and heading out into the night.

Colenso frowned. Why would Kitto be summoned to Fenton's office? Had the manager worked out who'd been turning the souvenirs she'd fashioned? Or had Kitto ignored her warning and spoken to him about their relationship? He was a proud man and fiercely protective of her.

The door clattering open interrupted her musing, and her mamm scuttled in, closely followed by her brother.

'Waited round the corner till your father disappeared into the alehouse. Couldn't face all his questions as to why I was late,' Caja said.

'We've just come from there ourselves,' Tomas explained. 'A fight broke out earlier and one of the men got hurt. Only a split lip but it wouldn't stop bleeding so I got Mamm to look at it.'

'Oh?' Colenso asked, her eyes widening.

'Don't worry, sis, no one you know,' he winked, then looked serious. 'Though a certain someone would do well to keep his mouth shut about his theories on how long the serpentine will last in the cities. Doesn't do to upset this new manager. He's got big plans and won't let anyone get in his way.'

'What plans?' Colenso asked, thinking of her father's earlier comment.

'To expand the works further so he can supply more shopfronts and mantle surrounds to the finest stores and houses in London. He's impatient to start straight away but it's caused bad feeling between the quarriers and labourers,' he said, throwing his cap on the nail next to hers then settling himself in his father's chair.

'Just you go and wash before you sit yourself down, Tomas Carne,' Caja remonstrated.

'Yes, Mamm.' He gave a wry grin but duly got to his feet again.

'Why has it caused bad feeling?' Colenso asked.

'The quarriers have been promised bonuses if they bring in larger pieces of the best-quality serpentine. One of them was boasting how much he could earn and that was it. Surprised

Father wasn't there, being as how he's always complaining about his pay.'

'Got his sights set on higher things, has Father,' Caja replied, looking pointedly at Colenso. 'Now go and wash, Tomas, so we can eat.' Then she saw the teal top on the table and her eyes widened. 'Nice bit of fabric, that. Glad to see you've taken Father's advice,' she winked, running her hand over the soft silk. 'Don't suppose you've got a spare bit for me?' Colenso shook her head.

'Emily kindly gave me enough material to make myself a decent top. In return I'm to help her with the new orders she's received.'

'Decent?' Caja hooted. 'That'll send old Fenton's pulse racing like one of them steam trains.' Seeing the look in her mamm's eye and not wishing her to see what else she'd been working on, Colenso quickly folded the material back in the brown paper. As she was putting it away in the dresser, she remembered something Kitto had said the previous day.

'You promised to let Mrs Rowse know I wouldn't be able to meet him last Sunday, but Kitto never got any message, Mamm.'

Caja slapped her hand to her forehead. 'Why, in all the excitement of meeting Mr Fenton, I clean forgot. I am sorry,' she said, sounding anything but. Clearly she would have to make her own arrangements in future, Colenso thought, vowing to see Kitto before the weekend.

However, much to her disappointment, as she was stealing out of the cottage early the following morning, her father caught her by the arm.

'Sneaking off, was you? And what's this?' he hissed,

trying to wrench the ring from her finger. 'Give it here, now.' Glowering, he held out his hand and Colenso knew she had no choice but to give him the ring. She watched in despair as he hurled it into the distant bushes where there was no chance of her ever finding it.

'Try leaving again before Sunday and you'll feel this like never before, defiant wench,' he shouted, cracking his belt in front of her face. 'It's your mother's fault for not being strict enough, so disobey again and she'll get it too, understand?'

Hearing a squeak and seeing her mamm's frightened face peering down the stairs, Colenso knew she had little choice.

*

That Sunday, having suffered the agony of sleeping with her hair in rags, Colenso was made to follow the same bathing ritual as before. Then, feeling the need for as much protection from Fenton's leers as possible, she let the curls tumble around her shoulders. However, her mamm, anxious to keep her husband happy, was having none of it.

'Come here, Colenso. A lady doesn't wear her hair down,' Caja tutted, grabbing the brush and coiling her tresses artfully into a knot at the nape of her neck. 'Now, go and get changed. It won't do to keep Mr Fenton waiting.'

Reluctantly, Colenso went upstairs and donned her new top, smoothing it down over her everyday skirt for there was no way she could afford a new one. Still, she doubted Ferret Fenton would look low enough to notice. Checking her appearance in the fly-spotted mirror, she saw luminous dark eyes staring back from a white, pinched face. The teal of the top suited her colouring and at any other time she'd have been thrilled to be wearing it. However, the prospect of having to spend the afternoon with a fusty old ferret made her stomach turn. But neither did she relish the idea of being thrown in gaol, she thought, throwing on the shawl she'd smuggled upstairs earlier.

'Hurry up, maid. Mr Fenton'll be here d'reckly,' her father bellowed, but Colenso waited until she heard the trap pull up outside before descending the stairs.

'Oh, Colenso, you can't wear that old thing,' Caja cried, tugging the shawl from her shoulders. There was a stunned silence as her parents stared at her in dismay.

'What the 'ell you done with that top? You can't see them …' her father finally spluttered, waving his hand in front of her.

'A lady should never reveal too much flesh, Father,' Colenso replied sweetly. How clever it had been of Emily to suggest adding an overlay of spider-gauze edged with lace to the silk bodice. 'Now, if you give me back my shawl, I'll be on my way. You don't want me catching a chill, do you?' she asked. Reluctantly her mamm handed back the shabby garment, sighing loudly as Colenso knotted it tightly round her neck. Then, heedless of the fancy hairstyle, Colenso rammed her bonnet on her head and strode out of the door. If she had to go through with this farce, she'd at least be closeted in as many clothes as possible.

'Colenso, my dear,' Fenton smiled, his eyes lighting up when he saw her. 'Allow me,' he added, holding out his hand to help her up.

'The church is only over there so we can walk,' she told him, gesturing to her right. He frowned, then shook his head.

'No need to muddy our shoes, my dear. Come along.' Reluctantly she took his proffered hand, grateful he was wearing buckskin gloves so that she didn't have to actually touch him. Smartly dressed in a dark greatcoat and top hat, with black leather brogues to match, he looked out of place amongst the villagers who were eyeing them curiously. 'I'm looking forward to our little outing,' he said before shouting to the driver to take them to Ruan.

'But you won't find a better example of serpentine workmanship than that of Grade lectern, Mr Fenton ...' she began.

'Leave the detail to me, my dear. And do call me Henry,' he smiled, patting her knee. 'I would have preferred to use the carriage but Dobson said he wouldn't risk driving it down these rutted tracks. 'Now, tell me something about this, er, hamlet you live in. Cadgwith is an unusual name, is it not?' Resigned to her fate, she nodded.

'Cadgwith – or Porthcaswyth as it used to be called – means cove or landing place of the thicket. I think that's quite fitting really, don't you?' she said, making a sweeping gesture from the sea below, where the fishing boats were pulled up on the beach, to the trees above from where the calls of warblers and chiffchaffs sounded. 'The view is quite beautiful.'

'Indeed, it is,' he murmured, staring at her and not the scenery.

'And it's a friendly place. Everyone helping each other, you know? Of course, we all have to work hard,' she gabbled, feeling more disconcerted by the moment.

'Quite,' he nodded, his gaze seeming to devour her. Just when she thought she'd scream with frustration, his attention was caught by a cottage they were passing. 'Good heavens, whatever is that door doing up in the air?' he asked, frowning up at the entrance beneath the eaves of the roof. Several feet above the ground, it had no steps leading up to it.

'That's what they used in the old days to empty out the gazunders,' she said, trying not to laugh when he cringed. Of course, it would never do to reveal that it was as an escape route for when press gangs descended upon the village. Luckily, before he could ask any more questions they'd left the village behind and were passing Mammwynn's resting place. Colenso silently promised to visit her soon and then they turned the corner and Ruan church loomed before them. Jumping down, she pointed to the stonework of the tower.

'Good serpentine blocks, eh, Mr Fenton?' He gave a nod and followed her inside.

To Colenso's relief, even though it was between services, the church bustled with visitors. Fenton clicked his teeth in annoyance and after a cursory glance at the font, he took Colenso's arm and ushered her back outside.

'Very good, but I had no idea it would be so busy,' he frowned, handing her up into the trap.

'The carved bench ends are quite magnificent too,' Colenso told him, moving as close to the edge of the seat as she dared as he sat down right beside her. He nodded then instructed his driver to take them straight to Mullinsa.

'It's too cold a day to be roaming the countryside,' he murmured by way of explanation. 'The establishment I've been recommended has a roaring fire and does splendid refreshments,' he added, turning to face her again. Then the trap lurched and his gaze lowered to her front, eyes widening like saucers as her bosoms were rocked from side to side.

'I'm sure Mamm would make us some,' Colenso said quickly, grabbing the side and willing her body to stay still.

'Very kind, I'm sure, but we don't want to put her to any trouble, do we?' he replied, regaining his composure. Then, to her relief, his attention was distracted by the scattered mounds of spoil from the small quarries along the cliffs.

She relaxed back in her seat, her thoughts turning to Kitto. She wondered what he was doing. How she longed to be with him instead of this creepy works manager with his oily smile and fancy way of speaking. Why, he didn't even notice the Cornish Heath that only grew on the serpentine or the mauve heather, golden gorse, purple betony, or creamy primroses that were blooming in the hedgerows. Kitto would have stopped and picked her a posy to take home. Kitto! If she ate her tea quickly, perhaps she'd be home in time to call and see him.

Even as her spirits rose, she knew it was a futile thought, for dusk fell quickly this time of year. Besides, it was rumoured a smuggling run was due in and no sensible person ventured out after dark then. Although the preventatives were vigilant, the seasoned smugglers who fiercely believed in their right to free trade went to great lengths to ensure nobody came between them and their booty. The village and caves were a veritable warren of secret tunnels and cellars where contraband was hidden until it could be safely moved on.

As they traversed the breadth of the flat peninsula, she remembered the story of old Mrs Arthur who, having a fondness for brandy, refused to move from her chair when the customs officers descended to search her cottage. Apparently, she'd clutched her chest and groaned until – afraid she was having a heart attack – they'd fled. Then, with a grin, she'd got to her feet, removed the rug covering the hatch and calmly climbed down her cellar steps to celebrate with a fresh bottle.

'Well, here we are, my dear.' She jumped as she felt a hand on her arm then realized they'd stopped outside an imposing stone building perched high on a cliff. Even on a dull day like this, you could see right across Mounts Bay to Penzance. 'Our competitors are over there,' Fenton announced, as if telling her something new. She shook her head, for everyone on The Lizard knew they competed for business with the works at Wherrytown.

'By the time I've finished here, Poltesco will be booming and they will be but a distant memory. Dead as the dust in their works,' he boasted, turning to her with a satisfied smile. 'We've all the resources and men we need at Poltesco. The materials come in through the back door and are wheeled out of the front, straight onto the boats.' Colenso bit her tongue, for again he was telling her things she already knew. But the Ferret was in his stride. 'Railway or not, there's no way they can compete with that.' Then his expression changed. 'Still, enough of business, it's time for us to get to know each other better, is it not?' he murmured, moving closer until his thigh was resting against hers.

Seeing that glint spark in his eyes once more, she could stand it no longer and leapt down from the trap.

Chapter 8

Colenso heard a muttered oath, followed by a thud and then footsteps hurrying after her. However, when Fenton reached her side, he just smiled knowingly and took her arm.

'The finest hotel on The Lizard,' he announced grandly. 'I take it you've not been here before?'

'I can't say I remember,' Colenso replied sweetly, refusing to rise to his gibe. She could never afford to come somewhere like this and he knew it. These fine new places were springing up all over the peninsula to cater for the tourists and artists who, inspired by the beautiful serpentine gifts and unusual flora and fauna, had begun descending in their droves. They had money to spend and the hotels were quick to capitalize on it.

A blast of warmth hit them as they entered the grand foyer with its plush red carpets and huge log fire blazing in the ornate stone fireplace. A man sporting a dark uniform with a red waistcoat hurried to greet them and, much to Colenso's consternation, insisted he take their outer garments.

'Won't feel the benefit when you go outside again, else,' he whispered, seeing her dismay. 'Your table is ready for you, Mr Fenton,' he announced, showing them through to a private lounge overlooking the water where another fire was burning brightly, this time in a magnificent fireplace of green serpentine. Colenso stared around the smallish room with its solitary table set for two. For the second time that afternoon, she vowed to eat as quickly as she could, and when the waiter appeared bearing a tray laden with triangles of sandwiches, scones, cream and jam, she realized it would be no hardship. And the Ferret couldn't expect her to make conversation because it was rude to talk with your mouth full, wasn't it?

However, she hadn't bargained for Mr Fenton's own table manners. Apart from ensuring her plate was never empty, he tucked into his own food, staring thoughtfully out across the bay. It was only when they were sipping their tea that he spoke.

'Well, that was delicious, don't you think?' he asked, leaning so close she caught the tang of his lemony cologne. However, he was more interested in trying to peer through the oyster spider-gauze covering her blouse than in her answer. Instinctively she sat back in her seat and his lips curled into a smirk.

'I expect this is rather different to the way you normally spend your Sunday afternoons.'

'Yes,' she agreed, thinking that, however lavish the food had been, it was the company that mattered and she'd rather be sharing a picnic of stale bread and cheese with Kitto.

'This could become a regular occurrence, you know,' he told her, nodding his head as if to add weight to his words. She watched the whiskers beneath his nose bob up and down and thought how much like a ferret he really did look. Then when he removed a pristine handkerchief from his pocket and dabbed at his lips with paw-like hands, she had to turn away before she burst out laughing.

'I understand that it was Mr Rowse who did the turning on your, er, craft works, Colenso,' he said. The tone of his voice told her this was more than a casual remark and she sobered immediately.

'Er, yes,' she replied, endeavouring to keep her voice steady.

'And a splendid job he did too,' he smiled.

'Kitto is very talented and wants to become a master craftsman,' she told him proudly. Henry Fenton studied her for a long moment.

'Like him much, do you?' Colenso nodded and his expression hardened. However, the next moment he was smiling again.

'I too am an ambitious man, my dear. And when I set my heart on something, I do anything and everything to make sure I get it.' He paused and stared at her, grey eyes like pebbles. Suddenly she felt the necklace tighten and put her hand to her chest to stop it from digging in. He flushed, his eyes widening as they followed her movement. Cursing silently, she placed her hands in her lap.

'You were telling me about your plans,' she reminded him. He continued staring for another moment before raising his head.

'It is my intention to have a showroom built at Poltesco similar to the one we already have in London. Obviously, it will exhibit only the finest quality pieces.'

'You mean I can continue with my work, then?' Colenso asked excitement rising, for she missed the satisfaction she derived from seeing the dull stone turn into useful items gleaming with vibrancy.

'Alas, no. Quite apart from the fact there will be no more offcuts, as you call them, the works I have in mind will be of a more exclusive nature. Ornamental clocks, tables, barometers, decorative vases, bowls, tazzas, that kind of thing. Resplendent polished red serpentine placed on plinths, they will complement our larger works of mantlepieces and shopfronts handsomely. Anyway, my dear, we are here to get better acquainted not to talk shop,' he smiled, sitting back in his seat. Remembering her brother had asked her to find out as much as she could about his plans for the works, Colenso returned his smile.

'Actually, Mr, er … Henry, I find your plans most interesting. Won't all this mean you'll need to have extra stone quarried?' His face lit up and he leaned closer again.

'You are one canny woman, Colenso. It does indeed and everyone will benefit. The quarrying of extra stone will mean more money for the workers.'

'All of them?' she ventured, remembering what Tomas had told her about the dissent amongst the men.

'Well, no, we have to show a profit, and the works already pay the highest wages around these parts. However, the exhibits required for the showroom could mean more for Mr Rowse, as long as he stops bleating about the stone failing. I mean, I ask you, do you know what serpentine is made of?' he laughed.

'Actually, I do, Henry,' she grinned, grateful that Kitto had explained it to her. 'Basically, it's composed of three elements: magnesium, silicate, and water trapped in its hydrated crystals,' she told him. There was silence as he stared at her in astonishment.

'Er, yes, precisely,' he murmured. Then, seeming to remember his point, he continued. 'As I reminded young Rowse, the church towers here on The Lizard have stood the test of time for four hundred years or more. They've endured gales, rain, and fog not to mention the hot sun, so I think that rather proves my point.' He sat back in his chair, smiling benignly. Eager to wipe the complacent look from his face, she shook her head.

'There was an article on the subject in the *Illustrated London News*, pointing out that here on The Lizard we don't suffer the same frosty weather as the cities and ...' she stuttered to a halt as he held up his hand.

'No more shop talk, please,' he insisted, holding up his hand. 'What did you think of my humble abode, Colenso?' She could tell by the tone of his voice, he thought his home anything but modest.

'Lovely, Mr, er ... Henry,' she assured him.

'And could be lovelier still. I believe I already mentioned it needs a woman's touch. So what do you think, Colenso, could you be she?' he asked, staring fixedly at her like an animal with prey in its sights.

'I don't think Mrs Grim would take kindly to any of my suggestions,' Colenso replied. To her surprise, he roared with laughter, his shoulders shaking.

'My dear girl,' he spluttered. 'Mrs Grim is an employee and does as she's bid. She's there to work not pass opinion.' Is that so, Colenso thought, remembering the housekeeper's disdainful manner, but the Ferret was in his stride. 'You have a good if somewhat modest taste in clothes, so I'm sure you will know better than I which draperies will benefit my house. Dobson will collect you next Sunday and then you can see what you think. I'll get Mrs Grim to lay on a proper afternoon tea. Where I come from we have fruit cake accompanied by a goodly slice of strong cheese.' As he sat back in his chair with a satisfied grin, the clock chimed the hour and the waiter reappeared.

'May I get you anything else, madam, sir?' he asked.

'No thank you,' Fenton replied, waving him away. Seizing the opportunity, Colenso jumped to her feet.

'We are just leaving, thank you,' she said, making her way quickly towards the door and out to the foyer.

During the journey home, she steered the conversation back to the works, asking question after question about his plans so that by the time they drew up outside her cottage, he hadn't had the opportunity to return to their previous conversation. However, as she made to jump down, he caught her arm.

'I have enjoyed this afternoon, my dear. You have proven to be very good company and I shall look forward to hearing your ideas for improving my house next Sunday afternoon.'

'Ah yes, about that. I'll ask Mamm to accompany me, she has more experience of these things,' she told him sweetly. He frowned and cast a sceptical look in the direction of their tumbledown cottage.

'Very well, if you insist,' he acquiesced. Then, as relief flooded through her, he added: 'But remember you are still indebted for my not handing you over to the authorities, and Henry Fenton always ensures his debts get repaid,' he said, patting her knee. She was about to protest when her father's voice boomed out.

'Mr Fenton, sir, I thought it was you sat outside in your fine conveyance.'

'Thank you for a lovely afternoon, Mr Fenton,' Colenso said quickly, taking the opportunity to jump down from the trap.

'Till next Sunday, Colenso Carne,' he replied, tipping his hat. Leaving them talking, she hurried indoors.

'Did you have a good afternoon?' her mother asked, looking up from her darning. Colenso was saved from answering by the clattering of the latch as her father appeared.

'He's calling for her again next Sunday,' he told Caja, rubbing his hands with glee. 'I'll break open that new bottle of brandy we got, er, given,' he chuckled.

'Well done, you've obviously made a good impression,' her mother smiled, turning back to Colenso.

'He just wants a woman's opinion on his draperies, Mother. I volunteered your services too, so you'll be accompanying me.'

'Well, it's a start, I suppose,' Caja frowned. 'And if you do a good job on his home and he sees how well you look in it, well …'

'I'm tired and going to bed,' Colenso interrupted, unable to listen to any more of her mamm's scheming. 'I promised Emily I'd go in early tomorrow and help with her orders and I intend going,' she told them. To her surprise her father nodded.

'Good idea, then you can nab another bit of that silk, maid. This time though, make a top without that netting stuff over it.'

'Yes, you can't be seen out with the works manager wearing the same blouse,' her mamm added. Colenso shook her head. All her life she'd been told to make what she had last, and now she was expected to produce a new top each week. Well, she wouldn't be asking Emily for any more material, she was already in her debt as it was.

*

'And neither should yer have to, maid,' Emily agreed. 'A man should takes yer as yer is, not worry about what yer wearing.' They were sitting by the fire, taking their noontime break after a frantic morning of cutting, sewing and pressing, and Emily had asked how her afternoon with Fenton had gone. 'Them parents of yers wants shooting, if yer don't mind me saying. Keep within yer own class and cut yer coat according to yer cloth, I say. Mind yer, I was asked this morning if I was interested in some French lace,' she winked. Colenso smiled.

'I was relieved to have that gauze covering my blouse. If Ferret Fenton's nose got any closer I'd have smacked it.' Emily eyed her sharply.

'Don't you let him take no liberties, maid.'

'I won't, don't you worry, though he gets so close I can smell him. It gives me the shivers.' Emily looked thoughtful for a moment.

'Yer grandmother used to hum a tune if a person she didn't like got too near. She said it cast a ring of protection round her.'

'You're right, she did,' Colenso exclaimed, remembering how she used to do that when Father was pontificating. 'I'll try it. My singing's that bad it will send anyone fleeing to the moors anyway,' she grinned.

'Well, there yer are, then,' Emily chuckled.

'Would it be all right if I finish early this afternoon? I promise to come in again tomorrow. Kitto didn't turn up for our meeting the other evening and then Father banned me from leaving the cottage. I need to tell him about yesterday before he hears it from someone else. You know what Father's like once he's had a drink. He'll have exaggerated everything out of proportion and I don't want Kitto getting the wrong idea.' Emily nodded.

'Be sure he understands yer his girl. He's a good 'un, is young Kitto, and yer'll do well together. Yer'll need to finish that skirt for Mrs Tallis before yer leaves, mind. Can't afford to have my reputation ruined, young love or not.'

*

And love was the crux of the matter, Colenso mused as she hurried down the lane later that afternoon. Kitto was her beloved. He was young and attractive, but most of all he set her pulses racing whilst the Ferret was ancient and repulsed her. If only she'd stuck up for herself more forcefully when he accused her of theft she wouldn't feel like a fly trapped in a web with the silken thread tightening around her.

Whilst it was heartening that the evenings were beginning to draw out, she didn't want her father to see her. As soon as she heard the ring of scutes on the rocky path and the workers began appearing, weary and dirty after their long day's work, she slipped into the shadows of the hedges. She frowned as they passed by, for some were arguing whilst others earnestly voiced their opinions. What could have upset these equable workers, she wondered. Usually they'd be keen to get home to their supper. Her musings were interrupted by a piercing whistle and she stared around in surprise. Then it came again and she saw Kitto beckoning to her from behind a large elm tree.

'What are you doing?' she whispered, slipping over to join him.

'Coming to see you but I daren't risk bumping into your father.' He fell silent as the next huddle of men noisily passed by. 'He's been trying to cause trouble with Fenton,' he continued, his voice low.

Chapter 9

'What do you mean?' Colenso asked, staring at Kitto in dismay.

'I think he was hoping to stab me in the back and get me fired, but you could say his plan backfired,' he chuckled, then became serious. 'I've missed you, Cali.' He pulled her closer and she snuggled against him, revelling in the warmth of his body.

'I waited ages by Mammwynn's seat,' she told him.

'Sorry, but Fenton called me into his office just as I was leaving. Said your father had told him it was me who'd turned those things for you. Thought I'd had it, I can tell you.' Colenso shuddered as she pictured the scene. 'Come on,' he murmured. 'Let's go somewhere warmer. Jim's not back with the horse bus yet, so let's avail ourselves of his nice warm stables.' They waited while another row of dissenting workers tramped past then, like a couple of naughty children, ran to the shelter of the stalls.

'Sit down and make yourself comfortable,' he invited, mischief lighting up his eyes as he gestured to a nearby bale.

'Honestly, Kitto Rowse, you do know how to spoil a girl,' she quipped, wrinkling her nose at the ripe smell emanating from piles of dung and goodness knows what else. Still, paupers couldn't be pickers, she thought, easing herself down on the straw.

'Soon as I'm qualified I'll take you to the finest hotel where you will sit on a velvet-cushioned chair and feast on the finest food to celebrate our betrothal,' he promised. Remembering her outing with Fenton the previous day, Colenso shook her head.

'There's no need for that, Kitto. A picnic on the beach with you beside me will suffice.'

'You are funny, Cali. Most maids would jump at the chance,' he replied, leaning over and kissing the tip of her nose.

'Well, I'm not most maids,' she replied, wiping a dusting of powdered marble from her face. She was about to explain why she'd prefer a picnic with him, when he took her hand, emotion turning his eyes to molten treacle.

'And that's why I love you, Cali,' he murmured, staring at her intently. She returned his gaze and for one long moment they were lost in their own world. How she wished they could stay like this, but already he was pulling away.

'I need to finish telling you about my meeting,' he sighed. 'Fenton looked so serious I was expecting him to blow his stack. Instead, he told me he's impressed with my work and wants me to turn some display pieces for the new showroom he's having built.' Colenso stared at him in astonishment. Then she frowned, suspicion snaking its way round her insides.

'Really?' she asked. 'That's somewhat surprising, isn't it?'

'I'll have you know I'm good at my job,' he protested, puffing out his chest.

'I know you are,' she assured him quickly. 'But Fenton's not someone who does things for other people's benefit.'

'It's a great opportunity and will mean extra money for when we wed,' he continued eagerly, waving aside her protest. 'In fact, he asked me to work yesterday. Said he needed to begin building up stock, and the other turners are married so can't be expected to give up their family time.' Now Colenso was certain Fenton was pulling strings.

'He called on me yesterday,' she said, waiting for him to explode.

'In his pony and trap. Yes, your father made sure I knew that,' he shook his head. 'Don't know what he's got against me, I'm sure. I mean, I know my father's been transported but times were hard. Besides, I'm not like him.'

'Of course you're not,' she agreed. 'Father has this notion of bettering himself at the works.'

'Well, can't blame him for wanting to get on, I guess.'

'But don't you see, he's using me to do it?' she cried. He smiled and took her hand, running his thumb along her palm in the way she found comforting.

'Don't worry, Cali. Fenton knows you're my girl. He explained it was your parents who proposed you show him the local sights.' Before she could tell him that it had actually been Fenton who'd engineered the outing, he leaned closer and kissed her lightly on the lips. 'I really have missed you,' he murmured, kissing her again, harder this time. As his arms tightened around her, she stopped thinking and gave herself up to the moment. Then, work and Fenton forgotten, they settled back on the bales, enjoying the rarity of time spent together.

'When you didn't turn up the other evening, I called at your home but it was in darkness,' Colenso told him once they'd regained their breath.

'Mother was offered overtime at the inn,' he explained. 'The quarriers were celebrating their extra pay, lashing out on both food and drink. It's causing bad feeling with the labourers at Poltesco, I can tell you.'

'So that's why they were looking so angry,' she replied, the scene she'd witnessed earlier now making sense. He nodded.

'Anyway, Mother took Alys, Wenna and Daveth along to help make up plates of bread and cheese. Said they've never been so busy and she even brought some home for supper. Looks like we can all benefit from the ambitions of this new manager.'

'Not everyone,' she reminded him. 'The labourers at the works aren't.'

'And are planning to do something about it,' Kitto told her. 'Look, Cali, I love you and want us to be wed as soon as we can. That's why when Fenton offered me this opportunity I grabbed it with both hands. Even if it does mean working some Sundays.'

'But that's when we usually see each other,' Colenso cried.

'I know but, as Fenton said, it's only a temporary measure. Once the showroom is up and running, it will just be a case of replacing what's sold. This will help my career as well as setting us up for the future. I want better than a hovel when we set up home,' he told her. Colenso frowned. Although what he said made sense, she just knew the Ferret was up to something.

'I've to visit his house again on Sunday to give my

suggestion for new furnishings and draperies,' she told him. Now it was his turn to frown.

'Not sure I like that, Cali.'

'Mamm's coming too, but it still feels wrong. If only I'd stood up for myself more when he accused me of pilfering his bloomin' marble,' she cried.

'Thinking about it, Fenton did tell me I owed him for using the works' lathe to turn your bits for the tourists,' Kitto muttered. As the impact of their situation struck, they stared at each other in the gathering gloom. Colenso felt closer to Kitto than ever before, but she was also filled with anguish, because what they'd both admitted defined the situation they were now facing.

'I'm thinking we'll either have to elope or see this thing through,' Kitto said. Elope? Her heart soared at the prospect, only to plummet as practicality set in.

'I'd love to run away with you but we don't have any money,' she sighed.

'And if I leave Poltesco without my apprenticeship being signed off, I'll have no prospect of earning any either,' he said gloomily. 'Then of course, there's Mother, Alys and Wenna. They'd never be able to pay the rent without my money, and despite the men's moans, the works pay the highest wages around,' he groaned. Colenso nodded, for wasn't Kitto's sense of responsibility one of the things she loved about him? That didn't stop her feeling as if the silken thread was growing ever tighter though.

*

'Mr Fenton is waiting for you in the parlour,' Mrs Grim announced, her manner as hostile as it had previously been. Colenso nodded and, with the samples of fabric she had borrowed from Emily clutched tightly to her chest, followed the housekeeper down the hallway. Much to her parents' chagrin, she'd insisted on wearing her usual Sunday gold blouse, her hair braided and coiled around her head. Now she felt more confident than she would dressed up to impress an old man. She was here to do a job and would both look and act like it.

'Remember to act ladylike,' Caja whispered, as if reading her mind. 'Your father's relying on you.' Shouldn't it be the daughter relying on her parent, Colenso wondered.

'Good afternoon, ladies,' Fenton smiled, turning from the window. 'We'll have tea in one hour exactly, please, Mrs Grim,' he added. He waited until the door closed then stared at Colenso's parcel. 'I see you have given consideration to my furnishings, so take a seat and tell me your ideas.'

'Our Colenso's spoken of nothing else all week,' Caja smiled as she settled herself happily on the faded couch. Colenso stared at her in surprise, for in truth she'd taken the swatches of material Emily had given her without even looking at them.

'I've picked the most expensive and written the prices on the back. He can afford it and we can make som'at out of it,' she'd chuckled.

Anything would be an improvement on the present drab drapes, Colenso thought, glancing at the faded ones at the window.

'Good, good,' Fenton smiled at her. 'Spread everything out on the table and we'll take a look.' Slowly Colenso did as he suggested, disconcerted to find him still staring at her and not the samples.

'Of course, you can only tell how they'll look by holding them up,' she said, snatching up a square of plush cranberry velvet and hurrying over to the window.

'That looks perfect, my dear,' Fenton nodded, following her and standing so close she again caught the strong smell of his lemon cologne. Remembering Emily's suggestion, she began to hum a tune that Mammwynn used to sing to her. Startled, Fenton took a step back.

'Perhaps you would bring the other samples through to the dining hall, Mrs Carne,' he said quickly.

'You have a dining hall?' Caja cried, stressing the word hall. 'And it's Caja, Mr Fenton,' she gushed, smiling sweetly as she followed them through to the next room. 'Why, it's huge,' she gasped, staring at the long, polished table adorned with silver candelabra, the matching sideboard set with cut-glass decanters of various drinks.

'This is where I entertain important guests and clients,' Fenton replied, clearly pleased he'd impressed her. 'I believe it is usual to have the chair seats matching the drapes but I'm sure, being an accomplished seamstress, you will find that quite an easy task, my dear,' he said, smiling at Colenso. She did a quick count, ten standard chairs and two carvers. That would take some doing, surely. Her mamm nudged her side impatiently.

'Yes, of course,' she agreed, realizing he was waiting for her to respond.

'That is why I need help selecting the correct fabric. Appearance counts for everything, as I'm sure you'll agree.'

As he stood there, nose twitching like a ferret catching the scent of a rabbit, Colenso shuddered. 'Of course, I will also be needing a good woman by my side, but I won't be requiring any assistance in my choice there,' he continued, staring meaningfully at Colenso. Feeling uncomfortable, she looked down at the fabric in her hand. Her one aim was to get out of here as quickly as possible. The question was how could she do it without appearing rude? Then inspiration struck.

'As the rooms lead into each other, perhaps you should keep the colours the same,' she said, again holding up the velvet sample.

'My dear Colenso, that is a marvellous idea. Brains as well as beauty,' he beamed, his fingers touching hers as he went to take it. 'Such soft skin,' he murmured, a gleam sparking in his eyes. Quickly she snatched her hand away and hurried over to the French doors. Holding up the swatch, she nodded.

'If you agree, Mr Fenton, I think this will be the perfect choice. Now, if that's all ...'

'Ah, but it isn't, my dear. There are other rooms to consider.' Beaming widely, he turned to Caja. 'Would you do me the greatest of favours and return to the parlour ready to receive our afternoon tea?' Colenso watched as her mamm blushed prettily.

'Why, of course, Mr Fenton,' she purred and head held high left the room.

'Now, my dear, we will take these through here,' he said, opening another door. As that gleam glinted in his eyes once more, Colenso felt a prickle of unease.

'But I thought you were going to have the same fabric in all your rooms,' she mumbled.

'Not all of them, Colenso. Chambers require the personal touch, do they not?' he murmured, waving his hand towards the covers adorning the huge, carved bed that dominated the room. Quickly, Colenso averted her eyes, but he moved closer, reaching out with his paw-like hands. Her feet were rooted to the spot but just when she felt she would faint, the necklace began stabbing at her chest. Summoning her strength, she dashed over to the window, snatched the tape from her neck and began measuring. As he stood watching, his lips curled into a lustful smirk, she once again began to hum. Immediately, his demeanour changed.

'Forgive me for saying, but I do not think music is your forte, my dear,' he said, stealing up behind her. Reaching out, he spun her round to face him, that gleam lighting up his eyes.

'Come now, my dear, you surely know how I feel about you,' he murmured. His breath was coming in heavy gasps as his hands began folding back her shawl. Colenso opened her mouth to scream but it was his voice that roared. 'Why you …' he cried, his hand going to his cheek where, to her surprise, she saw blood spurting. 'That thing jabbed me,' he accused, pointing to her front.

Staring down, Colenso saw the pentacle had somehow worked itself free from the neck of her blouse. Hurriedly, she pushed it back inside the material then knotted her shawl firmly around her shoulders. The Ferret watched her every movement, then taking his kerchief from his pocket carefully wiped his cheek.

'Don't worry, my dear, I like a bit of sport. The thrill of the chase and all that.' His eyes alight with excitement, he took a step closer and Colenso moved back until she felt the wall pressing into her back. 'Come along, Colenso, one little kiss isn't going to hurt,' he murmured.

Revulsion flooded through her as she realized she had nowhere to go. Then they heard a door opening and movement coming from the hallway. Muttering an oath, Fenton moved away from her. 'Regretfully, our fun will have to wait, for I can hear Mrs Grim arriving with our refreshment.'

Weak with relief, Colenso followed him back into the parlour where Caja, having affected a hoity-toity voice, was telling the housekeeper exactly how she liked her tea.

'Of course, it's really not proper to have cake and cheese on the same plate.'

''Tis the master's wish,' Mrs Grim replied tersely as she handed Colenso her cup. 'Will there be anything else, Mr Fenton?' she asked in a martyred voice.

'No, thank you,' he replied. 'Where I come from, Caja, a slice of fruit cake and cheese is a speciality and go together like your scones and cream, but if you'd prefer something else …?' he left the question hanging.

'That's quite all right, Mr Fenton. It's unusual to have savoury and sweet on the same plate, but I suppose it will take time for you to adjust to our civilized ways.' Oblivious to the fact she'd offended her host, she took a bite of the cake. 'Not bad,' she conceded. 'But our Col here makes a much moister one.'

'Does she indeed?' he asked. 'It would appear your daughter likes to keep her talents hidden, Mrs Carne,' he added, eyeing Colenso speculatively. She almost choked on her tea, for this time there was no mistaking his meaning. Desperate to escape his appraising look, she hurriedly put down her cup and jumped to her feet.

'I'll just go and measure up for those curtains in the dining hall,' she muttered, wishing to get away from him.

'No need, my dear,' he said, putting out a hand to detain her. 'My housekeeper will write down all the measurements, and the driver can deliver them to your cottage along with the requisite materials.'

'Oh, Emily will be happy to provide the fabric,' Colenso told him.

'And take a cut, no doubt. Your talents clearly do not extend to financial matters, my dear. Happily mine do, so you can leave the business side to me. Now, how long do you think it will take to make my drapes and whatnots for my chamber?' He sat eyeing her with satisfaction, as if he'd cornered his prey and was waiting to see what move it was going to try next. Determined not to be browbeaten, she stared boldly back.

'Colenso's anxious to please you, Mr Fenton, sir. She'll sew day and night to have everything made for when you wants to entertain,' Caja said, answering for her daughter.

'That's splendid,' he grinned. 'I'll have Dobson collect the materials from my merchant in Falmouth and deliver them to you by the middle of the week at the latest, my dear. Unless you think the job too big for you to handle.'

'Of course not,' Colenso replied indignantly. Immediately that gleam sparked in his eyes, and with a sinking feeling she knew she'd played right into his hands.

Chapter 10

On their return journey, while her mamm chattered excitedly about 'that nice Mr Fenton and his lovely home', Colenso silently fumed. How dare he make advances like that? How could her mamm not see what he was really like? Her hand went to the necklace at her throat. That it had saved her from the Ferret's fumbling advances, she had no doubt, though she still couldn't work out how it had swung loose and caught him on the cheek. Her mother, a nurse who could spot blood at a thousand paces, hadn't even noticed. She'd been far too busy playing the happy hostess.

How had she got herself into this situation? And how was she going to tackle all that sewing by herself? The task was far more onerous than she'd anticipated and the Ferret hadn't even mentioned paying for her time. As soon as she got home, she'd take herself upstairs and work out a fair rate for the job. When the driver delivered the material, she'd hand him an invoice for the Ferret, then he'd see that her talents did indeed extend to financial matters. Feeling somewhat mollified, she followed her mamm into the cottage.

'What the devil's been goin' on?' Caja gasped. Following her gaze, Colenso stared around the living room in dismay.

Furniture was overturned, one chair rocked precariously on broken legs, while the floor was strewn with shattered crockery. In the midst of all the upheaval, her father sat in his chair, puffing his pipe, an empty brandy bottle at his side.

'It were the fault of that son of yours,' he mumbled, his words slurred. 'High and mighty upstart.'

'Where is Tomas?' Colenso asked, fearing she already knew.

'Gone. Told him to sling his hook, didn't I?'

'Not Tommy as well,' Caja cried. 'Can't leave you two alone for a couple of hours, can I?'

'You won't have to any longer, cos I told him not to come back – ever,' he shouted, picking up the empty bottle and glaring at it. 'I need a drink.'

'Oh no you don't, Peder Carne. You'll help clear this mess up,' Caja told him, bending to pick up the broken shards at her feet. 'My poor dishes. And look at my table – it's all scratched – and my best chair. How do you expect us to live now?' she wailed, wringing her hands together.

'It don't matter, do it? Colenso here will see us right. She'll wed Fenton and he'll give us a decent home and all the furniture and pots you needs. You just have to make it sooner now, maid,' he muttered. Colenso opened her mouth to protest but he sank back in his chair and closed his eyes. Moments later his snores rocked the room but there were no bowls left on the dresser to bang together. She turned to her mamm.

'You know it's Kitto I'm wedding so isn't it about time you stopped all this nonsense?' she demanded. To her dismay, her mamm's eyes filled with tears.

'Father's set his mind on us all having a better life. If you refuse Fenton, I don't know what he'll do,' she cried. Colenso opened her mouth to say the only thing the Ferret had asked her to do was make curtains, but her mamm was so distraught, she left the words unspoken.

'Go to bed, Mamm,' Colenso said gently. 'Things will look better in the morning,' she added, not knowing what else to say.

By the time Colenso had cleared up the broken crockery and set the room to rights, it was late. Leaving her father to his snorts and snores, she snatched up the candle and took herself upstairs to bed. The door to the closet she'd shared with Tomas was hanging open, his few belongings gone. She threw herself down on her mattress, all thought of costings forgotten. Things must have been really bad for Tomas to have broken his promise. Never had she needed Kitto more, she thought, cradling the serpentine heart to her chest. She'd creep out and see him first thing in the morning when hopefully her father would still be sleeping off the effects of all the brandy he'd consumed.

However, exhausted by the day's events, she fell into a deep sleep and it was late by the time she rose the next morning. Her father had already left for the works and she knew Kitto would have done too.

'I'll go and help Emily this morning,' she told Caja. 'I still owe her some hours to make up for that material she gave me.' To her surprise, her mamm shook her head.

'Father says you're to stay in and give this place a clean. And he expects som'at filling for his supper.'

'Well, he's not here so he won't know if I go out, will

he? On my way back I'll pop up to Mammwynn's and pick some Alexanders. I'm sure Father's system could do with something cleansing after all that brandy,' she grinned. Her mamm stared at her forlornly.

'I've to stay in too, keep an eye on you. He were in that foul a mood, I daren't disobey. At least we've got one decent pot left to make a stew in, though it'll have to be roots again cos there's no money to buy anything else.'

Colenso saw her mamm wince as she lifted it from the range, and guessed her father had taken his temper out on her before he'd left. He was always evil after a night on the bottle.

'Here, I'll do it,' she said, taking the heavy pot from her. 'You go and lie down.' Her mamm nodded but halfway up the stairs she stopped.

'Best call me if someone knocks wanting the sick nurse. Being poor is no way to live, Colenso. I know you've set your heart on marrying Kitto, but it'll be years before he can afford to look after you properly. Mr Fenton could give you so much more. A lovely home with furnishings you'd be proud to show off, servants to run around after you. You'd never have to struggle to make ends meet like your father and I do.'

But Kitto didn't squander money on liquor like her father did, Colenso nearly said, but held her tongue. Besides, she didn't want servants running around after her, she wanted to look after her own home. All these thoughts kept spinning round in her head as she automatically chopped vegetables and crumbled dried herbs into the pot. She put it on to simmer, then shook out the remaining flour from the sack and made the smallest loaf imaginable. Whilst she could understand her mamm hating the constant scrimping and saving and wishing a better life for them all, it was up to her who she married. The sooner she fulfilled this so-called obligation to the Ferret, the sooner she could prepare for her handfasting to Kitto.

Setting the dough to prove, she took pencil and paper from the dresser and sat down to work out her costings. She remembered Emily explaining that, depending on the task, she either charged an hourly rate or gave a price for the job itself. Thinking of all the curtains and covers she needed to make, she decided an hourly rate would be more beneficial. Then there was the amount of material involved. But of course, she hadn't got the measurements so she couldn't get any further.

Sighing in frustration, she pushed the paper to one side. Seeing the dough had risen, she set about knocking it back, then floured the table and kneaded it into shape. As her hands performed the rhythmic motion, her thoughts turned to Kitto. When would she see him again?

'*Visualize him, Colenso.*'

'Yes, Mammwynn,' she replied automatically. Closing her eyes, she concentrated on his image, eyes like molten treacle, gentle smile, his warmth, the smell that was his very essence, his physical presence beside her.

A knock at the door made her jump, snapping her out of her envisioning. Thinking it was someone wanting the sick nurse, she wiped her hands on the cloth and hurried to open the door. Her eyes widened in surprise.

'Surely you haven't forgotten me already?' Kitto laughed.

'What are you doing here?' she gasped. She knew the

power of visualization was strong, but surely she hadn't really conjured him up?

'I needed to see you, Cali,' he explained. 'I intended calling home first but was seized with the strongest feeling. It was almost as though something was pulling me here. Can I come in?' Instinctively, Colenso looked over her shoulder.

'Don't worry, your father was barking orders at the other labourers when I left the works.' Still staring at him in amazement, she stepped back to let him in.

'Mamm's upstairs resting. She's, er, not feeling well today.'

'Sorry to hear that,' he said, giving her a knowing look. 'Does that mean I can steal a kiss from my favourite girl, then?'

'Your favourite …' she began then saw he was teasing and let him pull her close. He kissed her lips, lightly at first then more fiercely as their need for each other surfaced. For long moments they stood enfolded in their own world, each revelling in the warmth of the other's embrace. With a sigh, he reluctantly pulled away.

'Something smells good,' he grinned, sniffing the air appreciatively.

''Tis only root stew but you're welcome to a bowl,' she offered, wondering how many dishes were left intact after yesterday's fracas.

'Regrettably I can't stay that long, Cali. I've to sail out with the schooner on the next tide. The shipment includes an ornamental barometer and clock ordered by some lord or other who attended that second major craft exhibition in London last year. He's an important bigwig and Fenton's hoping he'll put more business our way, that's why he's

104

entrusting me with their delivery. He says as I helped with the turning it would be a good idea to see them in their setting. Then I'm to take a look at their showrooms. Get some ideas for the one they're building here.' Colenso studied his excited face, suspicion mounting.

'You mean he's paying you to be away from your work?' He nodded happily.

'Better than that, he's even promised me a bonus. I shall put it towards a ring for you, Cali, being as how you don't see fit to wear my brass offering,' he said, lifting her left hand.

'Father threw it in the bushes,' she admitted. 'But like I told you, the ring's not important.'

'It is to me, Cali. I love you and want everyone to know we're betrothed. If I can ever get your father to give his permission, of course. I'd like you to wear my ring every day, as you do that necklace.'

'It was Mammwynn's,' she said, lifting the pentacle from inside her blouse. 'Funnily enough, I was going to take it off but something stopped me. I swear it keeps me safe,' she sighed, staring up into his brown eyes.

'Then you must continue wearing it,' he insisted, his lips grazing hers. 'Especially as Tomas is no longer here.'

'Blimey, how do you know that? He only left yesterday,' she muttered, recalling the ugly scene they'd returned to.

'Heard your father boasting to Fenton he could cut the stone quicker than Tomas.'

'Oh, for heaven's sake,' Colenso snapped. That he could turn on his own family never ceased to amaze her. But Fenton was equally ruthless. 'What happened?'

'Tomas showed Fenton the iron toothless saw and

explained it was the rubbing action of all the sixteen blades that cut the stone into flat pieces ready to pass through to the polishing frame. He offered to give him a demonstration but even Fenton could see it was a process that couldn't be hurried. Gave your father a right bol … telling off for wasting his time.'

'Good. Perhaps he'll stop interfering in all our lives now, though I doubt it.'

'Me too, I'm afraid,' he sighed. 'But what about you, Cali? How will you spend your time while I'm away?' he asked.

'I've got to sew those bloomin' curtains and covers for Fenton's house. There's loads of them,' she sighed. 'I was trying to work out the costings earlier,' she told him, gesturing to the paper on the corner of the table.

'Want some help?' he asked, picking up on her mood.

'Thanks, but I can't get any further until I have the measurements.'

'Is Emily supplying the material then?' he frowned.

'No, Fenton insists on buying some from his merchant in Falmouth. Said it would cut out the middleman. I wanted to hand the costings to the driver when he delivers it, but until I know how much material there is, I can't, can I?'

'But Cali, if Fenton is buying the material you can't charge him for it, can you? Just let him know your rate and then tell him how long it's taken you to finish the job.'

'Yes, of course,' she said, shaking her head. 'I should have known that.'

'Pleased to be of service, my lady. Now regrettably, I really must go,' he said, pulling her close and kissing the top of her head.

'How long will you be away?' she frowned.

'Don't fret yourself. I shall be back in time for the Cuckoo Fest.'

'Fest?'

'Colenso Carne, don't tell me you've forgotten the fair. Why, last year you had me in fits the way you insisted on riding them dobbies. Round and round you went till I thought you'd be sick.'

'I didn't realize you'd noticed,' she smiled, remembering how she and her friend had spent all their money on riding the painted horses. Jenna was working up at the manor now and Colenso really missed her.

''Twer the night I really noticed you for the first time. "Kitto," I says to myself, "that's the girl for you."'

'Get away with you,' she protested, a warm glow belying her words.

'Be good while I'm away and I'll treat you to as many rides as you want,' he promised, his lips grazing hers. 'I'll meet you by the dobbies at 5pm,' he grinned. Then, with a rueful grin, he turned and left.

'Was that someone wanting me?' her mamm asked, peering down the stairs.

'No, Mamm,' she replied truthfully. 'I'm just about to take the bread out of the oven if you're hungry,' she added, hurrying over to the range. While the loaf was cooling, she folded the sheet of paper with her costings on and put it in the dresser. She would be sure to mark down every hour she worked and charge the Ferret accordingly.

What was the man up to, sending Kitto all the way to London? Important order or not, it seemed strange for a turner to be delivering finished items. And did he really need to visit the showrooms? Surely it would be more worthwhile for Kitto to spend his time turning the items to be exhibited there. The more she thought about it, the more she was certain Fenton had engineered the trip to get Kitto out of the way. The now-familiar stabbing at her chest only served to reinforce her suspicions.

Chapter 11

Colenso and her mamm had just finished their late luncheon when a fierce pounding on the door startled them.

'Who's that?' Caja squeaked, still jumpy after her earlier ordeal.

'Soon find out,' Colenso said, snatching up the poker and opening the door a crack. To her surprise, she saw Fenton's driver standing on the step, and behind him a large carriage almost blocking the lane.

'Afternoon,' he greeted, tipping his hand to his cap. 'Delivery for Miss Carne.'

'But I wasn't expecting it until midweek, and then I thought you'd be delivering it in the trap,' she replied.

'Well, I ain't taking it back. Got sent to Falmouth last night so as to collect all this fabric first thing. It needed keeping dry, else there's no way on this earth I'd risk bringing the carriage down these rutted tracks. Now, I'll start fetching everything in, if that's all right with you?'

'Yes, of course,' she replied, opening the door wider. Incredulously, she watched as he carried bolts of rich burgundy velvet into the cottage. 'I had no idea there would be so much,' she gasped.

'Ain't finished yet, Miss,' he puffed, throwing down another bundle and going back outside. As he began unloading yet more material and boxes, Colenso noticed neighbours had gathered outside and were speculating as to the meaning of the delivery.

'Started up in competition to Miss Tucker, have yer?' Mrs Buller called.

'Won't be happy if yer poaching her business,' her companion added.

'It's nothing like that,' she assured them, standing aside to let the driver pass with another box.

'Think that's it,' he puffed, throwing it down on top of the rest.

'Just as well,' Colenso muttered, frowning at the bales and boxes that now took up their entire living room.

'Oh yes, and there's a note from Mr Fenton,' he added, pulling a crumpled sheaf of papers from his pocket. 'You're to sign this copy for me to give back to him, confirming receipt of …' he paused and squinted, 'three bales of burgundy velvet, two of emerald green and one gold, plus two large boxes of fringing. The other copy is for you to keep, along with the measurements.'

'But that's six bolts of material,' Colenso cried.

'Well, if it's for drapes, the 'ouse do have lots of windows,' Dobson shrugged.

'And you've to do the seat covers in the dining hall,' Caja reminded her. And the bed coverings, she thought, shuddering at the idea.

'Now, if you could just sign them papers, it's been a long day.' Quickly she did as he asked then closed the door behind him and stared helplessly at her mamm.

'It'll take weeks if not months to sew all this. How am I going to manage?' she wailed.

'More to the point, where are we going to store it before your father gets back?' Caja replied. 'He'll go berserk if he sees all that cluttering his home.'

'Well, it was you who offered Fenton my services,' Colenso retorted. Then, seeing her mamm's face crumple, she sighed. 'I'll put it on Tomas's bed for now. Though goodness knows what'll happen if he comes back.'

'He won't,' Caja replied sadly. 'He's lodging over Ruan side, but don't tell your father.'

*

The next morning, Colenso waited until her father had left the cottage, then took one of the bolts downstairs, unfolded a length of red velvet and spread it across the table.

'Oh Mamm, this velvet's so thick, there's no way my scissors will cut through it neatly,' she frowned, running her hand over the plush pile. 'I'll call on Emily and see if she can help.' Caja looked up from the pot she was cleaning.

'I'll probably be out when you return. Mrs Pascoe's rheumatics are playing up again and I promised to drop by with some nettle unguent.'

'That reminds me, I promised Emily some,' Colenso said, throwing her shawl around her shoulders.

'That's all we've got. I'll need to look out the receipt to make some more,' Caja told her, taking the last two pots from the drawer and handing one over.

'I'll gather more nettles later,' Colenso promised, eager to have an excuse to spend some time in the fresh air.

Outside, the wind almost blew Colenso off her feet. March was certainly roaring through like a lion, she thought, hurrying down the lane. She could hear the waves crashing onto the beach where the boats were drawn up. There'd be no fishing today, she thought making her way through the village to Emily's cottage.

'Oh, 'tis yer, is it?' the woman snapped, giving her a gimlet stare through the half-opened door. 'Surprised yer had the cheek to show yer face.'

'I brought that unguent I promised you,' Colenso told her.

'Think that'll salve yer conscience?' the old woman glared. 'Years it took Clara and me to build up our little business and now I hear yer doin' yer best to steal it, right from under me own eyes.'

'Oh no, Emily, you've got it all wrong,' Colenso began, her hand going to her bonnet as another easterly gust threatened to send it flying.

'Yer mean there weren't no fine carriage unloading half a warehouse of plush velvet at yer door?' Colenso shook her head as understanding dawned. The gossipers had been at it. 'Well, were ther or weren't ther?' Emily persisted.

'Yes, there was, but the material is for those drapes and covers Fenton wants making. I showed him your samples but he insisted on purchasing his own fabric from a merchant in Falmouth.'

'Well, why didn't yer say,' the woman cried. 'And why are yer standing ther letting all my warmth out?' she asked, stepping back so Colenso could enter.

112

'Hi, Colenso,' a cheery voice greeted her from the front room, where a fire was glowing in the grate.

'Alys, what are you doing here?' she cried delightedly. 'Don't suppose you've heard from Kitto?'

'No, but we don't expect to, this is his big chance so he'll be busy, won't he? Anyhow, London's like another country, isn't it? I'm helping Auntie Em 'til I start at the manor,' Kitto's sister replied, holding up a length of material. 'Isn't it exciting?'

'Yer won't think so if yer don't get that seam finished,' Emily chided before turning back to Colenso. 'Guessed yer be too busy to help and I got to keep my customers happy.'

'I'm sorry but I really don't think I'll have any time for anything other than sewing all those drapes and covers for the Ferret.'

'Who's the Ferret?' Alys asked, looking at Colenso curiously.

'None of yer business, young lady,' Emily told her. 'And remember, yer on trial.' The sober words jolted Colenso back to the present. She really needed to get on with her work or she might still find herself on trial yet. Setting the little pot of ointment down on the table along with the samples, she turned to Emily.

'The material Fenton's bought is so thick my small scissors won't cut through it.'

'So even though yer don't have an order to place with me, yer expecting me to help?' Emily asked, shaking her head so that silver tendrils bobbed under her cotton cap. Colenso stared at the floor. 'Don't fret yerself, maid, cors I'll help. Did he buy tape for the hooks to hang by?'

'I hadn't even thought of that, but no, he didn't.'

'So, we can still make som'at from him, then,' Emily grinned. 'What about thread?' Colenso shook her head. She'd been so overwhelmed by the amount of cloth delivered, she hadn't thought beyond cutting it to size.

'I'll be needing burgundy red, emerald green and gold.'

Emily stared at her thoughtfully then bustled over to the cupboard in the corner of the room. 'Here, you might as well have this,' she said, handing Colenso a large wicker basket.

'But that was Clara's workbox,' she protested.

'And she'd be pleased for yer to have it,' Emily said, her eyes suspiciously bright. 'Go on, take it afore I change my mind. Yer'll find everything you need in there. Prided herself on keeping a goodly supply of everything, Clara did.'

'Oh Emily, thank you,' Colenso cried, leaning forward and kissing the old woman's paper-thin cheek.

'Get away with yer,' Emily protested. 'Just remember to cost yer time and charge Fenton well for that tape and thread. Yer can pay me back when he settles up.'

*

As March continued roaring its way through the rest of the month, Colenso sewed like a woman possessed, completing curtain after curtain according to the measurements Mrs Grim had provided, before making a start on the chair covers. To her delight but her father's chagrin, there had been no further communication from the Ferret. Thank heavens for small mercies, she thought, stabbing her needle viciously through the material. Although she tried not to dwell on their last meeting, images of him advancing, paw-like hands outstretched, continued to plagued her. Although she didn't know how, she was certain it was Mammwynn's pentacle that had saved her.

'It's been over three weeks since you last saw Fenton,' Peder moaned, over supper that evening. 'He don't even stop and speak at work no more.' Hardly surprising, Colenso thought, remembering how Kitto had told her Peder had tried to get Tomas fired. That he could do such a thing to his own son was despicable, yet not wishing to enrage her father, she held her tongue.

'You did say he was sorting out that dispute at the works cos the owner's coming to look over them next month,' Caja ventured.

'True, and I'm sure he'll introduce me to him. Me being one of his key workers an' all that,' Peder crowed, puffing out his chest. Colenso stared at her father in astonishment. Only he would have the gall to consider himself important enough to be introduced to the owner.

'What you staring at, maid?' he asked, turning on Colenso. 'If you've done som'at to put Fenton off, I'll …' his voice trailed off, his fingers going to his belt. Then, seeming to change his mind, he smiled. 'You'll have to do som'at to entice him, maid. Make him think he can't live without you. How else will we ever make a better life?' Colenso stared down at her plate and wondered when the nightmare her life had become would ever end.

*

115

As the days lengthened and lightened into April, Colenso's mood darkened until all she wanted to do was escape. She missed Kitto so much and, even using Clara's thimble, her fingers were sore from continually pushing the needle through the thick fabric. The bolts of material that had taken over her bedroom were gradually being replaced by the finished curtains and covers, but having to measure, cut and sew at the table downstairs then take everything back upstairs again before her father came home was both tiring and time-consuming. Even though he took himself off to the alehouse each evening after supper, he still refused to have his space cluttered with cloth, as he put it.

Then one Saturday an envelope was delivered to their cottage. It was addressed in copperplate writing to Mr and Mrs P. Carne. Hardly able to contain his excitement, Peder drew out the thick card and scanned the contents, his usual scowl turning to delight.

'Here, Mother, listen to this.'

> *Mr Henry Fenton requests the company of Peder and Caja Carne, along with their delightful daughter Colenso, for luncheon next Sunday 19th. The carriage will collect you at noon.*
>
> *You are hereby notified that the signatory has a matter of great import to discuss.*
>
> *There is no need to r.s.v.p. Your acceptance is presumed.*
>
> *Henry J. Fenton*
>
> *P.S. It would be greatly appreciated if the finished drapes and covers were conveyed at the same time.*

'Well, what do you think of that?' he grinned.

'But all the covers aren't finished yet,' Colenso protested. Immediately her father's expression changed.

'See that they are, then, or you'll be sorry,' he snapped, his hands going to the buckle on his belt.

'I'll help,' Caja said quickly. 'It wouldn't do to let that nice Mr Fenton down.' Colenso nodded gratefully, for she'd been dreading making the covers for the chamber. The very thought made her shudder.

'Wear your low-cut top,' Peder instructed. 'But without that netting stuff. Makes your bos—, er, front look like a couple of caged ...'

'Father!' Caja chided. 'Besides, look at the state of you. You can't go to Mr Fenton's looking like that,' she added, gesturing to the hole on his knee. 'You'd best go and see Mr Tailor. Get measured up for a new pair of barrigans.'

'I ain't wearing no stiff moleskin,' he protested. 'It's taken me years to wear these in and if you thinks I'm standing there while the old fool goes on about "fis, faps or awls", you can think again.'

'It's not his fault he has a stammer, Peder. And you could help by telling him if you want a fly, flap or hole at the front so he doesn't have to ask.'

'Pah, I've a meeting to go to. Important things to discuss,' Peder added, snatching his cap from its nail and all but running out of the door.

'He'll be spreading the news of our invite,' Caja said, looking delighted at the prospect. 'Now, what material are you using for those covers and where are they for?' she asked, turning her attention back to Colenso.

'Gold and it's for the principal bed chamber,' she muttered. 'I'll go and get it,' she added, grateful for the excuse to get away from her mamm's scrutiny. However, when she returned with the material, her mamm was still bubbling with excitement.

'Oh my, imagine having covers of velvet on your bed,' she gushed, running her fingers over the soft nap. She'd rather not, Colenso thought, snatching up the paper detailing the measurements.

'He wants six identical covers made, would you believe?'

'Six!' Caja exclaimed, her eyes widening. 'Blimey, maid, we'd better get stitching, there's only a week till we go to his house.'

'And he wants this edging added as well,' Colenso told her, holding up a box of heavy fringing. 'Oh, I'll do that,' she added quickly as her mamm began unrolling the gold material, but she was too late.

'What's this?' Caja frowned, holding up lengths of thread knotted at the top.

'They're mine,' Colenso replied, snatching them up.

'But what are they for?'

'To mark the days until Kitto returns.' She didn't add that it was only the removal of one each night that kept her going through the long weeks.

'Seeing that nice Mr Fenton is more important than worrying about when your friend's coming back.' As eyes similar to her own stared accusingly at her, Colenso shook her head.

'No, Mamm, you've got it the wrong way round. Kitto is more important than Fenton. He'll be back for the Cuckoo

Fest at the beginning of May and I intend going to it with him.' There was a heavy silence then Caja let out a heavy sigh.

'You'll not get another chance to make a better life for yourself. Your father's already pointed out the benefits of marrying nice Mr Fenton.'

'But he's not nice,' Colenso protested. 'He's old, smells and has hands like a ferret.'

'That's not much to contend with when you can have a fine house, servants and no money worries. Besides, we're relying on you to get us away from this place,' Caja said, looking around the room with disdain. 'What can Kitto offer you in comparison?'

'Love and kindness for a start, but married to Father, you wouldn't understand attributes like that,' she cried.

'Believe it or not your father had his moments. Shame that's all they were,' Caja sighed. She reached out and grasped Colenso's hands. 'But they don't pay the bills, do they? You won't get another chance like this.'

'Aren't you presuming an awful lot? Fenton hasn't even mentioned marriage yet.'

'No, but he will. And when he does, maid, best you accept. You've all the romantic notions a young girl has of marriage, but believe me, real life's not like that. None of my patients can afford to settle their bills so we've not got the money to pay the quarter's rent. We're relying on you.'

Colenso stared helplessly at her mamm. She was well and truly trapped, the silk thread slowly but surely being wound ever tighter.

Chapter 12

Despite the lavish meal, Colenso was unable to eat a thing. She'd been seated directly opposite the Ferret and each time he raised his fork to his mouth he gazed intently at her chest. Thank heavens she'd kept the spider-gauze overlay on her blouse. She winced as her father tucked into his food like a pig at a trough, while her mamm simpered down the table at Fenton.

'Nice bit of beef this, Mr Fenton, sir,' Peder said, looking longingly at the remains of the roasted meat on the silver carver.

'Do help yourself to more,' Fenton offered, looking aghast as the man speared the leftover joint with the carving fork and popped the whole thing onto his plate before helping himself to the last of the crispy potatoes.

'Tasty,' Peder grinned through a mouthful of food. Colenso looked away in disgust. Really there was nothing to choose between the two men, she thought. Both were swine out to sate their differing appetites. Feeling the Ferret's eyes on her again, she stared boldly at him.

'Is something wrong, Mr Fenton?' she asked. He raised his eyes.

'Far from it,' he smiled. 'I was merely thinking that a gold necklace would look more becoming than that heavy star thing you always wear.'

'It belonged to my grandmother and is the dearest thing I have,' she cried, her fingers automatically reaching up to touch it. His gaze followed her move and she quickly put her hands in her lap.

'I would be delighted to buy you something more, er, delicate and dearer,' he replied, deliberately choosing to misunderstand.

'Very kind, Mr Fenton, sir,' Peder said quickly.

'But I don't ...'

'That's very generous of Mr, er ... Henry, isn't it, Colenso?' Caja said, shooting her a warning look before turning back to him. 'Our Colenso's made a fine job of your drapes and covers.'

'I would expect no less,' he replied.

'You'll find an invoice with them,' Colenso told him. 'I had to purchase tape and thread and of course there was my time.' Taking no notice of her mamm's sharp intake of breath, she continued. 'I'm sure you will agree that I have now more than repaid your debt?' He raised his brows but chose to ignore her question.

'I expect your cooking is far superior to the humble fare we've just eaten.'

'But I was ...' she began, seeking an answer to her question.

'Cooks lovely, she does,' Caja interrupted. 'Would be the perfect hostess too,' she said.

'I'm sure she would,' Fenton agreed. 'Now if you've had

121

enough to eat,' he said, looking pointedly at Peder's plate before smiling at Caja and Colenso. 'Perhaps you ladies would like to adjourn to the parlour and I'll get Mrs Grim to bring some tea. Mr Carne, if you would like to join me for a port or brandy, there is something I wish to discuss with you.' Her father beamed knowingly at Colenso and her spirits plummeted.

'Yes, sir. Of course, sir. Off you go, women,' he said, shooing them away like dogs. Charming, Colenso thought, although she was only too pleased to escape the confines of the dining hall.

'This is a lovely room, isn't it?' Caja enthused. 'Although it will look a lot better when those nice drapes are hung. You could make some matching cushions for these chairs, put up some pictures, make it real homely.'

Colenso, busy staring out of the window, didn't reply. Down below, she could see that construction of the show-room was already taking place and the workshops had been extended. The Ferret obviously worked quickly. She wondered how Kitto was getting on in London. Dare she ask if he'd heard anything?

The arrival of Mrs Grim with the tea tray interrupted her musing. Her mamm, presuming the role of lady of the manor, was telling the housekeeper exactly how she liked her tea.

'No good if you can't stand your spoon up in it, oh and I'll have three sugars, if you're asking.'

'I wasn't,' the housekeeper sniffed, making a great show of measuring out the sugar. 'What about you, Miss Carne, do you have any specific wishes as to how you'd like your tea served?' she asked curtly.

'In a cup, please,' Colenso smiled.

'Oh, ha, Colenso, that's funny,' Caja chuckled. Clearly the housekeeper thought otherwise, for having poured the tea, she sniffed again and strode from the room.

'Seen happier corpses,' Caja mused, holding her cup high and eyeing the bottom. 'Ooh, Royal Worcester, no less.' Hearing the door to the dining hall open, Caja put down her cup and turned to Colenso. 'That didn't take long,' she whispered.

'Ah ladies,' Fenton greeted them. 'I'm wondering if we should be celebrating with something more festive.'

'Celebrating?' Caja squeaked, almost falling off the chair with excitement.

'Indeed. Your husband has just given permission for me to ask for your daughter's hand in marriage,' he said, beaming so widely Colenso felt sick.

'Course I did. All we has to do now is set the date. June be a really good month for a wedding,' he declared, rubbing his hands together.

'But I haven't said anything yet,' Colenso began.

'Forgive me, my dear. We are being somewhat presumptuous. You wish for time to think?' Fenton asked, although from his expression he clearly thought it a foregone conclusion.

'I do,' she replied, seizing on the excuse. 'It's a big decision and I would like to give it careful consideration,' she added, smiling at him sweetly.

'Now come on, Colenso, 'tis no good playing hard to get,' Peder scowled. 'Mr Fenton, er ... Henry here ain't got all day.'

'On the contrary, I'm happy to wait until Colenso feels happy to accept. I, myself, shall be busy for the next two weeks showing Mr Quinn around the works and quarries.'

'Our Colenso could act as hostess for you,' Caja offered excitedly.

'Had Colenso felt able to accept my proposal today then, I agree, that would have been an excellent idea. However, under the circumstances, it wouldn't be right or proper.'

'But …' Peder began. 'Say something,' he growled, glaring at Colenso.

'Now, Peder, this has obviously come as a wonderful surprise to your daughter. She needs time to take in her good fortune,' Henry Fenton said magnanimously. He turned to Colenso, for once staring her in the face. 'Of course, when you accept, my dear, you can consider your debt repaid in full.'

Seeing his triumphant grin, she was seized with the urge to slap it from his face. Clearly he'd planned this all along, she thought, clenching her fists at her side. Oblivious to her turmoil, he continued.

'In the meantime, Mrs Grim can hang those beautiful drapes and covers you've made. Although of course, I shall be saving the principal bedroom cover for a special occasion.' He gave Colenso a smirk, his meaning so obvious she had to turn away.

'Ooh Colenso, did you hear that,' Caja gasped. 'Imagine it.' She'd rather not, Colenso thought, her stomach threatening to bring back the little food she'd managed to force down.

'Now, regrettably, with the owner arriving tomorrow, I have things to attend to. Thank you for coming and I shall see you on the evening of Sunday 3rd, my dear, when I trust you will have the right answer for me.'

'But I can't make that …' she began, thinking of her date with Kitto.

'Of course, she can, Mr Fenton,' Caja interrupted, almost curtseying to him as she left. 'Thank you for a splendid meal.'

'Don't worry, Mr Fenton, sir. I'll see Colenso gives you the right answer. She's a good girl really.'

'Not too good, I hope,' he chortled. 'Until the 3rd, my dear. The evenings are lighter now, so we can revisit that nice hotel to celebrate.' He rang the bell, only for the housekeeper to appear immediately. From her expression it was clear she'd been listening to their conversation. 'My guests are just leaving,' he told her.

'About time too, coming in here traipsing mud all down me clean floors,' she muttered, leading them back down the hallway. With a sniff, she grudgingly took their outer garments from the big carved stand and held them out at arm's length.

'Wait till you has to iron me shirts as well,' Peder hissed.

It was pouring with rain outside but the wet didn't do anything to cool Peder's temper. As soon as the trap moved away he turned to her and shook his fist.

'Stupid idiot,' he raged. 'Didn't I tell you to say yes when he proposed?'

'You've let us down good and proper,' Caja wailed. 'To think, at this very moment, we could have been planning your wedding. And you could have been entertaining Mr Fenton's important guest.'

'Yes, and I would have been invited to dine with the owner of the works,' Peder growled.

'Well, he's been spared the embarrassment of your dreadful table manners,' Colenso retorted. Tired and overwrought, she'd had more than enough for one afternoon.

'Why, you …' he began, his hand going to his belt.

'Leave it, Father,' Caja cautioned. 'Colenso's a good girl. She'll do the right thing and accept.'

'She'd better,' Peder grunted. 'But in the meantime, you're to spend your days learning to cook proper dishes. And I mean proper. No more guts of a gudderin gaverick. I want roast beef and all the trimmings like we had today.'

'Then you'd better pay for it instead of squandering your money in the alehouse,' she cried.

'Money won't be a problem when you accepts. We'll have all we need, your mamm and I, soon as you wed,' he boasted.

'What do you mean?' Colenso frowned.

'Promised us a lump sum for you, Fenton has. One of them dury things,' he grinned.

'Dury? You mean dowry, Father,' she told him. 'But you've got it the wrong way round. It's the father who pays the dowry.'

'Not this time,' Peder boasted, rubbing his hands together gleefully. 'And I stood out for me pound of flesh, what with you being built sturdy, like.'

'What? You mean you're selling me, your own daughter?' she spluttered, staring at him incredulously.

'Always knew you'd come in useful for som'at.'

Just then, the trap lurched as it rounded the bend towards Cadgwith. Unable to take any more, Colenso leapt down.

'Where the 'ell do you think you're going?' Peder

bellowed. 'I ain't finished yet.' But ignoring both him and the sheeting rain, she ran towards Mammwynn's final resting place.

'Oh Mammwynn, you'll never guess what's happened,' she cried, throwing herself down on the wet grass. The rowans rustled and, knowing her grandmother was listening, she poured out her tale of woe.

'To think Father intends selling me. Well, I won't marry that man, I won't,' she cried. The rowans rustled as if in agreement. 'I knew you'd understand,' she told them, feeling calmer. 'The question is what do I do now?' The necklace pricked her, gently this time and she sat back on her heels and looked around.

In the weeks since she'd last been here the little patch had sprung to life. Herbs and flowers were beginning to flourish, along with the weeds that were threatening to choke them. Heedless of her bare hands, she began tugging at their roots. She worked until the plants were free and, as she did, she found her mind working too. Of course, she cried, jumping to her feet. All I have to do is play along with Father until Kitto returns. Then I'll meet him at the fair and tell him what's been going on. The necklace pricked gently again and she knew she'd made the right decision.

'Thanks, Mammwynn,' she cried. 'I can't tell you how much better I feel.' As the rowans rustled in reply, she smiled properly for the first time that day.

With the rain having eased, she removed her turnover but kept on her gloves and began picking the tops off the new nettles. As well as making more unguent, she'd make nettle soup for the next day's supper. After all, her father had told her to spend her time cooking something different, hadn't he? she thought, grinning down at her laden shawl.

*

An uneasy truce existed in the cottage as Colenso skirted round her father, meekly doing as she was told. In turn Peder, thinking he'd won, was trying his hardest to be nice to her.

'We only want what's best for you, Colenso,' he murmured over supper the next evening. He took a mouthful of the soup and she tried not to laugh as he grimaced.

'I know, Father, and I listened to what you said and spent today making this soup. Apparently, it's the very thing to serve at dinner parties,' she told him, crossing her fingers in her lap.

'Oh, er, very nice, yes,' he muttered, forcing down another spoonful. 'Cors, when you weds Fenton, your mother will have a fancy kitchen to cook in too.'

'Will you, Mamm?' Colenso frowned, wondering what was coming next.

'I will cos that nice Mr Fenton's promised me a lovely new home,' she beamed. 'Can't say I'll be sorry to leave this place,' she added, staring at the damp walls that had needed lime washing for years, the broken furniture and remains of her crockery set. 'Might even get some new dishes.'

'You can have all you want, Caja dear,' Peder offered, waving his hands expansively. 'When I'm the caretaker of that fancy new showroom, I shall need a smart house to come home to.'

'Caretaker?' Colenso cried.

'Oh, didn't I tell you? As well as one of them dury things, Mr Fenton is setting us up in a nice new cottage down by the works and giving me a promotion too. Seen how important I am to him,' he bragged, puffing out his chest as was becoming a habit. 'So you wedding him is the best thing for all of us.'

Seeing his excited face, Colenso almost felt sorry for the disappointment he had coming to him. But then she thought of the way he'd had no qualms about selling her, and hardened her heart.

'Glad you enjoyed it, Father. You were right about me needing to expand my cooking repertoire so if it's all right with you, I'll wander up to Mammwynn's plot tomorrow and gather some more Alexanders. They'll go nicely with a parsley sauce.' She looked at him expectantly.

'Very well. I'm glad you're taking this cooking seriously. As well as all your feminine wiles, the best way to a man's heart is through his stomach. That drop of green stuff was very, er, interesting but needed more salt,' he said, getting to his feet. 'Now, I've an important meeting to go to.'

She helped her mamm clear away then stealing up to her room, she snatched up the tassel of bright red threads she'd so carefully counted and knotted together. It was growing gratifyingly thinner she noticed, as with trembling hands she removed another one. Only eleven remained. Eleven days and then she'd see Kitto again. Her heart raced at the thought of his treacle eyes lighting up when he took her in his arms. As long as she managed to keep up this farce with her father, all would be well. The alternative didn't bear thinking about.

Quickly she undressed and climbed under the covers. Fenton could keep his fancy velvets, all she needed was Kitto to keep her warm. Cradling the polished heart to her chest, she closed her eyes and dreamed of the time she could marry the man she loved. Having worked on all that red, green and gold fabric, she knew the colours she wouldn't be using for their handfasting ties.

Chapter 13

The day of the Cuckoo Fest dawned at last. Heart racing, yet trying to act normally, Colenso went downstairs to find her mamm, bag in hand, about to leave the cottage.

'Ah, there you are. Why, you look positively blooming,' she cried. 'Don't our Colenso look radiant, Father? Still, it is an exciting day, isn't it?'

'It certainly is,' Colenso replied truthfully, turning away as her father gave her a searching look.

'Well, must go,' Caja continued, oblivious. 'One of them fair people's sons got his leg caught under a wheel when they were setting up in farmer John's field last night. The father's waiting outside to show me to their van.'

'Not having no travellers in here,' Peder growled. 'Don't know where they've been or what they're carrying. If it were up to me …'

'Well, it isn't,' Caja said, interrupting his mutterings. 'Don't worry, Colenso, I've a fair few patients to see today but I'll be back in plenty of time to help you get ready for when Mr Fenton comes. In the meantime, heat some water, take a bath, wash your hair. You should know the drill by now,' she laughed.

'Soon as she accepts that proposal, you can stop running round after other people, especially gyp …' but he was talking to thin air for Caja had already left, the door clattering shut behind her.

'Didn't you say you had to work extra hours today, Father?' Colenso asked as he continued sitting in his chair staring at her.

'Yep, Fenton wants to prove to that Mr Quinn how prosperous his works are. Still, he ain't likely to tell off his prospective father-in-law, now, is he?' he chuckled.

'I suppose not,' she gulped.

'Suppose you'll need all day titty whatsin to look your best. Though I has to say your mamm's right, you do have a kind of glow about you this morning. Excited, are you?' he asked, studying her closely. Feeling her face growing hot, Colenso turned away and began clearing their breakfast things from the table. He watched for a moment then shrugged and got to his feet. 'Well, best be off and check the men aren't takin' flippin' liberties. Wait 'til I'm promoted, they won't know what's hit them. Don't worry, I'll be home early to greet Mr Fenton properly when he calls.'

'Oh,' Colenso muttered, her heart sinking like a stone. Her father frowned.

'Look at me when I'm talking to you, maid,' he ordered. Reluctantly, she did as he said. 'That's better. I'll be checking you looks your best when I gets back, so make sure you take that bloomin' netting off yer top or I'll be doing it for you. Understand?' Wishing he'd hurry up and go, she nodded quickly and with a final searching look, he snatched up his cap.

As the door slammed behind him, Colenso let out a long whoop of delight. Excited at the thought of seeing Kitto, she wasn't sure she could have kept up the Ferret farce in front of her father any longer.

Then reality hit her like a bucket of iced water. She'd planned to make her way to the fair before her father left work, but if he was coming home early, how was she going to avoid him? Sinking into a chair, she pondered her problem. Finally deciding there was only one way to solve it, she spent the morning titty whatsin as her father called it, enjoying the luxury of having the cottage to herself.

Feeling refreshed and knowing it would be hours before she ate again, she helped herself to a portion of salted pilchards from the earthenware bussa and sat down at the table to enjoy them with a heel of bread. How wonderful it would be when Kitto and she had their own home and they could dine together like this, she mused.

Kitto. She'd need to leave shortly if she were to evade her father. Running upstairs, she dressed in her Sunday best and tied her hair back with the yellow ribbon that matched her blouse. Then leaving the fancy silk top in the closet, she bundled up her few remaining things and hurried back down. Breathing a sigh of relief that her mamm was still out, she opened the front door and bumped straight into her father.

'Oh,' she cried.

'I knew you was up to som'at,' he snarled, pushing her back inside. 'Thought you'd do a runner while my back was turned, did you?' Snatching the bundle from her, he threw it across the room. He was obviously drunk as like some demented demon, he advanced, towering over her, his eyes red with rage. 'Should have guessed, when I saw that rat Rowse getting off the boat earlier.' So Kitto was back. Despite her father's ranting, her heart sang with happiness.

'You're marrying Fenton, Colenso Carne, and that's final. Do you hear me?' he growled, jabbing his finger at her. Suddenly, she felt something snap inside her and all the frustration of the last weeks came flooding out.

'I am not marrying Fenton, Father, and you can't make me,' she shouted.

'Really? Well, we'll see about that,' he hissed, forcing her back until she fell into the chair. Deftly he removed his belt, snapping the leather straps together. She put up her arms to protect herself but instead of lashing out, he caught hold of her hands and bound them tightly together.

'A fine sight I'll look when Fenton arrives,' she said, bravado masking her fear.

'Ah, but he ain't coming till tomorrow now as that Mr Quinn's still there.' Thank heavens for small mercies, Colenso thought, but his next words sent shivers of panic down her spine. 'And as I said how distressed you'd be, he loaned me his trap to come home. So, maid, we'll take a little trip, you and me. I know the very place to make you see sense.'

Taking a bottle from his pocket, he sprinkled liquid on his grimy kerchief and held it to her face. She caught a whiff of something bitter before her senses began to swim. Vaguely she was aware of being pulled to her feet and pushed outside. As the fresh air revived her, she tried to lash out but her limbs wouldn't work. There was that smell again, then a harsh laugh. Her father's? She couldn't be sure, for she was feeling woozy once more. Then she was

134

tossed in the air, landing with a thump on a hard surface and everything went black.

'Wake up, you good-for-nothing wench.' Her father's voice sounded as if it was coming from far away. She blinked, the light hurting her eyes as she felt herself being dragged off the back of the cart and falling to the ground. 'On your feet,' he growled. He grabbed her arm and she felt herself being frogmarched along a dark tunnel towards a speck of light. There was the smell of damp and she heard the crashing of waves, distant at first but growing ever nearer. Then she was squinting in the daylight, could feel fresh air on her face, smell the tang of salt.

As he started to untie the leather belt from her hands, she felt a glimmer of hope that was dashed when, with a manic laugh, her father thrust her arms behind her back and she felt them being tied again with ropes. Although she wasn't fully conscious, the necklace began digging into her chest and she knew she was in danger.

'Nothing like a dose of dread to concentrate the mind,' her father hooted, thrusting his florid face in front of hers. 'Now, I'll leave you to have a good think. Be back for your answer when the tides turns. You'd better make sure it's the right one or …' he shrugged and gestured to the crashing waves. 'Your life depends on it, Colenso, as does our future.' With a mocking wave, he turned and walked away. Moments later he'd disappeared back into the tunnel, which she vaguely recognized as part of the underground warrens that ran from Grade down to this trig. Once used for collecting limpets at low tide, the caves were now commandeered by smugglers for storing their booty.

It was all too much, and her eyes closed as she began to feel faint from fear and the effects of the sedative. Her legs buckled and she slumped forward, stopped from falling only by the ropes lashed to the rock face.

*

The noise of the rising tide advancing towards the Devil's Frying Pan jolted her back to consciousness. She shivered as she saw the turbulence created by rough seas surging through its entrance. Her father had chosen his spot well. Desperately she tugged at the ropes binding her hands, only to wince as the damp hemp tightened, cutting deeper into her flesh.

As white-tipped waves swirled ever closer to her feet, she shuddered. In the distance she could hear the sounds of the organ from the travelling fair. Loud and brash, its purpose was to attract the crowds and, judging from the shrieks of laughter coming from the villagers on the green, it was doing its job. Nobody would hear her screams and Kitto, dear unsuspecting Kitto, would be waiting for her.

The light was fading now, the wind rising, bringing with it a thick bank of rolling mist. She licked her salt-coated lips. The crescendo from the waves pounding the tidal cave and reverberating around the serpentine rock was deafening now, blotting out all sound of the fair. Her father had promised to return for her decision before the tide was in full spate but, intent on his mission and wishing her scared witless, she knew he was deliberately cutting it fine. He'd have a wasted journey though, for she had no intention of changing her mind. Nothing on this earth would induce her to marry that odious Ferret with his grasping paws and suggestive sneers. Her heart belonged to Kitto, and without him her life would have no purpose. She would take her love to the grave if need be. And if it was deemed to be a watery one then so be it, she thought, as spray from the advancing swell covered her feet before receding to allow her respite, albeit momentarily.

She gave a laugh that came out as a high-pitched shriek. How ironic that her name Colenso should mean 'from the dark pool', for now it looked as if she would be returning to it much sooner than she'd thought.

'Colenso.' Yes, that's my name. 'Colenso.' She must be dreaming now. Do you dream before you die, she wondered? Then she heard the crunch of shingle. 'Oh, dear God, what has he done to you?'

'Mamm,' she whispered, for she had no strength left to talk.

'Don't worry, we'll save you.' More crunching, another figure hovering above her. She felt someone hacking at the ropes behind her back. Her hands were suddenly free, but her limbs were too numb to move. She felt rubbing on her arms and legs, the warmth of a blanket around her shoulders. With arms supporting her, she let herself be led back along the dark tunnels. Then everything went black once again.

When she came to, she was lying on a soft bed, her mother stroking her hair and talking softly to her.

'You're awake,' Caja cried. 'Mara, she's awake.' Eyes black as coal peered down at her, carmine lips smiling.

'My, you gave us a fright,' the woman said. 'Your poor mamm's been out of her mind with worry. Drink this, it'll warm your blood.' She eased Colenso into a sitting position then held out a silver goblet. The liquid was sweet on her tongue but as it hit the back of her throat, she began to cough and splutter. 'That's better, your colour's returning. You'll be all right, now.'

'How do you feel now?' her mamm asked.

'My throat's sore and it feels like someone's banging my head with a hammer, but other than that, I'm fine,' she smiled, hoping to reassure her mamm, who was looking whiter than the sheet covering her.

'When I returned home and saw all your clothes on the floor, well, I didn't know what to think. I found Peder in the alehouse but couldn't get any sense out of him. He kept muttering about you coming to your senses before the tide turned. Worried me sick, he did. If it hadn't been for Mara doing one of her readings and consulting her crystal ball … well, I don't know how we'd have found you.'

'Here, girl, eat this,' the black-eyed woman said, bustling back with a bowl of fragrant-smelling broth. 'Got lucky with a chicken this morning,' she winked.

It was some time later, when Colenso had finished her soup and felt the strength returning to her body, that she was able to take in her surroundings.

'Where am I?' she asked, looking around the wagon-like interior. It was like a miniature home with a stove, its chimney seeming to disappear out of the roof, utensils hanging from the walls, tiny cupboards, brightly coloured cushions on the bench-like seat opposite on which her mamm was sitting.

'This is Madam Mara's travelling van,' Caja told her. 'She's a fortune teller with the fair.' Colenso stared at the woman properly for the first time, taking in the shiny dark curls spilling from her headscarf to her carmine lips and the brightly coloured bracelets that jangled from her wrists.

'The problem is, what are we going to do with you, dearie? You can't go back to that monster of a father, it would be criminal, and from what your mother's told me the man he proposes you wed ain't much better.' Colenso stared at her mamm in surprise, for until now the Ferret could do no wrong in her eyes.

'I learnt things in the alehouse, terrible things about what he did to his first wife. He used to beat her but one day he went too far and …' she shook her head and shuddered. 'You've got to get away from here, and fast. Mara has offered you a ride in her van.'

'You'll have to stay hidden, though, cos Big Al don't allow no hitchers along, especially young female ones. Like I told your mother, you'd have to pretend to be a boy in case you was spotted.'

Colenso shook her head but the thought of facing either her father or Fenton again sent shudders shivering down her spine.

'I must see Kitto first,' she said.

'No time,' Mara replied. 'We leave at first light.'

'I'll tell him what's happened,' Caja said. 'Where are you headed?' she asked Mara.

'Best you don't know, then nobody can get it out of you. We don't want her father getting wind and following. Colenso can send you a card further down the line when things have cooled down.'

'But …' Colenso began.

''Tis for your safety, dearie.'

'Mara's right,' Caja sighed. 'Father'll be mad as a March hare when he finds you gone. As for Fenton, I only wish I'd known sooner what he was really like. Forgive me, Colenso. I'm going to miss you so much,' she murmured, leaning over and kissing Colenso's cheek.

'Me too,' she replied. Realizing she had no choice in the matter, she reached up and unfastened her necklace.

'Please give this to Kitto with all my love,' she murmured, fighting back the tears as she handed it to her mamm.

Chapter 14

Through a mist of tears, Colenso watched her mamm disappear. Was she really in so much danger? Mara obviously thought so, for bangles jangling, she took up a pair of fancy handled scissors and slid elegantly into the seat Caja had vacated.

'Best get you disguised before someone comes knocking on my door. Lovely hair you've got,' she sighed, taking a handful and cutting it off somewhere near Colenso's ear. 'By the time it grows back we'll be on the other side of the county. Still, it's a small thing compared with the ordeal you've suffered. Lucky for you the crystal ball never lies,' she added as she snipped with quick efficiency. 'Right, now let's get you changed. I've scavenged some old clothes from one of the tinkers but first we need to bind your chest.'

'What?' Colenso spluttered.

'Well, you've got a fine bosom – too fine for a lad,' the woman laughed, wrapping a band of material so tightly around Colenso she could hardly breathe.

By the time Colenso had squeezed into the boy's shirt and trousers, she was exhausted, but as she went to lie back down again Mara shook her head.

'Can't risk you being discovered. Make yourself comfortable in here,' she said, jumping up and lifting a hinged lid on the seat she'd just vacated. Colenso shivered as she remembered the dark tunnels, and stared dubiously down at the confined space.

'Will I have to stay in there for long?' she asked nervously.

'By the time you wake we'll be well on the road,' Mara told her. Still in a daze, Colenso did as she was bid. 'Whatever happens, don't climb out until I tell you it's safe, though judging by the look of you, you'll have the sleep of the angels.' Mara chuckled, her black curls bobbing as she bent over to cover Colenso with a blanket.

*

Colenso woke with a start. Where was she? Why was someone banging on her head with a hammer? Why was her chest so tight? And why was she being rocked from side to side? As she screwed up her eyes trying to remember, she became aware of the clip-clopping of hooves and the metallic trundle of wheels. In the dappled light filtering through a gap in the wooden slats, she could make out the outline of trees and hedges passing by, feel the cool breeze on her cheeks. She went to sit up but banged her head and everything went black again.

When next she surfaced, so did her memory. She was in a van travelling to who knew where, dressed as a boy. As her hand went to ease the band at her chest, the roof above her was raised and the cheery face of Madam Mara smiled down at her.

'Foretold you'd sleep well, didn't I?' she grinned through carmine lips. 'Still, better dead to the world than dead full stop,' she muttered. 'Blood runs cold every time I think of what that father of yours did. Still, he'll get his comeuppance. What goes around comes around.' Colenso smiled at the woman's avowal, for hadn't Mammwynn always said the same. A thud followed by a dragging noise came from outside, making her jump.

'Only the kumpania setting up camp for the night. Best stay where you are for now,' Mara added, as Colenso made to climb out. 'How does supper in bed sound?'

'Supper?' Colenso frowned. 'But I've only been asleep a little while.' Mara chuckled again.

'You've slept through the moon, stars and rise of the sun, dearie. Now it's sinking beyond the sea like a pink orange ball. How are you feeling?'

'My head's all muzzy and itches like mad,' she replied, lifting off the woollen cap she'd covered her cropped hair with.

'Best keep that on, dearie, in case anyone comes. This hedgerow tea will soon clear your noddle.'

'Thank you.' Colenso took the proffered cup and drank gratefully, for her throat was dry as dust.

'Now for the bokoli. It's one of the few dishes that tastes better when Queenie cooks it,' Mara smiled, gesturing to the corner. Puzzled, Colenso looked over to see who this Queenie was, but there was only the cast-iron stove upon which Mara placed a skillet. 'Usually I'd be broiling on the chitties over the yag with the others, but not tonight,' she explained.

Bokoli, chitties, yag? It was like another language, Colenso mused, her head spinning, but the tea was comforting and she sat back and savoured its unusual flower-like taste. Soon an appetizing aroma filled the little van, making her stomach rumble.

'Here we are, dearie,' Mara said, handing her a tin plate then sitting on the seat opposite. So bokoli must be a pancake, Colenso thought, tucking in ravenously. The batter was light as a feather and filled with a mixture of bacon trimmings and cheese sprinkled with some spice she didn't recognize.

'Thank you, that was lovely,' she said, handing Mara her empty plate.

'I'll have to do a lot of dukkering if you're going to eat like that,' Mara chuckled. 'That's fortune-telling to you,' she added as, bangles jingling, she got to her feet and peered through the drawn curtain. 'The others are still eating so if you want the privy, best go now.' Colenso stared around the tiny wagon. 'Not here, outside. I'll wash the dishes further downstream while you do what you need in the bushes.'

Cramped and stiff, it took Colenso a few moments to extricate herself from the wooden box before struggling into the coarse jacket she'd been given to complete her disguise. Following Mara out of the little door, she just had time to take in the group of people sitting around a crackling fire over which a blackened pot was swinging from a crook. Beyond was a circle of wagons, a huddle of trailers and horses munching the grass to one side. The woman gestured towards a row of trees then, with plates clattering, took herself off in the other direction.

'Not joining us, Mara?' a man called.

'Not tonight, Jimbo, I need to make more tisanes and teas for the next fair.'

'Still got a few days for all that …' But Colenso had reached cover and the rest of the conversation was lost to her.

Back in the van, feeling much better for her rinse in the flowing water, she went to climb back into her box, but Mara shook her head.

'Don't worry, dearie, the others will soon be making merry. They'll not bother us tonight, though they'll be up at break of dawn to strike camp. Come and tell me about yourself,' she said, patting the seat beside her.

'There's not much to tell, really,' Colenso shrugged. But as she sat in the dying light, heat from the stove warming her chilled body, she found herself opening up. 'One minute I was happily arranging my handfasting to Kitto, the next that Mr Fenton arrived at the works. For some reason he decided he wanted to marry me, and Father encouraged it.'

'Hmm, your mother explained about that. Got to know her quite well when she came to treat young Domo's leg. He'd been carried in here and between us we fixed him up. When she returned later in the day, we shared a brew and got chatting. Right worried about you, she was, yet couldn't explain why.'

'But she was as bad as Father for encouraging me to wed Fenton. They were going to sell me, can you believe?' Colenso cried indignantly.

'Avarice,' Mara tutted. 'It can turn a person's head.' She shook her head so that the golden hoops at her ears flashed in the glow from the stove. 'Can't understand this obsession with material things myself. Give me the open road, the wind on my face and my little home any day.'

'So, what do you actually do?' Colenso asked, intrigued by the striking woman and her funny way of speaking.

'Live life, my dear, and enjoy doing it too. I travel round the country with the kumpania, visiting the fairs and feast days, earn money by dukkering, forage for food.'

'It sounds a lovely way to live,' Colenso sighed.

'It is. New people to meet, acquaintances to catch up with and of course the friends I travel with. Although it's hard work pitching and striking camp at each new place. By the end of the season I'm ready to take things easier.'

'You mean you have a real home like a cottage to go to?'

'This is my real home, dearie,' Mara chuckled, gesturing around the van. 'I have everything here that I need. But tell me about this man you're betrothed to – Kitto didn't you call him?' At the sound of his name, Colenso's heart flipped, and as she began telling Mara about him the woman listened attentively.

'Sounds like a decent young man to care for his mother and siblings so. And he must be handsome to have caught the eye of a pretty young girl like you.' As Colenso's hand went to her shorn locks, Mara reached over and patted her shoulder.

'By the time you see Kitto again, your hair will be back to how it was. In the meantime, I promised your mother I'd keep you safe, so remember to stay well hidden. No use escaping one web just to be caught in another, now, is it?' Colenso nodded thoughtfully, for hadn't she been feeling like a fly being drawn ever closer to the spider's mouth?

'Of course, you're bound to be spotted sooner or later, but hopefully by then we'll be on the other side of the county,' Mara continued, placing a little ornately carved chest on the table.

'Now, let's see what's in store for us,' she said, raising the lid.

'Goodness,' Colenso murmured as the woman pulled decorative cards from beneath a covering of gemstones and herbs.

'Need to protect the tarot else they can pick up negative forces that affect the reading. Here, you shuffle them and let them pick up your energy,' she instructed, handing them to her. 'That should do it,' she said, taking them back moments later. 'Now to put them in order.' Colenso watched as she laid them out in rows of three on the little pull-out table. 'Right, now let's see what the spread says. Oh ...' her voice trailed off.

Colenso briefly caught a glimpse of staring faces and figures before Mara hastily gathered them together and returned them to the chest. 'Not working tonight,' she shrugged. 'Time we were abed anyhow.'

As Colenso climbed into her hidey-hole under the settle, she glimpsed Mara peering into a crystal globe and could tell the woman was troubled. But too exhausted to think anymore, she closed her eyes and fell into a deep sleep.

*

Men were shouting, banging things around. The clattering of hooves resonated.

When Colenso stirred, the van was swaying gently from side to side. Peering through the wooden planks, she could make out the outline of buildings, horses and carts, people walking. Her limbs were cramped and she needed some air, so she pushed on the lid above her head. To her surprise, it gave way easily and she climbed gingerly out. The room was empty and she guessed Mara must be outside steering the pony. Everywhere was immaculate, the things they'd used the night before neatly stowed away. The pans and brass handles on the cupboard and drawer were polished to a sheen and, although the space was smaller than their living room at home, it felt homely and loved.

Suddenly, the van lurched to a halt and, unable to resist taking a peek, she lifted one edge of the chintz curtain. They'd drawn up in a field, which to Colenso's eyes seemed to be crowded with vans and trailers. She just had time to glimpse big burly men erecting what looked like stalls, when the door opened and Mara appeared.

'Get away from there,' she growled. 'Have you not got the sense you were born with?' Colenso stared at the woman in bewilderment. Gone was her smile and kindly eyes.

'I was curious to see where we were,' she murmured.

'And you know what curiosity did,' Mara countered, slumping down onto the settle and thumping one of the brightly coloured cushions into shape behind her head. She looked dirty and dishevelled, smudges of purple beneath her eyes.

'Has something happened?' Colenso asked.

'Nothing for you to worry about. Just got here a bit earlier than planned.'

'Where's here?'

'Helston. We come every year and set up our stalls ready for the Feast of St Michael – or Flora Day as they call it here. It's a celebration of the passing of winter and the arrival of spring. Lovely it is, with dancing and everyone wearing lily of the valley, which is the town's symbolic flower. You never been before?' Colenso shook her head.

'Never been off The Lizard in my life before.' Mara's eyes widened.

'Then you've never lived,' she replied, her voice softening. 'This is one of the biggest fairs we attend. Over the next few days other wagons and trailers will be arriving with all manner of attractions.'

'You mean it's bigger than the Cuckoo Fest at Cadgwith?' Colenso asked.

'I should say,' Mara hooted. 'Anyhow, I'm whacked. Weren't taking no chance of being followed so left before dawn. Old Ears weren't happy at being hurried, I can tell you. Still, he's getting on in pony years so you can't blame him. Now, let me get some shut eye, will you? There's a couple books in that drawer to help pass the time,' she said, gesturing towards the kitchen area. 'But for both our sakes, don't venture outside. Promise?'

'I promise,' Colenso replied.

'We'll have a brew when I wake,' Mara mumbled, her eyes closing. A few moments later she was snoring gently.

Colenso sat listening to the sounds of banging and shouting coming from outside. From the little she'd seen, the men were obviously setting things up for the fair, and she was seized with the urge to go and look. Still she'd promised Mara she wouldn't.

Instead, she reached out and opened the drawer, marvelling again at how close at hand everything was. The first book contained handwritten recipes of strange-sounding dishes like Kerrit Bora, made with mutton, vegetables and wild ransoms; Ballivas, a suet pudding filled with bacon scraps and herbs; Coro Shoshoi which on reading she realized was jugged hare or rabbit depending on what was caught; rook or pigeon stew and Panni Sappor which translated to stewed eel. So, Mara hadn't been joking when she said she foraged.

There were also receipts for treating ailments. Ginger cordial for colds or bringing down a fever, sarsaparilla for cleansing the blood, lemon barley water for disorders of the bladder, raspberry vinegar for sore throats, elderflower junket for sneezes. Colenso smiled, remembering how Mammwynn had always maintained that nature provided the cure for any illness. Automatically, her hand went to her throat, but of course the necklace wasn't there. She hoped by now her mamm would have given it to Kitto and explained what had happened. Unless she'd conveniently forgotten to pass on her message – again.

'You look like a wet summer's day,' Mara said, sitting up and eyeing her shrewdly. 'Time for that brew,' she added, snatching up her kettle and going to the door. 'Remember, if anyone knocks don't answer.'

When she returned a short time later she was bearing two fragrant-smelling pasties along with her filled kettle.

'One good thing about these parts is the food,' she grinned, her spirits fully restored.

Although she was ravenous, as Colenso bit into hers, she couldn't help thinking of the one she'd made for Kitto. Why did everything remind her of him? The answer was obvious, of course. It was because she loved and missed him. So much had happened recently, she couldn't help wondering if she'd ever see him again.

Chapter 15

'The big vans have arrived,' Mara announced, peering through the window the next morning. 'I'll go and feed Ears then get my tent ready for the first punters.'

'Why is he called that?' Colenso asked,

'Because he doesn't miss anything,' Mara laughed. 'Never known a pony like it. We complement each other though, him with his hearing and me with my sight.'

'What can I do while you're out?' Colenso asked. Having just finished a hearty breakfast of pancakes laced with some kind of fortifying cordial, she was eager to help.

'Lie low,' the woman replied, setting the little chintz curtain back in place. 'It'll be pandemonium while they set up the stalls and rides so nobody should come knocking. I'll try and nip back later but can't promise as it's always hectic on opening day,' she added, tying a red scarf around her hair and rubbing liquid from a little glass phial over her lips until they were the same bright colour. Then, gathering up the velvet bag with its crystal ball and the carved casket, she disappeared outside.

With a sinking feeling, Colenso watched her go. How was she going to get through another long day with nothing to do? Then she remembered the other book and settled down to read it. This one was written in beautiful copperplate and illustrated with colourful drawings of sweetmeats and other wonderful confections she'd never seen before. Eagerly, she turned the pages, enthralled to read recipes for preserving fruits and nuts with sugar, candied orange slices, clotted-cream fudge. Although Mammwynn had taught her to make a tablet concocted from flowers, this was entirely different. Fascinated, she lost all sense of time and had just reached the page detailing bullseyes and rose rock when Mara returned, closing the door quickly behind her.

'Just got time for a brew before the fair opens,' she announced, scuttling over to stoke the stove and place the kettle to heat. 'Fair parched, I am,' she added, grinning at her pun as she collapsed onto the brightly coloured cushions which turned into her bed at night. 'Find that interesting, do you?' she asked, pointing to the book.

'I had no idea you made such things,' Colenso told her.

'I don't,' Mara laughed. 'Jago the Journeyman does, or rather his mother and sister do. He left his grandmother's journal here last year. You might get to meet him, though not until we're well clear of here. Still too close to home for you yet.'

'Let me make it,' Colenso offered, jumping up as the little kettle whistled.

'Save the leaves in the jar with the rest for brewing again,' Mara told her. 'There's always those who want a reading.' Colenso stared at the woman in admiration. Was there no end to her talents?

'Got the gift passed down from my grandmother,' Mara

said as if seeing into her mind. 'Didn't understand what it was at first. Thought everyone saw the things I did.'

'What do you mean? What did you see?' Colenso frowned.

'Spirits of people who'd passed over. First happened with my dear Grandma. Loved her so much and was devastated when she died. Anyhow one day our dog Benjie started barking excitedly and there she was beside us. I was chatting away to her, telling her everything that had happened, when Mother came into the room and asked who I was talking to. Thought I was making it all up cos she couldn't see Grandmother herself. It happened a few times but I learned to keep it to myself. Not many have the gift, you see.'

'Mammwynn used to say her pentacle foretold things,' Colenso told her.

'The one you gave to your mother,' Mara nodded.

'Which I hope she remembers to give to Kitto with my message,' she sighed.

'If it's written in the stars then it'll happen,' Mara told her, patting her hand. 'For now, let's enjoy our drink.'

After Mara had left, Colenso settled back to her reading. However, it wasn't long before the tea made its inevitable journey. Knowing she couldn't wait any longer, Colenso dragged on the jacket, pulled her cap right down over her face then stole outside. The organ was churning out its brash music while the field rang with an assortment of strange noises and laughter. Certain she wouldn't be spotted amongst the melee, she hurried towards the edge of the field. However, when she emerged a few minutes later, she heard a man yell.

'You boy, over here.' She broke into a run but the man followed and moments later caught her firmly by the arm.

'Think you can disobey me? Well, think again. We don't carry no shirkers here,' the swarthy man with greying hair roared, pushing her roughly towards a queue. 'These people are waiting for the overboats, so look sharp and start turning that handle.'

'I can't …' Colenso began, but he'd already turned away.

'Right folks, two at a time please, two at a time,' he told them, taking their money and slipping the coins into a leather pouch at his side.

'Well, get to it, we ain't got all day,' he snapped as the lads seated in the boats stared at her expectantly. Grabbing the handle, she began turning. 'You'll have to go faster than that or they'll be wanting their money back,' the man shouted.

As the fair organ with its brass trumpets emulated the sound of a military band and people milled around, laughing and shouting, Colenso lost all track of time. She could hear the shot of rifles, the crack of balls against the coconut shies, the cries of delight when people won. Conscious of people watching the ride, she tried to pull the cap down further over her face.

'Put your back into it, boy,' the man cried, taking fares from yet more punters. The smell of frying onions wafted on the breeze, making her stomach churn as she turned and turned the handle. Her arms were aching and the band across her chest constrained her breathing, inhibiting her movements. But there was no respite, for no sooner did one ride finish than the boats were refilled with yet more people eager to experience the thrill of being swung into the air.

Finally, her arms went dead and, unable to carry on any longer, the handle slipped from her grasp. As the punters voiced their disapproval, the swarthy man turned on her.

'What the hell you playing at?' he roared, grabbing her by the shoulders. Then he stared at her closer. 'Why, you ain't no boy.' As people stopped and stared, wondering what all the fuss was about, Colenso saw Mara pushing her way through the crowd.

'Leave her alone, Al,' she called.

'What's going on, Mara?' he growled. 'You know my rules, no hitchers.'

'Not here. Come to my van and I'll explain.'

'Flippin' 'eck, I got a show to run,' he huffed, hands on hips.

'All the more reason to get this sorted without making one, don't you think?' she asked. Then linking her arm through Colenso's, she began walking towards her van. He swore under his breath before, calling to a straw-haired youth to see to the ride, he followed her.

'This had better be good,' he growled as Mara shut the door behind them.

'Regrettably, Al, it's not good at all. In fact, it's the most despicable story you ever heard. Sit down and I'll get us all a stiff drink.'

With a glare at Colenso, he sank onto the cushions while Mara poured rose-coloured liquid into tiny glasses. She handed them round and Colenso sniffed hers tentatively.

'Get it down you, it'll do you good,' she encouraged before turning to Al. His face remained stern but he listened without interrupting until Mara had finished telling him how Colenso had come to be here.

'I should throw you out of the fair, Mara,' he grunted. 'You know the rules.'

'But you won't because, for all your bluff and bluster, you hate bullying. Besides, I'm one of your biggest draws.' The man gave a sharp intake of breath and as he ran a rough hand through his thatch, Colenso was certain Mara had gone too far. To her surprise though, he raised his glass, the hint of a smile on his lips.

'Touché, Madam Mara. But if the girl's to stay she must earn her keep. Obviously she's too weak to be of any use on the rides, so what do you suggest?'

'Colenso's willing to work her way, but we're still too near The Lizard for her to risk being outside. There's no telling what those evil men will do. My conscience simply won't allow her to risk being spotted.' Mara shuddered and took a long mouthful of drink. Then to Colenso's surprise she changed the subject.

'By the way, Jago's sister burned her hand testing the rock and can't make up the cones for his Nelson's buttons and bullseyes. It's a shame for you know the punters will pay more if the sweets are nicely wrapped. They do like a little memento to take home.' She paused, then as Al took a sip of his drink, winked at Colenso.

'What say the girl makes up the cones in here?' he cried, his blue eyes brightening as he gestured around the van.

'Why Al, what a marvellous idea,' Mara gushed. 'What do you say, Colenso? Isn't Big Al here clever to think of such a solution?' she asked, turning to Colenso.

'Er, yes,' she replied, trying to keep a straight face, for clearly Mara had outfoxed him.

'Well, after what Mara's told me, it wouldn't be human to throw you out,' he muttered in Colenso's direction. 'Can't have no fancy names so you're to answer to Col and keep dressed like a boy, all right?'

'That's fine and I really do appreciate ...' Colenso began but he'd already turned back to Mara.

'Don't want no trouble so I reckon she should stay in the van until we reach Zennor.'

'That sounds sensible, Al,' Mara agreed, again making it sound as if he'd come up with the plan she'd originally devised.

'Right, well, better get back. I've a show to run out there, you know,' he grunted, draining his glass. 'Nice drop of sloe gin, that.'

'The hedges were generous with their bounty last autumn,' Mara grinned. 'I'll speak to Jago first thing tomorrow.' She waited until he'd left then turned to Colenso. 'Right, now that's sorted, let's get you cleaned up. Colenso frowned down at her blood-encrusted hands then winced as Mara gently dabbed them with a kerchief soaked in the gin. 'You'll have blisters come morning but could have been worse.'

'Why are you helping me like this?' Colenso asked.

'What am I meant to do, leave you to the mercy of those beasts?' Mara muttered.

'But ...'

'No buts. Let's just say someone once helped me when I needed it and now it's my turn to return the favour. Right, all done. You get some shut-eye while I go back to my tent. There's a goodly crowd out there with money burning holes in their pockets. I can't afford to miss the opportunity of having my palm crossed with silver,' she grinned and, before Colenso could thank her, disappeared outside.

158

'Have you made cones before?' Jago asked her the next morning. With his hazel eyes and shock of white hair, he appeared older than Colenso had expected. However, his gentle, unassuming manner soon put her at her ease.

'No,' she admitted.

'Oh well, 'tis easy. Must be, else Karla would never manage,' he grinned. 'Look, all you do is cut out circles of paper, fold each into four, unwrap, and slice down the creases,' he said, demonstrating deftly. 'Roll each one into shape, mould the pointed end like so, then paste the edges,' he said, dipping his finger into the flour-and-water mixture. 'Then, hey presto,' he said, triumphantly holding up the finished cone. 'Now you try.'

It took Colenso a couple of goes before she'd grasped the technique to his satisfaction but finally he nodded.

'That's good. Sometimes for special occasions like the Flora Day, Karla fashions scallops out of the edges of circles before she cuts them but that's up to you. I'm just mighty obliged for any help you can give me.'

'Let me master this, then I'll give the fancy ones a try. The time passes slowly cooped up in here so I'll be happy to have something to do. Not that I'm complaining,' she added quickly in case he thought her ungrateful. 'And I really enjoyed reading your sweetmeat journal.'

'Did you?' he asked, looking pleased. 'It was Grandmother's life's work to ensure all her receipts were recorded. She drew all the pictures of how they should look, too. When you're allowed out, as it were, come and see me at the Panam stall. I'll be delighted to show you what we sell.'

'Do you and Karla make all the sweets?'

'Mostly, although it varies from fair to fair, depending on how long we stay in each place. I've gotten to know ladies who make different confections that I collect along the way. Adds variety to the Panam and gives them the opportunity to earn some money. Don't know how long Karla will be out of action though. Her hand turned nasty so I told her to stay home with Mother until it heals.'

'How did she manage to burn it so badly?'

'Testing the consistency of the syrup,' he sighed. 'Didn't get her finger out in time,' he shrugged.

'That's terrible,' Colenso gasped, her blisters suddenly seeming mild by comparison.

'Occupational hazard,' he shrugged. 'Don't look so shocked, she knew the risk. Besides if she hadn't been day-dreaming about her follower, it wouldn't have happened.' Follower? How old was his sister then? Perhaps Jago was younger than she'd first thought for, although he had that shock of white hair, his eyes were clear, his skin smooth.

'Well, I'd better leave you to it,' he said, interrupting her musing as he got to his feet. 'Get Mara to drop those over to the Panam when you're done.'

'Do you sell a lot of sweets?' she asked.

'Oh yes. If the men don't win something on the stalls for their ladies to take home then they have to purchase them a gift or their lives wouldn't be worth living. Then there are the children who want to spend their precious pennies on rock or barley-sugar twists,' he grinned.

Pleased to have something useful to do to pass the time, Colenso pulled out the little table and settled down to making the cones. It was an easy enough task, even within the confines of the little van and with all the noise and kerfuffle going on outside.

As the pile grew, she found her mind wandering. She thought of Kitto and wondered how he was getting on. Had her mamm given him her necklace yet? And if she had, what would his reaction be? Would he be able to get time off from work to follow after her? His family were reliant on his wage after all.

With a shudder, she thought of the Ferret, recalling what her mamm had heard about his first wife. Would he really try and find her? He would have been furious at having had a wasted journey to their cottage. But no doubt her father would have made up some story to cover his tracks. However, there was no getting away from the fact that, without her accepting his proposal, there would be no promotion for her father or new cottage for her mamm. Her father wasn't one to let an opportunity like that slip through his fingers, so perhaps Mara was right and he would come after her.

She shivered in the dying light. As shadows crept slowly round the little van, the extent of the danger she could be in finally sank home and she vowed to lie low until they reached this place called Zennor, wherever that might be.

Chapter 16

'Sorry, dearie, but you'll have to get out and walk. Ears can't manage these hills with you in the van.' Colenso looked up in surprise to see Mara peering down at her.

'Is it safe?' she asked nervously, her dreams having been haunted by images of the Ferret and her father coming after her.

'Put your cap on and keep your head down,' she ordered. 'Come on, look sharp or we'll never make it to Zennor in time.' Colenso looked at Mara with her red scarf tied elegantly round her head then glared at the itchy, woollen hat she'd come to hate. Still, it was worth suffering the discomfort if it meant she could be outside, she thought, ramming it on top of the tufts of her hair.

Used to the confines of her little hidey-hole now, she climbed up quickly and put her head out of the top part of the little stable door. Blinking in the bright light, she jumped down the step, wincing as the stones pierced the thin soles of her boots. Ahead of them, the other vans were continuing their journey, ponies blowing and snorting as they laboured their loads up the long incline. Men and women walked alongside while children and dogs darted in and out of the golden gorse, setting its coconut scent wafting on the early-morning breeze. Birds swooped low, gathering food for their hungry chicks while in the distance she could see the sweep of the moors with the tall chimneys and gaunt engine houses of tin mines dotted around the landscape. Colenso stretched, glad to be out in the fresh air again, then hurried to join Mara who was leading Ears along the dusty lane.

'I didn't realize you were making such an early start,' she said, staring in wonder at the crimson sun rising above the hills, bathing them in its rosy glow.

'We have a full day's travelling ahead of us for the Feast of St Senara, which is where they reckon the name of Zennor comes from, by the way. Starts on Sunday.'

'St Senara?' Colenso frowned. 'Can't say I've heard of him.'

'Well, you wouldn't because Senara was a woman – a Breton queen, no less,' Mara grinned. 'According to legend she was thrust into a barrel and thrown into the sea by a jealous husband. Whilst there she gave birth to a son who went on to become St Budoc, another famous Cornish saint. Anyhow, Senara created the church and by all accounts was a popular saint, worshipped by the men who fished the dangerous waters near the village.'

'Even so, it's a long way to travel just for one day, isn't it?' Colenso asked.

'Except the feast lasts for a whole week. Families who've left the village return home, and people visit from miles around. There's all manner of celebrations so it's well worth setting up the fair. There'll be other attractions too, as long as they can get their wagons along the narrow lane to the church.'

'And I can manage to walk on all these stones,' Colenso cried as another sharp stone cut into her foot.

'What's wrong?' Mara asked, stopping and frowning as she was shown the holes in Colenso's boots. 'Hardly appropriate for walking any distance, are they?' Before Colenso could answer, the woman put two fingers to her mouth and gave a sharp whistle.

'Hey, Tinks,' she shouted. A thin man weighed down under the weight of various bags with shoes and boots dangling from his shoulders, turned to look at them. 'Got a suitable pair of boots for Col here?' He nodded then began rummaging through his motley stock while he waited for them to catch up.

'How about these?' he asked, holding up a pair of scuffed but serviceable boots as they pulled up alongside. 'Could let you have them for a shillin'.'

'A shilling,' Mara cried. 'You old reprobate. And after I let you have some of my rabbit stew last week. You can swap them for Col's old ones here and a bottle of my sloe gin as long as she hasn't got any blisters when we arrive,' she told him. The tinker grinned.

'Done deal,' he said, spitting on his hand then holding it out. As Mara shook it, Colenso took off her old boots and donned the new ones. They were a bit big but the soles had plenty of wear left in them.

'Better?' Mara asked, handing her old ones to the tinker when she nodded. As the tinker went on his way, Colenso turned to Mara.

'But I've already got blisters.'

'Shame. Old Tinks likes his gin,' Mara winked. Colenso

laughed, for the woman really was incorrigible. 'I suppose your father intended buying you new ones?' Recalling how he'd ignored her discomfort on the journey to the works, she muttered something noncommittal but Mara shot her a knowing look.

They spent the next few hours traversing the undulating hills, passing through tiny hamlets and farmland criss-crossed with hedgerows until they reached the saltings at Hayle, where they stopped for a break.

'Oh, this is much better,' Colenso cried, breathing in the sea air as she perched on a rock and watched the gulls wheeling over the gently lapping waves. 'The countryside is pretty but it does feel hemmed in.'

'Well, make the most of it for we've a fair few miles of country to pass through yet,' Mara told her. 'Mind you, I can't say travelling the open road has ever made me feel hemmed in as you put it. Come on, finish your bread, the others are preparing to move on.'

Having made their way through winding lanes with blackthorn and bracken high on either side of them, passed through Halsetown and skirted around St Ives, they started to climb a steep hill. The vista of the sea opened up as the land fell away sharply to their right, while rock-strewn, bracken-covered moorland towered above them on the left. After the procession had struggled up the tortuous tracks, it was late afternoon when they finally reached their destination. Zennor was set in a deep valley with a cluster of granite cottages, sprawling farms, and a magnificent church beyond which the moors rose like a battlement. Thinking they would be taking a break, Colenso offered to fill the kettle from the stream then make them some tea. To her surprise, Mara hooted with laughter, setting the hoops at her ears dancing.

'Take a rest?' she spluttered. 'We've to help set up the fair before we can even think of taking a rest.' Colenso peered around, wondering how she could have missed the frenzied activity that was now taking place. Rides were being manhandled into position by burly men with tattoos decorating their muscular arms, stalls already erected were having their contents artistically displayed, while the big wagons carrying their heavy equipment were being directed onto the field. Villagers stood avidly watching whilst their children, hopeful of earning a few pence or free rides, were clamouring to help.

'I've never seen so many people in one place before,' she cried.

'Well, you were hidden in the van at Helston. Just you wait until tomorrow. Won't be able to move for bodies,' Mara replied, setting Ears free from the wooden shafts. Bending down, she then began pulling poles and bags out from the racks under the van.

'Well, don't just stand there with arms the same length – grab hold of these and help me carry them over there,' Mara said, thrusting the poles at her while trying to point towards the church at the same time. 'If we don't get a move on, the best places will be taken. Jostling past others, all with the same intent, Mara headed towards a vacant spot near the graveyard. 'Adds to the atmosphere,' she winked.

Much later, when her little round tent had been erected

and the folding table and chairs set out to her satisfaction on the hessian rug, Mara turned to Colenso.

'How's your feet?' she asked.

'Tired but these boots are much better, thank you.'

'Good. Well, I don't know about you but I'm ready for supper,' she said, pointing to a fire that was blazing in one corner of the green before striding towards the kumpania she travelled with. As Colenso followed, she could smell woodsmoke mingling with the appetizing aroma of stew. She guessed it was coming from the huge iron pot that was swinging from the chitties spiked into the ground alongside the yag, which she now knew was what they called the campfire. She sat down on the ground beside Mara, who began introducing her to her companions.

'This is Col who's helping Jago whilst Karla is indisposed,' she explained. At first, Colenso was wary but they welcomed her cordially, asking no personal questions, and she guessed Mara had already briefed them about her situation. By the time a plate of rabbit swimming in rich gravy was passed to her, she felt relaxed enough to enjoy her meal.

The sun was sinking behind the hills and she watched as the sky darkened to inky black and the first stars twinkled their nightly appearance. Excitement bubbled up inside her. Although she was exhausted and her legs ached, tomorrow she was to help Jago at the Panam and she couldn't wait. Surely now she could shed these horrible, itchy garments and wear her own clothes again.

*

'Oh good, you've come bearing gifts,' Jago greeted Colenso when she arrived at the Panam stall weighed down with the cones she'd spent the morning making. 'I see you're still in disguise,' he added. 'Shame, a pretty girl always draws the punters.' Colenso sighed and stared down at her coarse attire.

'Mara insisted. Ears woke Mara in the night with his whickering and she was convinced someone was prowling around outside.' She didn't add that the woman had wanted her to stay in the van and had only relented when she'd insisted she couldn't let Jago down.

'Well, Mara will know who to speak to about that. Now, let me show you my little emporium,' he quipped, gesturing round the compact stall, its red and white bunting flapping merrily in the light breeze. Cones already filled with sweets were attractively displayed alongside containers of assorted coloured confections. Setting down her latest batch of cones, she walked round the Panam, trying to take in the vast array of goods.

'There's always a good choice at the beginning of the fair,' Jago explained. 'Though, of course, I'll be pleased if there's little left by the end. Now, let me explain the different varieties. Feel free to try any,' he offered, raising his voice to be heard above the peal of church bells.

'These are striped bullseyes flavoured with lemon, Nelson's buttons, barley-sugar twists, fruit drops, humbugs, striped lollipops, assorted flavoured rock, which as you can see are shaped like walking canes, and of course no Panam would be complete without gingerbread,' he said, his fingers running along the various confections. 'Naturally, it varies over the

168

year depending on what's available – nuts and apples in autumn, spiced confections in the winter.'

'These are just wonderful,' Colenso exclaimed, bending to inhale the various heady scents. 'This rock gleams like polished serpentine.'

'You sound an authority on the subject,' he said, looking at her in surprise.

'I used to fashion it into trinkets for the tourists.'

'Did you now? And loved your work, by the sound of it. I'm sure Karla would show you how all of this is made. We'll be stopping off at Truro next month and I'll need to pick up more supplies. Hopefully her hand will have healed by then.'

'That would be wonderful,' she cried.

'Right, better get ready for the rush,' he said, rubbing his hands together as the organ started up to herald the opening of the fair.

The noise was deafening as it competed with the ringing of the church bells but nobody seemed to mind as they swarmed onto the field, laughing and jostling to be first on the rides. Colenso was kept so busy filling the cones to customers' requirements she didn't notice someone watching her from the shadows.

'What's your name, boy?' Colenso jumped as a tall man leant over the stall and studied her closely. He was more formally dressed than the other customers, his hair slicked back under his topper. As his eyes lowered to her chest, she felt a prickle of unease. His look reminded her of the Ferret except, instead of leering, the man was frowning.

'Is something wrong?' Jago asked. Although his voice was

casual, Colenso could tell from his eyes that he hadn't taken to the man either.

'What's the matter, can't the boy speak for himself?' the man asked, emphasizing the word boy.

'I pay him to work, not stand here talking,' Jago replied. 'Get to it, boy, those cones won't fill themselves and there's customers waiting,' he grunted, pretending to cuff Colenso's head but pushing her cap down lower in the process. 'Now, sir, if there's nothing you want, perhaps I could ask you to move, the people behind are waiting to make their selections.'

With a grunt of irritation, the man turned away and Colenso watched as he was swallowed up by the crowds.

'Didn't like the look of him,' Jago muttered. 'Let me know if you see him hanging around again.'

Although Colenso tried not to let the incident mar her afternoon, there was no getting away from the fact the man had unsettled her. As the sun began to sink behind the hill and the lamps were lit, she found herself jumping at the slightest movement, which didn't go unnoticed by Jago.

'Look, we've nearly used up all the cones. Go back and make some more for tomorrow, eh?' he suggested, patting her shoulder.

'I will,' she replied, nodding gratefully. 'I can come again tomorrow?' she asked.

'Same place, same time,' he grinned.

As Colenso began making her way behind the stalls, a man stepped out of the shadows. With his blonde hair and muscular physique, he looked like a giant haystack. She quickened her pace but he reached out to detain her. She opened her mouth to scream but he smiled and shook his head.

'I mean you no harm, miss,' he said, his gentle voice belying his looks. 'I work for Big Al and he's sent me to escort you back to your trailer. Can't be too careful round here.'

'Oh, well, that's kind of him,' she murmured, reassured by his presence.

To her surprise, Mara was waiting when she entered the van. The stove was lit, emanating a welcoming warmth, and Colenso felt her spirits lift.

'Titan see you back, did he?' she asked.

'Is that his name?' Colenso replied, sinking onto one of Mara's brightly embroidered cushions.

'Heard you'd had an unwelcome visitor at the Panam,' the woman continued, shooting Colenso a penetrating look.

'Gracious, this place is worse than Cadgwith,' she exclaimed. 'But yes, there was this strange man.'

'Top hat, slicked-back hair, smartly dressed.' Colenso stared at her in surprise. 'I spread the word for people to keep an eye out. You didn't recognize him then?'

'No, although the way he was looking at my, er, chest was strangely familiar. Except he seemed puzzled, disappointed almost.' To her surprise, Mara hooted with laughter.

'I'm sure he was. Comes looking for a female with nice womanly assets only to find a boy flat as the proverbial pancake. So what does that tell you, girl?'

'That he's a friend of the Ferret?' she asked, the penny dropping.

'More likely someone employed by him to find you. Don't worry,' she added as Colenso's eyes widened in horror. 'Old

Titan's a champion at Cornish wrasslin' and he saw to him good and proper. Don't think old nosey-nocks will be snooping round here again.' As the kettle began to whistle and Mara went to make the tea, Colenso felt relief wash over her.

'Mind you, that Ferret, as you call him, must be awfully keen on you to go to all this bother, so best be vigilant.'

Chapter 17

With Titan assigned to escort her to and from the Panam, Colenso's days fell into a comfortable pattern. In the mornings she helped Mara prepare their simple breakfast and then, whilst the woman went out to wash the dishes, she tidied the little van.

'It's a good job there's always a stream next to the camp, isn't it?' she said when Mara returned carrying a kettle full of water.

'Oh yes, the villagers always lay one on for us,' Mara replied, her face deadpan. 'Now young lady, although it's three days since old nasty-nocks paid a visit, I don't want you taking any chances,' she told her, gesturing to the cap on the seat beside her. 'So no going out without that.'

'But surely it's safe to wear my own clothes now?' Colenso protested, reaching under the shirt to ease the band around her chest.

'Big Al reckons if we've not seen hide nor hair of the man by the time we reach Bodmin, then you can resume being a girl.'

'But these clothes are so scratchy,' Colenso sighed, running her fingers under the collar of the coarse shirt, 'and my chest feels tight.'

'Well, if you can still feel then you know you're alive,' Mara pointed out briskly. 'Now, I've people to see, readings to do and you've plenty more cones to make. Jago's pleased with you, says you're a natural with the children, but then I guess it's not long since you were one yourself.'

'It's like another lifetime away,' Colenso sighed.

'So why not live in the present and enjoy life on the road?' Mara suggested. Then, giving one of her customary winks, she snatched up the tools of her trade and left. As Colenso picked up the first sheets of paper, she thought about what Mara had said. There was no denying she enjoyed helping the customers make their selection, and Jago was easy to work for. He was also vigilant in keeping a look-out for anyone suspicious prowling around. And hadn't he promised to take her to meet his sister, Karla? The thought of seeing how the rock and sweets were produced made her fizzle with excitement.

As she cut, folded and pasted, it wasn't long before her thoughts turned to home and Kitto. He must have received her necklace by now. Of course, there was no telling what her mamm would have told him, but she felt in her heart he would be wishing her well. Why, even at this very moment he could be searching for her. Though how would he know where to look? Then she remembered Mara saying something about her sending a card home when they'd moved away from The Lizard. She'd send him one from Bodmin, for if it was deemed safe for her to wear her own clothes then it would surely be safe to send a communication.

The strident notes of the organ starting up brought her swiftly back to the present and she scooped all the cones she'd

174

made into the wicker foraging basket Mara had loaned her. Everyone was being so kind, she thought as the three knocks heralding Titan's arrival sounded on the window. Dragging on the dreaded cap, she opened the door, blinking in the glare of the afternoon sun.

'Lovely out here, it is,' Titan beamed as he took her basket and she stepped outside with him. 'The missus is picnicking by the water with the little 'uns.' The thought of the giant having little anything made Colenso smile. 'Good to see you looking happier. Thought when you'd finished at the Panam you might like to take a look round the fair. Don't suppose you've seen much, having been cooped up like a chicken. Some of the fair will be moving on soon.'

'I thought Mara said we'd be here a week,' Colenso frowned, glancing over to the little round tent beside the graveyard.

'You will. Mara's is one of the most popular draws. People visit her year after year. Say her predictions always come true. Most of the villagers have been parted from their hard-earned dough though, so the big rides don't hang around.' He gave a devilish grin.

'So why do the others stay?'

'The locals have cricket matches and various other competitions arranged between local villages. The remaining stalls including the Panam will all move over to where Mara is.'

'I'd love to look around later, as long as you think it'd be safe,' Colenso murmured, automatically looking over her shoulder. When she could see no one following, she turned back to Titan. 'Don't you get tired of all the packing up and moving on?' He gave a loud belly laugh that boomed above the sound of the organ and the noise already emanating from sideshows they were passing.

'The missus and I get a rest when we haul up at Penzance at the end of the season. Take any available work to put food on the table.'

'Do you stay in your van over the winter then?'

'Yep, neither of us could imagine living in brick. Well, here you are, delivered safe and sound,' he grinned, handing back her basket. 'Afternoon, Jago,' he called. The vendor waved, then turned back to the buxom woman he was serving. Sporting her Sunday best, she was clearly doing her utmost to charm him.

''Ow much can I get for a farthing?' a tiny voice asked. Colenso looked down to see a grimy urchin, sporting tattered rags and staring at her hopefully.

'Is that your pocket money?' she asked. The boy looked uncomfortable.

'Found this on the grass,' he admitted, holding out a small coin. 'I never 'ad no sweets afore.' Seeing him glancing wistfully at the glistening rock, she gathered up a couple of the crooks and popped them in a cone. Delightedly, he snatched it from her and ran off, fearful she might change her mind.

'Putting me out of business, are you?' Jago grunted, shaking his head.

'You can take it out of my wages,' she said recklessly.

'Expecting to be paid as well as looked out for, are we?' he tutted, then changed the subject. 'It's good to see you looking happier. Now, if you wouldn't mind, there's a group of children over there clamouring to be served.'

'Seems to me everything around here clamours,' she replied

as the church bells began pealing their daily competition against the organ.

The afternoon passed in a flurry of activity, the tantalizing smell of lemon and mint mingling with the spicy gingerbread tempting her taste buds. Colenso sighed, eager for the time when she could learn the secrets of making the sweet confections. Whilst the livestock auction was taking place on the green, Jago went for a break, leaving her to refill the containers. Who would have believed they could get through so many, she thought, filling yet more cones with an array of assorted sweets. As she stepped outside the Panam to check everything looked enticing, a shot rang out making her jump. Heart beating wildly, she scurried back behind the stall.

''Tis only the rifle range over there, lover,' the man from the Hammer Bell Striker called, gesturing behind him. 'Got moved cos of all the noise,' he groaned, raising his bushy brows.

'Oh, er, thank you,' she murmured, glad for once his attraction was quiet with no menfolk queueing to test their strength. The ringing of the bell when it was hit set her teeth on edge, although luckily it didn't happen that often. The crack of rifles would be an entirely different matter though.

The excited hullabaloo of the crowd returning signalled that the auction had ended, and to her relief she saw Jago approaching.

'See it's our turn for the rifle range,' he sighed. 'Oh well, they'll be moving on soon.' As customers began clustering around the Panam, Colenso turned her attention back to helping the children make their important choices. As they often asked what the sweets tasted like, she decided to sample every single one of the confections to give them an informed opinion. The glistening candy coats made her mouth water and during a lull she popped one of the striped bullseyes in her mouth. She was just savouring the tangy, lemon flavour when Titan appeared.

'Not slacking again, Col? Have to dock those wages of yours,' Jago teased as she went to move from behind the stall.

'Blame me, Jago. I offered to show Col around before the rides start packing up,' Titan said, taking her basket from her.

As they wandered through the stalls, he swung it easily back and forth and Colenso couldn't help comparing it to the way her father had let her carry her laden basket to the works.

'I had no idea the fair was so big or so dangerous. I mean, how can she bear it?' Colenso shuddered, stopping by a stall where a tall woman dressed as a red Indian squaw stood without flinching as knives were thrown onto the board around her.

'Don't worry, Blade's being doing that for years,' Titan laughed. 'He's a true showman and makes it look more terrifying than it is. Besides, Lottie would have his scrotum for supper if he ever hit her.'

'Oh,' she murmured, moving quickly on to the next stall, only to wish she hadn't when she saw a lady with bright painted lips under which a mass of black facial hair hung. She was perched on a stall and smiling. The effect was decidedly weird.

'Only a penny to find out if the lady's beard is real,' a man sporting a topper and red-striped jacket grinned, showing a mouthful of yellow stained teeth. So that really was a female? Colenso couldn't resist taking another look. 'Go on, stroke it, find out what it'll feel like when you can grow one, boy,' he invited, holding out the long beard. 'Oh, hello Titan, didn't see you there,' he added his expression changing.

'No, I'm hard to spot,' Titan chuckled, taking hold of Colenso's elbow and moving her on. 'As you can see, some stalls are more tasteful than others. And more fragrant,' he added, wrinkling his nose at the smell of frying offal. 'You wouldn't believe what some people buy.' They walked on past the swing boats where Colenso had spent that awful time turning the handle for what seemed like hours, until finally Titan came to a halt.

'How about a ride on these splendid fellows?' he suggested, pointing to the dobbies. As memories of the previous year came flooding back, Colenso shook her head. 'Perhaps another day, then,' he said, mistaking her look. 'Don't worry, old nosey-nocks won't come calling again. His legs won't allow it,' he grinned. Then seeing her puzzled look, he shrugged. 'You learn a lot of useful moves in my job. Besides, Mara said she feels the presence has moved away. Come on, it's getting late and she'll be wondering where you've got to.'

While they'd been wandering round, the shadows had gathered over the fairground, and now light from the lamps cast pools of murky yellow over everything. Leaving the noise and hustle behind, they wandered back to the relative quiet of the site where the kumpania had lit their campfire. It had been quite an afternoon and Colenso was keen to be back in the security of Mara's cosy van.

'Want me to see you inside?' Titan asked. She shook her head.

'No, you get back to your family. Thank you for showing me around, Titan. It's been most enlightening,' she smiled.

'My pleasure,' he said, handing over her basket. 'The little 'uns would love a couple of cones sometime,' he grinned, then with a mock salute made his way past the kumpania to the other corner of the field where his van was.

*

It was the end of the week and, having packed up their things, they were on the road again. Although it was early, the air was already hot, the road dusty. Colenso sighed at the thought of the long trek ahead of them.

'Don't you ever get bored with all this walking?' she asked. Mara, who'd been murmuring encouragement to Ears, looked up and frowned.

'Bored? Whatever do you mean, child? How could you possibly get weary with all this to look at?' she said, gesturing to the countryside around them. 'Apart from anything else, you should be keeping your eyes peeled. It's a fine time of year for foraging nature's bounty. Ramsons, elderflowers, nettles, and if it rains we could even strike lucky for dryad's saddles – that's mushrooms to you.'

'Funny name.'

'Dryads are the wood nymphs who inhabit trees, and they say the mushrooms are the saddles they ride on. Don't look like that,' she said when Colenso rolled her eyes. 'They're found at the base of dead trees so it could be true, you know.'

'Maybe but I wish we were heading that way,' Colenso said, pointing to the sea to her left.

'Ah, a mermaid born and bred, eh?' Mara chuckled. 'The local lads will have to watch out.'

'Pardon?' she asked, wondering what tangent the woman was going off on now.

'Legend has it that a very beautiful lady periodically attended the church in Zennor. No one knew who she was or whence she came, but she had the sweetest of singing voices. A local man called Mathey Trewella, himself a fine singer, was beguiled by her beauty and followed her one day but never returned. 'Twas said she was a mermaid who'd enticed him to her abode deep below the sea.'

'Really,' Colenso burst out laughing. 'Apart from the fact my father said I'm built like a bal maiden, my singing would wake the dead not entice anyone.'

'True or not, the story put a smile on your face. Anyhow, just think, when we reach Bodmin you can transform back to a girl. Surely that's enough to spur you on.' Immediately, Colenso brightened. To be able to wear her thin skirt and blouse would be bliss after these coarse clothes especially as it seemed summer had arrived. She stared around at the primroses and dog violets in the hedgerows. Everything seemed to bloom later here in the north of the county compared with on The Lizard.

'Them mauve beauties be good for the treatment of piles,' Mara said, following her gaze. 'Still, those periwinkles winking over there might be more appropriate for you. 'Tis said if a woman and man eat the leaves together love will blossom between them.'

'Hmm,' Colenso murmured sceptically. 'But that reminds me, I'm going to send Kitto a card when we arrive,' she told Mara. 'What address will I give him?'

'The Kumpania of Cornwall,' the woman quipped. 'Seriously

181

though, you'd better give the address of the post office at Truro. We'll be there for the June fair. Make sure you seal the envelope though. Don't want it getting in the wrong hands.'

'I can't wait until we get to Bodmin,' she cried, eager to write and tell Kitto where she was. She'd ask him to tell her what he'd been up to in his reply.

'Well, you'll have to hold your fire for another three days, my girl, for that's how long it'll take us.'

'Oh,' Colenso murmured, her heart sinking like a stone.

Chapter 18

As the sun rose higher, Colenso felt herself flagging. The trail of wagons, their owners and children alongside, were leaving the moor behind and descending towards a valley where, to her relief, the lane was shaded by trees that were coming into leaf. It still amazed her that these people carried all their worldly goods and the wherewithal to make a living, along with them. True, they didn't have many but then, what worldly goods did she possess? It was a sobering thought to think she only had her clothes and the boy's cast-offs she was wearing to her name.

Suddenly through the bushes she saw an enormous round granite rock on the ground. It must be as high as their wagon, she thought, stepping closer and looking up at it.

'Whatever is that?' she asked.

'Legend has it that stone was used by the giants Trecrobben and Comoron to play Boule,' Mara replied delightedly.

'Not another one of your myths,' Colenso said, shaking her head.

'I prefer the word legend and there are hundreds of them around these parts. Of course, nobody really knows how that boulder got there, but it's fun to imagine a couple of big men playing with it,' Mara laughed.

'Well, I'm too hot and tired to even think of playing,' Colenso sighed.

'It's not far to the river where we'll be stopping to rest and have a cooling drink.'

Sure enough, minutes later they came to a mill and above the creaking of its wheel Colenso could hear the brook chuckling. Ears picked up his pace, coming to a halt on the bank where Mara released him from the shafts. While he drank thirstily, the children kicked off their boots and jumped laughing and shrieking into the water. Colenso was tempted to do the same, but Mara was holding out the kettle for her to fill.

'I'll rack up the stove and we'll have a nice brew afore we go foraging,' she told her. 'This is a good spot for chickweed and cuckoo flowers, then further on we might find some three-cornered leeks to go with them. Should have the makings of a good garlic soup and salad tonight,' she said, rubbing her hands together delightedly.

Later, refreshed from their rest, they went in search of the wild plants Mara had spoken about. The woman's knowledge and enthusiasm for them reminded Colenso of Mammwynn and she couldn't help feeling a pang for the grandmother she'd loved so much. And yet, almost without realizing it, she knew she was beginning to come to terms with her loss. The cycle of life, she thought, placing the fresh green ramson leaves carefully into Mara's basket.

With the basis for a good supper neatly stored in the tiny kitchen area, they rejoined the group and headed north where the country gave way to grime and dirt as they passed the iron foundry belching out plumes of black smoke. Trundling along the long straggling street, local people stopped to observe their progress. Some smiled but others glared.

'Why are they staring at us like that?' Colenso asked.

'Probably making sure we're not camping here. They don't trust the folk of the fairs. Regrettably there are some who steal, or worse, which gives us all a bad name,' Mara sighed.

Having left the buildings behind, Mara hopped up on the cart and gestured to Colenso to do the same.

'Nice and flat for quite a while now, so we can give our legs a break,' she said, wiping the perspiration from her brow. To Colenso's delight, they followed the line of the sand dunes for some miles and she revelled in the tang of the salty air and the cries of wheeling gulls. Then the vista changed as they reached the dirty, noisy towns of the tin- and copper-mining area.

The smelters and factories were blanketing the sky with smoke and soot, while the constant hiss and clunk from stream-driven pumps in the engine houses reminded Colenso of the noise at the serpentine works.

'Down we get again,' Mara sighed, as they reached the hilly main street and Ears began to labour. It was lined with grand granite houses, but as Colenso peered down the side streets she saw they were crammed with smaller run-down terraced cottages. Beyond them, ragged children played barefoot among the spoil and slag heaps.

'This is terrible,' she shuddered.

'I know, there's no vegetation at all so there'll be no foraging here,' Mara said sadly. 'Too much copper and arsenic in the ground.'

That wasn't what Colenso had meant, but they'd begun to

leave the oppressive area behind them and she let the subject drop. When they reached the open moorland again, she raised her face and breathed deeply of the fresh air.

'Bet you don't think the countryside's so bad now,' Mara said, giving her a wry look. They continued the journey on foot, over undulating hills, past farm fields bordered by hedges, until they reached Blackwater where they set up camp for the night. After the hullabaloo of the previous days, Colenso revelled in the gentle company of the kumpania as they sat around the fire.

'Looks like you enjoyed that,' Mara said, gesturing to her empty dish.

'It was delicious. I never knew you could make such wonderful meals with a few flowers and leaves.'

'We'll make a country girl of you yet,' Mara grinned.

*

The next day followed much the same pattern as they trekked on through the countryside, passing yet more farms bordered by high hedges. The sun beat down relentlessly, and by the time they'd climbed the steep hill out of the valley at Zelah, Colenso could feel the perspiration dripping down her back. How she wished she could throw off that wretched cap and jacket.

Finally, they reached their destination of Summercourt, a hamlet of terraced stone cottages built around a crossroads.

'We'll be coming back for the fair in October,' Mara said, as they turned into a field beyond the alehouse, but Colenso was so hot and dusty it was all she could do to murmur an answer.

She helped Mara unhitch Ears and set up the van for the night, then unable to bear the itching any longer, followed the tiny stream until she came to a pond in the woodland. Noticing how quiet it was, she tore off the scratchy clothes and band binding her chest then, heedless of the murky water, dived in. She hardly noticed the cold puckering her skin as she revelled in the relief of being free from restraint. Flipping over, she floated on her back, watching the sun-streaked sky turning from crimson to rose and apricot.

A splash in the water close by disturbed her reverie. There was a rustling in the grass and she saw two amber eyes and a lolloping tongue staring at her from the bank. Her eyes widened as another figure appeared. Crouching further down in the water, she covered her breasts with her hands, her heart pounding so loudly she was sure he would hear it.

'I say, boy, could you retrieve that stick?' the man called. 'Threw it a bit hard and old Bosun here won't go anywhere near water.' Colenso swallowed hard and looked over to where the twig was hovering just out of reach. How could she retrieve it without revealing herself? Careful to keep beneath the water, she inched her way towards it. Grabbing it with one hand whilst keeping herself covered with the other, she aimed it arrow-like at the man.

'I say, good shot,' he cried. 'Mighty obliged, boy. That water looks so inviting. Could be tempted to take a dip myself.' As he leaned over, his shadow edging towards her, Colenso's stomach sank. 'Still, got to think of the dog. Thanks again, boy,' he said and much to her relief, bent and retrieved the stick. He threw it in the opposite direction and then followed after the dog. She waited until he'd disappeared then let out the breath she'd been holding. Laughter bubbled up inside her. Boy indeed. If only he knew. Although the old clothes had served their purpose, she felt so invigorated there was no way she was putting the coarse garments back on again.

'I'd like to wear my own blouse and skirt now,' Colenso told Mara when, holding the jacket in front of her to protect her modesty, she entered the van.

'I told you, we need to check with Big Al that it's safe,' the woman frowned. She'd removed her scarf and was sitting on the cushion, combing out her curls. As the light caught the sheen of her long tresses, something snapped inside Colenso.

'You're meant to be the fortune teller so why don't you consult your crystal ball?' Mara dropped her comb in surprise. 'I want to be a woman again,' she added, her voice softer now.

'Very well,' Mara said, taking down the velvet bag. 'But I think you should put those clothes back on before we see what it has to tell us.' She covered the globe with her hands then removed them and peered closely into it. Her eyes widened but, instead of saying anything, she went pale.

'Well, what does it say about me?' Colenso asked impatiently as she sat down beside her.

'Me, me, me, that's all you think of,' Mara roared, jumping to her feet and running from the van. Colenso stared after her before turning back to the crystal. Although she gazed hard into its depths she could see nothing but swirling mist. A knock on the door brought her back to the present, and looking up she saw Jago staring worriedly at her.

'Everything all right in here?' he asked.

'I didn't know you were here,' she smiled, pleased to see him.

'Only arrived a few minutes ago. I heard shouting and then saw Mara stomping down to the stream.'

'I asked her to look in her crystal ball but she wouldn't tell me what she saw.'

'Oh,' he murmured. 'Well, whatever upset her, I'm sure she'll be back soon. In the meantime, are you joining us for supper?'

The others looked up curiously as they took their places beside the fire but nobody said anything. Colenso accepted her plate and ate her meal automatically, hardly tasting the herb-laden potage. She watched the flames becoming brighter as the shadows around them lengthened.

'Mara's not back,' Sarah said when they'd all finished eating. 'Shall I go and check she's all right?'

'Probably wants a bit of space. Not used to sharing her home, she isn't,' her husband replied. Colenso stared at them in dismay. She'd been so caught up in her own problems she hadn't given any thought to the generous lady who'd taken her in and cared for her these past few weeks.

'I'll go,' she said, jumping up and hurrying towards the water. She followed the path along the bank for a while until she spotted Mara sitting under a tree, her back leaning against its thick trunk.

'I'm really sorry, Mara,' she apologized.

'Don't be, it comes to us all,' the woman sighed, getting to her feet. 'Reckon you can wear your own clothes tomorrow,' she added. Colenso was so delighted that it was only later she remembered the woman's first remark. By then Mara was snoring gently and she resolved to ask her about it first thing in the morning.

The pleasure of pulling on her soft blouse over skin not constrained by the tight band made her shiver with happiness. She was just running her fingers through the tufts of hair, the delight of not having to wear the itchy cap again outweighing the loss of her long tresses, when Mara returned, Jago following behind.

'Well, look at you,' he said, his eyes widening in surprise. 'Scrubbed up well, eh Mara?'

'No more than I would have expected,' Mara smiled, her black mood of the previous day having disappeared.

'Should draw more punters in now,' Jago said, rubbing his hands together gleefully.

'Jago has to pick up supplies for the Panam so is leaving for Bodmin now. He wonders if you might like to accompany him?'

'Really?' she asked, hardly able to contain her excitement. 'But won't you need help packing up?' she asked.

'Managed perfectly well afore you arrived so I'm sure I'll cope,' Mara replied. 'Besides, it'll be nice to enjoy the peace of the countryside without you asking stupid questions every few minutes.' Although her voice was brusque, Colenso saw her lips twitching and knew she was teasing. Impulsively, she kissed the woman's cheek, surprised at how papery it felt, but she had little time to dwell on the matter, for Jago was already heading out of the door.

His van was larger than Mara's but the woodwork was plain and looked dull compared with the brightly painted flowers that adorned hers. However, his horse was also larger and capable of pulling the wagon uphill with them in it as well. Seated beside Jago, she watched as they passed moorland covered with bracken, golden gorse and yet more low, scrubby trees.

'Mara seems like her old self again this morning,' Jago commented. 'But it will probably do her good to have some time to herself.'

'You mean you engineered this trip?' Colenso asked, turning to him in surprise.

'I need to collect more confections, for that is my job of a journeyman after all.' Well that told her, she thought. Then he turned towards her and smiled. 'Thought you'd like to meet some of the people who make them.' They travelled on in silence and Colenso couldn't help thinking how much nicer it was to be riding rather than walking along the dusty roads, especially as she was wearing her skirt again.

'They're the china-clay workings over there.' She wrinkled her nose at the large mountains of dirty white spoil beyond the boggy moorland.

'Going to be another hot day by the look of it,' Jago sighed, gesturing to the sun rising like a great yellow ball in front of them. 'I'll have to make sure the sweets don't melt.'

'Do you want me to check them for you?' she asked.

'Later perhaps. Let's use the time to get to know each other better. You know I hail from Truro, but where are you from?' Not wishing to divulge any personal information, Colenso gestured to the tin mines they were passing.

'I didn't realize there were so many around here,' she commented. Giving her a knowing look, he nodded and lapsed into silence again. After a while, the landscape became less rugged, with more fields farmed. Jago tugged on the reins and the horse obediently turned down onto a track.

'Mrs Manning has the farm here. She ran it with her husband until he got caught under the wheels of his cart. Nasty business. Caitlin's carried it on since his death, yet still manages to concoct her speciality for the Panam in her spare time. She's from Scotland and makes their native tablet. I've told her I'll understand if it gets too much, but she insists she finds the process therapeutic,' he said. He gave another tug on the reins and the horse trotted round to the yard. The moment they pulled up outside a grey, formidable-looking farmhouse, the door opened. A pretty woman in her late twenties with auburn hair coiled around her head smiled and waved, but as soon as she saw Colenso her expression changed.

'Caitlin, how are you?' Jago asked, oblivious. 'I've brought Colenso with me. She's been helping me on the Panam.'

'Och, how kind,' she replied in such a patronizing voice Colenso wanted to pull tongues at her. However, she refrained and smiled back politely. 'Forgive me, Jago dear, but I'm all behind today. It's hard managing by myself, though as you know, I do my best,' she simpered.

'And very well you do too,' Jago replied gallantly. 'Do you need a hand packing up the tablet?'

'I need help making it,' Caitlin giggled, batting her eye-lashes at him. So that was the way of things, Colenso thought.

'Now don't you worry, Colenso here wants to learn how to make our sweet confections so she can stay and help you.'

'But I thought you could,' Caitlin pouted, laying a hand on his arm.

'I'm afraid I've other collections to make before the fair opens tomorrow. Look, I'll call back early this afternoon, that should give you enough time. You'll give Caitlin a hand, won't you?' he asked, turning to Colenso.

'Delighted to,' she smiled, trying not to laugh out loud as the woman's lips tightened into a line.

'Surely you'll stay for a drink like usual?' she asked, her Scottish lilt becoming more pronounced.

'That's kind of you, Caitlin, but I'd hate to delay you.' With a quick nod, he turned and walked back to his wagon. There was a strained silence as they both stood there staring after him.

Chapter 19

The wagon disappeared in a cloud of dust and Caitlin turned to Colenso, eyeing her critically. Thank heavens she was wearing her own clothes, she thought, for clearly the woman had dressed up for Jago's visit.

'Well, come on then,' Caitlin snapped, leading the way into an outhouse.

'I thought we'd be making it in the kitchen,' Colenso murmured as they entered the cool interior of the dairy.

'I will be,' she said, emphasising the word 'I'. 'You can start by greasing these.' She pointed to rows of shallow tins set out on the cool surfaces, then to a dish of golden butter. With a baleful glare, she stomped back outside. It didn't take Colenso long to finish the simple task, and while she waited for Caitlin to return, she took a look around. Everything was spotless, with jugs and pans lined along a shelf, and dishes, moulds and cutters on another, while in the corner stood a cheese mill. It was easy to see what the milk was used for, she thought, gazing through the window where reddish brown cows contentedly munched the grass. Lucky you, having your meals provided, she thought as her stomach growled, reminding her she hadn't eaten since the previous day. Fed up with waiting for Caitlin to reappear, she made her way outside and following the sounds of pots being banged found her way to the kitchen.

'All done,' she said brightly. 'What would you like me to do now?' To her surprise, instead of snapping at her, the woman's lips widened into a grin.

'If you really want to help, you can scrape down the insides,' she said, indicating the huge pan she was stirring. Colenso's eyes widened as she saw the mixture bubbling and frothing up the sides. 'Well, jump to it, else crystals will start forming,' she added brusquely, inclining her head towards the pastry brush. As the woman stared challengingly at her, Colenso snatched it up and did as she'd been asked.

The heat rising from the mix was unbearable, burning her skin and making her eyes water, but she continued wiping the mixture back down until the woman grudgingly told her to stop. 'Test time now. You putting your finger in or am I?' Colenso stared at the seething inferno and thought she was joking until she remembered Jago telling her about his sister. 'Och really,' the woman tutted, sticking her finger into the pan then quickly removing it and licking off the liquid. 'It can come off the heat now,' she nodded, lifting the pan onto a big trivet on the kitchen table. Then taking up a big wooden spoon, she began beating it hard.

'What are you doing?' Colenso couldn't resist asking.

'Beating it until the mixture begins to form crystals.'

'So now you want crystals?' Colenso asked, staring at her in surprise.

'Och aye, of course. 'Tis called graining.' Colenso watched fascinated as the woman thumped the mixture with all her might before slowing to a stir. 'You and Jago sweethearts?' Caitlin asked without stopping what she was doing.

'Good heavens, no. I'm betrothed to a man from Cadgwith,' Colenso replied, her heart flipping at the thought of Kitto. Immediately, the woman's manner changed.

'Is that so?' she grinned before resuming her stirring. 'Right, that's it, we're away to the dairy now,' she said, picking up the heavy pan and carrying it outside.

Back in the dairy, the woman tilted the pan and poured the mixture quickly into the prepared tins. Taking up a knife, she spread it evenly then tapped each one on the surface.

'This releases any bubbles,' she explained, seeing Colenso's puzzled look. 'Right, all done. Just got time for a wee cup before we need to score the surface.'

Once she knew Colenso wasn't a threat, Caitlin proved to be entertaining company, and by the time Jago returned, the tablet was set, cut into pieces and wrapped in muslin.

'So how did you find the redoubtable Mrs Manning?' Jago asked as they rejoined the road to Bodmin.

'She was fine once she knew I didn't have any desires on your affections,' Colenso replied truthfully.

'You don't?' he asked, raising his brows enquiringly.

'Of course not. You're much too old,' she grinned.

'Oh, how you wound a man,' he cried, theatrically slapping his hand to his chest.

'Mrs Manning certainly desires you, though.' When he didn't answer, she changed the subject. 'At least I got my first lesson in sweet-making.'

'Ah, now you're talking my language, woman,' he quipped. 'So what's her secret receipt?' he asked, looking serious.

'Receipt?' she frowned. 'I don't know, Caitlin had already mixed everything by the time I'd got back from greasing the pans.'

'The first rule of sweet-making is to gather as many receipts as possible. That's how my grandmother started,' Jago told her, trying to keep his voice calm. 'Can you remember what ingredients she used?'

'There was milk and cream in the kitchen, oh and a big cone of sugar,' she said excitedly.

'All confections contain sugar,' Jago groaned. 'Oh well, it's my fault for not having mentioned it earlier. In future, remember the golden rule.'

'Yes, Jago,' she replied.

'We'll soon be in Bodmin so you might as well sit back and enjoy the rest of the ride.'

They had left the moorland behind, and Colenso stared in fascination at the fields that were rectilinearly partitioned and looked like a gigantic patchwork quilt.

'I need to stop in the town and buy a card,' Colenso said as they approached the outskirts and the horse laboured up the long slope.

'The fair is on the west side before we enter the town itself and I daren't make a detour in this heat or my stocks will melt.'

'But I need to send one,' she told him, frowning as they veered off the road and bumped their way down a track towards the field.

'Don't worry, we'll be here for quite a few days so you'll have plenty of opportunity. My, it's busy already,' he said, nodding to where stalls had already been erected. 'And look, there's Mara's little tent over by the graveyard. Don't know how she manages to find one, but she always does. No, not yet,' he said, putting out his hand as Colenso made to climb down. 'We'll find out where your kumpania are camped and I'll deliver you to Mara's door.' She was about to protest, but when she saw the crowds of people, vans and wagons converging onto the field, changed her mind.

'Wondered where you'd got to,' Mara grunted as they drew up beside her van. She was sitting on the step and Colenso just knew she'd been waiting for them to arrive.

'I'm going to check my stocks and set up the Panam, so I'll see you later,' Jago said as Colenso climbed down.

'Do you need any help?' she offered.

'No ta,' he replied. 'All right, Mara?' She nodded and went inside, leaving Colenso to follow.

'Been having a tidy-up,' the woman said, pointing to the hidey-hole Colenso had been sleeping in. It was now topped by a brightly coloured crocheted blanket and matching cushion.

'Oh yes, so I see,' Colenso frowned. Obviously, the others had been right and Mara wanted her own space back.

'Don't look like that,' Mara said. 'Stands to reason that now you're wearing your own clothes, you won't need to stay in there anymore.'

'No, of course. I'll go right away. Before I do though, I'd like to thank you for looking after me.'

'Go? Where are you going?' Mara cried, looking alarmed.

'Well, obviously you want your van to yourself and ...'

'Fiddle. I might like my own company but you've still so much to learn about the countryside. Whilst I appreciate your love of the sea, it's my duty to teach you about Mother Nature's bounty, so you'll make a good wife to that Kitto of yours. Now, kettle's boiling, so stop talking rot and make us some tea.' Relief rushing through her, Colenso nodded and hurried over to the stove.

'I want to send Kitto a card as soon as I can,' Colenso told her as she poured water over the leaves.

'Good idea,' Mara nodded.

'I was wondering if I should send Mamm one too,' she frowned.

'Not a good idea,' Mara said emphatically. 'Could get into the wrong hands. I'm sure Kitto will let your mamm know you're safe.'

'Yes, of course,' she replied, knowing what the woman said made sense.

'I've finished setting up my tent, so we can walk into the town first thing tomorrow. The show here is a big one and when it gets going things become hectic.' Once she'd poured the tea and settled on the bright cushion opposite Mara, Colenso asked the question that had been niggling her since the previous day.

'Why are you looking after me like this?'

'I took on the responsibility for you, and I've never been one to shirk my duties,' Mara replied, sipping her drink. Not sure she liked being thought of as a duty, but knowing she had much to thank the woman for, Colenso held her tongue.

*

Although they were up before dawn, the fair people were already getting things ready for the opening.

'Morning, ladies,' Titan called, appearing as if by magic as they stepped out of the van. 'I hear we're shopping this morning.'

'Are you coming with us, then?' Colenso asked, her eyes widening as he took the basket from her.

'I am,' he nodded. 'And, if you don't mind me saying, you look far better dressed as a woman.'

'That's because she is one,' Mara snorted, making them smile. 'Now, you can make yourself useful and tell Colenso something about this place. I'm trying to educate her, see.'

'Right. Well, Bodmin boasts the county asylum, institutions, the gaol, the barracks ...'

'For goodness sake. Can't you do better than that on this fine morning?' Mara cried. But Colenso hardly heard her for her attention had been caught by the display in the shoemaker's window. Right in the centre was a pair of red shoes adorned with silver buckles.

'Bodmin is renowned for its shoe-making,' Mara said, noticing her interest. 'However, some are more practical than others.'

'But they're beautiful,' Colenso cried.

'And utterly frivolous. Now, I thought it was a card you wished to buy.'

'Yes, of course,' she replied as Titan darted her a sympathetic look. They walked past the shambles with all its butcher's shops, and the fish market bustling with customers, turned down another street with its gas street lights, clock tower and three-storey bank, before coming to a halt outside the post office.

'You can buy your card and send it from there,' Mara said, holding out some coins. 'And don't look like that, it's what you've earned at the Panam,' she added as Colenso opened her mouth to protest. 'Now, I've business to attend to so I'll see you back at the van. And make sure you don't take all day.' Before Colenso could answer, she strode back down the street, the way they'd come.

*

'Took your time, didn't you?' Mara asked, looking up from a document she was studying. 'Get that card sent, then?'

'Yes, I did, thank you. And I put the return address as Truro post office, like you said,' she told the woman.

'Well, it'll be another ten days or so before we arrive there so he'll have plenty of time to reply. Which is more than you've got. Jago dropped by with paper for you to make up more cones,' she said waving her hand at the pile on Colenso's seat-cum-bed. 'Said you'd need to make a goodly supply as there are a lot of other sweet stalls and carts, so competition will be fierce. In a right mood, he was, on account of him arriving late yesterday and not getting his usual spot. Said you'll find him on the north side at the back.'

'Oh,' Colenso said, staring in dismay. 'I'll never be able get all those done in time.'

'That's what I said. He seemed quite put out you weren't here. Anyhow, he said you'd best roll and twist the paper instead of pasting. Right, I'm off to wander the crowds,' she said, bangles jangling as she folded her paper and popped it into her pocket. 'It's good to let people see there's a dukkerer in their midst. No use sitting in me tent if no one knows I'm there,' she winked, taking herself outside.

Colenso smiled. What a mixture the woman was. On the one hand she communed with nature, whilst on the other she possessed the acumen any businessman would envy. As Colenso began rolling and twisting the paper, her thoughts returned to the card she'd posted to Kitto. How surprised he'd be to receive it. She knew he'd be relieved to know she was safe, and could hardly wait until they reached Truro to hear from him.

Heart singing, she quickly worked her way through the pile of paper, and by the time the organ started up, her basket was filled with cones.

Outside the sun was beating down as crowds of laughing people jostled their way around the stalls, seeking out the best attractions. The air was filled with the smell of onions and cooking meat, then she heard the ring of the bell as someone proved their prowess with the hammer bell striker. It took her a few minutes to find the Panam and, when she did, she was greeted by a scowling Jago.

'I've made all these,' she said brightly. 'Shall I start filling some?'

'Probably won't need them stuck right out here,' he muttered, staring gloomily across the ground to a cart surrounded by clamouring people. 'Taylor's pinched my pitch.' Leaving him to his mood, she began packing an assortment of the coloured sweets into cones. But by the time she'd finished, they still hadn't had one single customer.

'What does he sell that you don't?' Colenso asked.

'Don't know,' he growled, determined to stay in his dark mood.

'Well, I'll go and have a look, shall I?' she asked, desperate to do something.

She made her way back through the crowds until she reached the cart. To her surprise, the sweets were similar but not nearly as varied as the ones on the Panam and she could see no evidence of any tablet or rock canes. She watched as the man served a small boy, handing over his purchase in a nondescript twist of paper. Remembering what Mara had said about there being lots of other sweet vendors, she made her way around the various stalls, trying to get an idea of what they were selling.

'Well, hello,' a man with a shiny black moustache said from the doorway of his tent. 'This could just be your lucky day.' She smiled politely but, when she went to pass, he stepped forward to block her way. 'Not so fast, darling,' he drawled, glassy blue eyes eyeing her up and down from under his tall hat.

'Sorry, I'm in a hurry,' she murmured.

'Don't you know who I am?' he asked, raising his dark brows when she shook her head. 'I am Marvellous Marco, Illusionaire Extraordinaire. And who, pray tell, are you?'

'Colenso,' she replied, immediately wishing she hadn't.

'An exotic name for an exotic beauty.'

'Sorry, I must go,' she said shaking her head and hurrying away. Exotic beauty, she thought, running her hand through her shorn locks. Except, instead of wiry tufts, she could feel short but silky hair. Mara had been right. By the time she saw Kitto it would have grown somewhere near back to its normal length. She wondered how he'd got on in London and what he'd been doing since his return. How long it seemed since they'd last been together.

'Where did you get to?' Jago muttered, still looking dismal. 'As you can see I've been rushed off my feet in your absence.'

'Sorry, Jago,' she replied, ignoring his sarcasm. 'I had a brilliant idea but then I got stopped by this funny man, Marvellous Marco or something.'

'You want to stay away from him,' he said, giving her a sharp look. 'That man's bad news. His assistant went missing after the last show and she's never been heard of since.'

Chapter 20

'Anyhow what was this great idea of yours?' Jago asked.

'I thought, if the customers won't come to us, we'd go to the customers, or rather take the confections to them,' she told him excitedly.

'What do you mean?'

'I could pack the filled cones into my basket and walk around the fair selling them. These are so colourful,' she said, gesturing to the glistening sweets. 'But it's no use having them if no one knows they're here,' she added, thinking of Mara's earlier words. He stood mulling things over then, after another glance at the crowds thronging around his rival, nodded.

'Certainly worth a try. I'd do it myself but a pretty girl like you will be more of a draw. Promise me you'll stay away from Marco, though. Mara would have my guts if she thought I'd allowed you to go anywhere near him,' he added, helping her pack the basket with colourful cones. Then he delved into his money pouch and handed her some coins.

'In case you need change,' he said when she looked askance.

'Of course. And thank you for the wage. I was able to buy my card.' This time it was his turn to look puzzled. 'You didn't give Mara any money, did you?' she asked. He shook his head.

'I know I owe you but, truth to tell, after paying Caitlin for the tablet and settling my dues with Big Al, it's left me a bit short.'

'You have to pay Big Al?' she frowned.

'We all have to. He arranges all this,' he said, waving his hand around the fair. 'Then there's his cut of our takings, protection money …' He trailed to a halt as if he'd said too much. 'Don't worry, I'll see you get paid for all your hard work … as long as we sell all those.' He tapped her basket.

'Well, I'd better get started then.' She gave him a bright smile and set off, her thoughts in overdrive.

So Big Al wasn't the kind-hearted man he purported to be. And Titan had been paid to look out for her. How naive she'd been and what a lot she had to learn. Well, Colenso Carne was capable of looking after herself and, what's more, she'd show them all exactly what she could do. Purposefully, she made her way to the centre of the fair where it was busier.

Although people eyed her basket curiously, they didn't stop. Spotting a group of children waiting for their turn on the dobbies, she strode over and held her basket invitingly.

'Freshly made confections, bullseyes, barley twists, tablet, rock canes,' she called. Their heads turned, eyes widening as they took in the bright cones filled with glistening sweets. Squeals of delight were followed by clamours to parents, and moments later her basket began to empty.

Flushed with success, she made her way to the next attraction, where the same thing happened. Before long she'd sold everything and, coins jangling, she made her way back to the Panam to replenish her stocks.

'Well, I'll be,' Jago exclaimed, eyes widening when he saw her empty basket. She handed over the money she'd taken, and this time he whistled happily as he helped her restock.

By the end of the afternoon, Colenso was feeling tired but exhilarated. She must have returned to the Panam at least a half a dozen times more, and each time Jago's smile had become brighter.

Now though, the crowds were thinning, but instead of returning directly to the Panam she decided to have a look around. Some of the stallholders called out in greeting, but there were many new attractions and people she didn't know. Showmen were trying to drum up custom for their evening performances and she shuddered as she caught a glimpse of a woman holding a snake in her arms, its head poised by her open mouth.

'Only a tanner to see Soukie swallow the serpent,' the man called, flicking down the flap of the tent and hiding the act. 'Watch as it wriggles and writhes its way to her stomach.'

'Want a ticket, darlin'?' the woman cackled when she spotted Colenso watching through the gap. Horrified, she shook her head, yet a weird fascination compelled her on to the next tent, where a very tall man was extolling the virtues of his unusual phenomenon.

'Roll up, roll up. The show starts in five minutes. Only a few seats left, ladies and gents. Don't miss this rare opportunity to see Lisa and Lana, twins extraordinaire. Joined at the hip, separate in thought and deed. You won't believe the antics they get up to.'

A beautiful girl, golden braid cascading over one shoulder, winked at her. She was about to smile back when the girl shuffled round and another almost identical face, plait over the other shoulder, winked. Then they turned again and she saw them, side by side, their scanty outfits revealing that they were indeed joined at their side. Seeing her incredulous look, they giggled.

'Right, girls, that's enough. Back inside and prepare to do your dastardly,' he grinned, rubbing his hands together. With a joint tinkling laugh, they turned and Colenso just had time to see that they both had two arms and legs before they disappeared through the flap of the tent. The man held out his hand. 'Cost yer to see more, darlin'.'

'Oh, er, sorry, I'm working,' Colenso muttered and scurried off as the man scowled. Heavens, you never knew what you were going to see next, she thought, wiping beads of perspiration from her brow.

'Here, have a drink, love.' She looked up to see Sarah from the kumpania holding out a cup.

'Thank you,' she murmured, taking it and sipping gratefully. 'Why, that's the loveliest lemon drink I've ever tasted.' The woman beamed, showing pink gums.

'Looked like you needed it. I know it's only nearly the end of May but I've never known it as hot as this in all my naturals. Still, it makes the punters thirsty. How's Mara?' she asked, her clear eyes giving Colenso a penetrating stare.

'She's fine,' Colenso replied. 'When I last saw her, she was off to drum up some business.'

'Like she needs to do that,' Sarah laughed. 'Biggest draw here, she is. People come for miles to have one of her readings. Never got anything wrong yet, so they say. Make sure she doesn't overdo it, won't you?' Before Colenso could ask what she meant, the woman had turned to serve a customer.

Refreshed from the drink, and all thought of the strange sights she'd seen forgotten, she began making her way back to the Panam.

'So, we meet again, my exotic beauty.' As the dark-haired man stepped out in front of her, Colenso stared at him in dismay. Mindful of Jago's warning, she'd kept to the other side of the fair, away from Marco's tent. 'I've been watching you going around selling sweets from your basket. Such a waste,' he tutted, shaking his head.

'I've enjoyed it actually,' she replied, determined not to be intimidated by his glassy-eyed stare.

'As I said, such a waste.' He let out a theatrical sigh. 'You have the grace of a swan yet the charm of a cygnet and would draw the crowds.' As Colenso tried not to laugh, he leaned closer and she caught a waft of the pomade he used to curl his moustache in that upwards, outwards, ridiculous way. 'How would you like to be part of my act, hmm?' Recalling what Jago had said about his previous assistant, she suppressed a shudder and shook her head.

'Must go,' she said.

'I could make you famous,' he called after her.

'You keep away from her or you'll be off this fair before you know what's hit you,' a voice of authority snapped. As he fell into step beside her, Colenso saw it was the swarthy man with greying hair. 'He's right in some ways, mind. The ragged urchin has turned out to be a stunning swan.'

'Fiddle,' she said, subconsciously emulating Mara. Big Al gave her an uncharacteristic grin.

'So, how's you doin'?'

'I'm fine. In fact, I'm more than fine.' Determined to show him she was, she held up her empty basket. 'I've managed to sell lots of Jago's confections,' she told him.

'Have you now?' he asked. Although he spoke casually, she could tell he'd taken note and wished she'd kept her mouth shut. Would Jago have to pay him more now?

'Well, here we are,' he said, moments later as they reached the Panam. 'It's getting late. Do you want me to send Titan over to escort you back to the van?'

'No thank you,' she said quickly, in case he charged for that as well. He gave her a considering look then shrugged. 'Well, Mara knows where to find me should you need any help.' With a smile he turned to Jago. 'I hear your bonbon girl is doing you proud,' he called.

'Oh hi, Big Al,' he said, sliding his leather money pouch quickly into his pocket. 'It's only thanks to Colenso that I've sold any sweets at all, stuck out on this godforsaken pitch. Probably won't take half as much as I usually do, though.'

'Is that so?' Big Al replied, quirking his brow. 'Well, we'll have to see, won't we?' With a curt nod he strode away and Jago turned to Colenso.

'Whatever were you doing with Big Al?'

'That Marco man waylaid me and he told him to leave me alone or he'd be thrown off the site.'

'But I warned you to stay away from Marco,' Jago frowned.

'I did, but like I said, he intercepted me on my way back

here,' she shrugged. 'Anyhow, here's the rest of your money,' she added, emptying out the coins from her pocket.

'Well done, girl,' he said, his eyes lighting up. 'You didn't tell Big Al how much you made, did you?'

She shook her head. 'Don't know exactly how much I took,' she said truthfully.

'Well, you've sold twenty times more than I have. Do the same tomorrow and I'll pay you double, my little bonbon girl,' he said, grinning as he filled her basket with paper to make yet more cones.

'Twice of nothing is still nothing,' she quipped, grateful the subject had been diverted away from Big Al and Marco.

That night over a simple supper of the cold meats and onions Mara had brought back to the van, Colenso told her about Jago not getting any customers and how she'd taken her sweets around the fair.

'Well done, dearie. Good to see a bit of initiative. Hope everyone was nice to you.'

'Mostly, apart from that Marco man.'

'Marco?' Mara frowned, setting down her dish with a clatter.

'Don't worry, Big Al came along and told him to leave me alone or he'd be off the fairground. Jago said his last assistant just disappeared.'

'Hmm. She did. Not sure whether she scarpered or … Anyhow, you'd do well to steer clear of him if you can.'

'I didn't realize Big Al charged protection money,' Colenso said, collecting up their empty dishes. Mara reached out and placed a hand on her arm.

'Got to make a living, has Al,' she said, eyeing Colenso

intently. 'Ours is a funny old world, dearie. Most people are honest and easy to get on with, but others …' she shrugged. 'That's when it's useful to have Big Al and Titan looking out for us.'

'But to charge …'

'Look,' Mara interrupted. 'Things aren't always as they appear, so don't go judging people by what you assume. Like I said, there are some funny people around.'

'I know,' she shuddered recalling some of the sights she'd seen earlier. 'There were these two girls joined together here,' she said, her hand going to her side. 'And this horrid, tall man was making a show of them.'

'That horrid man, as you call him, is Tiny Tim. He and his wife bought the twins when their mother was going to abandon them after they were born.'

'You mean she took money for them?' Colenso gasped.

'Only too happy to be rid of them, apparently. Anyway, Mr and Mrs Tiny nurtured the girls and gave them a happy childhood when they would otherwise have been destined for the poorhouse, or worse. They share a blood and nervous system, so who knows what might have happened to them,' she sighed. 'In return, Lisa and Lana are happy to put on a show – freak shows, they're called – for the benefit of the public. They use their, er, unique condition to satisfy people's curiosity, which pays for their keep. Can't argue with that, can you?'

'No, I suppose not,' Colenso muttered, swallowing hard. 'But it doesn't seem right somehow.'

'Who's to say what's right? Look, dearie, when you've lived life as long as I have, you learn not to judge.'

'Gracious, you make it sound as though you're old,' Colenso laughed, embarrassed by her assumptions.

'Well, I've seen more than a few seasons and many a moon, my girl,' she said, yawning loudly. 'And sometimes I feel every one of them.' Remembering Sarah's words, Colenso stared hard at Mara. Despite the relentless sun of the past few days, there was a pallor to her skin and dark smudges under her eyes.

'Are you feeling all right, Mara?' she asked. 'Only you look a bit pale.'

'Well, I've been stuck in my tent all day, not gallivanting in the sunshine like some. It can be tiring telling plain, pudgy ladies that their prince will soon arrive to sweep them off their feet.'

'You never do!' Colenso giggled.

'Afraid so. That's all many of these country spinsters live for. It doesn't do any harm for them to have something to dream about while they're churning butter and milking cows.'

'But I thought you said the crystal ball never lies?' she asked.

'It doesn't,' Mara said, looking serious. Then she shook her head as if clearing it. 'Sometimes I just embellish a little. Now, what say we have an early night?'

Her mind still buzzing from the events of the day and the weird sights she'd witnessed, Colenso lay back on her cushion and stared out of the window. The inky sky was studded with sparkling stars. As she watched them winking and twinkling like tiny lanterns, she wondered if Kitto was looking up at them too. Only a few days more and she might hear from him. She imagined him reading her card then sitting down at his battered old table to pen a reply. Except …

'Oh no,' she exclaimed, sitting bolt upright on the little bed that served as a table during the day.

'Whatzat, what's the matter?' Mara mumbled.

'I've just remembered something.'

'Can't it keep it till morning?'

'No, it's too important and I can't believe I didn't think of it before.'

'What is this mighty revelation that won't wait?' Mara sighed, propping herself up on her own cushion.

'Kitto won't be able to reply to my card. He can't read or write,' she wailed. Mara stared at her in the gathering gloom and let out a long sigh.

'Blimey, is that all? I thought you'd forgotten to feed old Ears, the fuss you were making.' Mara huffed. 'Look, if Kitto's the resourceful lad you say he is, he'll find a way. Might even turn up at Truro. I mean it is the Cornwall Show, after all. Now for heaven's sake, let me get some sleep,' she muttered, pulling her blanket over her head.

Colenso stared at Mara, desperate to ask if she'd look into her crystal ball but, remembering the last time, didn't have the courage. Besides, the woman was snoring now. Colenso laid back on her little bed and stared back out at the stars, except they were fast disappearing behind a carpet of cloud. It was a bad omen, she could feel it in her heart.

Chapter 21

Reassured by Mara telling her that Kitto was resourceful and would think of a way to contact her, Colenso threw herself into her new job. With the Panam's pitch on the edge of the fair still failing to draw many customers, she continued taking her basket around the attractions, selling the cones filled with brightly coloured sweets. By the end of the week, she had become known to the children as 'the bonbon girl' and they were eagerly looking out for her. To Jago's delight, his stocks were almost depleted.

'Hope Karla's been making lots of confections while I've been gone,' he said as they began packing up the stall in readiness for the journey to Truro. 'This fair has turned out to be surprisingly lucrative,' he grinned, patting his bulging money pouch.

'Good to hear it,' Big Al said, appearing behind them.

'No thanks to this godforsaken pitch,' Jago said, quickly covering his bag.

'Then you've got Bonbon here to thank,' the swarthy man continued, winking at Colenso. 'Make sure you play fair, Jago, know what I mean?'

'Course, I will. You know me,' he replied airily.

'I do,' Big Al replied, shooting him a level look. 'Right, Bonbon, I take it you've had no trouble from Marco.' It was more statement than question and Colenso guessed he must have had a word with the Illusionaire.

'No, I haven't, although I've given his tent a wide berth.'

'Very sensible,' Big Al nodded. 'Got to help yourself. You'd do well to learn from your assistant here,' he added, turning back to face Jago. 'Remember what I said.' With a curt nod, he swaggered over to where swing boats were now being dismantled. Colenso grinned wryly, remembering the first time she'd met him. How different everything seemed now. Dressed as a girl again, she'd been accepted by the travelling people and was beginning to enjoy her new roving life.

'Ruddy Mr Know-All,' Jago growled after him. 'Lives off the back of us, he does.'

'Mara says he works hard,' Colenso replied. 'As have I,' she added, looking at him expectantly.

'Yes, well when we get to Truro I'll work out how much I owe you,' he muttered, turning back to his packing-up.

'But …' Colenso began, not sure how to pursue the matter. 'Look, Jago, it's only right you should pay me something now. I can't continue living off Mara's generosity.'

'When did a few wild leaves cost anything?' His voice was muffled as he'd started taking down the Panam and was hidden under folds of striped canvas. Colenso shook her head. Although Jago was happy when money was coming in, it was becoming increasingly obvious he didn't like paying any out.

'I'm looking forward to meeting your sister,' she said. 'And learning how to make sweets.'

'Good,' he mumbled. 'See you in Truro,' he added, bending down to roll up the Panam. Knowing the fair people came together then went their separate ways before meeting up again, Colenso nodded. Her money could wait another day or so.

*

As the sky lightened to a pearlescent pink, the kumpania began making its way south towards Truro. Colenso walked alongside Mara, happy to see the woman had regained some of her colour. They watched as mewling buzzards circled the gentle hills, inhaled the perfume of the rich pink whistling jack and blue columbines, picked comfrey and the hedge woundwort whose leaves contained antiseptic properties for treating wounds.

'And these make a good mattress-filler,' Mara told her, pointing to the hedges festooned with creamy white plumes of bedstraw. 'Sleep on those with your lover and your union will be blessed, as well as having a comfortable romp, of course.'

'Mara,' she gasped, feeling the heat stealing across her cheeks.

'Sorry,' the woman replied, sounding anything but. 'But if you make the most of nature's summer bounty, you'll be set up for the winter. I can't believe it's the first week of June. The summer solstice will be here before we know it.'

'Mammwynn celebrated Litha by rising before dawn to greet the sun on its day of greatest power.' Her smile was tinged with sadness as she remembered the excitement of sitting on Mammwynn's little seat and waiting for the first ray of light to appear. The air was always filled with a sense of expectation, which turned to wonderment as the grey sky turned to blush pink then rosy red.

'The day the reigns of the Oak and Holly Kings are reversed and old Lord Holly comes into his own once more,' Mara nodded, breaking into her thoughts.

'You understand,' Colenso cried excitedly, for there were many – her father included – who scorned such beliefs.

'Of course I do.' There was a moment's pause. 'I would have liked your grandmother,' Mara murmured. She said it in her usual straightforward way and Colenso knew the two women would have got on well.

'I shall miss celebrating with her this year,' she sighed.

'Well, we're going to Marazion after we've done Truro, so we can rejoice together on the beautiful Mount of St Michael. You couldn't wish for a more serene place to mark the solstice,' Mara said, reaching out and patting her arm. 'As long as your Kitto hasn't whisked you away on his white charger by then,' she chuckled.

Colenso fell silent as thoughts of Kitto began spinning around in her head once more. How was he and what was he doing? Would she hear from him? Although Mara seemed positive he would contact her somehow, so much had happened that she felt her confidence wavering at times.

'Look, you can see the china-clay workings over there, which means we're edging towards Bugle,' Mara said breaking into her thoughts.

'Jago pointed out the spoil heaps when we were on our way to Bodmin.'

'Well, you're about to see them close up, my girl. I know it brings vital work but those poor people who live here … well, look,' she sighed, gesturing ahead to little terraces of run-down granite cottages covered in white dust from the mining.

'Heavens,' Colenso exclaimed, grimacing at the spoil heaps that towered menacingly over the town.

'Something to be said for the open road with its fresh, green countryside, eh, my girl?' Mara said with a sideways glance.

'And definitely the roar and crash of the waves on the beach, the tang of salt in the air,' Colenso smiled.

They laboured up the hill then down the other side with overgrown white mountains of old clay waste on both sides of them. The sun beat down relentlessly from a cloudless sky and, as they trudged on, Colenso couldn't believe how far these people travelled between each fair. Finally, tired and thirsty, they came to a stream where they stopped to water the ponies and have a rest. It was then Colenso noticed Mara wasn't eating much. The pallor had returned to her skin along with the dark smudges under her eyes.

'Why don't you have a sleep in the van?' she asked as the kumpania made ready to leave.

'But I won't have to walk, the road is flat enough for us to ride from here to Grampound where we'll spend the night. Besides, who would steer old Ears?'

'Me, of course. I've watched you often enough and he should know me by now.'

Mara stared at her thoughtfully. 'Hear that, Ears,' she said, patting the pony's head. 'Behave yourself for Colenso and you'll get an extra feed.' The pony whinnied softly and Mara handed over the reins and climbed into the back of the van.

Colenso carefully steered them back onto the road then followed the trail of wagons as they passed through a valley blanketed with dense woodland before it opened out into farmland and scrub. It was then she felt the stabbing. Her hand went to her chest, except her necklace wasn't there. She stared around but could see nothing but fields and vegetation. Thinking tiredness was making her edgy, she tried to relax. The others were some way ahead and she urged Ears on, but the pony ignored her and continued plodding at his own pace.

Then she heard the sound of hooves and the rumble of wheels behind them. She turned her head but could only see the side of the vardo. A large, ornately decorated wagon drew alongside making her gasp. The lane was barely wide enough to accommodate both vans, and she held her breath as the two sets of wheels nearly collided. Instead of passing, the wagon slowed to their pace and to her dismay she saw Marco smiling menacingly at her. Slowly, inch by inch, he steered his horses closer. She pulled tightly on the reins but it was no good, the van tilted into a ditch on the side of the road. As she sat there stunned, she heard Marco's cruel laugh as he whipped his horses and they took off at an alarming rate, the wagon bouncing behind.

'What the blazes …?' Mara muttered, appearing beside her. 'You all right, girl?' she asked.

'I think so. It was Marco, he ran me off the road,' she shook her head, pointing ahead to where his wagon had veered off the lane and was heading north.

'Bloody man,' Mara shouted, shaking her fist at him before leaping down and patting Ears. 'There's a good boy,' she crooned. 'Many a pony would have bolted, but not Ears,' she told Colenso as she jumped down beside her. Together they studied the van. It was well and truly stuck, with both nearside wheels embedded in the ditch.

'It's no good. We'll never get that out, so we'll have to leave it here and walk,' Mara said, unhitching the pony. 'Get someone from Grampound to come and help us shift it.'

'I'm sorry,' Colenso murmured.

'Not your fault. That madman should be locked up.'

'But why would he do such a thing?' Colenso persisted.

'A proud man, is Marco, and you spurned him, didn't you? Asked you to be his new assistant, didn't he?' Mara added, seeing her frown. 'His ego wouldn't allow rejection, see? Illusionaire Extraordinaire, indeed. Come on, Ears,' she said, taking hold of his bridle.

'So what does he do exactly?' Colenso asked.

'Makes things and people disappear,' she said grimly. 'Literally.' Colenso shuddered as they began walking. As if to add to their mood, the sun disappeared behind the clouds that had gathered.

'Typical,' Mara muttered. 'Going to rain now. Still, I guess it'll wash some of the dust off us.'

They hadn't gone far when they heard hooves and the rumble of wheels. Spinning round, they saw Big Al waving to them from his wagon.

'What caused that?' he asked without preamble, drawing to a halt beside them.

'I was taking a nap in the back when Marco tried to run Colenso off the road,' Mara told him, her eyes narrowing to dark slits. 'Wicked, he is. Time someone put a stop to his trickeries.'

'Agreed,' he nodded. 'You all right?' he asked, turning to Colenso.

'Yes, except for landing Mara's van in a ditch and losing sight of the others,' she muttered, feeling foolish.

'Soon fix that. When we get to Grampound, I'll send Titan and his pal to retrieve the van and you can catch up with your kumpania. They'll no doubt have a fire going and be brewing up some concoction in their cauldron,' he laughed, holding out his hand to take the bridle from her before helping them up. Then, with Ears trotting behind, they continued their journey.

The rain was falling in big fat drops now, the leaden sky merging with the moors. Thankful to be under cover, Colenso sat back on the seat. Big Al and Mara had their heads close together and were muttering but she couldn't hear what they were saying. All she could think of was that malicious grin on Marco's face. The man was mad.

*

'Tinks and I are going to see if we can get some offcuts of leather from the tannery before we leave,' Mara told Colenso. Despite their eventful afternoon the previous day, they were up early and were enjoying their first cuppa of the day. 'I noticed old Ears's rein is getting worn when I was leading him yesterday.'

'It didn't take Titan and Tory long to recover your van, did it?' Colenso asked, amazed at the speed with which it had turned up. By the time they'd arrived here, the rain had stopped and the kumpania were cooking chitties over the yag.

Colenso still marvelled at the way everyone pulled together, for by the time they'd finished supper, the men had not only recovered the van but set it up alongside the others.

'Told you Big Al had things organized, didn't I?' Mara told her, winding the red scarf around her curls.

'Jago doesn't see things that way, does he?' Colenso asked.

'No, but then he doesn't like paying out for anything he deems unnecessary,' the woman replied. 'Talk of the devil,' she added as there was a brisk rapping and the door opened. 'Let yourself in, why don't you.'

'Morning to you an' all, Mara,' he grinned. 'Hear you girls had a spot of bother on the road yesterday.'

'That Marco had better not show his face, that's all I'm saying,' Mara growled.

'Blimey, that look would scare me,' he replied, pretending to cower. 'I'm going to see what delights Karla's making and I thought you might like to come with me,' he said to Colenso.

'I'd love to,' she cried, excited at the prospect of meeting his sister and seeing how the confections were created. 'If that's all right with you, Mara?'

'See you at the fairground in Truro then. Don't forget to call in at the post office on your way through, cos you never know,' she winked.

'What might you never know?' Jago asked as they rode through the little town waymarked Probus.

'If there's a letter waiting for me,' she admitted, excitement bubbling in spite of her worries that there might not be. 'And if there is, I shall need to purchase a card and stamp,' she added, staring at him expectantly.

'My, it's busy today,' he murmured. Colenso stared at the

empty lane ahead and sighed. Getting money out of the man obviously wasn't going to be easy. She'd have to devise a strategy, she decided, sitting back and looking around.

The air was fresh after the rain and she breathed in deeply. They were crossing a river now and as two swans glided down, her thoughts turned to Kitto. Would he have found some way to reply to the card she'd sent?

Before long they drew up outside a little cottage on the edge of Truro. Although it was small and quite run-down, it was on a corner plot and when she followed Jago round to the back she saw that an outhouse of some sort had been added.

'Hello sister, dear,' he called brightly, pushing open the door and beckoning Colenso to follow him into the steam-filled room. A woman in her thirties, dark hair piled messily on top of her head, white apron covering her dress, looked up from the big pan she was stirring. 'I've brought Colenso here to meet you.'

'Yer've brought a girl home, Jago? Well I never,' she exclaimed, nearly dropping her spoon into the mixture. ''Tis good to meet yer, dear,' she smiled warmly at Colenso. 'I'd like to say any friend of my brother's is a friend of mine, but sadly that's not always true.'

'This is Karla,' Jago said, looking uncomfortable. 'Learn what you can from her and I'll be back later.'

Chapter 22

As Jago scuttled back outside, Karla burst out laughing.

'Forgive me, dear. Bit of sibling banter. Must have got to him cos he forgot to take those,' she chuckled, gesturing to the jars of brightly coloured sweets that were lined up along the cupboards. 'I'll just put this pan in water to arrest the cooking then we can get to know each other.' There was a hiss and spitting before she turned back to Colenso. 'Sit yerself down and tell me how yer got caught up with my brother.'

'Thank you,' Colenso said, perching on a seat beside the huge, scrubbed table. 'I work on the Panam, selling sweets with him.'

'Oh, yer not walking out, then?' she asked candidly.

'No,' Colenso spluttered, the very idea amusing her.

'Thought it was too good to be true. Mother said he wasn't normal, like. Does he pay yer?' Dark eyes surveyed her curiously. Colenso shook her head.

'He keeps promising but …' she shrugged.

'Same here,' Karla told her. ''Tis time we taught that brother of mine a lesson. I'll think on it while I'm finishing these,' she added, carefully adding drops from a little brown bottle to the mixture and stirring. A pungent aroma filled the air as she lifted the pan and set it down on the scrubbed table. Snatching up a spoon, she began dribbling the orange-coloured syrup over the tips of sticks that were laid out on large trays.

'Lollipops?' Colenso asked, staring in fascination as the liquid pooled into perfect circles.

'Yes, Jago says you can't have a Panam without lollipops. Course, they takes longer to make and I have the devil's own job getting him to pay me for my time, but yer not interested in that.'

'Actually, I might well be,' Colenso replied. 'And I'd like to hear more about your brother, for I really don't know him that well.' She smiled at the woman, thinking she might have found an ally.

'Perhaps you could start crushing that while we talk,' the woman said, pointing to an enormous cone of sugar. 'I've finished everything apart from the rock canes,' she said.

'I'd love to see how you make those,' Colenso told her as she set about her task.

'Yer can helps me shape them later, if yer like. But first, I needs to grease this then get on with my mixing. Timing's everything when yer making confections. That and temperature,' she said, setting down a huge tray that almost covered the length of the table. Colenso glanced around the room, taking in the range, the sink under the window and the row of cupboards, their tops lined with the jars of jewel-coloured sweets.

'Did you make all those yourself?' she asked, gesturing to the containers.

'Mother helped. It's how we makes our living, supplying

the fairs. When we gets paid, of course,' she sighed. 'Oh good, yer've finished enough for me to get started,' she said, scooping up the sugar Colenso had filed from the cone. As she tossed it into another huge pan on the stove, Colenso noticed the livid mark on her finger spread all the way down to her hand, and remembered how Jago told her she'd burned it.

'You need more?' Colenso asked, not wishing to be caught staring.

'Yep, yer gets through an awful lot of the stuff when you makes confections,' Karla laughed. 'Cors different ones need different textures so yer has to be careful how yer controls the melting and recrystallization process. Needs to know which part of yer range is hottest and which is cooler.' As she talked, she was busy spooning ingredients from different containers onto the sugar in the pan. Then she poured over a jug of water and stood back. Just has to let that start dissolving now,' she said, sitting down beside Colenso.

''Tis a shame Mother's not here but she's earning extra, helping them down at the fair. If Jago paid us she wouldn't have to. Yer've done enough now,' she said, nodding to the pile of sugar. 'Yer can put that into the jar there and place the rest of the cone back on the side. Those trays of lollies can go on the side too. We'll need all the table to work on.' They jumped up and she turned back to her stirring and before long the mixture began to bubble. Colenso did as she'd been asked then watched as Karla picked up the brush and began washing down the inside of the pan.

'I watched someone making tablet the other day,' she said, reminded of her morning with Caitlin.

''Tis a similar process 'til you get to the colouring and

kneading bit. Different ingredients other than the sugar, of course,' she grinned. 'Now for the tricky bit,' she frowned, quickly dipping the finger next to the scarred one into the pan and licking off the mixture. 'Right, that's done,' she said, taking the pan off the heat. 'Just need to leave that to cool down a bit. Fancy a drink?'

'Yes please. It's so hot in here, although it looks like you're very well organized,' Colenso told her as Karla poured lemonade from another jug on the dresser and handed her a glass.

'Hot? More like a raging furnace,' the woman said, downing her drink in one. 'Phew, that's better. Jago got one of his, er, friends to help him add on this room. Said we could make more sweets and more money. Ha ha to the second. How did yer come to be working with him?'

'It's a long story but I'm travelling with Mara in her van and, well, thought it would be a good way of contributing towards my keep.'

'Mara the fortune teller?' Karla asked. 'I keep meaning to have mine told. I've heard she's good. Mind yer, I think I already know my future,' she said, her hand going to her stomach.

'You mean …?' Colenso said, her eyes widening. Karla nodded.

'Not that Jago knows. Denny, that's my follower, and me are getting wed. Cors it'll have to be sooner rather than later now,' she chuckled as she crossed the room and lifted the pan into the sink. Luckily Colenso was saved from answering, as the noise of hissing and spitting filled the room.

'I thought Mother'd go mad, but Jago's away so much she

quite likes the idea of having a man around the house. Says we'll be the only ones to make her a grandmother anyhow,' she said, lifting out the pan and stirring before pouring the syrup into the prepared tray. She let it cool for a moment then cut it into two portions, one twice the size of the other.

'Right, now we add flavouring to the bigger piece,' Karla said, carefully shaking out two drops from a tiny phial.

'That smells so good,' Colenso cried, inhaling the floral aroma. 'It's just like roses.'

'Rose rock, see? If yer wants to help yer can wet yer hands and start kneading this,' she said, placing the flavoured piece in front of Colenso. 'I'll colour the other portion.' She added a couple of drops from a phial and began massaging it in. As Colenso worked her mixture she was surprised to see it turn from clear and glass-like to white and satiny.

'It's like magic,' she cried.

'Alchemy, they calls it,' Karla grinned. 'Now, you roll the mixture into a long sausage while I roll the red one into a strand. They need to be the same length. That's it,' she said, taking her red one and placing it deftly over Colenso's white. 'Now I'll roll them together like so.'

Colenso watched fascinated as the combined mixture was rolled to twice its original length before being folded so that they became two red stripes. Then taking up a pair of scissors, Karla began snipping the mixtures into six-inch lengths.

'Right, you can help me roll and bend the tops back into the shape of a crook like this, see?' she demonstrated. Colenso smiled as she saw the formed shape of the walking cane then tried herself. 'That's it,' Karla said moments later. 'Now we can take a rest while they cool.'

'That was fun,' Colenso said as they collapsed back onto their chairs.

'Don't know about that, but it's bloomin' bakin',' Karla groaned, fanning her face with her hands. 'Want another drink?'

'I'll get them,' Colenso replied, jumping up and refilling their glasses. She handed Karla hers then ran her fingers along the jars lined up in the cupboards. 'They're like priceless jewels,' she murmured.

'Well, Jago certainly thinks they're beyond price,' Karla moaned. Then her lips widened into a broad grin. 'That's it. We won't hand them over until he pays what he owes.' She jumped up and began hiding the jars in the cupboards. 'The lollies are set now, so help me pack them into cones then we can hide those away too,' she said, snatching up a little pile and placing them on the table. 'Can't believe I didn't think of this before.'

By the time Jago came back, they'd cleared everything away and the room was looking neat and tidy.

'There's people milling around all over the fairground. Should bode well for selling lots of sweets,' he grinned, rubbing his hands together. Then he frowned as he took in the clear table and bare work surfaces. 'Where are they?'

'Where's what, brother dear?' Karla asked innocently.

'All those sweets you were busy making.'

'Yer mean the ones yer intend selling for lots of money?'

'Of course, er … well, hopefully,' he amended as they both stared stonily as him.

'Yer'll get the sweets when we get our money,' Karla told him, holding out her hand.

'I haven't the time to play games,' he blustered.

'Best get on with it then,' Karla countered. He stared at them for a moment then, realizing he was beaten, took out his leather pouch. Slowly he counted coins into their outstretched hands. 'And the rest, you skinflint,' Karla urged. 'Mother helped as well.' With a muttered oath, Jago handed over a few more coins.

'Thank you, brother dear,' Karla said sweetly while Colenso stared at her money with relief. She had enough to give Mara a fair amount for her board and to purchase another card and stamp should she receive a reply from Kitto. Her heart leapt at the thought and she pocketed her money before helping Karla unpack the confection from the cupboards.

By the time Jago had loaded them onto his wagon and Colenso had thanked Karla for the lesson in sweet-making, it was late afternoon.

'I'd like to stop at the post office, please,' she told him as they headed down a road of elegant Georgian houses with their splendid walled gardens and on past the newer townhouses that led into the town.

'Not sure I've got the time,' Jago muttered, still sulking from being outmanoeuvred by his sister.

'Well, drop me off here then and I'll walk. Mara told me the green is only just out of the town.'

'I suppose I could take you, as long as you promise to help me arrange everything in the Panam. This fair's only on for two days so I'll need to make the most of every minute if I'm to earn any profit at all. And we'll need more cones as well,' he added, letting out a long sigh.

'I'd be happy to help,' she told him sweetly. The sooner she could get to the post office the better. She was longing to find out if there was anything waiting for her. As Kitto had never learned to write she couldn't see how he could possibly reply, but Mara had seemed so sure.

And Mara was right. A letter was waiting for her. Hugging it to her body, she almost danced out of the building and clambered back onto the wagon.

'Happy now?' Jago asked, urging his horse on.

'Very,' she smiled widely, tempted to open it there and then. Somehow she resisted and happily watched as they made their way out of the town and along the estuary towards Sunny Corner. Seagulls swooped and called, boats bobbed on white-tipped waves. She had a letter from Kitto and she was happy.

They arrived at the green to find it bustling with noise and activity. As ever, burly men assembled the attractions while children ran in and out of the stalls laughing. Flags flew from tent tops and there was an air of anticipation and excitement.

'Got a good pitch right in the centre this time. Old Taylor's here but his cart's up by the road,' Jago grinned.

'Good,' Colenso smiled, relieved he was happy at last. 'I can see Mara's little tent over by the water. Oh, and there's her van under the trees. I'll see you tomorrow,' she said, preparing to jump down.

'You could at least help me unpack the confection,' Jago muttered.

'I'll help tomorrow,' Colenso called, leaping to the ground as the horse slowed. All she wanted to do was open her letter and find out what Kitto had said.

Heart thumping, she let herself into Mara's vardo, for once thankful to have it to herself. Slumping down on the cushion, she studied the bold writing on the envelope until, unable to resist any longer, she ripped open the flap and drew out a sheet of paper.

Dear Colenso

> *I was so pleased to hear from you and to know you are safe.*
> *Mary Anne, the schoolmistress, read your letter to me. When I expressed my disappointment at not being able to reply, she kindly offered to help me.*
> *We have been meeting each evening and she is teaching me my letters. She has been really sweet and patient for I do not find it easy.*
> *As soon as I'm able, I will follow after you, so please let me know where I can reach you.*
> *I am keeping your pentacle safe until we meet.*

Miss and love you.
Kitto

As Colenso read the letter through again, her initial elation turned to dismay. Mary Anne was as pretty as she was clever, and Kitto, her betrothed, was spending each evening with her.

'What's up with you?' Mara asked, entering the van and slumping down on the cushion opposite. 'I'd have thought a letter from your lover would make you happy not sad. That is from him, I take it?' She pointed to the letter and looked at Colenso expectantly.

'Yes, it is,' she sighed, ignoring the woman's choice of word.

'Well then?' Mara frowned.

'He's only spending every evening learning his letters with the schoolmistress,' she cried, throwing the note down on the seat beside her.

'May I?' Mara asked, reaching over and picking it up. When Colenso nodded, she scanned the contents, her lips curling into a smile. 'Well, that's a nice letter and he's keeping your necklace safe. He's obviously keen to communicate with you if he's prepared to spend his free time learning his letters, so what's wrong?'

'He's learning with Mary Ann, who is fair-haired, slender and the prettiest girl in Cadgwith, that's what's wrong,' Colenso wailed, running her fingers through her tufts of hair. 'That and the fact that she has always had her eye on Kitto.'

'What's for you won't pass by you,' Mara said gently.

'Oh, you and your silly sayings,' Colenso shouted.

'Calm down and think about it. You said Kitto loves you, and presumably you still love him?'

'Of course I do,' she cried.

'Then shouldn't you trust him?' Mara asked, staring at her intently.

'What do you know about it? You've never been married, have you?' Colenso was so overwrought, she hardly noticed the woman flinch.

'No, that's true, I haven't. But I was promised to someone once. Someone I loved with all my heart.'

'So what happened?' Colenso asked, feeling a pang of remorse as she saw the desolation in Mara's eyes.

'He died in a mining accident,' she whispered. Then she went silent, a faraway look in her eyes. Colenso watched as, with a supreme effort, the woman continued. 'They thought they'd found a new vein of copper and he was offered a goodly sum to go deeper underground and investigate. I had a dreadful feeling about it and pleaded with him not to go. However, we were saving to be married and, knowing the extra money would come in handy, he insisted but ...' Her voice quavered then petered out. Colenso rushed over to the woman and put her arm around her.

'It's all right, you don't have to tell me,' she murmured.

'But I do,' Mara said, her voice quiet. 'The roof collapsed and he was buried under tons of soil and rock. It was too dangerous for anyone to go back down so his body was never found.'

'Oh Mara, that's terrible. I had no idea.'

'How could you?' Mara shrugged. 'But love is a precious thing, Colenso, so think hard before you throw it away on perceived grievances. Now, if you don't mind, I'd like to turn in.'

'Thank you for telling me. I'll write to Kitto tomorrow.'

Chapter 23

After a restless night tossing and turning, her dreams punctuated by the fair-haired schoolmistress smiling adoringly at Kitto as he sat learning his letters, Colenso woke to hear Mara rooting through her little cupboard.

'What are you doing?' she muttered, rubbing the sleep from her eyes.

'I was thinking last night that you could do with something new to wear and I remembered these,' she said holding up a green skirt and matching top. 'You can't go around in those old clothes any longer,' the woman told her. 'They're all worn and torn.' Colenso stared at the brightly coloured garments then laughed.

'But I'll never get into those. I'm much too big.'

'Have you taken a look at yourself lately? All that walking has paid dividends, my girl. I've even found an emerald scarf for you to tie around your head. Go and try them on whilst I go and get some water for a brew.' Before Colenso could reply, she snatched up the kettle, unbolted the little door and hurried outside.

Colenso ran her fingers over the pink and yellow daisies that had been embroidered on the blouse then noticed they'd been replicated around the flounce of the skirt. How lovely it would be to wear clothes as pretty as these. Hardly expecting them to fit, but not wishing to offend Mara, she jumped out of bed and slipped them on. To her amazement not only did the buttons on the blouse do up, the skirt skimmed her hips. Delighted, she danced around the tiny room, revelling at the swishing sound the fine material made. Running her fingers through her growing tresses, she twirled the scarf around her head, letting the ends drape elegantly down her back as Mara did. Peering in the tiny mirror beside the cupboard, she gasped in surprise. No longer plump and awkward, her reflection showed a slender outline with sparkling dark eyes and skin that was tanned and healthy. The bright green of the outfit seemed to bring her colouring alive somehow.

'Well, look at you,' Mara beamed, returning with the filled pot. 'All you need now are some golden hoops in your ears and you'll really look the part.'

'These clothes are so pretty. Can I really wear them?' Colenso asked.

'Why bless you, they're yours to keep, dearie.'

'Really? How much do I owe you?' Colenso asked, taking the coins out of her basket. 'Jago finally paid me yesterday,' she explained. 'His sister insisted.'

'Well, I'm glad about that but you keep your money. It will be lovely to see the clothes being worn at last after the hours I spent stitching those daisies.' She blinked and looked out of the window, her expression taking on that faraway look.

'I'm sorry, Mara,' she murmured, guessing their conversation of the previous evening had stirred up sad memories.

'Don't be, it was all a long time ago.' She forced a smile. 'Now, put those coins somewhere safe.'

'But you haven't taken anything for my keep and …'

'Money holds no import for me. I have everything I need and, as you've seen, Ears and I always find enough to eat and kindling to heat along the way. Now,' she continued as Colenso made to protest, 'Sarah and I are going into Truro before the fair opens, so get that reply written to Kitto and I'll post it while I'm there. While you're doing that, I'll make us tea and nettle champ. Opening day's always hectic so we'll need a good breakfast inside us.'

Colenso took out the card she'd bought the previous day, addressed and stamped the envelope then reread Kitto's letter. She let out a long sigh.

'What's the matter now?' Mara asked, looking up from the potatoes she was chopping.

'He didn't say much so I'm not sure how to answer.'

'Well, if he's been learning his letters it probably took him all his time to write what he did,' she pointed out. 'Tell him you're pleased to hear from him, you miss him and can't wait to see him, but as you're travelling around at the moment he should send his reply to the post office at Marazion.'

'Right, I'll do that.'

'Now, come and eat. I see you've lots more cones to make,' she added, nodding towards the pile of paper in her basket.

'Hmm, Jago wants them by this afternoon. I suppose I'll have to wait ages for him to pay me again. I never realized he was so mean.'

'He is careful with money, I agree. Have you ever wondered why, though?' Mara said, handing her a plate of food.

'Suppose he wants to keep it all for himself,' she said, eagerly tucking into the fried potatoes mixed with nettles and onions.

'Since he was little, Jago had to make a little money go as far as possible. His father ran off with a younger woman, leaving him to fend for his mother and sister. It was through his own hard work that he was able to set up the Panam. Then, when he saw an opportunity for them to make some of the sweets, he built an outhouse to work in.'

'Yes, Karla said one of his so-called friends helped him do that.'

'Sounds like a true friend to me if he was prepared to assist.' She paused and stared at Colenso intently. 'As I said last night, friends come in many guises, so don't be too quick to judge.'

*

Colenso settled down to make the cones, her thoughts moving as quickly as her fingers. Was she too quick to judge? When she'd first read about Kitto spending time with the pretty schoolmistress her reaction had been less than charitable. As Mara had said, he wouldn't have bothered learning his letters if he hadn't cared deeply for her, and she would focus on that. As for Jago, now she understood his preoccupation with money, she would be more tolerant. And, like Mara, she'd be more accepting of people. Although she wasn't sure she'd ever be able to accept what her father and mamm had done to her. Poor Mara, life had dealt her a terrible blow and yet she spent her time giving hope and pleasure to the countless people who flocked to her little tent.

Hearing the music start up, Colenso piled the cones into her basket and headed out into the sunshine. No longer did the ticking of the clock rule her life; she moved to the beat of the organ now.

She walked along the banks of the estuary, revelling in the feel of her new skirt swishing around her ankles. A heron was standing motionless in the shimmering water, seagulls screeched as they wheeled overhead and, for the first time in a long while, she felt contented. Ahead she could see the stalls already thronging with people.

'You're looking bonny, Bonbon,' Big Al grinned, falling into step beside her. Colenso glanced down at her new outfit, a rush of pleasure tingling through her.

'Mara's been so kind,' she replied by way of explanation.

'Most folk here are. There's always the exception, of course. Talking of which, you needn't worry about Marco anymore.'

'Oh?' she asked, looking askance.

'Let's just say that dirty deed was his last. Were you to catch sight of him again, it *would* be an illusion extraordinaire,' he guffawed. Whatever did he mean, Colenso wondered, watching him stride away. However, she didn't have time to dwell on his strange statement, for Jago was calling for her to hurry.

'Thought you were coming early to help me set up the stock,' he grumbled, frowning as she slipped behind the stall. 'Suppose you've been frittering your money on gewgaws and furbelows being as how you're all done up like a dog's dinner. Doesn't excuse you for being late, though.'

'I've made up lots of cones so I hope we'll be busy,' she

smiled. Having learned it was better to ignore his moans, she tilted her basket and emptied them out onto the stall. 'I really enjoyed learning how to make these,' she told him, rearranging the rock canes into an artistic fan.

'Doesn't mean you can alter my display,' he growled. His frown turned to an indulgent smile as children began swarming around, holding out coins in their grubby little hands. Colenso helped them make their selection, not minding what mix of sweets she made up for them. Seeing their looks of wonder and delight made her feel warm inside and she couldn't decide what she liked more, making the sweets or selling them.

Later, when the children had gone home for their supper, she made her way through the fair towards the van. The sun was like a rosy red ball as it sank beyond the estuary and, as ever, the lapping of the water filled her with contentment. Hearing the sound of rifle shot, she spun around. Her eyes widened in astonishment as she saw the targets on the range were covered with pictures of Marco. As another shot rang out, hitting him right between his glassy eyes, she laughed out loud. So that was what Big Al had meant. They'd sought their revenge on the ostentatious, evil man in the way they knew would hurt him the most. An illusion extraordinaire indeed.

*

It seemed no time at all before they were packing up and back on the road again. This time it was only the small kumpania travelling together. As ever, Jago was to join them once the fair was set up.

'Don't you get fed up with moving around all the time?' Colenso asked as they descended the long hill to Carnon Downs.

'Not at all. When you travel your thoughts move along with you. It stops you living in the past or dwelling on petty niggles,' Mara replied, smiling knowingly at her. Colenso was pleased to see the woman had regained her humour after her recent outpouring. 'Besides, it increases one's knowledge both of the area and the flora and fauna. For example, this stone bridge spans the wide drying creek to Perranwell. And see that pretty woodland over there?' She pointed to the trees in the distance. 'That's Kennall Vale, which houses the old ruins of gunpowder mills. Now, you didn't know that before, did you?'

'No,' she laughed. 'And I suppose you have other pearls of wisdom to impart?'

'Well, if you're interested, there's the Giant's Chair. And if you're good, when we stop later, you can sit on it,' Mara grinned. 'But first we need to forage for food and gather some kindling. Keep your eyes peeled, for this area's good for fat hen.' Colenso stared at the woman sceptically. Surely you couldn't find fat hens in the hedgerows? Mara snorted as if picking up on her thoughts.

'It's a bit like spinach, although the leaves are green on top but creamy white underneath. Goes well with ramsons but they've probably finished by now,' she told her. 'You'll thank me for sharing this knowledge with you when you and Kitto wed and have a family to cook for.'

Kitto – her heart flipped at the mention of his name. He should have received her letter by now. Why, even now he might be penning her a reply.

'Anyhow, best start looking, for when we reach the granite quarries there'll be nothing but spoil heaps,' Mara said, bringing her back to the here and now.

Although they walked a fair distance, Mara kept up her knowledgeable commentary on the topography, and Colenso found the time passed quickly. When they finally reached Godolphin Hill where they were to stop for the night, her brain was buzzing with facts and their little van filled with the makings of a good supper and a goodly supply of sticks for the stove.

The kumpania set up camp and once again Colenso was amazed at the way the travellers quietly pulled together. Soon the appetizing aroma of supper simmering in a pot over the yag filled the air. Later, when they sat down to eat it in the gathering shadows, she couldn't help contrasting the serenity with Karla's steamy outhouse.

'Did you enjoy your supper?' Mara asked when they'd finished their potage.

'I still can't believe you can eat so well on a few leaves.'

'It's what you do with them,' Mara laughed. 'The alchemy.'

'Like turning raw sugar into glistening jewel-like confections,' she replied.

'You're learning, girl. Of course, the food we forage is far more nutritious, although you do need to supplement it with bread or potatoes or your stomach would be growling from here to Goldsithney. Now do you want to sit on the Giant's Chair before we turn in?' When Colenso nodded, they climbed up the steep-sided hill and ambled over to a mass of rock rising out of the gathering darkness.

'Goodness, it really does look like a huge seat,' Colenso

said, surveying the smooth hollow with the back slanting off at an angle.

'Let's see if we can follow the giant's example and hurl these blocks of granite to Prospidnick. It's only about four miles as the crow flies,' she laughed.

'Might have known you'd have another yarn to tell me,' Colenso snorted. 'Come on, time for bed,' she said, holding out her hand as the woman yawned.

It was only later, when Colenso looked back on that evening, that she realized it marked the turning point in their relationship.

Chapter 24

Raindrops drumming on the roof of the van woke Colenso. Peering through the window, all she could see was grey, swirling mist. Mara was still sleeping, her blanket rising and falling along with her gentle snoring. Dressing quickly, Colenso unbolted the little stable door and slipped outside. Ears whickered softly and, shivering in the cold wet of the morning, Colenso fondled his soft muzzle and gave him some oats. Then after a quick rinse in the stream, she filled the kettle and hurried back inside.

After feeding kindling into the stove, she set the pan to boil and began making breakfast. How she'd grown to love this cosy little kitchen which, although basic, had everything necessary to prepare and cook their meals. Humming softly, she made their pancakes and was just tipping them out onto their plates when noises from outside told her the kumpania was making ready to strike camp.

'Come on, lazy bones,' she joked, leaning over and shaking the woman gently. 'The others are preparing to leave and you don't want to be left behind now, do you? I've made us tea and bokoli, although there's no bacon or cheese so I've flavoured it with herbs.'

'Taking over my kitchen now,' the woman grumbled, climbing out of bed and peering through the curtain. 'Mizzly as misery out there, but you're right, the others are almost ready to leave,' she added, quickly pulling on her skirt and winding the red scarf around her hair.

'Don't worry, Mara, I've seen to Ears so we only have to hitch up,' she soothed. 'I'll steer the van if you like.'

'And we all know what happened last time you did that,' Mara snorted, taking a bite of her breakfast. 'Not bad, though a bit more seasoning would have helped.' Seeing the woman was out of sorts, Colenso turned her attention to her own food.

By the time they were ready to leave, the rain had stopped and the other vans were already trundling off into the distance.

'Good job Ears knows the way,' Mara said when Colenso took the reins.

As they wandered along, the mist slowly began to lift, and by the time they reached Marazion the sky was bright blue. Colenso stared at the white-tipped waves sparkling to the left of them then peered at the island that rose prominently out of the rocky bay.

'Oh, that is so beautiful,' she sighed, breathing in the sea air. 'I suppose that mount was named for St Michael.'

'Doesn't take a genius to work that one out,' Mara retorted.

'Just interested,' Colenso replied, deciding to humour her. It worked, for the woman turned and smiled.

'Then we shall continue with your education. The Archangel St Michael is said to have appeared on the west side of the island and warded fishermen from the danger of the rocks. Ever since, pilgrims, monks or people of any faith really, have visited to pray and give praise.'

'It looks so peaceful. I can't wait to visit for Litha,' Colenso replied.

'I agree there is something mystical about the island – all this area, in fact,' she said gesturing around.

'This is glorious,' Colenso murmured as they joined the kumpania on a field overlooking the wide expanse of water. Out in the bay, fishing boats were hauling in their seine nets, the inevitable seagulls swooping low. 'It's just like being back home.'

'Miss it, do you?' Mara asked.

'Sometimes,' she nodded. 'Especially Kitto. Although I still couldn't face seeing Father and Mamm.'

'Well, that's hardly surprising,' Mara exclaimed. 'I think spending the summer here will do us both the world of good. Rest, sea air and a bit of dukkering to keep the wolf away,' she sighed contentedly.

'Are we really staying that long?' Colenso asked, excitement rising. Mara nodded.

'We don't usually, but Jago suggested we try it. He reckons the railway brings lots of day-trippers and holidaymakers here.' She pointed ahead to the steam of a train chugging out of the station, little puffs of white clouds rising into the blue sky above. 'And they're people with money to spend.'

'That sounds like Jago,' Colenso laughed. 'So what's that big yard for?'

'To store and transport the perishables from surrounding farms and harbours. Talking of which, we'd better start unloading.'

'I'll do that,' Colenso said as Mara struggled to free the canvas and poles from their racks beneath the van.

'Blooming rains made them heavy as Hades,' she muttered. Colenso frowned down at the equipment that was bone dry, then up at Mara. Despite having ridden all the way here, she was looking fatigued.

'Want some help, ladies?' Jago said as he pulled up in his van. Relief flooded through her, for she could see Mara was struggling.

'Always managed before,' Mara replied.

'Come on, Mara, let Jago do his manly bit,' Colenso quipped, shooting him a grateful look.

'I'm parched. Don't suppose you've got the wherewithal for a cuppa?' he asked.

'Course I have,' Mara snorted, climbing back into the van.

'Come on, I know where she likes to do her dukkering,' Jago said, hoisting up the little tent and setting off across the field towards the water. 'Swears blind that Mount over there transfers some of its spirituality to her,' he added. Colenso stared at the island rising like a magical castle out of the sea, and nodded. She couldn't wait for midsummer to explore it.

The days flew by in a frenzy. With Mara still frail, Colenso had taken over the chores. In the mornings, when the tide was right, she would forage the shore for its rich pickings of sea beet, kale or the spear-leaved orache for their evening meal. She'd then return to the van to make up the cones before working on the Panam in the afternoons.

As Jago had predicted, the day-trippers and holidaymakers arrived with money to spend, and eager children swarmed around the stall, clamouring for sweets before making their way onto the beach, brightly coloured cones clutched in their hands.

Before Colenso knew it, the evening before Litha – or the summer solstice, as Mara insisted on calling it – had arrived.

'Where do you think you're going?' Jago asked as Colenso scooped up her basket and made her way out of the stall.

'I told you, Mara and I are going over to the Mount for the summer solstice.'

'But there are still some people milling around and they might want to buy sweets,' he frowned.

'Then you'll have to serve them yourself, Jago. I'll see you tomorrow afternoon as usual,' she said, trying not to laugh at his indignant look. Having been rushed off her feet all afternoon, he wasn't going to make her feel guilty for leaving a couple of hours earlier than usual. 'I'll dock it from your wages.'

'What wages?' she asked.

Excitement bubbled up inside her as she hurried over to Mara's tent. She was pleased to see the woman was in fine spirits as they made their way down to the beach. For the past week or so she'd been withdrawn and preoccupied, spending her mornings looking out over the island or chatting earnestly with Sarah before taking herself off to her little tent. After supper she went straight to bed. Mara hadn't once teased Colenso about her choice of sea plants for their meal, and she missed their bantering.

'We'll walk over the causeway to St Michael's Mount and climb up the pilgrim's path to the castle. It's the best place to watch the sun rise,' Mara told Colenso as, shedding their boots, they stepped onto the cool sand. With the water lapping over their feet, they made their way towards the island.

Despite her earlier excitement, when she saw the outline of The Lizard in the distance, her spirits plummeted. She'd visited the post office earlier that morning and there was still no letter from Kitto. Despite Mara's assurance, she couldn't help wondering if he'd succumbed to the schoolmistress's charms after all. But she couldn't stay gloomy, for they'd reached their destination.

'Well, here we are,' Mara said, sinking down onto a rock and slipping into her boots. 'I think we'll take a little rest, it's a steep climb to the top,' she added as Colenso bent and tied her laces.

'I've brought us some of Jago's confections,' she grinned, extracting a cone of bullseyes from the basket and holding it out to the woman. They sat sucking the striped, lemon-flavoured sweets while watching the activity going on in the harbour. Colenso was sure she'd never seen so many boats.

'Could bloomin' break your teeth on these things,' Mara moaned, taking the sweet from her mouth and throwing it into the water. 'Come on, let's get moving.'

'Goodness, they've got cows here,' Colenso exclaimed, staring at the small black animals in amazement.

'How else will they get milk and butter?' Mara snorted as they joined the throng of people wending their way up the steep path. The views from the top were breathtaking, a carpet of green meeting the azure of the sea. Although Mara looked tired, she was adamant they secure their spot on the eastern side ready to see the sun rise.

The sky was just darkening to grey by the time they settled

on a rocky crest along with all the others who had come to keep vigil together for the rising sun. Colenso pulled a blanket from the basket and gently covered the woman.

'If things had been different, I'd have liked a daughter just like you,' Mara murmured. Colenso turned to the woman in surprise, but she'd already closed her eyes and was snoring gently.

Colenso sat in the gathering shadows, watching pale lights flickering on the mainland, listening to the lowing of the cattle and the gentle lapping of the waves, and thinking of all that had happened over the past months. She could hardly believe that only a short time ago she'd had her life all mapped out and was planning her handfasting ceremony. She wondered what Kitto was doing on this special night, and then, when the image of him with the fair-haired Mary Anne surfaced, wished she hadn't. Her eyelids grew heavy and she must have slept, for the next thing she knew Mara was prodding her side.

'Look,' she whispered. There was a collective gasp around them as a trace of light peeked above the hills. They watched in silence as it grew bigger, rays of red and gold spreading wider across the sky. 'Sol Invictus,' Mara whispered, rising to her feet. 'Let us draw strength and energy from the triumphant sun and concentrate on our outgoing energies.' Colenso stared at Mara in surprise, for it could have been Mammwynn speaking and, not for the first time, she thought what friends they might have been had they met. 'Attune to the energies of the waters, the origin of life,' Mara murmured, stretching her arms out wide to the sea and closing her eyes.

'Now you must discover the magic of the rock,' Mara

said, her eyes shining as she turned to Colenso. 'Come on,' she said, leading the way to an old church. 'This is where the highest point of the bedrock is seen. It's a mystical place but to fully benefit you need to touch that stone. Go on,' she urged. 'Now close your eyes and make a romantic wish.'

'Really,' Colenso protested.

'Go on. It has to be romantic, mind.' Seeing the woman wouldn't be satisfied until she did, Colenso closed her eyes and wished.

'You don't really believe in that myth, do you?' she asked as they made their way carefully down the path.

'If a romantic wish is made before marriage, it will be granted,' Mara insisted.

*

Colenso remembered the woman's words each time she visited the post office. But by the end of the summer, when the had sun lost its heat and the leaves on the trees had turned from green to gold, she still hadn't heard from Kitto and gave it up for the myth she'd suspected. As for the reason Kitto hadn't responded, well, it didn't take a genius to work that out.

'The tourists have gone home and it's time we moved on,' Mara said, returning from her discussion with the kumpania.

'Are you sure?' Colenso asked, noting the woman's pallor. Not travelling over the summer had done her good but she was still frailer than she'd been when Colenso had first known her. 'Wouldn't you rather stay here?' The woman shook her head.

'No, we always visit the fair at St Just for Samhain.'

Samhain! Colenso's heart flipped, but Mara was continuing. 'The festival's important, marking the end of the year and …' her voice faltered, her eyes taking on that faraway look that had become more prevalent of late.

'Mammwynn said it was also the beginning,' she ventured.

'And she was right,' Mara sighed. Then her voice became brisk again. 'We'll be meeting up with Big Al and everyone. Jago's gone for more stock and says he'll join us there. Did he pay you before he left?'

'No, he didn't,' Colenso frowned. He hadn't paid her since Truro and she was down to her last few coppers. Hoping to tempt Mara's appetite, she'd been buying potatoes and fish, although it was indicative of the woman's increasing frailty that she hadn't noticed. Now the weather was getting colder and she needed to buy a shawl. She'd tackle him as soon as she met up with him in St Just.

As they made their way out of Marazion, Colenso looked out over the sea. What a lovely summer it had been. She'd met so many people, explored the shore, visited the Mount. All too soon, they were turning away from the place she'd come to love and were making their way slowly up the hill. It wasn't long before Mara began to tire and Colenso insisted she rest in the van. Unusually the woman didn't protest, and even when they turned along a lane that was flat and ran parallel to the coast, she remained inside.

As they passed through the village of Heamoor and onto the road to St Just, Colenso stared around at the changing countryside. Here the land was mainly cultivated, with a scattering of tumbledown houses which, despite their sad state, appeared to be lived in.

Further on, the working tin mines with their leats and reservoir reminded Colenso of the works at Poltesco. Her thoughts turned to Kitto but she pushed them firmly away. He'd had all summer to write and hadn't. She felt as abandoned as the old mines up on the moor.

'Right, jump up, we're turning off here,' Mara said, jolting Colenso out of her reverie as she emerged from the van.

'But the others are continuing this way,' she protested, gesturing to the vans ahead.

'Well, we're not.'

Hearing the firmness in the woman's voice, Colenso knew better than to argue and climbed onto the seat beside her. Although she looked refreshed from her rest, Mara seemed thoughtful as they plodded higher up a narrow lane with bright-green boggy moorland spreading out on either side. Finally, they came to a tiny chapel and Mara pulled on the reins.

'Stay here,' she ordered as she clambered down.

'But …' Colenso began.

'A few moments privacy, that's all I ask,' the woman interrupted, and there was something in her expression that forbade further argument.

Colenso watched as Mara slowly climbed down and made her way inside the granite building. It was a few minutes before she emerged, then instead of coming back to the van, she seemed to disappear behind it. Colenso was about to jump down to check she was all right when the woman popped up again. To her astonishment when she climbed back up beside her, the woman's face and hands were soaking wet.

'Blessed by the holy water and left a cloutie on the tree,' she grinned, holding up her ripped scarf. 'Probably too late, but it made me feel better. The veil is lifting.' Although Colenso looked askance, Mara ignored her, calling instead for Ears to walk on.

They eventually rejoined the road and, after travelling a short distance, saw the tall granite tower of a church rising above the rooftops of St Just. After passing through the triangular market square they turned into the Plen an Gwarry where, to Colenso's relief, she saw the kumpania was already camped with other vans and wagons alongside them. Mara had been strangely jubilant after her visit to the chapel, and Colenso wanted to discuss her peculiar behaviour with Sarah, who she hoped would understand these things.

But she didn't get the opportunity, for Mara was strangely insistent that Colenso sit with her after she'd retired to bed.

'Hold my hand,' she whispered.

'Are you all right, Mara?' Colenso asked, worried she'd overdone things.

'Never better,' she replied. 'Thank you for today and for your company.' Colenso turned to her in surprise, for the woman was not given to sentiment, but Mara had already closed her eyes, a smile of contentment on her face.

Pulling the cover over her, Colenso felt a rush of tenderness for her friend and was glad she'd conceded to her wishes to visit the chapel. Knowing Mara, after a night's rest she'd be rushing around getting things ready for her dukkering, Colenso thought, climbing into her own bed.

*

When Colenso woke in the early hours of the morning, everything felt unusually still. She glanced over and saw Mara lying in the same position, the smile still on her lips.

It was then she realized the woman wasn't merely sleeping. 'Oh Mara,' she wailed.

Chapter 25

With tears streaming down her cheeks, Colenso watched as the orange flames licking at the wood turned into a raging inferno, devouring the beautiful little van that had become her home.

'We should have stayed in Marazion,' she wailed. Sarah shook her head.

'It wouldn't have made any difference, it was her time, love. She should have let go weeks since but she made herself hang on till Samhain. Seen the veil in her ball, see. Knew it was a sign.' Colenso nodded, remembering that evening when Mara, upset after consulting her crystal, had fled to the water's edge.

Colenso looked back at the fire. It was dying down now, a blackened pile of wood the only testament of a life lived.

'But why did they have to burn her van with her body inside it?' she cried.

''Tis our way, love. Come with nothing, leave with nothing. The remains of ash will be returned to the ground. Her old body ain't no use where she's gone, and it was her wish that she be set free under the trees. Fancied thinking of her earthly form as a bluebell swaying in the breeze.'

Sarah's laugh came out as a sob and it was Colenso's turn to comfort her.

She stared around, noting for the first time that it wasn't only the kumpania that had turned out to send Mara on her way. The whole of the fair had gathered, heads bowed as they paid their respects. As the fire gave a final crackle, Titan's wife bent and laid a nosegay beside it, and Colenso had to bite her lip from crying out loud when she saw it had been fashioned from Mara's favourite herbs and flowers.

'Everyone loved her,' Sarah murmured.

'They did,' Solomon her husband agreed.

'Oh look,' Sarah grinned, pointing to a ray of sunshine breaking through the thick cloud. 'She's letting us know she's arrived safely.'

At that precise moment, Ears, who'd been standing watching, gave a distressed whinny before keeling over beside the burnt remains of his mistress. 'Even old Ears,' she sighed, pulling Colenso back as she moved towards the pony. 'He's gone too, faithful to the end.'

Titan, who'd been standing with his wife, signalled to a couple of the men.

'Better cover him over before some wise guy sells him for glue and pet food.' He turned to Colenso. 'She was the best,' he muttered, his eyes bright with tears. 'Let us know if you need anything.'

'Thank you,' she whispered. 'I don't know what I'll do now.'

'Well, for a start you're coming with us for a hot drink,' Sarah said. 'Ain't that right, Sol?

'I'll be along soon. Best help the others,' he replied, limping over to where the men had begun digging. With a final look at the burnt remains and the loyal pony lying beside them, Colenso let herself be led away.

She sat in Sarah's van, which was similar though slightly bigger and more cluttered than Mara's had been, sipping her drink whilst trying to come to terms with events. Everything had happened so quickly.

'If only I'd done more for her,' she cried.

'Oh love, if you only knew how much joy you brought her these past few months. Said when she first saw you, she recognized a lost soul, just as she'd been. Helping you blossom lent purpose to her life,' Sarah said. 'Especially once she'd seen the veil and knew her time was coming.'

'But she looked so happy and was smiling, I ...' her voice trailed away.

'Expect her lover came for her,' Sarah nodded. 'She were ready and waiting.'

'But she was acting so strange on the way here, insisting we stop by a chapel, even though I've never known her visit one before.'

'It were the blessed well she really wanted to see, to leave a cloutie and make one last wish for her heart's desire. Not many people know where that well is these days and she wanted to respect that by letting the rest of us go on ahead. She made her peace and it would appear her wish was granted. You helped her do that, so be thankful not sad. It was her heart's desire to pass at Samhain and she did. Said it would befit the ending of this life and the starting of a new.' Colenso felt warmth begin to seep into her body, for wasn't that exactly what Mammwynn had wanted too? She took another sip of her drink, almost spluttering when she saw the crystal ball on the shelf.

'That's Mara's,' she gasped.

'It is,' Sarah smiled, her eyes glistening with unshed tears. 'She gave it to me before we left Marazion, along with her cards and little tent. Knew she hadn't long left and began dishing out her things.'

'You mean she gave her things away before she ... before ...' A lump rose in her throat, she shook her head.

'That's the way we do things. Give our prized belongings to those we love and leave the rest to be burnt along with our earthly body. We don't carry any worldly possessions into our afterlife, see? She gave Titan her best cups and saucers, Al her glasses, Tinks her sloe gin, and this she left for you,' she said, lifting up Mara's basket.

'Oh,' Colenso gasped, taking it from her with trembling hands and staring at the items piled neatly inside it. 'I ... I'm ...'

'Not ready to look,' Sarah finished for her. 'Well, no hurry, love. Wait until you've come to terms with things a bit. Look, you've had a nasty shock so let's have something a bit stronger,' she added, jumping up and pouring pink liquid into their empty mugs. 'She gave me some of her gin as well, so let's drink a toast. To Mara, my best friend in this world and hopefully the next,' she said, raising her mug.

'To Mara,' Colenso echoed. They sat for a few moments, each lost in their own thoughts. 'How did you get to know Mara?' she asked, realizing she really didn't know much about the woman she'd been living with.

'We met when she took to the road after losing her

beloved. She was bereft, as you can imagine, and came to me for comfort. I have the sight too, you see. That's why she wants me to carry on her dukkering. She were very good at it.'

'She didn't always get it right,' Colenso murmured, thinking of her prediction that Kitto would continue corresponding. A loud rapping on the window interrupted her musing.

'Come in, Al,' Sarah said as his head appeared through the open top of the stable door.

'We're just toasting Mara, want some?' she invited, holding up the bottle.

'Later perhaps. Just thought you should know we won't be opening the fair today out of respect. We'll start up tomorrow, then stay an extra day to keep the locals happy. Sol says you're moving on today.' Sarah nodded.

'We've no heart for the fair here now so we'll start making our way east. Sol likes to spend the winter somewhere drier. The Cornish mist gets into his bones and then we both suffer,' she said, raising a brow theatrically.

'What about you?' he asked, turning to Colenso.

'I, er, don't know. Stay with the fair, I suppose.'

'Penzance is our last stop after this, then we disband for the winter,' he frowned.

'Disband?' Colenso muttered. 'Oh, I hadn't realized.'

'Probably best if she comes with us, then. We can see her safely to Penzance,' Sarah told him. She turned to Colenso. 'It will be easier to make your way home from there.'

'There's nothing for me to go back for,' she sighed. Seeing Kitto with the schoolmistress would be more than she could bear. As for her father and the Ferret … the very thought sent shudders sliding down her spine.

'Whatever you decide, you'll need some money,' Big Al told her, passing her some notes.

'But why would you give me money?'

'To tide you over. Can't live on fresh air, girl. Besides, Jago hasn't seen fit to show up and I bet he didn't pay you for working on the Panam all summer.'

'No,' she sighed. 'He said he'd settle up with me here.'

'Well, you'll soon find something else, pretty girl like you. Probably be easier than when you was pretending to be a boy, Bonbon,' he grinned.

'Mara said you looked out for me, so thank you,' she murmured, remembering her manners.

'My pleasure,' he said, tipping his hand to his thatch.

Sarah followed him out of the door and, as they stood talking on the step, Colenso's thoughts were running amok. How could Jago take her for a fool? Now she had no job or money of her own. Why, she hadn't even realized the fair was disbanding. Although, now she came to think of it, Titan had said some of them spent the winter in brick. Where would she go? What would she do?

When Sarah returned and saw Colenso's bleak expression, she sat down beside her and patted her arm.

'Perhaps you should see what Mara's left you?' she suggested, bending down and lifting the basket onto Colenso's lap. Under Mara's red scarf with its jagged tear were her golden hooped earrings.

'My, you'll look lovely in those,' Sarah exclaimed. 'They'll go a treat with that green outfit. What else have you got?'

262

'Jago's books,' Colenso cried. 'Oh, and there's a note inside.'

Dear Bonbon,

Don't feel guilty about taking these. If my hunch is correct, that scoundrel Jago won't be reappearing with the money he owes you. You seemed to enjoy making the confections, so use the recipes to your advantage. Whenever you pick Mother Nature's bounty or hear the wind whispering in the leaves, think of me and know you made my last months on earth happier than I ever could have wished.

Your friend,
Mara

As another lump rose in her throat, Colenso blinked back her hot tears and delved into the basket again. There was Mara's fine, lacy shawl, and underneath were the beautiful red shoes she'd admired in the shop window in Bodmin.

'Oh, my goodness, I don't know what to say,' she gulped, running her fingers over the soft leather.

'Mara bought those when you went to the post office with Titan. I remember she was glowing with glee when she showed them to me.'

'I had no idea,' Colenso said, shaking her head.

'Course not, she wanted them to be a surprise. Gawd knows you need something to lighten your life. What will you do now, love?'

'I honestly don't know. I'll have to wait until my mind clears then have a good think.'

*

Having insisted Colenso spend the night in their van, Sarah and Solomon dropped her off on the outskirts of Penzance. She was wearing the golden hoops in her ears and, knowing she'd be seeking employment, had ensured her green outfit was looking presentable.

'Good luck,' they called. She watched until they were a speck in the distance then, hefting her basket over her arm, made her way towards the town. The first thing she needed to do was find a job and then somewhere to stay. It all seemed so daunting, and already she was missing Mara. For all her funny sayings and grumpy ways, she had been good company and a true friend.

She'd just started walking when she was almost overcome by the smell of sulphur coming from a huge tin-smelting works that mixed with the pungent odour from the tannery next door. What a welcome to Penzance, she thought, hurrying as fast as she could towards the sea.

Breathing the bracing air deeply, she headed towards the quay, mentally listing her talents. She could sew, cook, fashion serpentine. Serpentine, that was it. Wherrytown was on the other side of the town. She remembered the Ferret saying the finished works were shipped out of the harbour here, so surely they'd be looking for people to finish the stone.

Feeling optimistic, she walked briskly, passing the fishing boats, barges and lifeboat, then on along the promenade until she came to a gloomy-looking building bearing the name Wherrytown Serpentine Works. Gathering her courage, she marched inside. Although the men glanced curiously in her direction, nobody stopped what they were doing. The place was very large, dusty and noisy, and it took her a while to locate the works manager's office. Boldly, she knocked on the door.

'Enter,' a voice boomed. Squaring her shoulders, she walked into the room and smiled. A man of middle years, wearing an ill-fitting jacket, looked up and frowned over the top of his round spectacles.

'Good morning, sir,' she said. 'I've come about a job.'

'Tavern's two doors down,' he snapped, staring her up and down before returning his attention to the papers on his desk.

'You misunderstand, sir. I've come about fashioning the serpentine.' He looked up in surprise, snatched off his glasses and sat back in his chair.

'You are a qualified turner or polisher?'

'Well no, but I have turned trinkets for the tourists and …'

'Character?'

'Very good,' she assured him. He let out a long sigh.

'I mean can you furnish me with a testimonial from your last place of employment?'

'Well no, sir. You see …'

'I thought not,' he snapped. 'This is a respectable establishment, Miss, er,' he waved his hand in the air. 'We employ men with families to provide for, not some woman of dubious nature.'

'I'll have you …'

'Shut the door on your way out,' he ordered, cutting her short. Placing his glasses back on, he stared pointedly back down at his papers.

'I pity your workers. No wonder they all look so miserable,' she snapped.

A woman of dubious nature, indeed, she fumed, stamping her way back outside and turning back the way she'd come. Rain was falling in great fat splodges and, with the day wearing on, she needed to find somewhere to stay. Some of the money Big Al had given her would buy a bed in a modest boarding house for a couple of nights, giving her time to find employment. Always supposing someone would engage her without a character.

As she passed the plush-looking Queens Hotel it began to rain but, realizing a room there would be way beyond her means, turned up the adjacent street lined with tall, elegant houses. Obviously some people had money to be able to afford such grand places, she thought, turning into another lane which led into the town.

The appetizing aroma of hot pies made her stomach rumble, reminding her she hadn't eaten since breakfast. Delving into the basket for her money, she gasped as someone thrust her hard against the wall. She just had time to glimpse a man with black teeth and foul-smelling breath, before the notes were snatched from her hand. Then he was gone, footsteps echoing on the cobbles.

'Stop, thief,' she called, but nobody took any notice. Shocked, shaken and berating her stupidity, she slumped down in the doorway, pulling her shawl around her. Sheltered from the driving rain, she sat there trying to collect her thoughts. Suddenly the door flew open, tipping her backwards.

'Be on your way. We don't want riff-raff darkening our doors.' Colenso stared at the irate man. He looked hot and sweaty, his clothes covered by a large apron.

'I was only …' she began, but he stood there shaking his fist until she got wearily to her feet and continued her journey.

Light-headed through tiredness and lack of food, she wandered aimlessly around the wet streets, not knowing what to do. Darkness was gathering and the lamplighter was going about his job.

'Hey darling, want to earn some money?' She spun round to see a sailor coming out of a nearby alehouse. He was clearly the worse for wear as he staggered and weaved his way towards her. 'Just been paid and looking for a bit of fun,' he leered. Eyes widening as realization hit her, she turned and fled down yet another lane. However, she soon realized her mistake. Here women, their clothes revealing more than they hid, were intent on parting seamen from their money as they plied their trade. Hastily averting her eyes, she ran back the way she'd come. She'd rather go hungry than resort to that.

Chapter 26

The rain was still falling in torrents, and the wind blowing in from the sea carried the tang of salt, making Colenso feel thirsty as well as hungry. Finding herself outside the tall church she had seen earlier and too exhausted to go any further, Colenso decided to seek refuge inside. However, the big wooden door was locked and so, biting back tears of frustration, she slumped down in the narrow porch. She shivered as an owl hooted then saw a pale flash as it swooped low in front of her. There was a piercing scream followed by an eerie silence. Pulling her shawl tighter around her, she realized it was going to be a long night. How could she have been so stupid as to pull her money from her basket in broad daylight? Grief must have dulled her senses, she thought, trying not to look at the lichen-covered gravestones that loomed luminously out of the darkness. Penniless and homeless, the threat of the workhouse or worse was fast becoming a reality.

The clock on the tower struck midnight, its mournful tones sounding loud in the quietude of night. She tried to formulate a plan but images of Kitto rose in her mind instead. Surprisingly, they no longer filled her with joy. He'd obviously had a change of heart and didn't care enough even to reply to her letter let alone follow her. Never would she put herself in such a vulnerable position again, she thought, her heart pricking with pain. She'd lock her emotions into a cage. No longer would she torture her mind, reflecting on what might have been. Somehow, she'd make a new life, though where and how, she had no idea.

She must have fallen asleep, for the next thing she knew the sky was lightening to grey. Mercifully, the rain had stopped and the grass smelled fresh, glistening like a carpet of diamonds. Stretching her stiff limbs, she picked up the basket and got to her feet. Onward and upward, she told herself as she made her way down the path and out onto the street again. Her stomach rumbled loudly and she thought longingly of the bokoli she'd shared with Mara. Dear Mara, she hoped her lover had come for her and that they were happy together in the afterlife.

Being early, the streets were deserted apart from the sewage cart collecting the night soil. Holding her nose, she hurried on until she came to the town with its sprawl of shops. She looked around, hoping to find one that was open, although how she was going to purchase anything, she had no idea.

The tempting smell of baking lured her to the back of a shop where two men were busy taking loaves out of a huge oven.

'I'm seeking work, do you have any positions?' she asked, eyeing the bread hungrily.

'We don't employ vagrants here,' a woman said, appearing from a door behind.

'But I'm not ...' Colenso began.

'Be off. Scat,' she said, shooing her away with her cloth.

Vagrant indeed, Colenso fumed as she made her way further up the street. Hearing the sound of hooves, she turned to see a man driving a donkey cart laden with a milk churn, ladle clanking on the sides. Her mouth watered and she raised her arm to hail him before remembering she had no money.

Realizing she needed to concentrate on getting a position, she crossed the road to the raised pavement where the better shops were. As she stood on the granite paving deciding which way to go, her nose twitched. There was an acrid smell coming from the premises in front of her. She tried the handle then, when it didn't turn, peered through the window but couldn't see anyone, only rows of jars lined up along a counter.

With the smell of burning growing ever stronger, she hurried down the side passage where smoke was pouring out from an open door. Rushing inside, she blinked in the steam-filled room then spotted a huge copper pot, its contents boiling over and spilling onto the range. Snatching up a cloth, she carefully removed the pan from the heat and set it in the sink, where it sizzled and spluttered as the seething mass began to settle. Whatever it had been was black and beyond saving.

A snort followed by a snore made her jump, and spinning round she noticed an old man asleep in a chair in the corner of the room. As the smoke cleared, she saw he had a long white beard that rested on his chest. He looked so peaceful she didn't like to wake him. Instead she walked around, taking in the huge cone of sugar on the cupboard, funny long thin tables that appeared to be made of tin, a strange-looking roller. Shelving housed different moulds and rows of little bottles, some brown others clear. Utensils hung from nails, and two large hooks were set incongruously on one wall.

'Can I help you?' a voice asked as a man appeared in the doorway. He was carrying a sack over his shoulder, which he dumped unceremoniously on the floor as his hazel eyes surveyed her. He was sporting a white apron over his twill shirt and looked to be in his late twenties.

'I smelt burning and saw a cloud of smoke but couldn't find anyone,' Colenso told him. 'Whatever was in that pot was boiling over.' She gestured to the sink. 'I'm afraid it's made a dreadful mess of your stove.' At another snore from the corner, the younger man sighed.

'That was sugar syrup and you have clearly saved us from disaster, Miss …?'

'Carne, sir. Colenso Carne.'

'Well, Miss Colenso Carne, you have my undying grati-tude. I am Garren Goss and the man asleep at his post is my father, the proprietor here. We were making rock and ran out of supplies. He was meant to be watching the mixture while I went out to the store cupboard, but obviously he had to rest his eyes as he calls it. Probably be asleep for a while now.' Although he stood shaking his head, Colenso could see he was clearly fond of his aged parent.

'Glad to have been of help. I gather you run a confec-tioner's here then,' she added, remembering the jars on the counter in the front of the shop. He nodded.

'Father and Mother ran it quite successfully until she was taken ill.' His eyes clouded with painful memories.

'I'm sorry. You're clearly busy so I'll leave you to it,' she said, picking up her basket and heading for the door.

'I was about to make some tea and toast,' he said, shaking himself back to the present. 'Would you care to join me, Miss Carne? It's the least I can do under the circumstances.' The mention of food set her stomach growling and she grinned ruefully.

'Thank you, it's quite a while since I last ate,' she explained. His eyes lit up, gold flecks turning his eyes jade, but as he stood looking at her his smile turned to a frown.

'Perhaps you would like to clean up while I prepare everything. You'll find the, er, outhouse and pump in the yard.' How rude, she thought, then following his gaze saw her skirt was stained and crumpled, her boots coated in mud and goodness knows what else. No wonder the woman at the bakery had thought her a vagrant.

'Thank you, yes,' she said quickly. Ashamed to be seen in such a state, she hurried outside.

The yard was enclosed by a limewashed stone wall, a wooden structure which was clearly the privy at the bottom, while a pump stood on a slab of granite nearby. She set about making herself as respectable as possible before, feeling refreshed and ravenous, she went back indoors. The smell of toasting bread greeted her, setting her stomach rumbling again.

'Do take a seat,' he invited, setting down a plate piled high with slices of browned bread. There was no tablecloth but the little round table was now set with china and cutlery. As she sat down, he began pouring tea from a brown pot. 'Forgive the basic ware, Miss Carne. Mother would have had her best china laid out, but regrettably she was laid out herself earlier in the year.'

'Sorry for your loss,' she murmured.

'Mercifully she went quickly, and life has to go on. Although Father hasn't really recovered from the shock. Anyway, here's your tea,' he said. 'Help yourself to milk and sugar.' Colenso stared at the steaming earthenware mug and thought she'd never seen anything so wonderful in all her life. She was so hungry, she finished her toast in minutes and eagerly accepted another slice. It was only when they'd eaten and had drained the pot dry that Garren turned to her.

'Your accent tells me you're Cornish but not from Penzance, so what brings you to these parts?'

'It's a long story,' she sighed. 'Suffice to say I find myself without a roof over my head and no job with which to buy food. I am indebted to your kindness, sir.'

'Garren, please,' he corrected. A loud snort emanated from the corner. 'Father's well away,' he smiled, looking towards the old man. 'He's really too old to be helping in the shop. Since Mother died he's lost all interest, losing himself in sleep. Still, at least I can keep an eye on him – when I'm not replenishing stocks, that is,' he grinned. 'Mind you, it's taking me ten times longer to do even the most basic chores. I can't be in here making the sweets and serving in the shop at the same time.'

'So this is a workshop as well as a kitchen, then,' she said, the strange tin tables and equipment now making sense. 'And now you'll have to make more syrup for the rock,' she said, nodding towards the big pan in the sink. He stared at her in surprise.

'You know about such things?' he asked, his eyes widening.

'I spent the summer working on the Panam at the fair.

Jago, the journeyman, sometimes took me with him to collect supplies and I saw how rock and lollipops were made,' she smiled, remembering her time with Karla.

'And judging by your expression you clearly enjoyed it, but you spoke in the past tense, so what happened?'

'The woman I lived with died then the fair disbanded for the winter,' she sighed. He sat looking at her for a long moment.

'Well, Miss Carne, I need an assistant who knows how to make sweets and you are in need of a job so perhaps we can help each other. I can't pay much but there is a little box room next to the workshop, which you'd be welcome to use. Father and I live upstairs so you wouldn't be disturbed.'

'That would be the answer to my prayers, Mr, er, Garren,' she cried, her spirits lifting only to fall when she remembered the derision of the manager at the Wherrytown Works. 'But don't you require a character?'

'I think I'm a good judge of character, Miss Carne, and you look good to me,' he grinned. 'Why don't we give it a trial of one month? If either of us isn't happy during that time we can revise the situation.' He held out his hand and, unable to believe her good fortune, she shook it firmly. There was another snort from the corner followed by gentle snoring, making them both laugh.

'I think Father will be asleep for quite a while yet, so why don't I show you around?'

'Oh, yes please,' she replied, a quiver of excitement tingling her spine.

She followed him past a staircase and through a little arched door that led into the shop itself. The walls were lined with wooden shelves with drawers beneath them, their golden handles gleaming in the gloomy interior. On the counter was a set of brass scales, tiny weights in a tin alongside and the empty jars she'd seen earlier. On the shelf behind were trays of glistening sweets waiting to be decanted into them.

'These will go in the windows when they're filled, but luckily we haven't been that busy of late,' he explained, pointing from the jars to the bays with their tiny panes of glass. Luckily? What a strange thing to say, Colenso thought. Seeing her puzzled look, he grimaced.

'I mean obviously I want more custom, but with Father the way he is … well, those that have the money to buy confectionery expect prompt service and …' he shrugged. Colenso nodded and stared around the room, gathering an overall impression. Everywhere was clean but clinical, and the dim interior was hardly conducive to tempting people through the door. She could see how a woman's touch could make it look more inviting, but guessed everything had changed when Mrs Goss had died.

'How do you serve the sweets?' she asked.

'Why, in twists of these,' Garren replied, holding up a pile of thin, plain paper. 'Although Mother used to tie ribbon around if it were purchased as a gift. Now, I think I can hear Father moving about so let's go back through and I'll introduce you.'

Colenso followed him back through to the kitchen.

'Father, this is Miss Colenso Carne. She has kindly agreed to come and work for us. My father, Edwin Goss,' Garren said.

'Didn't hear you arrive, where did you spring from?' he frowned, staring at her from under his white bushy brows.

'You fell asleep whilst the syrup was boiling, Father. Luckily Colenso here smelt it burning or we could have had a nasty fire in here,' Garren explained.

'Only rested my eyes for a few minutes. I am old, you know,' the man muttered defensively.

'I do know, Father, and now Colenso can take over some of your duties,' Garren told him. The man scratched his head, and it was evident he wasn't sure if he really wanted to relinquish any.

'Of course, I'll appreciate any advice you can give me,' she told him. Immediately the man's eyes brightened.

'Taken me years to learn everything, it has,' he told her. 'Make everything proper here. None of that bulking out the others do. Everything is pure, well, apart from those colours,' he said, pointing to the little bottles. 'Some come from coal tar waste, they do, and can be toxic for those who don't know what they're doing.'

'Quite,' Garren said quickly. 'That's why I thought I'd make the confections while Colenso takes care of the shop. Now, where are your things?' he asked, turning back to her.

'Here,' she said reaching for her basket.

'That all you got?' the old man asked. 'Where are all your clothes?'

'These are the only ones I possess,' Colenso told him.

'Well, you'd best get on and make some new ones. We get a good class of person in here and they expect to be served by someone looking neat and tidy at the very least. I ain't having you serving in my confectionary looking like a scarecrow.'

'Father, really.'

'No, it's all right, Garren. Mr Goss does have a point,' she sighed. 'No one will want to be served by me looking like this,' she said, gesturing to her tattered green attire. Then, hefting the basket over her arm, she made for the door. She was about to step outside when she heard the old man chuckle.

'Come back and sit yourself down. Likes a bit of spirit in a girl, I do, livens up the day. My Meggie were like a frosted fruit too. Sweet on the outside but with bite in the centre,' he sighed, the light going out of his eyes. Not wishing to upset him, Colenso let herself be led back to the chair she'd been sitting on earlier.

'Good, that's decided. You're staying,' Garren said, looking relieved. 'Now I'll show you to your room.'

'Not so fast, son. Don't suppose you thought to test her capabilities.' The man turned to Colenso. 'If you really want to work then you can begin now,' he said, staring Colenso straight in the eye. 'That pot isn't going to wash itself and look at the state of the stove.' Knowing he was throwing down the gauntlet, she set down her basket and went over to the sink.

'It's a good job I'm not wearing my best clothes or they'd be ruined,' she quipped, snatching up the cloth.

'She'll do, son,' the old man chuckled. 'Mind you, I'd hate to see standards slip, my Meggie always looked fresh as a daisy when she served in the confectioner's.'

Chapter 27

Tired but happy, Colenso sank onto the little daybed, pulling the blanket over her. The room had been used as a store but, after clearing sacks and jars out of the way, Garren had apologized for the lack of furnishings and left her to settle in. It must have been fate that led her here, for hadn't Mammwynn always declared that destiny dictated?

She yawned and stretched out, running her fingers through her hair and was gratified to find it now almost reached her neck. After the dramas of the previous night, this seemed like paradise, and she could hardly believe her good fortune as she thought back over the day.

After the old man had gone upstairs to rest his eyes, Garren had set about making more sugar syrup while telling her about his plans for building the business up again. She'd helped by washing down the sides of the pan with the brush, then winced as he'd put his finger in to test the boiling concoction.

'They've got sugar thermometers in America but regrettably they're very expensive. Still, who knows? One day,' he grinned. 'Now, let's get this poured.' She watched as he tipped the mixture out on the tin tables, which he explained were called cooling tables.

Then, by the light of the lantern, they worked together colouring, flavouring and kneading the mixture before cutting it into lengths. When she'd told him how Karla had formed them into crooks, he'd agreed they looked more decorative but explained that straight sticks could be packed into jars.

'However, it's good that you take an interest in what you're doing. I can see you are going to be a real asset to the business, Colenso,' he told her.

Now, with his words of praise ringing in her ears, she closed her eyes. She was just planning how she was going to help Garren set out the little shop, when there was a shuffling noise outside. Then came a rap on her door. She sat bolt upright, pulling the shawl around her shoulders. Garren had assured her she wouldn't be disturbed and she'd thought him genuine, but then he was a man. Recalling the degrading sights of the day before, she shuddered. There came another, more insistent knocking. Well, if he thought she was that kind of woman, he could think again.

Jumping out of bed, she opened the door a tiny crack.

'Oh,' she cried when she saw the old man standing there, a bundle in his hands.

'I'm sorry to bother you, my dear, but I can't help thinking I was rather rude earlier,' he said, smiling ruefully.

'No, you were quite right, Mr Goss. I can't serve customers looking like a scarecrow. Luckily Garren has offered to loan me an apron,' she told him.

'Well, I can do better than that,' he said, grinning widely as he held out his offering. 'I bought this for my Meggie's birthday but she died before … I thought perhaps you could use it,' he said, thrusting the parcel into her arms before shuffling away.

'Thank you, Mr Goss,' she called but he'd already disappeared into the darkness.

Impatient to see what he'd given her, she lit the candle. Pulling back the brown paper she saw a length of material, its vibrant pink reminding her of the thrift that garlanded the cliffs back home. Running her fingers over the soft cloth, she could visualize the dress she would make. Then she remembered the red shoes and delving into her basket brought them out and held them next to the material. They toned perfectly, the bright colours reflecting her excitement. 'Oh Mara, if you could see me now,' she whispered. Of course, it could have been coincidence that made the flame flicker, but she knew in her heart that it wasn't.

Colenso was up bright and early the next morning and, covering her stained clothes with the big white apron, let herself out of her little room. Hearing pans and spoons clattering in the workshop, she let herself straight into the shop. Humming happily, she filled the jars with the sweets, marvelling at all the different types and inhaling their aromas. As well as the bullseyes, barley twists, Nelson's buttons and the rose rock she was familiar with, there were also confections smelling of acid, peppermint and aniseed, reminding her of the herb Mammwynn used to make a tisane when she'd had a cough. Others were little jewel-like confections, their multi-coloured hues like the stained-glass windows in a church. Taking the filled jars over to the little bay windows on either side of the door, she set about arranging them in a way she hoped would catch the attention of passers-by.

She was standing outside, trying to judge the effect, when a smartly dressed woman came out of the adjoining shop.

'I hope you're going to clean your frontage,' she said haughtily. 'We pride ourselves on keeping our facades pristine, and frankly yours lowers the tone of the place.' Nodding curtly, she disappeared back inside. And good morning to you too, Colenso thought. Staring down at the ground in front of her, she saw that it was covered in mud and mess. Remembering she'd seen a besom in the yard the previous day, she hurried to retrieve it, and had just finished sweeping the muck into the gutter when Garren appeared in the doorway.

'I don't expect you to do that,' he told her, taking the broom from her. 'Goodness, that's a fine display,' he added, spotting the jars through the window. 'Looks just like a rainbow. If that doesn't draw in the customers then I don't know what will.'

'Glad you approve,' she replied,

'I came to tell you I've just made breakfast, so let's go and eat.' Before she could reply, he was heading down the side passage and she had no choice other than to follow. Inside the workshop-cum-kitchen the aroma of toast mingling with the smell of oranges and lemons made her mouth water.

'Got to keep up supplies,' Garren said, gesturing to the sweets he'd just made. 'I call them St Clements Drops,' he added. 'My speciality is stuffed dates. Popular with the genteel ladies but time-consuming as they need making up every day. Still, got to keep everyone happy. Now, help yourself to toast.'

'Is your father not joining us?' Colenso asked, taking

281

a seat at the little table. He handed her a mug of tea then shook his head.

'Said he had a late night and needed to rest his eyes. I heard him moving about his room, pulling out drawers and muttering to himself long after I'd retired. Goodness knows what he was doing.'

'I think he might have been looking for the material he brought me. He suggested I make something to wear in the shop.'

'Don't tell me he visited your room?' Garren groaned.

'Well yes, he said he was worried he might have been a bit rude earlier.'

'A bit,' Garren exclaimed then shook his head. 'I'll have to have a word with my father about propriety.'

'Please don't, he was merely being kind. And he was right, I do need to look decent, although I shall have to wait until I can purchase cotton and scissors. I didn't bring anything with me.'

'No, I noticed you were travelling light,' he grinned. 'Leave it with me and I'll see what I can do, although I'm not in a position to advance you any wages.'

'Good, because I'm not in a position to accept charity,' she retorted.

'Father was right, you do have Mother's bite,' he grinned. 'Now, if you've finished eating, I think it's time we opened up,' he added, getting to his feet. Scooping the sweets he'd made earlier into a jar, he led the way through to the shop.

Although Colenso knew she should be grateful for his generosity, she was fed up with taking things from other people. She couldn't wait to receive her wages and start paying her way.

'This is where we keep the cash,' he said, taking out a little tin box from a drawer under the counter. 'We start with a £2 float so that we can give change to anyone who requires some. All the prices are written on the labels, as you've probably already seen. Now to the scales.' He picked up one of the little brass weights and set it down on one side, then using a serving scoop, dropped some of the orange and lemon sweets onto the other until they balanced. He then tipped them onto a square of paper, brought up the corners and twisted them together at the top.

'On the Panam, we used to pop sweets into a cone so that they were all ready to hand over.'

'I'm sure that was all right for a fair, but you'll find the customers here like to see their sweets being weighed in front of them. Protocol, I think it's called. Of course, barley-sugar twists and rock sticks you can sell individually.'

'Of course,' she replied, but he had turned away and was frowning at the wall behind the counter.

'Good grief,' he murmured, snatching down a black cloth. Immediately the room was flooded with light reflected from the windows. 'We covered that mirror out of respect when Mother passed, and completely forgot about it. Now, if you'd like to turn the sign around to open, I'll go and make more sweets.'

'More?' she gasped, staring at all the full jars.

'Got to keep supplies up. Nothing worse than a sweetshop without sweets,' he grinned. 'I'll leave you to it. Call me if you need any help.'

Colenso turned the sign then, with a final check that all the jars were neatly aligned, took herself back behind the counter. As she stepped in front of the mirror, she nearly did a double-take. The woman staring back scarcely resembled the one she remembered. Her eyes sparkled, her skin still bore the tan of a summer spent in the fresh air, while her hair curled softly beneath the green scarf, the golden hoops shining as they caught the light. Why, if it wasn't for her torn hem and stains on her blouse, she'd look quite presentable, she thought happily.

The ringing of the little bell interrupted her musing and, spinning round, Colenso smiled as an elegant woman in her early twenties entered. She perused the jars before asking: 'Do you have any of those delectable dates? Mother so adores them.' The woman's smile turned to a frown as Colenso tried to remember seeing any.

'Ah, good morning, Miss Veryan,' Garren said, appearing from the workshop. 'I have just this moment finished making them.'

'That is most opportune,' she replied, a dazzling smile replacing her frown.

'As if I would let my favourite customer down, Miss Veryan. Your mother is keeping well, I trust?'

'If her grumbling is anything to go by, she is hale and hearty,' the woman replied, with a roll of her eyes. While they exchanged pleasantries, Garren weighed out the dates and wrapped them.

'Here you are, Miss Veryan. I have added an extra one for yourself,' he told her.

'How kind you are, Mr Goss,' she said, handing him a coin. 'Good day to you.' Without a glance in Colenso's direction, she glided from the shop.

'Well,' Colenso muttered.

'She is a good customer so I often add a little treat. But not for everyone, you understand, or I would soon be out of business,' he replied, completely missing her point.

The bell jangled and two grubby little boys came in, eyeing Garren hopefully.

'Got any broken bits, mister?'

'As a matter of fact, I have,' he winked. Taking a little bag from behind the counter, he handed it to the older one.

'Cor, thanks, mister,' they chorused, almost running out of the shop in their haste to eat their treats.

'But they didn't pay,' Colenso exclaimed.

'They're from the orphanage. I collect up the bits from the bottom of the jars each evening so it doesn't really cost me anything. Now, I'll leave it to you to make our fortune,' he grinned and disappeared back to the workshop.

There was a lull during which Colenso carefully placed the dates into a clean jar and put it in the window. She had just returned to her place behind the counter when a harassed-looking woman entered, followed by three young children who immediately ran over to the sweet jars, gazing longingly at the contents.

'Three barley-sugar sticks,' the woman said, giving Colenso a weary smile.

'Aw Mamm, can't we have some of these?' the little boy said, gazing longingly at the sugar-glass sweets.

'No, we wants these,' the girls chorused, pointing to the Nelson's buttons.

'Which is why you're having a barley stick each,' she replied. 'If you're good you can eat them in the park on the way back.'

'Do you want them wrapped?' Colenso asked, unscrewing the lid and counting out the three sticks.

'No ta, be lucky if they last as far as the park.' Eager hands grabbed the sweets, and the children immediately began to devour them. 'See what I mean?' the woman sighed, proffering her money.

'Good morning,' she called, as the little bell rang their departure. Her first sale, she thought, carefully placing the coins in the cash box. It wouldn't make Garren a fortune, but it was a start.

For the rest of the morning, the little bell hardly stopped jangling and she was rushed off her feet, serving well-heeled ladies and gentlemen stuffed dates, Nelson's buttons and humbugs. Then came a surge of busy mothers with excited children wanting barley-sugar twists and rock sticks. By the time Garren closed the shop for lunch, the jars were almost empty.

'Well done,' he said, grinning as he looked around. 'While you've kept the customers happy in here I've had time to make plenty more.'

'I was surprised how many ladies came in with their children,' Colenso told him.

'Pay days are always busy. Mothers call in here after they've been to the butcher's. Sugar is a cheaper way of filling up hungry bellies, which of course they don't complain about. The women can then feed their men more meat, which keeps them happy too.'

'Really?' Colenso asked. How different things were here, she thought, recalling Mammwynn's fresh herbs and vegetables, fish when the boats could get out or the pilchards showed up, scraps of meat from old Buller in return for a few hours' help.

'There is a lot of industrial work around here, which is hard graft, and the men need nutrition to keep them going. Talking of which, I've prepared luncheon. Just a bit of bread and ham,' he said when he saw her expression.

'This is becoming a habit and I can't keep eating your food,' she replied, taking her place at the table.

'Board and room is part of the deal, remember? However, I gather from your earlier comment that you find it awkward accepting things, whether it be material or human assistance. But perhaps you could look at it from my point of view. I can't be in two places at once, and whilst you've been serving the customers, I've been able to make more sweets than I have since Mother died. As you've gathered, Father tries but he's really too old to be of much use.'

'I know, but it was kind of him to give me that material.'

'It was. However, he has no idea that dresses take time to make and he will expect you to be wearing the new one when he next sees you.'

'What …' she began, but he held up his hand to stop her.

'I know, these things don't happen just like that,' he said, snapping his fingers. 'And you're probably waiting until you get paid to purchase things like thread and buttons or whatnot.' She stared at him, surprised a man would know about such matters. 'Mother made all our clothes, which is why I was going to ask if you would like to look through her sewing drawer and see if you can make use of anything – and before you protest again, you really do need to look the part of a smart shopkeeper. I believe you met Miss Chenoweth from the shop next door.'

'Oh yes, she commented on the state of the pavement.'

'And later she saw fit to comment on the state of your dress. She prides herself on running an upper-class establishment and expects everyone else around here to conform to her standards. I wouldn't mention it other than she implied you would be letting the street down if you continued looking like a … well, dressed like that.'

'And we can't have that, can we?' Colenso retorted. 'In order to save embarrassment all round, I would be pleased to look through your mother's sewing drawer, provided you deduct the cost of anything I use from my wages.' He gazed at her intently, a smile hovering on his lips. 'You think that funny, Mr Goss?'

'Actually, Miss Carne, I am impressed by your integrity. Most of the women I know would be only too pleased to be handed things on a plate.'

'Well, I am not most women,' she retorted.

'Indeed, you are not,' he replied quietly, and Colenso saw the spark of admiration in his eyes. Having been rejected by Kitto, it was solace to her soul.

Chapter 28

A few days later, having spent her evenings frantically cutting and sewing, Colenso appeared in the workshop wearing her new outfit. She'd added the lace they'd found in the sewing drawer to the collar and cuffs of the dress and there'd been enough of the pink material left to make a matching scarf. Seeing how terrible the worn black boots looked against the beautiful bright material, she'd discarded them in favour of the new red shoes.

'Goodness, what a transformation,' Garren cried, looking up from the rock he was making. You look like one of those French bonbons, all shiny and tempting.' Seeing the look of admiration in his eyes, she turned away. She liked Garren, but he was her employer and she didn't want to complicate matters. Besides the cage around her heart was still firmly locked. 'Sorry, that remark was out of order,' he added.

'It's just that I was known as Bonbon at the Panam,' she told him, seizing on the excuse so as not to offend him.

'Bad memories, eh?' he asked, looking searchingly at her. 'Well, don't worry, I won't mention it again.'

'You will deduct the cost of the materials from my wages, won't you?' she asked, eager to change the subject.

'I promised, didn't I?' he replied, turning back to his task. Colenso watched as he cut the glistening mixture into sticks, releasing the fragrance of the rose flavouring.

'Now that I've finished sewing, I wondered if I could help make the sweets in the evening?' she asked. Scissors poised mid-cut, he looked up and shook his head.

'Sorry, I didn't mean to intrude,' she sighed.

'You're not,' he laughed. 'It's just that one minute you insist I charge you for material and a scrap of lace, the next you're offering to work on after the shop closes. You're most welcome to, of course, but regrettably I can't pay you any extra at the moment.'

'All the same, I'd love to learn how to make the sweets as well as sell them,' she said, excitement bubbling at the thought. The whole process of taking raw sugar and mixing it with a handful of ingredients to turn them into the jewel-like confections fascinated her.

'Very well. You can have your first proper lesson this evening after supper. Now, you'd better take these through and replenish the jars. I can't believe how quickly the last lot disappeared. If I didn't know better, I'd say you'd been sampling them yourself.'

'I wouldn't do that,' she retorted, then saw he was teasing. 'Oh you,' she muttered, gently slapping his arm before taking the tray through to the shop.

Colenso loved the quietude of the early morning as she prepared the displays ready for opening. There was something almost magical about the sweet-smelling atmosphere, she thought, pulling the big white apron over her new dress. Humming happily, she restocked the jars then set about dusting the counter and shelves. Catching sight of herself in the mirror, she couldn't help smiling. The material looked even brighter in the daylight, putting her in mind of the vivid camellias she loved so much. In her new pink dress with the matching scarf holding back her dark hair, she looked quite the part of the sweetshop assistant and would be a match for that snooty proprietress next door. Remembering the woman's jibe about the pavement, she snatched up the besom and hurried outside.

With autumn turning to winter, the air was colder now, the wind whipping in from the sea and bringing litter from the docks with it. At least it was dry and she was spared from having to sweep in the mud, she thought, catching sight of her bright red shoes.

'Look at you all dolled up like a fancy trollop. Hasn't taken you long to get your feet under the table, has it?' Colenso looked up to see the shopkeeper from next door glaring at her.

'Good morning, Miss Chenoweth,' she said, ignoring the barb. For some reason the woman had taken a dislike to her, but Colenso was determined to be pleasant.

'Think you're going to lure him by prettying yourself up, do you? Well, handsome is as handsome does and Garren Goss likes a bit of class,' she sniffed before, with her nose in the air, she stomped back inside. Bemused, Colenso shook her head.

'Don't mind her,' Mr Goss said, appearing at her side. 'Had her sights set on Garren ever since her parents took over the shop. Luckily, he's more sense than to fall for the wiles of a wisp of spun sugar.'

'You mean she's not the proprietress?' Colenso asked.

'Good Lord no, 'tis her father who runs the place. Mind, it's her that insisted on turning it into an epicurean though,' he sighed. 'Was always a normal grocery store before.' Colenso's spirits soared. For all her hoity-toity ways, it seemed Miss Chenoweth was just an assistant, the same as her.

'Well, that's a turn-up for the books,' she grinned.

'Might I say how attractive you look in that new outfit. Knew that colour would bring a bloom to your cheeks. It were a good day Garren took you on,' he winked. 'Oh, and he told me to let you know breakfast is ready.' Colenso smiled as he shuffled down the street towards the seafront. Not having to help out in the workshop had already done wonders for his well-being.

The day sped by in a flurry of serving customers, replenishing the little jars, and tidying up. Before she knew it, she was preparing for her first proper lesson in sweet-making.

'The fundamental thing to remember is that time is money,' Garren told her, his hazel eyes serious. 'A sweetshop proprietor needs to keep up with demand or he'll never turn a profit and, believe you me, the margins are small to start with. Ingredients are too expensive to waste. Might seem obvious, but if you really want to learn how things are done, you need to start with the basics.'

'I'm interested in every single detail,' she told him. 'Mammwynn used to say magical results come from mundane beginnings.'

'Sounds a wise woman,' he nodded. 'Right, as you know, as the mixture cools it firms and so you need to work quickly before it sets. Therefore, it pays to set out all your ingredients and have your equipment ready before you begin. Tonight, we are making lemon drops, one of the easiest confections, as the acid helps prevent crystals forming in the hot liquid. It's still important to start over a low heat to give the sugar a chance to fully dissolve.' Colenso watched as he stirred, helping him wash down the sides of the pan when it reached the boil. Once he'd transferred the pan to the heatproof mat he turned to her and smiled.

'Right, now you can add the colouring and flavouring.' Excitement bubbled as she reached for the two little bottles he'd selected. 'A couple of drops of each at most,' he told her, brows furrowed in concentration as he watched her pour. 'That's enough, too much and the taste will be overpowering.' Picking up the copper, he poured the lemon mixture onto the cooling table and turned it with a knife a couple of times. 'Right, it's beginning to hold its shape so you can knead and fold it over. Good,' he said as soon as Colenso felt it stiffen.

'Oh, it's turning opaque,' she exclaimed.

'It's ready then,' he said, forming it up into a sausage shape and throwing it over the hook on the wall. 'Now we stretch it to incorporate the air.' She watched in fascination as he pulled it, threw it back over the hook and repeated the process. 'And now for the shaping,' he said, taking the elongated sausage and feeding it into the press. He turned the handle and her eyes widened as it came out the other end looking like a flat worm. 'See those indentations?' he asked. 'Well, start snapping them apart. That's it,' he nodded as the yellow mixture broke into sweet-shaped lozenges. 'All we do now is leave them to harden completely before packing them away into jars.'

'I suppose you can leave them overnight to do that,' she said.

'You would think so, wouldn't you?' he replied, eyes twinkling with mischief. 'However, one must never presume, Miss Carne. Because sugar, even in this form, absorbs moisture from the atmosphere, it is imperative the sweets are stored in airtight containers as soon as they are completely cold.'

'Oh,' she said, feeling stupid.

'I would rather you asked questions and voiced opinions, Colenso, for that is the only way to learn. It also means you have been paying attention.' His grin was so infectious she found herself smiling back. 'Now let's have a cuppa while we're waiting. I always put water on to boil once the mixture has come off the heat. Efficient use of energy, see?'

'Oh, excuse me,' she said, trying to stifle a yawn.

'Would you would prefer to retire? It has been a long day,' he said, glancing at the clock.

'A cup of tea would be most welcome,' she replied. 'I didn't realize making sweets was such thirsty work.'

'That'll be the fumes from the colouring. I did say they were potent,' he grinned, pouring water into the teapot on the little round table. 'I must say you looked as though you enjoyed your sweet-making session.'

'I did,' she agreed, then took a welcome sip of her drink. 'In fact, I can't wait to do it again.'

'Good, for tomorrow we shall be making barley-sugar twists and sugar-glass plate. It can get a bit steamy with two coppers on the boil so I hope you won't mind.'

'Mind? Why should I mind?' she frowned.

'Some women worry about their hair getting frizzed,' he said, his eyes clouding.

'Well, I'm just pleased mine is growing back,' she said without thinking. 'Oh, and of course, my scarf protects it,' she added quickly. He was quiet as he poured them more tea.

'Tell me a bit about yourself, Colenso,' he invited. 'Do you have any followers?'

'I don't think so,' she replied. 'I mean, I did but he didn't pursue things so ...' she shrugged.

'More fool him, if I might be so bold,' he smiled, reaching out and patting her hand. 'Sorry,' he apologized. 'Truth to tell, I feel comfortable in your company, even ... well, something I haven't felt for many a long year.' She stared at him curiously but he changed the subject. 'Well, those sweets are ready for packing. No, I'll do it,' he said as she jumped to her feet. 'You've done enough for one day.'

*

The next weeks followed a similar pattern and Colenso revelled in her new work. She was getting to know the customers, even predicting what some wanted as soon as they entered the shop. Garren was generous in his teaching and she was enjoying learning how all the sweets were made. She felt comfortable in his presence and an easy relationship formed between them, often ending with them sharing a cuppa at the end of the long day. Mr Goss senior, relieved to be free from the burden of working, took himself off to play cards or dominos with his friends and no longer appeared in the workshop.

One morning as Colenso was preparing the shop for opening, Garren appeared looking serious.

'Do you realize it's December next week?' he asked.

'Really? Goodness,' she gasped, for in truth the days were passing so quickly she'd lost track of them. Is something wrong with those?' Colenso asked, seeing him frowning at jars in the window.

'Not as such. I was just thinking we'll need to make some special sweetmeats in preparation for Christmas. Miss Chenoweth told me earlier she was surprised we hadn't changed our window display. Apparently, the other confectioners in the town are already advertising their seasonal treats.'

'Well, I suppose it does make sense to start planting ideas in the children's minds. Reel them in with irresistible creations, remind them Father Christmas will soon be coming,' she grinned, getting quite carried away with the idea.

'Mother used to say the same,' he admitted. 'And she was a dab hand at making red and green streamers to hang everywhere.'

'I'd be happy to decorate the shop,' Colenso volunteered, remembering how Mammwynn used to love festooning her little cottage with holly, ivy and fir cones.

'Would you?' he replied, his expression lightening. 'I'm afraid I don't have much spare cash but I'm sure there are some scraps of green and red material upstairs. I'll have a look later. First though, I need to post some letters. After which I might just take a detour and see what the competition's up to,' he chuckled. Once again, she couldn't help thinking how much younger he looked when he smiled.

It was while he was out that she remembered Jago's books.

She was certain she'd seen receipts for Christmas confections when she'd been reading them in Mara's van. As ever, thoughts of Mara made her feel bittersweet. On the one hand she hoped the woman had found happiness in the Summerlands with her lover, on the other it made her realize how much she missed her friend's company and wise ways. Still, if there was one thing Colenso had learned from her, it was to make the most of the life you were currently living and not to dwell in the past. Unlike Jago, Garren paid her without fail every Thursday. Although it wasn't much, not having to pay for her room or food meant she could save.

The jangling of the little bell brought her back to the present and she smiled down at the two children who dashed in ahead of their mother.

'Uncle Sam's given us money for sweets,' they chorused, holding out their precious farthing.

'What a nice uncle. Now, what would you like?' she asked, smiling as they stood gazing longingly at all the jars.

'Come on, you two,' their mother urged. 'We've still more shopping to do.' She turned to Colenso and shook her head. 'I knew I should have gone to the market first but they were so excited. It's a rare thing for them to be able to come in here. Oh, do come on,' she urged as they dithered between barley-sugar sticks and the rose rock.

'Why don't you have half of one of each?' Colenso suggested. They nodded eagerly and watched wide-eyed as she selected the two sticks and cut them, making sure the pieces were equal, before wrapping them.

'Thank you so much,' the mother said, smiling wearily and ushering them out of the shop.

She'd just finished serving two elderly gentlemen with their twist of Nelson's buttons and humbugs when Garren returned.

'I have something for you,' she greeted him. She was about to ask him if he would mind the shop whilst she went and got Jago's receipt books when he held out a letter.

'And I have something for you too,' he replied. 'Apparently, it's been forwarded from Marazion. It was the name scrawled on the top that made the man in the post office ask if I knew who it might be for,' he added, holding out an envelope. Recognizing the writing, her heart began thudding wildly, demanding to be freed from its cage.

'Thank you,' she stuttered.

'I can see from your face it's important, so why not take it to your room to read? I'll mind the shop,' he added, solemnly.

Chapter 29

Colenso sank onto her bed and stared at the envelope. It was addressed to her c/o Hawkins Fair but Marazion had been crossed out and Penzance written in its place. Goodness, she hadn't even known Big Al's name was Hawkins. Beside her name, the question 'Bonbon?' had been added in another hand. With trembling fingers, she tore open the flap.

Dear Colenso

I was really happy when I received your letter. Forgive the delay in replying but so much has happened since then.

It grieves me to have to tell you that Mother and Wenna met with a terrible accident when the drayman's horses reared out of control. Sadly, they are both now buried in the churchyard.

The good news is that Alys has secured her position at Bochym Manor while Daveth has been taken on by the seining company and is lodging with Mrs Trevallis. Which means, Cali, that at long last I am free from responsibility and can follow after you. I leave with the carter first thing in

the morning. He has agreed to take me as far as Helston, after
which I will head for Marazion and be with you as soon as
I can.

Love
Kitto xx

Poor Mrs Rowse and Wenna. What a terrible thing to happen. She let out a long sigh as she remembered how kind Mrs Rowse had been and the pranks mischievous Wenna had delighted in playing. Then her heart flipped. Kitto still loved her and he was on his way to Marazion. Only she wasn't there. However, if his letter had been forwarded to Penzance, then surely the post office would direct him here too, she reasoned.

She couldn't wait to see him again. But when would he arrive? Snatching up the envelope she saw it was postmarked 30th October, the date they'd left Marazion. Why, that was nearly a month ago. If he'd secured a lift as far as Helston, what could be keeping him? Perhaps he'd had an accident on the way? Been hijacked even. Her imagination ran riot until another thought hit her. Perhaps he'd changed his mind, she thought, her spirits sinking.

Remembering she'd left Garren taking care of the shop, she returned the letter to its envelope and placed it in her basket. As she did, she noticed Jago's books and snatched them up.

'Everything all right?' Garren asked, staring at her intently when she joined him behind the counter.

'Yes. It was a letter.'

'Well, I gathered that,' he grinned. 'The postmaster asked if I knew anyone by the name of Bonbon, what with me having the confectioners. I remembered you saying you used to be called that at the Panam. Of course, the envelope also had your full name on, but he didn't know anyone called Miss Carne.' He looked at her quizzically.

'It was just from an old friend,' she murmured, not wishing to pursue the subject. 'Anyway, talking of the Panam, you remember me telling you about Jago the journeyman? Well, these books here contain his grandmother's receipts, some of which are for Christmas confections.' Garren's eyes lit up as she placed them on the counter.

'It's nearly noon so let's shut up shop and take a break. We can peruse them in peace while we enjoy a cuppa,' he said excitedly.

As they sat at their customary seats at the table in the workshop, exclaiming with delight as they leafed through the pages, Colenso felt her earlier tension draining away. Of course, she'd have known if anything bad had happened to Kitto. Realizing Garren was talking, she pulled herself back to the present.

'Jago's grandmother must have been talented to pen such detailed illustrations,' he marvelled, pointing to candied orange peel that looked as if it was shimmering with sugar.

'And those sugar mice and jellied pigs look positively real,' Colenso smiled. 'I'm sure they'd sell well so shall we make some?'

'Why not. Should be easy enough now we have synthetic dyes and colourings. Those natural plant ones were messy and time-consuming and didn't always give even coverage.'

'Can we make sugar plums and jewelled lollies as well? They'd look beautiful displayed in the window.'

'They would,' he agreed, snapping the book shut. 'I'll see about the ingredients right away and we've got plenty of decorative starch trays,' he said, pointing to the moulds on the shelf.

'I'll look forward to seeing how those work,' she told him.

'Good, because you'll be using them many times between now and Christmas. We'll also make some cheap jellied sweets. Although sugar's coming down in price, the orphanages and the workhouse still can't afford it so we always ensure the children there get a few confections on Christmas morning.'

'That's nice of you,' she replied, staring at him in surprise.

'Well, Mother always used to say "there but for the grace of God".'

Colenso shivered, knowing the truth of that, for if she hadn't been taken on by Garren, who knew where she might have ended up. Realizing he was speaking again, she once more pulled herself back to the present.

'If we manage to make all the confections we've spoken about, our competitors won't know what's hit them,' he grinned. His enthusiasm was infectious and Colenso found herself fizzing with excitement as she reopened the shop.

Having made sure the jars were replenished, Colenso perched on the little stool behind the counter, mulling over the confections they were going to make and how she'd display them. They'd never really celebrated much at home, for Father would be propping up the bar in the tap room while Mamm always seemed to be called out to some emergency or other.

'Babies don't stop coming just cos it's Christmas,' she'd say, snatching up her bag and leaving Colenso to finish cooking their meal. She sighed, thoughts of home reminding her of Kitto's letter. If he really wanted to find her then he surely would have done so by now?

It had started raining, huge drops splattering against the window panes. The pavements were empty and she knew there'd be no more customers that afternoon. As the aroma of mint wafted her way, she decided her time would be better spent helping Garren in the workshop. Jumping down, she crossed the room ready to turn the sign around when the bell jangled.

'I was just …' she began, then saw who it was. 'Kitto?' she gasped, her heart thudding as she took in the handsome face that had haunted her dreams these past months.

'Colenso, I've been looking all over town for you,' he cried. They both spoke at the same time then gave an awkward laugh as they stood staring at each other.

'Cali, I can't believe I've found you at last,' he murmured.

'At last is right,' Colenso replied, the worry and uncertainty of the past months bursting out of her.

'I've been going from shop to shop, asking …' he began. 'Look, if you've finished making your purchase perhaps we can go somewhere more private,' he added.

'I was just going to suggest closing for the day so feel free to go out with your friend if you wish,' Garren told her, an unfathomable look in his eyes as he stood watching from the archway.

'Oh Garren, I didn't see you there. Thank you,' she said quickly, and without even thinking to introduce the two men, yanked open the door.

'Better take the umbrella or you'll get drenched,' Garren called, gesturing to the black gamp in the stand.

'Thank you, sir,' Kitto said, snatching it up and following her outside. From under its canopy, they stood staring uncertainly at each other. 'We'll catch our deaths in this. Come on, there's a little place by the market that does hot drinks.'

He set off at a brisk pace and, unless she wanted to get a drenching, Colenso had little option but to follow. They passed the other shops on the higher side of the pavement before crossing the road by the market. A few moments later he opened the door and ushered her into a small room with tables and chairs. She chose one furthest away from the fair-haired young girl behind a huge tea urn, who was eyeing them curiously.

'Usual mug of tea, Kitto, lover?' she called.

'Yes please, Polly,' he called cheerfully, shaking the rain off the gamp on the doorstep before joining Colenso. 'Tea for you too, Cali?' he asked, using the endearment she used to love hearing. After all this time though, it sounded wrong and far too familiar.

'Er, yes, thank you,' she replied when she realized he was waiting for an answer. Sliding into the seat opposite, he smiled. 'So what delights were you purchasing from the confectioners?'

'I wasn't. I work there,' she told him.

'So that's where you've been hiding, I …' he broke off as the waitress arrived with their drinks.

'Here we are, Kitto, a cup of tea just how you like it, good and strong. And one for …?' the young girl paused, looking at Colenso expectantly, 'your friend,' she finished, when there was no reply. With a raise of her brow in Kitto's direction, she scuttled off to serve another customer.

'I haven't been hiding, Kitto,' Colenso replied, staring at the almost red liquid with distaste. 'I've been working at the shop for nearly a month, which to my mind has given you ample time to find me – if you really wanted to, that is.'

Kitto's eyes widened in shock.

'Gosh, Cali, I don't remember you ever being like this before.'

'Well, I've never felt like this before. Your letter saying you were leaving Helston was posted almost a month ago. I thought you were coming by carter not camel.' The spark of amusement in his eyes didn't help her mood. Was he laughing at her? 'And it's obvious you haven't just arrived either, being as how you're well known here,' she continued, jerking her head towards the young girl who was staring in their direction.

'I have been here a little while, yes,' he agreed. 'When I reached Marazion and was told the fair had moved on, I made enquiries at the post office and was told my letter had been forwarded to Penzance. You knew I was coming and could have left me a forwarding address.' Dark eyes that moments ago had gazed at her lovingly now stared accusingly.

'For one thing your letter only reached me this morning. For another, when we left for St Just I had no idea the fair was disbanding for the winter. Mara, the lady I travelled with since leaving Cadgwith, died and I found myself without a home or job.' Feeling tears welling, she looked quickly down at her drink.

'That must have been tough,' he said, his voice gentle as he reached out to take her hand. His touch sent shivers of delight up her arm but, not wishing to show it, she pulled away. Hurt flickered in his eyes but he shook his head. 'It seems we have both been through difficult times recently,' he added quietly.

'I was sorry to hear about your mother and Wenna. They were lovely people,' she murmured. He nodded, his pain evident now. 'It's been a distressing year all round. I can't tell you how shocked I was when I heard what had happened to you. Which reminds me, I've kept this safe for you,' he said, delving into his breast pocket and drawing out her necklace. 'Carried it next to my chest all these months, Cali, I mean Colenso,' he said quickly as he held it out.

'Thank you,' she murmured, taking it and holding it tight. The familiar feel of the metal was reassuring and she felt herself thawing slightly. 'I suppose nothing has changed with Father and Mamm?'

'Everything's changed. After Fenton was dismissed, your father took to spending all his time in the alehouse. Seems our dear manager was caught misappropriating the funds. That's why Mr Quinn, the owner, stayed so long. He got rid of Mrs Grim too, said she was too depressing. Anyway, a new manager's been appointed and your mother has moved in as his housekeeper. Said she wasn't prepared to put up with Peder's drunken rages any longer. At least she's got a room in that nice house to live in, but he's lost the cottage and has to sleep in a net loft. Your mother said to tell you she's sorry for everything that happened and, could you ever bear to return, she'd love to see you.'

'Goodness,' Colenso gasped, trying to take everything in. She was pleased her mamm was making a new life, but to think she'd been fretting about the Ferret finding her when he had already moved on.

'Just as well Fenton moved on, because when I heard what had been going on in my absence I ... well, let's just say I could have killed Fenton and your father too.'

'And is the new manager agreeable to work for?' she asked, trying not show she was pleased to hear he cared so much.

'I don't know. By the time he was appointed, I was busy sorting things out at home. It was a terrible time. Alys and Daveth were inconsolable,' he shook his head and took a gulp of his tea. Without thinking, she reached out and squeezed his arm. He stared at her sadly.

'I've found a job at the Wherrytown works, but I can see that I've left it too late,' he shrugged. 'That man in the sweetshop seems nice.'

'Garren? He is. He and his father have both been very kind to me. I'm learning to make confections as well as serving in their shop.' Kitto nodded.

'Your eyes light up when you talk about them and I must say, even slightly bedraggled, you're looking beautiful. That pink puts me in mind of one of those camellias you love so much.' He gave a tentative smile and she could feel her lips twitching in response for hadn't they always thought alike?

'How long have you been working at Wherrytown?' she asked.

'Three weeks or more.'

'And you've only just managed to find me?' she asked indignantly.

'I couldn't begin looking until I had a job and something to offer you,' he replied. 'I always said I wanted to give you something better than a brass curtain ring.'

'Oh,' she said, jumping up. 'I've just remembered I promised Garren I'd help him make a start on the Christmas confections.' As she reached for the umbrella, he put out a hand to detain her.

'Before you go, Cali, tell me; is there anything between this Garren and you?'

'What?' she laughed. 'Good heavens, no. He's a lovely man but he's not ...' She'd been about to say he's not you, but pride prevented her.

'So it's not too late for us, then? You'll come with me and choose a new ring?' Seeing the love shining from his eyes, she thought her heart would burst out of its cage. Then she remembered that while she'd been fretting, he'd been working nearby for these past few weeks and the cage door clanked shut again.

'I honestly don't know,' she murmured.

'Give us a chance eh, Cali?' he pleaded. 'Perhaps we could start by walking out again. May I call on you at the shop on Sunday, take you for afternoon tea perhaps?' As she stood there looking at his earnest expression, the necklace gently prodded her hand. The last vestiges of anger dissipated.

'Very well,' she replied. 'But I'll meet you here. If the weather's better perhaps we could walk along the seafront.'

Chapter 30

Seeing the little shop in darkness, Colenso let herself in through the workshop.

'The wanderer returns,' Garren said without looking up from the wooden moulds he was working on. 'Have a good time, did you?' Although he sounded casual, Colenso had the feeling her answer was important to him.

'I did and thank you for the loan of the umbrella,' she replied, leaving it to dry beside the door. 'As you might have guessed, that was Kitto who called in earlier.'

'Ah, your follower,' he said, keeping his eyes averted.

'Yes. Things were a bit awkward at first but I said I'd walk out with him on Sunday afternoon. If that's all right with you?' she asked quickly.

'You're entitled to time off,' he replied. There was a pause, followed by a thump on the table that made her jump.

'Oh, you've started on the mice,' she cried, seeing the little shapes staring up at her.

'Yes, I've made them in white fondant but they'll need their eyes coloured and strings added for their tails. Perhaps you'd like to do that while I begin on the jelly mixture for the pigs. Unless you're too tired?' he said, looking up and studying her.

'No, of course not,' she frowned. Why would she be tired this early? Hadn't she spent the previous evenings working with him? But he'd turned away and was already scooping a heap of sugar into the copper pan. 'Goodness, you have been busy,' she said, staring at the depleted cone.

'Filing sugar's therapeutic,' he muttered. 'Now, please can you get on with those mice before the fondant sets?'

Obediently, she began cutting the string into suitable lengths and pressing them into the fondant. Then she took up the food colouring and began painting their eyes. The effect was quite realistic and she giggled at the rows of pink-eyed mice with their curly tails.

'Right, if you've finished that, perhaps you'd like to pour those almonds into the shallow wide pan ready to go on the heat when I've finished here. While they're heating you need to melt the sugar and gum arabic to coat them.'

'Oh, can't I help you make the jelly pigs?' she asked, dying to see how the starch trays worked. But he shook his head.

'Not tonight. I want enough confections to fill the window tomorrow.' Although he said it pleasantly enough, she couldn't help feeling he was keeping his distance. Still, she did as he asked and, once the gum arabic mixture had cooled sufficiently, poured it over the nuts and began working it through with her hands. Who'd have thought sugar plums were actually coated nuts?

'The coating is very thin,' she said, frowning.

'That's why you have to let the nuts cool and then keep repeating the process until you've built up a good covering,' he replied.

'Oh,' she said, looking up and seeing him pouring the

310

jelly into the moulds. Although she was enjoying what she was doing, it wasn't the same as working on the confections together.

By the end of the evening, they had sufficient fondant mice, jelly pigs and sugar plums for a credible window display.

'Luckily these confections will last, so we shouldn't have any wastage,' Garren smiled. 'Right, that's enough for tonight. You go off to bed and I'll cover them over. Goodnight and thank you for your help.'

'Oh, goodnight,' she replied, staring at him in surprise. Usually they finished the night with a pot of tea but clearly that wasn't forthcoming tonight.

Although tired, she couldn't sleep. Her head was spinning with the events of the day. And what a day it had been, she thought. First, the letter from Kitto, then him turning up like that. She smiled into the darkness, then frowned. Did he still love her? Could things ever be the same between them? 'He's here, Mammwynn,' she whispered, her hand going to the pentacle at her neck. A feeling of hope and reassurance flooded through her as she felt the answering jab. However, although he'd explained his reasons for securing a job before coming to find her, she couldn't help feeling aggrieved he'd taken so long. Why, if the situation had been reversed nothing would have prevented her from hurrying to his side. Still, she'd be seeing him again on Sunday. While Colenso didn't give a fig for the Ferret or her father, she was pleased her mamm was making a new life for herself and hoped she was happy.

She'd enjoyed her sweet-making session with Garren tonight. Although she hadn't had a lesson as such, he had a lovely way of explaining things and she knew she'd remember everything she'd done. He'd seemed a bit distant, though. Perhaps he was tired – he did work long hours. Tomorrow, she'd make sure she helped him in the workshop as soon as she'd finished serving in the shop. She began thinking how she would display their seasonal confections, yet it was Kitto who filled her dreams.

*

'I think that looks wonderful,' Colenso said, standing back and admiring the window display. Garren had been up early, making jewelled lollies and cheap jelly sweets to add to the mice, pigs and sugar plums they'd made the night before.

'Well, the proof will be in the pudding – or in this case, the sugar plums,' he grinned. Then as if remembering something, he frowned and hurried back to the workshop, leaving Colenso gazing after him.

She turned back to see a group of children, noses pressed against the window panes, gazing excitedly at the Christmas confections and tugging at their mother's sleeve. To her surprise though, apart from the odd mouse or a few sugar plums, it was the normal sweets that sold.

'I can't understand it,' she told Garren, going through to the workshop, where the delectable aroma of fruit and nuts made her stomach rumble.

'You haven't sold all the seasonal fare already?' he asked, looking up from the pan he was stirring.

'No. Everyone exclaimed how wonderful it all looked but hardly anyone bought anything. The children have had their noses pressed against the window all morning yet they didn't come inside.'

'Well, they wouldn't,' Garren said. 'Christmas is too far away for their parents to be thinking about buying confections. The window display is to create attention, remember. Don't worry, those children will now be pestering for Father Christmas to bring them sugar mice, jellied pigs or whatever they desire. The week before the big day we'll be rushed off our feet, you'll see.'

'Yet you've been busy making more sweets,' she cried, gesturing to the cooling tables laden with almond-paste sweets coloured and shaped like fruits, glistening dates stuffed with red and green paste, candied orange and lemon peel slices and, incongruously, yet more of the cheap jelly sweets.

'For the well-heeled for whom presenting a seasonal treat to guests is de rigeur,' he explained. 'Apart from those jelly sweets, of course, which is probably all parents will be able to afford between now and Christmas.'

'Goodness, I have so much to learn,' Colenso exclaimed.

'We both do,' he replied. Although he said it lightly, she had a feeling he wasn't referring to sweets.

'Well, it's almost noon so shall I put the kettle on to boil?'

'Yes, by all means,' he said, reaching out for the brush to wipe down the sides of the pan. 'Help yourself to bread and cheese.'

'Shall I cut enough for both of us?' she asked.

'No, I'll have something later,' he said, lifting the pan from the heat. 'Want to get these glass-plate sweets finished.'

And that seemed to be the way of things for the rest of the week. Although Garren was polite and helpful, he never seemed to take his break when she did. Even when they worked on together in the evenings, he assigned her jobs that were at the other end of the workshop. However, Colenso was so busy helping to make the sweets and serving in the shop, she hardly had time to think. By the time her head hit the pillow at night, she was so exhausted she fell asleep straight away.

That Sunday, putting the thumping of her heart down to needing a break, she checked her appearance in the mirror over the counter. She'd sponged the stains from her green outfit, tied the matching scarf around her head and clipped on the golden hoops. Then, as the day was fine but brisk, she slipped Mara's shawl around her shoulders. Calling to Garren that she was leaving, she let herself outside then, unable to resist checking the window display, smiled at the fondant pigs and jellied mice peering out from the dishes of sugar plums.

'Very nice, Cali.' She spun round to find Kitto grinning at her. He was wearing the heavy serge jacket and flat cap she remembered but whether he was referring to the window display or her, she couldn't tell.

'I thought we were meeting by the market,' she replied.

'Couldn't wait,' he quipped, holding out his arm. Not wishing to appear churlish, she took it and just had time to glimpse the look of glee on Miss Chenoweth's face in the window as they set off down the street.

'Have you had a good week?' she asked brightly.

'Not really. Being the new boy's not easy. Even though I was taken on as a turner, I get given the rubbish jobs nobody else wants to do. Still, let's not waste time talking about that. The day is dry so I'm guessing my lady would like a stroll along the prom.' Her heart leapt at his words. Careful, Colenso, she chided. Better to take things slowly this time. If only her heart would stop beating at the door of the cage. 'Well?' he persisted. Seeing him look askance, she nodded. 'Have you seen much of the town?' he asked.

'No, not really. I've been so busy I've not really had time to venture out, apart from the other day. What about you?'

'Saw quite a bit when I was searching for you,' he replied. 'There are some beautiful buildings here. Very different from the thatched cottages on The Lizard, some of them. I mean, did you know that here is called Market Jew Street?' he said as they walked down the steps that led to the lower side. 'It means Thursday Market, in Cornish. That fine granite building with the tall columns in front of us is the Market House.'

'What does the writing mean?' she asked, staring up at the engraved letters.

'It's not Cornish so no one seems to know, although Polly overheard a customer saying it was opened in the 1830s like the rest of the big buildings in the town centre.'

'I never knew you were interested in things like that, Kitto,' she replied, looking at him in surprise.

'Wait until you see the next building I've come across,' he grinned, leading her down a narrower street. 'How would you like to live in a house like that?' he asked, gesturing to his right.

'That would be just wonderful,' she gasped, staring at the magnificent busts of two Egyptian women that proudly graced the ornate pillars above the entrance. The front of the building was painted in red, orange and gold, picking out mouldings, figures and patterns. A black cormorant perched under the eaves, and the intricate metalwork to the windows made the whole building look exotic.

'Don't think we can quite run to a house like that when we're wed, Cali, but I do want us to have a nice home.'

'Perhaps we should concentrate on getting to know each other again before thinking of things like that,' she told him as they made their way past a couple of old alehouses and a fine merchant's house. He shot her a puzzled look but she hardly noticed, for the church with the tall tower was looming before them. Gazing up at the porch she'd huddled in, a shiver ran down her spine.

'Apparently that tower acts as a waymark to seafarers,' he started to say. 'Hey, you've gone all pale, are you all right?' he asked, frowning at her.

'Just impatient to get to the sea,' she murmured, not wishing to dwell on that dreadful night.

'Well, if we turn down here,' he said, leading her down a little lane. 'There,' he cried, gesturing ahead. Sure enough there was the sea, wind whipping up the white horses as it hit the wall and splashed over onto the promenade. 'Don't think we'll get too close unless you fancy a soaking,' he quipped. Standing well back, they watched the boats pitching and rolling in the swell, even though they were sheltered from the west by Mousehole.

'So, how's life in the sweetshop?' he asked as they began walking along, carefully keeping to the edge of the promenade away from the breakers.

'Very busy. We've been making those Christmas confections I mentioned the other day.'

316

'You mean you made those mice and pigs?' He stopped walking and stared at her, clearly impressed.

'Well, actually I did the sugar plums. Do you know they're not made of plums at all?'

'Well, I did have an inkling. I mean, since when do you get plums in December? Still, they did look very good,' he said quickly when he saw her frown. 'Look, the wind's freshening, shall we go and have a hot drink and scone or something?' he said as another wave washed over the wall, splattering the promenade with pebbles and seaweed.

'Good idea,' she agreed, pulling her shawl tighter round her as they turned and hurried back the way they'd come, although this time he turned up a different lane.

'Everywhere leads to the town,' he explained when she looked askance.

Two minutes later they were entering the warmth of the tea room. As before, the fair-haired girl beamed a smile of welcome at Kitto before nodding briskly at Colenso.

'A pot of tea for two and a couple of scones, please, Polly,' he called, as they made their way to the table by the window they'd occupied before. He sat staring at her for a long moment.

'Is something wrong?' she asked.

'I was just thinking that you never used to wear a scarf around your hair. Not that you don't look very nice, er, lovely in fact,' he said quickly, colour creeping up his cheeks.

'In order to escape from Cadgwith, I had to pretend to be a boy, which meant having my hair shorn,' she told him.

'Oh Cali, I had no idea,' he gasped.

'Don't worry, it's almost back to normal now,' she assured him when he grimaced.

'No, I meant I had no idea you were suffering like that. Your mother told me you were safe and that you'd be writing to me, so I waited to hear from you. That's why I learned my letters – so I'd be able to reply.' She was about to ask him about the schoolmistress but he was already speaking again. 'It was holding your necklace that gave me comfort.' Automatically her hand reached inside her dress.

'Yes, I missed it but I'm glad it helped you. I swear blind it has magical properties. Anyhow, in answer to your question, I took to wearing a scarf while my hair was growing and, well, have continued doing so. I quite like the effect, and of course it's practical when I'm making sweets.'

'I think you look wonderful,' he murmured, giving her that intense look she remembered. 'Quite like the hoops too, they make you look like a gypsy.'

'Here we are, lovers,' Polly said, her comment clearly meant for Kitto as she placed his mug in front of him. 'Wouldn't dare risk eating one of them meself,' she added, placing the scones down on the table and looking pointedly at Colenso. 'Wouldn't want to spoil me figure.' Turning to Kitto, she tittered and ran her hands over her slim hips.

'Luckily Colenso doesn't have to worry about that,' he replied. As the girl pouted and flounced back to the counter, Colenso stifled a giggle.

'Oops, I think you've upset your admirer,' she whispered.

'There's only one admirer I want, Cali,' he said, looking serious as he took hold of her hand. 'And I want her to wear my ring,' he added, delving into his pocket and bringing out a little box. Flipping open the lid, he held it out to her. Her eyes widened as she saw the little red stone winking up at her.

318

'It's a garnet, which represents constancy, faith and loyalty. I'm hoping you will accept this ring as a token of my love and intention,' he told her. 'I was hoping to offer this in a better setting but the seafront was too cold. Besides, I didn't want one of those waves washing it away. Well, Colenso, what do you say?' She looked from the ring to the earnest expression on his face, heard her heart trying to beat down the door of the cage. And yet, there was still that niggle that if he loved her as much as he purported, then the first thing he'd have done on arriving would have been to find her.

'Can I think about it?' she asked.

Chapter 31

The necklace stabbed frantically at Colenso's chest but she didn't need it to tell her she'd said the wrong thing. Her heart was doing that. Before she could say anything, though, Kitto had snapped the little box shut and replaced it in his pocket. She knew she'd hurt him, but by the time he turned to face her, he'd regained his composure.

'I'll not deny I'm disappointed, Cali, especially as being able to buy you a nice ring was the main reason for me taking the job at Wherrytown. But if you're not sure about us, well ...' he shrugged.

'I thought I needed time to think but ...' she began.

'You'll have plenty of that while I'm away,' he cut in, smiling sadly as he got to his feet. 'I'll be in touch when I get back.'

'Back?' she frowned. 'Back from where?'

'London. I've to supervise delivery of a cargo of serpentine shopfronts. Like I said earlier, being the new boy, I get given all the good jobs at the works.'

'How long will you be away?'

'Depends on the weather. Hopefully I'll be back for Christmas. Take care of yourself,' he said, hurrying towards the door.

'And you,' she whispered, too stunned to move. It was the pentacle's sharp stabbing that brought her to her senses. Why was she letting him go like this? Jumping up, she rushed to the door but by the time she'd got outside, he'd already disappeared. It was only then she realized she didn't even know where he was staying.

Tears welled as she stood there cursing her stupidity. A gust of wind blew in from the sea, bringing with it a squall of rain and, knowing it would be futile to walk around looking for him, she headed back to the shop. As she let herself into the workshop, Garren looked up from the copper he was stirring, his eyes widening in alarm.

'Whatever's the matter? You look half-drowned.'

'For heaven's sake, son, don't waste time asking daft questions,' Mr Goss snapped. 'Go and get out of those wet things, my girl. We'll have a hot drink ready when you get back,' he told her, putting down the mould he was using and gently leading her to her room. His caring concern brought a fresh flood of tears as Colenso hurried inside. Then, heedless of her wet clothes, she threw herself down on her bed, crying as if her heart would break.

It was some time later when, exhausted and with no tears left, she changed out of her wet things and emerged. Garren and his father were working at the cooling tables.

'Ah, there you are,' Mr Goss said. 'What do you think of this little lot?' Grateful for his tact, she went over and looked at the new batch of sugar mice. Their little pink eyes must surely reflect her own, she thought. 'Good eh? Thought it was time I supervised the making of the Christmas confections. Right, now sit yourself down, girl. Garren, have you got the tea poured yet? I could murder a slice of that shortbread her next door brought round earlier,' he added, rubbing his hands together. 'Thought there must be another fire, the way you rushed in,' he told Colenso.

His easy chattering and the hot tea revived her somewhat, although she was still cursing her stupidity. Still, Kitto said he should be back by Christmas and that was only three weeks or so away. She'd tell him she would be delighted to accept his beautiful garnet then.

'There's always so much to do at this time of year,' Mr Goss was saying. 'Although it won't be the same without Meggie.'

'Oh Mr Goss, I'm so sorry. There's me wallowing in self-pity while you're suffering.' Without thinking, she reached out and patted the old man's hand. 'And I'm sorry about earlier,' she said, feeling she should explain. 'Kitto, my follower, told me he has to take a cargo to London and I got upset because he'll be away for three weeks or so.' It was the truth if not the whole story, but she didn't feel up to admitting her folly.

'Life can be difficult, throwing unexpected things our way,' Mr Goss murmured. 'I thought having a bit of free time would be of benefit, but it's keeping busy that stops me moping. Silly old fool, I've only just realized that.' Knowing he was trying to help, Colenso smiled. As he sipped his tea, lost in his memories, she became aware of Garren watching her.

'I'll not be going out on Sundays between now and Christmas, so I'll be pleased to help with the extra preparations,' she told him. When he didn't reply, she added: 'If you want me, that is.'

'Oh, I do,' she thought he murmured but he'd buried his head in his mug and she couldn't be sure.

*

The days leading up to Christmas passed in a blur of making and selling sweets, and Colenso was able to keep her thoughts of Kitto at bay. It was during the long nights that she lay in bed thinking of him, rehearsing what she would say to him. She couldn't believe she'd been so insensitive. Sorry just didn't seem enough somehow. *Love is a precious thing, Colenso, so think hard before you throw it away on perceived grievances.* She heard Mara's words as clearly if she was standing right beside her. How could she have been so stupid as to worry that he hadn't come after her quickly enough? Surely the important thing was that he'd cared enough to come at all?

She remembered the red serpentine heart he'd polished and engraved with their initials. It must have taken him ages to do and proved he loved her, didn't it? What if she were to make him a similar token in order to prove her love for him? They were bound to be making more fondant and she was sure Garren would let her have some. She could fashion a heart, colour it red, then carve their initials into it. Happy with her idea, she fell asleep at last.

Just as Garren had predicted, the nearer it got to the big day, the busier the shop became. Even the windy, wet weather didn't deter the customers, and an air of excitement and anticipation hung in the air.

'Could I please buy a portion of that?' she asked Garren as he prepared the fondant to make their last batch of sugar mice.

'You can certainly have some but there's no need to buy it. Cut off what you need.'

'Thank you but I'd feel better if I paid,' she told him.

'Still the proud woman, I see,' he said, shaking his head. 'What do you want it for, if I might ask?'

'To make a present and if I may also use a drop of red colouring, I'd be grateful.' This time Garren threw back his head and laughed.

'You hear that, Father? Colenso, who's been serving in the shop by day and helping us in here each evening, would be grateful for a drop of red colouring.'

'Don't mock, Garren,' the old man remonstrated. 'It's nice to see a young girl with manners.'

'It is. Sorry, Father,' he replied, looking so chastened that Colenso had to stifle a giggle. 'We are truly obliged for all your help, Colenso. I was going to give you something for Boxing Day but you can have the fondant and colouring with our compliments instead,' he quipped, a gleam of mischief sparking in his hazel eyes. It was then she realized he'd been quiet of late and that she'd missed his teasing.

'Why, thank you, kind sir,' she replied.

'You'd better cover that fondant to work on later because while Father shapes the mice, we need to make more rock,' he said, nodding towards the piece she'd set aside.

'You know I told you we shaped the rock into canes at the Panam?' she said, duly wrapping her fondant in a cloth.

'I remember, and I explained why we kept them straight here,' Garren nodded, looking up from the sugar syrup he was now stirring.

'Well, why don't we colour this batch green and red then

324

shape them into canes or crooks, just for Christmas Eve,' she added quickly when he frowned.

'That's a good idea, girl,' Mr Goss nodded. 'We could capitalize on the nativity and sell them as shepherd's crooks. Shame we didn't think to do it earlier,' he said, darting his son a look.

They spent the rest of the evening kneading, pulling, colouring and shaping, and by the time they collapsed with their cups of tea, the cooling trays were lined with red and green canes and white sugar mice.

'Brilliant,' Garren pronounced, finishing his tea. 'Now I'll just fill the jars with the jellied sweets, ready for the orphanage and workhouse. Being Christmas Eve tomorrow, the children will be excited and we mustn't let them down.'

'I'll take them, Garren. I know you'll be busy with the centrepiece for the window,' Mr Goss said.

'Oh, what's that?' Colenso asked, looking up from the fondant she was carefully shaping into a heart. The red colouring made it glisten and all she needed to do was carve out their initials. She was sure this would show Kitto how she felt, better than words ever could.

'Ah ha, you'll have to wait and see,' Garren teased. 'All I'll say is, prepare to be surprised.'

*

Colenso woke early the next morning and, knowing they'd be extra busy, she quickly dressed and pulled on her big white apron. She could hear Garren moving around in the workshop and so, honouring her promise not to go in there until he said she could, she let herself into the shop. It was her favourite time of day and, humming a carol softly, she set about getting the shop ready for opening. The tantalizing smell of peppermint, fruits and nuts filled the air and she bustled around making sure the displays looked enticing. Garren had told her to leave the middle window empty and, although he didn't say why, she knew it must be for his centrepiece.

Seeing one of the jars half-empty, she refilled it with the jewel-like boiled sweets. A rare ray of sunlight shone on one of the red ones, making it glow. Reminded of the garnet Kitto had offered her, she snatched it up and held it against her finger, smiling as she imagined wearing his ring. Would it be today he returned, she wondered, excitement fizzing up inside?

'Ta-da.' She jumped as Garren came through bearing a platter high in the air. Hastily she returned the sweet to the jar.

'The *pièce de résistance*,' Mr Goss grinned, following his son into the shop.

'Oh my,' Colenso gasped, staring in astonishment as Garren carefully placed what looked like a boar's head in the centre window. Glazed with chocolate, glacé fruit for eyes, and holly in its pricked-up ears, it was truly magnificent. She watched as Mr Goss carefully arranged truffles around the base while Garren stuck spears studded with marzipanned fruits into the sides.

'It is a replica of what our dear Queen will be having, only hers will be a real one, of course,' he explained, standing back to study the effect. Mr Goss meanwhile was out on the pavement, giving the thumbs-up. 'That should draw in the customers,' he grinned.

Immediately a crowd gathered, pointing excitedly at the centrepiece and all the other confections. Then the little bell tinkled, and amid much exclaiming the day got off to a good start.

'We've not even had time for a cup of tea,' Garren moaned, but she could see he was pleased. The boar's head certainly proved a draw and they were so busy it took all three of them to keep up with the incessant flow of customers.

'Good idea, that,' Mr Goss said later as he put the last of the candy crooks into a bag. 'There you go, my lovely,' he said, handing it to a little girl whose eyes were shining with delight. 'Don't forget to think of the shepherds who visited baby Jesus, will you?' He turned to Garren. 'Which reminds me, I must get those jellied sweets over to the workhouse and orphanage or there'll be some very disappointed children. I'll pick up some bread and ham on my way back and expect a cuppa ready when I return.'

'Goodness, it's almost noon,' Garren exclaimed, looking at the clock above the door. 'No wonder I'm parched. You must be starving, Colenso, we didn't even get to break our fast this morning.' She was about to offer to put the kettle on to heat when the door opened and another group of excited children descended, their harassed parents following behind. They stood looking at all the sweets, trying to decide what to choose while the adults tried to hurry them along. Once they'd finally departed, bags clutched eagerly in their hands, Garren hurried to lock the door, declaring it was definitely time for a break. Snatching up the cash tin, he led the way through to the workshop where he began counting up the money while Colenso went outside to the pump.

The kettle was boiling, the mugs and plates set ready on the table when Mr Goss finally returned.

'At last, my stomach thinks my throat's been cut,' Garren sighed then he took a closer look at his father and frowned. 'Whatever is the matter? You haven't overdone it, have you?' he asked, his voice rising as his father slumped into a chair. The old man shook his head.

'I think you'd better sit down, Colenso,' he said, pulling out her chair. 'After I delivered the sweets for the children, I felt in need of a breath of air and went for a stroll. There were a group of men from the Wherrytown works gathered on the harbour. It would appear their barge got caught up in a storm and, I'm sorry, dear,' he said, taking hold of Colenso's hand. 'It's believed it went down, with all lives lost.'

'What? But that can't be right,' she gasped, shaking her head. 'I haven't given Kitto his present yet.'

Chapter 32

The grey, swirling fog that had engulfed Colenso stayed and wouldn't lift. It was as if she was on the outside of life looking in as she routinely went about her work. She couldn't believe Kitto was dead, didn't feel he was, and yet everyone assured her that he couldn't have survived the terrible storm that sank the barge. The pentacle stabbed relentlessly at her neck, until finally, with hot tears coursing down her cheeks, she wrenched it off and put it away in her basket.

Christmas had passed in a blur and, unable to sleep, she'd taken to walking down to the harbour early each morning in the hope of hearing something, anything. She'd expected a group of men to be waiting and looking, like the fishermen's wives did when their men were late back. There was never anyone from the works there though and, exhausted and dejected, she eventually gave up going, gave up going out at all.

'I can't believe he's dead,' Colenso muttered one morning as she helped Mr Goss make a new batch of barley sugar. As she couldn't bring herself to smile, Garren had agreed to serve the customers in the shop.

'I know how exactly you feel, my dear,' he replied. 'Even

now, I wake up some mornings expecting Meggie to appear, but of course she never does. I'm told it is part of the grieving process. Best get twisting that mixture before it sets too hard,' he urged gently as she stood staring into space.

'If only I'd said yes,' she sighed.

'If only we'd done a lot of things,' he agreed, a wistful look on his face. 'Shall we sneak an extra break, I could murder a cup of tea, oh …' he paused, looking embarrassed.

'I know what you mean,' she assured him. Snatching up the kettle she went out to the pump. Snowflakes were falling from a leaden January sky, coating everything in crisp white powder. The air was as icy as her heart, although thankfully the water hadn't frozen yet. Oh, why hadn't she accepted Kitto's ring? The thought that plagued her day and night, surfaced once again. As she stood there wondering what had possessed her to do such a stupid thing, her attention was caught by a cluster of snowdrops in the corner of the yard. Pearlescent fragility belying their toughness, they stoically stood, taking all the weather winter threw at them, and Colenso knew she would need to summon that same strength if she were to get through the coming months.

As was often the case in this more temperate part of the country, the snow didn't settle for long, and by the end of February it had thawed, although Colenso's feelings remained frozen, suspended in her last meeting with Kitto.

'Come along,' Garren urged late one afternoon. Business had been slow since the Christmas rush, and he'd closed the shop early ready to try out another of Jago's grandmother's recipes. 'We need something new to entice the customers in.'

'What are we going to make?' she asked, trying to show

an interest. Although life held no joy for her now, Garren and Mr Goss had been good to her, and she owed it to them to help keep their business going.

'As you've probably noticed, many of our customers have been sneezing and coughing, so I thought we'd try this receipt for aniseed humbugs,' he said, pointing to an illustration of little black and white cushions. 'These are larger and stronger than the ones I've done previously, so we can sell them as a remedy,' he grinned.

Once the sugar syrup was poured out onto the cooling tables, Garren cut it into two portions, one twice the size of the other. To the smaller portion he added a tiny amount of black colouring, to the other the aniseed flavouring he'd purchased earlier.

'Right, we'd better oil our hands or they'll be black for days,' he told her. 'I'll knead the black portion while you do the other one until it satinizes, then we'll press them together.' They pummelled them until the mixture turned from clear to satiny and then rolled them into a sausage and strand, ensuring both were the same size. Garren placed the black strand over the white and rolled the two colours together until twice their original length. The smell was heady by now and she began to feel lightheaded.

'Remedy working already, is it?' he grinned, seeing her expression. 'That's a good sign.' As he so often did these days, he took no offence when she didn't reply, merely answering his own question. 'Right, now we need to snip them into lozenges,' he said, passing her a pair of scissors. But she worked too slowly and the mixture cooled so that she was no longer able to cut it.

'It's too brittle, the rotten, stupid stuff,' she shouted, throwing it down on the table, where it shattered into shards. Horrified by her outburst of temper, she covered her eyes with her hands.

'It's all right, Colenso,' Garren said softly, leading her over to the table and easing her gently into the chair. 'Anger is the next stage of the grieving process,' he murmured, handing her his kerchief. 'I bought some angelica on the market and thought we might crystallize it tomorrow. It'll soon be Mothering Sunday and it would make a good cake decoration. Of course, the whole place will reek like a distillery for a week, for the stems smell like gin when you boil them. He chatted on without expecting her to answer, and before long she felt the rage that had bubbled up from nowhere, subsiding.

With the new remedies proving popular, Colenso found herself working alongside Garren as they spent most evenings and Sundays trialling both the receipts in the journal and developing some of their own. He never asked questions yet was always ready if she wanted to talk. Although she still felt guilty at the way she'd refused Kitto's ring, as February turned to March, she found the numbness easing slightly, leaving a heavy weight in its wake. She still couldn't believe he was dead; yet, as there'd been no news from Wherrytown, she slowly began to accept the inevitable.

'You need feeding up, my girl,' Mr Goss said, placing a boiled egg in front of her. 'Mrs Heava's hens is laying well so there's plenty more where they came from.'

'And I've even cut a slice of bread into soldiers for you,' Garren grinned.

'Really, boys, I'm not a child, you know,' she replied,

a smile hovering tentatively on her lips as she saw them watching like mother hens themselves.

'No, but you do need to eat a bit more,' Mr Goss pointed out. Colenso nodded, for it was true her clothes were hanging off her. Even when she'd retrieved her pentacle, it had felt too heavy to wear. 'Can't have a scrawny scarecrow serving in my confectioners,' he added, a twinkle in his eye.

'You're going to need the energy, for being Mothering Sunday tomorrow, I'm expecting a run on the last of those angelica stems. I'm pleased at just how popular they've proven to be.'

'What about you, Colenso? Do you have a mother to think of tomorrow?' Mr Goss asked.

'Mamm has made a new life for herself,' she replied, obediently tucking into her egg. It was enjoyable and the first thing she'd really tasted since hearing the news about Kitto. 'And we buried Mammwynn more than a year ago.'

'We shall be going to visit Meggie's grave tomorrow,' Mr Goss said. He looked so sad and, wanting to make him feel better, Colenso held up her empty egg cup.

'Thank you, that was delicious.' Both men smiled. 'Perhaps I could return the favour by cooking a meal for you tomorrow,' she offered. After exchanging a look, they nodded.

*

As spring flowers bloomed in the yard, so Colenso found herself slowly coming back to life. She'd never get over Kitto but, with Garren and his father's help, she found herself taking an interest in things again.

One Sunday morning as she took herself into the workshop for breakfast, she found Garren opening a present.

'Thank you, Father,' he said, shaking out a moss-green jumper. 'Just what I need,' he grinned.

'Happy birthday, Garren,' Colenso said. 'I'm sorry, I didn't realize or I would have bought you something.'

'Well, as it's my birthday and the weather's warm and sunny, why don't we pack a picnic and walk along the beach until we find a sheltered spot? We've all been working hard and you haven't been out anywhere in ages, Colenso. It will give me an opportunity to wear my new jumper,' he added as she opened her mouth to protest.

'That would be nice,' she found herself saying.

'What do you think, Father?' Garren asked.

'As you say, we've all been working hard and I'm feeling rather tired,' he replied, yawning for good effect. 'Think I'll rest my eyes a while. You two go, though.'

The day was indeed sunny, although there was a breeze blowing so that Colenso was glad of her shawl, and Garren his smart new jumper. Taking a different street than she had before, they strolled down towards the seafront. The birds were singing, camellias and primroses bloomed, a tulip tree was in full bud, and Colenso found herself feeling if not happy, then almost content. Her heart wobbled as they passed the boats in the harbour but Garren quickly guided her through a little tunnel opposite the smelting works and onto the beach.

'Shall we go barefoot?' he asked, grinning mischievously. 'We might even risk a paddle later if you want, although the sea will be perishing, oh ...' his voice trailed off.

'Why not,' she replied brightly, ignoring his faux pas as she perched on a rock to remove her shoes.

'Love the colour,' he grinned.

'Mara, the lady who took me in, bought them for me. I didn't know until after she passed,' she explained, letting out a long sigh.

'Poor Colenso, so much sadness,' he said, patting her shoulder. 'But today is my birthday and my wish is for you to relax and enjoy it with me. Come along, we'll walk down St Michael's Way. Have you been across to the Mount?'

'Yes, I saw the sun rise there at Litha – or the summer solstice, as Mara called it.' She let out another sigh, remembering how the woman had told her to make a romantic wish at the magic rock. A fat lot of good that had been, she thought.

'*Oh, ye of little faith.*' The words were so loud that for one moment Colenso thought Mara was at her side. She shook her head.

'Life is full of memories,' Garren murmured, staring out to sea. 'Still, as you haven't been out recently, we'll not go as far as there today, just settle for a gentle amble.'

With the Mount ahead of them, they began walking, their toes sinking into the still cool sand. In the distance, she could see three large black lumps of rock.

'That big one is Long Rock, for obvious reasons,' he laughed. She stared at the elongated shape and smiled. They walked for another mile or so before Garren suggested stopping for their picnic. As they sat in the shelter of a cove, feasting on bread and cheese, they each began to open up about their past.

'You mean Miss Chenoweth actually asked you to accompany her to a concert?' she exclaimed.

'Sinful, wasn't it?' he laughed. 'And in the church hall as well. As soon as they moved next door, she made it plain she had plans, as she put it, to combine her epicurean establishment with my confectioners.'

'You didn't fancy the idea?' Colenso asked, the reason for the woman's increasing hostility towards her now becoming clear.

'No fear. She'd have me wearing a starched collar and suit and offering my customers – or clientele, as she prefers to call them – violet and rose creams. Now, don't misunderstand me, there's nothing wrong with those confections but they're hardly for children, which was her idea. Nasty, smelly little blighters is how she referred to them.'

'But you love children,' Colenso cried, recalling how patient he was with them.

'Precisely,' he nodded. 'In fact, when I marry, it is my intention to raise a whole brood of them.'

'And do you have anyone in mind?' she asked. 'Oh sorry, that was dreadfully rude.'

'I did have but it turned out the woman I had in mind already had a follower.' He said it lightly but was staring at her so earnestly, she had to turn away. 'Of course, it's much too soon for me to declare myself but maybe one day,' he added quietly. 'Now, come along, we'd best get back or Father will be wondering where we've got to.' It could have been awkward on the walk back but he kept up such a flow of chatter about the sweets he was hoping to make for Easter that they were back outside the shop before she knew it.

'I've had a lovely time,' she told him, surprised to find that it was true. For a few hours at least, she had managed to put the tragedy out of her mind.

'Me too. Perhaps we could repeat the experience,' he replied.

As she lay in bed that night, she thought back over the day. Garren had been good company, undemanding but attentive, and she could enjoy spending more time with him as long as he realized she wasn't ready to take things further.

For her heart belonged to Kitto, it always had, and although she'd accepted he was never coming back, she couldn't envisage ever feeling the same about anyone else. In fact, she knew she wouldn't.

Chapter 33

'Sun, sea and sweets, what more can tourists ask for?' Garren asked as the door closed behind another gaggle of happy children clutching twists of confections in their hot little hands. It was early summer, and the warm weather and longer days had brought the visitors flocking to the seaside town.

'Laughter and lollipops,' Colenso replied.

'Lollipops?' he frowned, hazel eyes thoughtful.

'You said we needed to come up with a novel idea if we were to stay ahead of your competitors and I noticed how sticky the children's hands get in this weather. When I was working on the Panam, we sold lollipops, and it occurred to me that sweets on sticks might prove popular with the visitors.'

'That's a splendid idea,' he cried. 'We shall make some as soon as we close. What particular flavour did you have in mind, Miss Carne?'

'All sorts, Mr Goss. I can just picture the window now, a kaleidoscope of colour to stop the customers and tempt them in.'

'If it looks half as good as the roses on your cheeks, then we will indeed attract a lot of attention.' Although he said it lightly, the tone of his voice told her he meant it as a compliment.

Their gaze met and held. Embarrassed, Colenso turned and began tidying the counter. They'd been getting on really well together and recently Garren had been treating her more like an equal than an employee. She sensed his feelings for her were deepening and, although she liked him a lot, there was still that Kitto-shaped hole in her heart.

'Come on,' he said, going over and flipping the sign to closed. 'Let's have supper and you can tell me about the other ideas you've come up with. And don't say you haven't, because I've heard that brain of yours buzzing away like a bumblebee,' he added as Colenso opened her mouth to protest. Grinning, she followed him through to the workshop, not minding that a long evening of sweet-making lay ahead. As well as having to keep the stocks replenished, they needed to come up with new ways of attracting customers to stay ahead of the other confectioners in the town.

Over plates of cold ham and pickles, they discussed various colour and flavour combinations.

'Right, as this is your idea, you can choose the colourings and flavourings while I make the sugar syrup,' he said as soon as they'd finished eating. A tingle of excitement, which she hadn't experienced in months, ran through her as she looked along the little bottles, selecting orange, lemon, strawberry and even mint.

'Mint lollipops? You have the strangest of tastes, Miss Carne.'

'Or maybe I'm just more adventurous than you, Mr Goss,' she quipped.

'Is that so?' he frowned. He returned to his stirring and was quiet for a few moments. Goodness, she hadn't offended him, had she? Colenso wondered. But soon he was back to his joking self, and by the end of the evening the workshop was filled with the heady aroma of mixed fruits and mint, and the cooling tables lined with a rainbow of lollipops.

'A job well done,' Garren pronounced. 'Any other bright ideas, Miss Carne?'

'Yes, actually. I noticed how drab and dreary the paper twists look. If we are to complete with the other confectioners we need to address that. I believe I've mentioned the bright cones we used on the Panam. They were always well received by both children and parents alike and they would certainly stand out against the other confectioners' plain bags. As it's Sunday tomorrow, I could make some up and place them in the window.' He shook his head. 'Oh well, it was only an idea,' she said, wondering why he was against it.

'I was shaking my head about you doing it tomorrow,' Garren explained. 'Because surprisingly, Miss Carne, I have come up with an idea of my own,' he told her, eyes gleaming.

'Oh, and what may I ask are we making tomorrow?' she asked.

'Merry,' he replied.

'Merry what?' she asked, wondering if the effects of the colourings had gone to his head.

'Tomorrow, we are taking ourselves off to make merry.'

That night Colenso slept soundly and for once nightmares didn't torment her, so that she woke refreshed and eager for the day ahead.

'Oh, are we not going to the beach?' she asked when Garren turned towards the countryside.

'Time for a change,' he smiled, clearly enjoying his little mystery. 'Now, let's relax and enjoy the freedom of being in the great outdoors. Look at that heather, isn't it a riot of colour? It's a good job we don't have mauve colouring or you'd be making purple lollipops next.'

'And why not?' she asked. 'In fact, if we were to mix some red with blue, we could create some.'

'*Mon dieu*, the woman is mad,' he cried, waving his hands in the air. 'Ah listen, a skylark. Is that not the sound of summer?' She smiled. He was certainly in good spirits this morning.

They tramped on, venturing deeper into the countryside alive with golden gorse, its coconut fragrance wafting on the breeze.

'What that we could bottle that aroma,' Garren sighed. 'We'd make a fortune.'

'Fortune favours those who help themselves,' Colenso told him. 'At least that's what Mammwynn used to say.'

'She was probably right. Oh look, here we are,' he said as they arrived at a gentle sloping field.

'Goodness, what are all those?' she asked, hopping up and down as she stared at the circle of stones.

'Those, Miss Carne, are known as the Merry Maidens and you'd better not jig around like that,' he instructed, laughing at her puzzled expression. 'For I have it on good authority that these were once young girls who were turned to stone for dancing on the Sabbath.'

'You're joking, of course,' she chuckled.

'Maybe, maybe not, but it is the Sabbath so I wouldn't risk it,' he replied, his grin belying his serious tone. 'Look at the way they've been placed. See how they get smaller from the south-west to the north-east there,' he said, gesturing with his arm. 'Some tales suggest they were arranged to mirror the waxing and waning of the moon, though personally I prefer the Merry Maidens story,' he grinned.

'Hence making merry today?' she replied.

'Absolutely,' he nodded. 'And that stone over there tucked into the hedgerow is known as the Gun Rith Standing Stone, which could have formed part of the processional alignment with the Merry Maidens.'

'So this place was used for sacred ceremonies?' she asked, gazing around in wonder.

'Well, it was also known as Dans Meyn, which would suggest that here was used for rituals involving dance.'

'You can feel the magic in the air. Mammwynn would have loved it here,' she cried, surprised not to feel the necklace thumping madly at her chest. Then she realized she was no longer wearing it. She would put it back on tonight, she vowed. Suddenly, she became aware of Garren gazing at her intently.

'I can feel magic in the air too,' he said quietly. 'And I'm hoping it will look favourably on what I am about to ask.' He swallowed hard. 'Colenso, I have loved you from the moment I first saw you standing all bedraggled in my workshop. Would you … could you consider becoming my wife?'

'Oh,' she gasped, her eyes widening.

'I'm reliable and would always look after you,' he declared, taking her hand in his. 'We both love children and I could provide you and them with a good home, so ... what do you say?'

'Well, you've taken me by surprise,' she stammered.

'I know I can never replace your Kitto. I'm not half as good-looking, for one thing,' he gave a nervous laugh before continuing. 'However, we do get on well together and in time you might even come to return my affection.'

'I am fond of you, Garren,' she told him, blinking back tears as she stared at the stones. But was that enough?

'To my mind that's a good start,' Garren replied.

But what did she want from life? It was the first time she'd thought about it since Kitto had died. Kitto, her heart almost stopped for a moment. She still loved him, but he wasn't coming back, was he? He wouldn't have expected her to stop living, she knew that. She was only eighteen, after all, and didn't want to end up like Mara, remaining frozen in the past for the rest of her years.

Having her own home and family had always been her dream. Garren would make a good husband and father and, in return, she'd make sure she was a good wife and mother. Slowly, she turned back to face him.

'Thank you, Garren, I would be proud to become your wife,' she told him. His face lit up and, letting out a whoop of glee, he lifted her off the ground and swung her round and round in the air.

'I hope this doesn't count as dancing,' she laughed.

*

343

'Father, we have some good news for you,' Garren said, as they burst into the little upstairs living room where he was sitting.

'It had better be good an' all, rushing into the room like that. If a man can't rest his eyes in peace in his own home, then it's a poor show,' the old man grumbled, although Colenso could tell he didn't really mind at all.

'Colenso has agreed to become my wife,' Garren announced proudly.

'Has she now?' Mr Goss asked, eyeing her shrewdly. 'Well, in that case we'd best break out that port I keep for special occasions. It's in the dresser in my room.' He waited until Garren had left then turned to Colenso.

'And is this news good for you, my dear? Are you ready to move on? I wouldn't want to see Garren hurt.'

'I'd never do that, Mr Goss. I admire and respect him too much.'

'I didn't hear the word "love",' he murmured, just as Garren reappeared carrying a bottle. He went over to the sideboard and poured a small amount into three glasses before handing them round.

'To you both,' Mr Goss said, getting stiffly to his feet and raising his glass. 'I hope you will be as happy as Meggie and I were,' he added, his eyes looking suspiciously bright.

'Thank you, Father. Colenso has made me the happiest man. To our future,' he said, clinking his glass against hers.

'To all our futures,' Mr Goss said, settling himself back in his chair. 'Sit down, dear,' he added. 'The good news seems to have relieved my son of his manners.'

'I haven't been up here before,' Colenso said, taking a seat on the couch and staring round the bright, well-furnished room.

'Used to be Meggie's favourite room, this. Catches the afternoon sun. Still, you'll be wanting it for yourselves now.'

'Goodness, Mr Goss, I wouldn't dream of sharing it with you,' Colenso cried.

'Nor would I ask you to,' he assured her. 'I have been thinking of removing myself to the gentlemen's hotel. No, don't argue,' he went on as Garren opened his mouth to protest. 'I have a little money saved and, to be honest, my legs can't manage these stairs for much longer. The opportunity of having my meals cooked and laundry taken care of is too good to miss. Besides, I won't be here to call on when you get a rush in the shop.' His impish grin made him look like his son and Colenso couldn't help smiling.

'Well, if you're sure,' Garren said.

'Oh, I am, son. I am. Have you set a date for the wedding?' he asked.

'Goodness, Garren only asked me a few hours ago,' Colenso gasped, feeling everything was moving too fast.

'Ah well, I dare say it will give you time to get this place as you want it.'

'We shall visit the jewellers tomorrow and choose you a betrothal ring.' Unbidden, the memory of Kitto and his garnet popped into her head.

'I don't need any fancy ring, Garren. A wedding band will suffice,' she told him, turning away quickly when she saw his hurt look. 'It's only a token after all.'

'Fair enough,' he sighed.

Later, in her little room, she took the pentacle out of her basket but as she went to place it round her neck, the clasp came away in her hand.

The rainbow lollipops proved so popular they added rainbow rock to their repertoire and Garren was busy all summer keeping up with demand as holidaymakers and day-trippers flooded to Penzance. Colenso was rushed off her feet from the moment the shop opened until it closed late in the evening, and sometimes it was nine o'clock by the time they sat down for supper.

Mr Goss, eager to put his plans into action, had arranged to remove to the quiet little guest house near to the Gardens and promenade, where he was able to come and go as he pleased. The landlady, a large, amiable woman, looked after her regulars as if they were family, clucking round them like a mother hen.

Once they'd helped him settle in with his personal belongings, and Garren had been satisfied his father had enough put by to live on, they were able to turn their attention to themselves. Instead of making more confections, Garren insisted they spent Sunday afternoons getting the upstairs rooms ready for when they were married.

'As you can probably tell, we've not done anything up here since Mother died,' he said, gesturing around the little living room. 'Feel free to change things, move anything around, get the place how you want it before you move up here.' He hesitated. 'When I called in and saw Father today, he offered to take care of the shop so that we can have a honeymoon. I can only run to a couple of days but it will be a nice way to start our marriage, don't you think?'

'Yes, I do,' she told him. 'Have you anywhere in mind?' He tapped the side of his nose with his finger.

'Well, I hope it's somewhere restful, we've been so busy,' she told him, the idea of a holiday appealing.

'Peaceful yes, but should a honeymoon be restful I ask myself?' He gave her such an outrageous wink that she looked away in embarrassment. While he didn't set her pulses racing, he was a good man and she was determined to make him a good wife.

'We'll need to sit down and fix a date,' he told her. 'However, much as I would like to spend more time with my lovely wife-to-be, duty calls. I really need to make another batch of that rainbow rock or we'll have none to sell when we open in the morning.'

That night, for the first time in ages, her dreams were of Kitto.

Chapter 34

The next morning, her head still spinning from dreaming of Kitto, Colenso let herself into the little shop. She polished the counter, replenished the jars and set about arranging fresh lollipops and rock in their rainbow window. They would need to come up with a new theme for the autumn, she thought, standing back to check the effect. A face peering through the glass made her jump. It looked like Kitto, she thought, rubbing her eyes, certain they were playing tricks. A tap on the window, that cheeky grin. It *was* Kitto.

Heart pounding, she unlocked the door just as he hurled himself through it. Then she was in his arms and he was hugging her as though he'd never let her go.

'I thought you were dead,' she gasped when he finally released her.

'So did I. And for a long time, I nearly was,' he murmured, pulling her close and kissing her hard on the lips.

'Kitto,' she began but, unable to resist, gave herself up to his embrace.

Lost in the wondrous moment, they didn't hear Garren come in. It was only when he coughed that they realized he was there and sprang apart.

'Oh Garren, Kitto has come back,' she cried, tears of joy coursing down her cheeks.

'So I see,' he said quietly.

'I need some time with my girl, sir. Would you excuse her for a while so we can catch up?'

'Yes, of course. Take as long as you need, Colenso,' he told her, his eyes grave.

'But it's time to open the shop,' she began, suddenly aware of where her loyalties now lay.

'I'll see to the customers. You go with Kitto. I'm sure you will have much to discuss,' he told her.

Hands tightly clasped, as if by tacit consent, they made their way down to the beach. The sun was rising, bathing the bay in its rosy glow while the light early-morning breeze carried the tang of salt. Everywhere suddenly looked so vibrant, smelt so fresh.

'God, Cali, I've missed you so,' Kitto murmured, enfolding her in his arms. He kissed the top of her head and even through the material of her scarf, she could feel the warmth of his lips. 'I've dreamed of this moment so often over the past months, although I must admit I never envisaged you swathed in white,' he chuckled. Colenso stared down at her apron and grimaced.

'In all the excitement of seeing you again, I quite forgot to take it off.'

'Don't worry, it suits you. Oh Cali, you could be wearing anything or nothing for all I care.' Realizing what he'd said, he stopped. 'I was going to apologize but that conjures up such a wonderful vision, I'm not going to,' he told her. Too happy to object, she contented herself with giving him a playful nudge in the side, which led to more kissing and cuddling.

It was sometime later that they became aware of people watching and so they reluctantly broke apart. They wandered along the shoreline, not speaking, just savouring the pleasure of being together again. Only when they neared the hustle and bustle of the harbour at Newlyn did they seek the shelter and privacy the rocks afforded. He spread his jacket and made a sweeping gesture with his hand.

'If my lady would care to take a seat.'

'Why, thank you, kind sir,' she responded, entering into the spirit of things. They sat staring at each other for a long moment.

'How are you?'

'How have you been?' As ever, they spoke at the same time. Laughing, he took her hand in his, running his thumb over her palm in the way she loved so much. 'Good to see we're still in tune, Cali. These past few months have been hell.'

'I know,' she agreed. 'When I heard you were dead I wanted to die too. I was told that your ship had gone down with all hands lost,' she told him, her words breaking on a sob. He pulled her close.

'It's true the barge sank in a heavy swell. Never seen waves like it before and never want to again,' he shuddered. 'All I can remember is the water covering me, filling my lungs until I thought I'd burst. Next thing I knew I was waking up in some strange bed. Apparently, I'd been unconscious for quite some time.'

'And did they tell you what had happened?' she asked.

'Only that when the boat broke up on the beach I was

dragged onto the sands by fishermen who'd been watching from the shore. I'd busted my leg, fractured ribs. I was a sorry sight, I can tell you. If it hadn't been for the care of those wonderful strangers I would have been a goner.' He let out a long sigh, his eyes on the distant horizon, lost in another world, another time. She snuggled into him, revelling in the warmth of his chest, the familiar smell that was him.

'Then I am grateful to those strangers for nursing you back to health,' she told him.

'And you, Cali? How have you fared? Are you cross that I have taken so long to return?' he asked, dark eyes turning their gaze on her.

'No,' she sighed, remembering her accusations of the previous year. 'I'm just thankful you are alive and have come back.' He smiled and pulled her tighter.

'I'll not return to the Wherrytown works after this. Word has it they're in a pretty bad way anyhow. Shall we return home to Cadgwith? I'm sure I can get another start at Poltesco,' he asked. She smiled happily for, with the Ferret gone and Father existing in a stupor, there was no reason not to go back. Then, as if someone had thrown a bucket of icy water over her, she remembered her promise.

'Oh Kitto, I can't,' she wailed. 'If only you'd come back sooner.'

'So you *are* cross that I've taken this long getting back,' he sighed.

'I'm truly pleased you're safe and it's wonderful to be with you again but ...' her voice trailed off and she stared helplessly at him.

'But what?' he frowned.

'I'm promised to another,' she whispered.

'You what,' he shouted, his voice echoing as it bounced off the rocks. 'Hell's teeth, I've not been gone that long. Who ... oh, don't tell me, it's that confectioner, isn't it?'

'Garren's been very good to me, Kitto. He and his father looked after me while I was grieving for you. If they hadn't I don't know what would have happened to me.'

'What you're saying is, he's taken advantage of your helpless state. Well, in case you've forgotten, I'm your betrothed.'

'But I thought you were dead, Kitto. Please understand that I was trying to get over you. I've been so unhappy, desolate even. When I thought I had nothing to live for, he offered me comfort and hope for the future.'

He let out another long sigh. 'It's been hard on us both, I can see that. Come on, let's go back and speak with him. Ask him to release you from a promise made under duress.'

'But it wasn't. I like and respect him.'

'But do you love him?' he asked, gazing at her intently. Slowly, she shook her head.

'Well then?'

'I'm sorry, Kitto, I promised and I could never go back on that,' she mumbled, tears welling as she got to her feet. 'No, please don't,' she added as he made to follow. 'I'll go back by myself.'

'God, you're stubborn,' he muttered. 'But know this, Colenso Carne. I love you and will not rest till you are mine.'

Hot tears coursing down her cheeks, she stumbled back along the beach. How could the day that had seen her deepest dream come true end like this? Because you made a promise to a good and kind man, she told herself. A good, kind man who looked out for you in your hour of need and you will not renege on your promise to him.

By the time she got back to the shop, it was lunchtime. Garren took one look at her face and ushered her straight through to the workshop.

'You need tea,' he said, pushing her gently into a chair and pouring hot water into the pot. Unusually, there were no sweets set out on the cooling tables and she realized he must have spent the whole morning serving customers.

'The shop's been busy then?' she said.

'Yes, thank heavens. Nothing like keeping occupied to stop you from thinking,' he muttered, his hands shaking as he set down a mug in front of her. 'You were obviously delighted to see Kitto. So, what happens now?'

'You saw us earlier then?'

'Hard to miss with you all over each other.'

'It was a wonderful surprise to find he was still alive, and naturally I was pleased to see him,' she admitted.

'Was?' he asked, staring at her in disbelief. She nodded and took a quick gulp of her tea, hardly noticing that it burnt her mouth. 'I will release you from your promise if you want, you know.'

'Thank you, but my word is my bond, Garren,' she told him, staring him straight in the eye then looking quickly away when she saw the hurt there. 'When I was getting ready to open this morning, I noticed we're almost out of cones. As I had the devil's own job getting you to agree to them in the first place I'd better get on and make some more. Thank you for the tea,' she said, her voice cracking as she took herself back to the shop.

'You've hardly drunk any …' he began but, needing time to compose herself, she ignored him. While her hands automatically formed the paper into the cones that had become so popular, her thoughts span wildly around in her head.

Seeing Kitto again had been a shock. One that had only served to prove her strength of feelings for him. She loved him with all her heart, of that she had no doubt. But she was fond of Garren and wouldn't let him down. And yet could she really marry him now she knew Kitto was alive? Yet she'd have to, for hadn't she just assured Garren that she wouldn't break her word? Round and round her thoughts went. It was like being on the dobbies at the fair, she thought, pressing her hand to her throbbing head.

She didn't see Garren for the rest of the afternoon and assumed he was busy in the workshop making up for the time he lost this morning. The shop was busy, the incessant tinkling of the little bell making her headache worse. For the first time ever, she cursed her bright ideas of the rainbow window that constantly drew in the excited customers.

Her brain never stopped processing the events of the morning, and by the time she was able to close the shop she was certain her decision was right and honourable. She was just turning the sign to closed when Mr Goss appeared.

'Oh, I was just shutting,' she explained.

'Thought you would be,' he said abruptly. There was no trace of his usual smile as he made his way through to the workshop. 'I hear Kitto's turned up,' he said without any preamble. 'I'm pleased for him, of course, but need to know what that means for my son.'

'Nothing has changed, Mr Goss. I still intend honouring my promise to marry Garren.'

'Honour, promise, piffle,' he replied, snapping his fingers after each word. 'I don't want my son cheated, Colenso.'

'But I wouldn't ever do that. I will remain faithful to Garren both before and after our wedding.'

'Honourable words,' he agreed, then his tone softened. 'You are young, Colenso, and have the idealism of youth. However, I have lived life, and with age comes realism. Believe me when I say that whatever you might think, you will be cheating on him if you marry him when you love another. He deserves better than that, so please, I urge you, think carefully about your decision.'

All night, Colenso tossed and turned. Yet no matter how much she thought, it still came back to the fact that whilst she loved Kitto, she owed it to Garren to honour her promise. Whilst Mr Goss had a point, the fact remained that Garren had been good to her and there was no way she could let him down.

As the grey of morning filtered through the tiny window, Colenso dressed ready for another day in the shop. On impulse, she took her necklace from her basket and held it tightly in her hands.

'This is the right thing to do, isn't it?' she asked. But the pentacle remained cold and lifeless. 'Oh, you're no help,' she cried, throwing it back in despair.

To her surprise, Garren followed her through to the shop. He seemed on edge as he coughed and cleared his throat.

'Colenso, I have spent all night deliberating and ...'

He paused and cleared his throat again. 'I have decided it wouldn't be fair to hold you to your promise.'

'But …'

'Go to Kitto, Colenso. When I saw the way you were gazing at him yesterday, the love shining from your eyes like diamonds, well, I admit I was hurt. You've never looked at me that way and sadly, I know you never will.'

'But I am fond of you and …' she began but he held up his hand to silence her.

'Fond isn't love, though, is it? Like I said, Colenso, go to Kitto and be happy.' She stared at him sadly, knowing what he said was true.

'Thank you, Garren, for everything,' she whispered, wondering how it was possible to feel so sad and elated at the same time.

Epilogue

On a late autumn day, as the last red rays of setting sun cast their magic over Mammwynn's little garden, Colenso and Kitto, silver ribbons binding their hands, exchanged vows of love in front of family and friends. Dressed in a red dress that matched her shoes, a circlet of wild flowers and herbs bound with myrtle adorning her flowing tresses, Colenso had never felt happier.

'*Marjoram for love, rosemary to stimulate the heart and parsley for lust*,' Mammwynn whispered in her ear.

'*Myrtle for good luck, love and prosperity in marriage*,' Mara added.

Colenso smiled, content to know the two women who'd meant so much to her were here together on this special occasion. She'd chosen to hold their handfasting on the day when the veil between the two worlds was at its thinnest. Her hand stroked the pentacle that Kitto had mended and, feeling its warmth, she knew all was well.

As the sun disappeared behind the horizon, leaving them

bathed in the light of the flickering candles, Kitto leaned forward and kissed her passionately on the lips. He looked so handsome in the new jacket Emily had insisted on making him, a sprig of heather pinned to his lapel, but it was the love shining from his eyes that made Colenso's pulse race.

'Well, Mrs Rowse, wife and love of my life, are you ready to jump from your old life into our new one?' he asked, transferring the silver ribbon to the handle of the besom and holding it out to her.

'I am, Mr Rowse, husband and holder of my heart,' she replied, taking it from him. Then as the assembled well-wishers fell silent, she straddled the broom and made the symbolic leap towards him. Everyone cheered and applauded, but Colenso and Kitto only had eyes for each other as they sealed the magical moment with another kiss.

'We've finally made it, Mrs Rowse,' he murmured.

'Let's hope the road we travel together will prove less hazardous than the past year.'

'Road? Travel? I'll have you know we're not going any-where, wife of mine. We're going to settle in our cot and raise a whole brood,' he told her, eyes sparking with mischief.

'All in good time, husband dear. I have my new sweet-making venture to set up first. Who'd have thought the new baker would want to expand into confections?' she sighed. 'And it was nice of Mr Whitelaw to let us have that old cottage next to his house, wasn't it?'

'It was, but I think he might have had an ulterior motive,' he grinned, nodding over to where the works manager was smiling lovingly down at Caja. 'I think another wedding might be on the cards soon.'

'Mamm looks so happy. I'm pleased she's been given a second chance. She had such a miserable life with Father.'

'Well, she hasn't got to worry about Peder any longer, has she? I mean, he literally drank himself to death.' Colenso couldn't help shivering as she remembered that night at the Devil's Frying Pan. As if sensing her thoughts, Kitto pulled her close.

'I know, I'll help things along,' Colenso smiled, taking the circlet from her hair.

'Hey Mamm, catch,' she called, tossing the flowers towards her. They watched them sail through the air and land in Caja's outstretched hands.

'Nice one, sis.' She looked up to see Tomas giving her the thumbs-up. Alys was by his side, grinning widely.

'Oh, so that's the way of things, is it? I shall have to have a word with that brother of yours,' Kitto said as they came over to join them.

'Don't worry, Kitto, I'll look after Alys. You just make sure you take good care of Colenso,' Tomas declared.

'Looks like we might become sisters-in-law again, then,' Colenso squealed, throwing her arms around the girl, who beamed delightedly. 'And it's good to see you, Daveth. How you've grown up since I last saw you.'

As the boy blushed, everyone suddenly surged forward, eager to wish them well. Colenso smiled and greeted them all warmly.

Then, as the silver moon rose in the sky, someone took up an accordion and began to play. As jaunty music filled the air, Kitto turned to her and smiled.

'I believe it's traditional for us to lead the dancing, so shall we?' he asked, holding out his hand and leading her into the centre of the little garden.

His arms tightened around her and she smiled happily up at him as they swayed gently together. The others joined them and there was hardly room to move, but she didn't mind in the slightest. She was home with her love at last. The ending of one year, the beginning of the next.

'*I told you to have faith in the magic of the rock,*' Mara whispered.

'*There's a proper time for everything and everything has its season. This is yours,*' Mammwynn's voice drifted on the breeze. In the background the rowans gently rustled.

'*Blessed be,*' they cried in unison.

Colenso stared up at Kitto and knew she truly was.

Acknowledgements and

Heartfelt Thanks to...

Gary Hill at The Serpentine Works at Lizard Point, for allowing me into his workshop and showing me how the serpentine is worked and turned.

Pem, for his research on the places and dates all the fairs took place.

Teresa Chris, for her continued encouragement and passion for this story.

Kate Mills and her wonderful team at HQ, who are always so helpful and enthusiastic.

My friends at BWC, who continue to listen and give their invaluable feedback.

Thank you all.

ONE PLACE. MANY STORIES

Bold, innovative and
empowering publishing.

FOLLOW US ON:

@HQStories